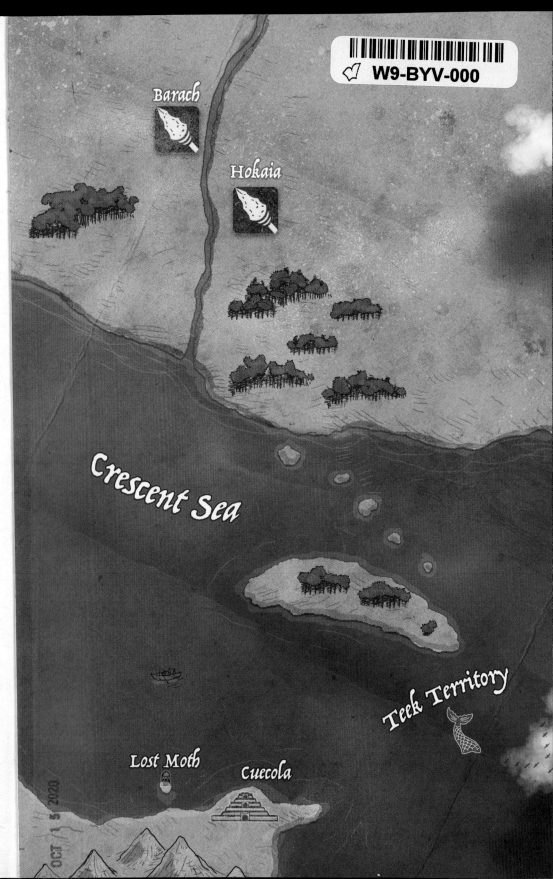

ALSO BY REBECCA ROANHORSE

Barach

Hokaia

Crescent Sea

Teek Territory

Lost Moth

Cuecola

BLACK SUN

BETWEEN EARTH AND SKY

BOOK ONE

REBECCA ROANHORSE

SAGA PRESS

LONDON SYDNEY **NEW YORK** TORONTO NEW DELHI

SAGA S PRESS

AN IMPRINT OF SIMON & SCHUSTER, INC.

1230 AVENUE OF THE AMERICAS, NEW YORK, NEW YORK 10020

Copyright © 2020 by Rebecca Roanhorse

All rights reserved, including the right to reproduce this book or portions thereof in any form whatsoever. For information, address Saga Press Subsidiary Rights Department, 1230 Avenue of the Americas, New York, NY 10020.

First Saga Press hardcover edition October 2020

SAGA PRESS and colophon are trademarks of Simon & Schuster, Inc.

For information about special discounts for bulk purchases, please contact Simon & Schuster Special Sales at 1-866-506-1949 or business@simonandschuster.com.

The Simon & Schuster Speakers Bureau can bring authors to your live event. For more information or to book an event, contact the Simon & Schuster Speakers Bureau at 1-866-248-3049 or visit our website at www.simonspeakers.com.

Interior design by Michelle Marchese

Manufactured in the United States of America

10   9   8   7   6   5   4   3   2   1

Library of Congress Cataloging-in-Publication Data

Names: Roanhorse, Rebecca, author.
Title: Black sun / Rebecca Roanhorse.
Identifiers: LCCN 2020012273 (print) | LCCN 2020012274 (ebook) | ISBN 9781534437678 (hardcover) | ISBN 9781534437692 (ebook)
Subjects: GSAFD: Fantasy fiction.
Classification: LCC PS3618.O283 B58 2020 (print) | LCC PS3618.O283 (ebook) | DDC 813/.6—dc23
LC record available at https://lccn.loc.gov/2020012273
LC ebook record available at https://lccn.loc.gov/2020012274

ISBN 978-1-5344-3767-8
ISBN 978-1-5344-3769-2 (ebook)

For that kid in Texas
who always dreamed in epic

THE PEOPLE OF THE MERIDIAN

• THE OBREGI MOUNTAINS •

Serapio – *The Crow God Reborn*
Saaya – *Serapio's mother*
Marcal – *Serapio's father*
Paadeh – *Serapio's first tutor*
Eedi – *Serapio's second tutor, a Spearmaiden*
Powageh – *Serapio's third tutor, a Knife*

• CITY OF CUECOLA •

Xiala – *The Captain, sailor, Teek in origin*
Callo – *First mate, sailor*
Patu – *Cook, sailor*
Loob – *A sailor*
Baat – *A sailor*
Poloc – *A sailor*
Atan – *A sailor*

Balam – *A merchant lord*
Pech – *A merchant lord*

• CITY OF TOVA •

THE WATCHERS
Naranpa – *Sun Priest, Order of Oracles (hawaa)*
Iktan – *Priest of Knives, Order of Knives (tsiyo)*
Abah – *Priest of Succor, Order of the Healing Society (seegi)*
Haisan – *Priest of Records, Order of Historical Society (ta dissa)*
Kiutue – *Former Sun Priest (deceased)*
Eche – *Dedicant, Order of Oracles*
Kwaya – *Dedicant, Order of the Healing Society*
Deeya – *A servant*
Leaya – *A servant*

THE SKY MADE CLANS
Yatliza – *Matron, Carrion Crow*
Okoa – *Yatliza's son, Carrion Crow*
Esa – *Yatliza's daughter, Carrion Crow*
Chaiya – *Captain of the Shield, Carrion Crow*
Maaka – *Leader of the Odohaa, Carrion Crow*
Ashk – *A stablehand, Carrion Crow*
Feyoue – *A healer, Carrion Crow*

Kutssah – *A giant crow*
Benundah – *A giant crow*
Paida – *A giant crow*

Ieyoue – *Matron, Water Strider*
Aishe – *Water Strider*
Zash – *Water Strider*
Tyode – *Water Strider*

Paipai – *A giant water strider*

Nuuma – *Matron, Golden Eagle*
Peyanna – *Matron, Winged Serpent*

THE DRY EARTH (CLANLESS)
Denaochi – *Brother to Naranpa*
Akel – *Brother to Naranpa*
Jeyma – *Father to Naranpa*
Zataya – *A witch*

You are the substitute, the surrogate of Tloque Nahuaque,
the lord of the near and far.
You are the seat [the throne from which he rules], you are
      his flute [the mouth from which he speaks],
he speaks within you,
he makes you his lips, his jaws, his ears . . .
He also makes you his fangs, his claws,
for you are his wild beast, you are his eater of people,
      you are his judge.

—*The Florentine Codex*, Book VI, 42R

CHAPTER 1

The Obregi Mountains
Year 315 of the Sun
(10 Years before Convergence)

O Sun! You cast cruel shadow
Black char for flesh, the tint of feathers
Have you forsaken mercy?

—From *Collected Lamentations from the Night of Knives*

Today he would become a god. His mother had told him so.

"Drink this," she said, handing him a cup. The cup was long and thin and filled with a pale creamy liquid. When he sniffed it, he smelled the orange flowers that grew in looping tendrils outside his window, the ones with the honey centers. But he also smelled the earthy sweetness of the bell-shaped flowers she cultivated in her courtyard garden, the one he was never allowed to play in. And he knew there were things he could not smell in the drink, secret things, things that came from the bag his mother wore around her neck, that whitened the tips of her fingers and his own tongue.

"Drink it now, Serapio," she said, resting a hand briefly against his cheek. "It's better to drink it cold. And I've put more sweet in it this time, so you can keep it down better."

He flushed, embarrassed by her mention of his earlier vomiting. She had warned him to drink the morning's dose quickly, but he had been hesitant and sipped it instead, and he had heaved up some of the drink in a milky mess. He was determined to prove himself worthy this time, more than just a timid boy.

He grasped the cup between shaking hands, and under his mother's watchful gaze, he brought it to his lips. The drink was bitter cold, and as she had promised, much sweeter than the morning's portion.

"All of it," she chided as his throat protested and he started to lower the cup. "Else it won't be enough to numb the pain."

He forced himself to swallow, tilting his head back to drain the vessel. His stomach protested, but he held it down. Ten seconds passed, and then another ten. He triumphantly handed the empty cup back.

"My brave little godlet," she said, her lips curling into a smile that made him feel blessed.

She set the cup on the nearby table next to the pile of cotton cords she would use later to tie him down. He glanced at the cords, and the bone needle and gut thread next to them. She would use that on him, too.

Sweat dampened his hairline, slicking his dark curls to his head despite the chill that beset the room. He was brave, as brave as any twelve-year-old could be, but looking at the needle made him wish for the numbing poison to do its job as quickly as possible.

His mother caught his worry and patted his shoulder reassuringly. "You make your ancestors proud, my son. Now . . . smile for me."

He did, baring his teeth. She picked up a small clay bowl and dipped a finger in. It came out red. She motioned him closer. He leaned in so she could rub the dye across his teeth. It tasted like nothing, but part of his mind could not stop thinking about the insects he had watched his mother grind into the nut milk to make the dye. A single drop, like blood, fell on her lap. She frowned and scrubbed at it with the meat of her palm.

She was wearing a simple black sheath that bared her strong brown arms, the hem long enough to brush the stone floor at their feet. Her waist-length black hair spilled loose down her back. Around her neck, a collar of crow feathers the shade of midnight, tips dyed as red as the paint on his teeth.

"Your father thought he could forbid me to wear this," she said calmly enough, but the boy could hear the thread of pain in her voice, the places where deprivation and sorrow had left their cracks. "But your father doesn't understand that this is the way of my ancestors, and their ancestors before them. He cannot stop a Carrion Crow woman from dressing to honor the crow god, particularly on a day as sacred as today."

"He's afraid of it," the boy said, the words coming without thought. It must be the poison loosening his tongue. He would never have dared such words otherwise.

His mother blinked, obviously surprised by his insight, and then she shrugged.

"Perhaps," she agreed. "The Obregi fear many things they do not understand. Now, hold still until I'm done."

She worked quickly, coloring his teeth a deep carmine until it looked like blood filled his mouth. She smiled. Her teeth were the same. Father was right to fear her like this, the boy thought. She looked fierce, powerful. The handmaiden of a god.

"How does your back feel?" she asked as she returned the bowl of dye to the table.

"Fine," he lied. She had carved the haahan on his back earlier that day at dawn. Woken him from bed, fed him his first cup of numbing poison, and told him it was time. He had rolled dutifully onto his stomach, and she had begun.

She'd used a special kind of blade he had never seen, thin and delicate and very sharp. She talked to him as she worked, telling him that if he had been with his clan, a beloved uncle or cousin would have carved his haahan over a series of months or even years, but there was no time left and it had to be her, today. Then she had told him tales of the great crow god as she cut curving lines—the suggestion of crow wings—across his shoulders and down his lateral muscles. It had burned like sticking his hand in the fire, perhaps because he hadn't drunk the full measure of the drink. But he had endured the pain with only a whimper. Next, she made him sit up and she had cut a crow skull at the base of his throat, beak extending down his chest, so it sat like a pendant in his skin. The pain was tenfold worse than the wings had been, and the only thing that had kept him from screaming was the fear that she might accidentally slice his throat if he moved too suddenly. He knew his mother's people carved their flesh as a symbol of their perpetual mourning for what was lost, and he was proud to bear the haahan, but tears still flowed down his cheeks.

When she was done, she had taken in her handiwork with a critical eye. "Now they will recognize you when you go home, even if you do look too much Obregi."

Her words stung, especially that she would say them even as she marked him. Not that he wasn't used to the observation, the teasing from other children that he looked not enough this or too much that.

"Is Obregi bad?" he dared to ask, the poison still making him overbold. Obregi was certainly the only home he had ever known. He had always understood that his mother was the foreigner here; she came from a city called Tova that was far away and belonged to a people there who called themselves Carrion Crow. But his father was Obregi and a lord. This was his ancestral home they lived in, his family's land the workers tilled. The boy had even been given an Obregi name. He had also inherited the curling hair and slightly paler face of his father's people, although his narrow eyes, wide mouth, and broad cheeks were his mother's.

"No, son," she chided, "this life, this place"—she gestured around them, taking in the cool stone walls and the rich weavings that hung from them, the view of the snowy mountains outside, the entire nation of the Obregi—"was all to keep you safe until you could return to Tova."

Safe from what? He wanted to ask, but instead he said, "When will that be?"

She sighed and pressed her hands against her thighs. "I am no Watcher in the celestial tower," she said, shaking her head, "but I think it will not be so long now."

"A month? A year?" he prodded. *Not so long now* could mean anything.

"We are not forgotten," she assured him, her face softening. She brushed back an unruly lock that had fallen across his forehead. Her dark eyes brimmed with a love that warmed him from head to toe. She may look frightening to his father like this, but to him she was beautiful.

Shadows moved across the floor, and she looked over her shoulder as the afternoon light turned strange.

"It's time." She stood, her face flushed with excitement, and held out a hand. "Are you ready?"

He was too old to hold her hand like a baby, but he was scared enough of what came next that he pressed his palm against hers and wrapped his fingers around tight, seeking comfort. She led him outside onto the stone terrace where the late-season winds chilled his bare skin.

The view was a feast for the eye. From here they could see the valley, still clinging to the golds and crimsons of late fall. Beyond them squatted the high jagged mountains where the ice never melted. He had spent many afternoons here, watching hawks circle the village that sat just on the edge of the valley, dropping pebbles off the ledge to watch them shatter to dust on the rocky cliffs below. It was a place of fond memories, of good thoughts.

"So cloudy," his mother fretted, her hand still wrapped around his, "but look, it changes even as we prepare." She beamed, showing her bloody teeth.

She was right. He watched as the sky cleared to reveal a tattered sun, hunched like a dull watery ball atop the mountains. And to its side, a darkness loomed.

The boy's eyes widened in alarm. Mama had told him the crow god would come today, but he had not fathomed the horror of its visage.

"Look at the sun, Serapio," she said, sounding breathless. "I need you to look at the sun."

He did as he was told and watched with a growing terror as it began to disappear.

"Mama?" he asked, alarmed, hating that his voice sounded high and frightened.

"Don't look away!" she warned.

He would not. He had endured her knife and her poison, and he would endure the needle soon, too. He could master the sun.

But his eyes began to water and sting.

"Steady," she murmured, squeezing his hand.

His eyes ached, but his mother tugged the delicate skin of his eyelids with her fingernails to keep them open. He cried out as she grazed his eyeball, and instinct more than desire made him buck. She pulled him tight, arms like a vise and fingers gripping his jaw.

"You must look!" she cried. And he did, as the crow god ate the sun.

When all that was left was a ring of trembling orange fire around a hole of darkness, his mother released him.

He rubbed at his stinging eyes, but she slapped his hands away. "You've been so brave," she said. "You must not fear now."

The edge of a bubbling panic crawled up his spine at what was to come next. His mother did not seem to notice.

"Hurry now," she said, ushering him back inside, "while the crow god holds sway over the world."

She pressed him to sitting in the high-backed chair. His limbs had grown heavy and his head light, no doubt from the poisoned cup. The panic that had tried to rise died on a soft, terrified half-moan.

She bound his feet to the legs of the chair and wrapped the cords around his body until he could not move. The rope stung where the haahan were still raw.

"Keep your eyes closed," she warned.

He did, and after a moment, he felt something wet press along the line of his eyelashes. It was cold and deadened the skin. His lids felt so weighted that he did not think he could open them again.

"Listen to me," his mother said. "Human eyes lie. You must learn to see the world with more than this faulty organ."

"But how?"

"You will learn, and this will help." He felt her slip something into his pocket. It was a bag like the one she wore around her neck. He could just reach it if he wiggled his fingers, feeling the fine powder inside. "Hide this, and use it only when you need it."

"How will I know when I need it?" he asked, worried. He didn't want to fail her.

"You will learn, Serapio," she said, voice gentle but firm.

"And once you have, you must go home to Tova. There you will open your eyes again and become a god. Do you understand?"

He didn't understand, not really, but he said yes anyway.

"Will you come with me?" he asked.

Her breath hitched, and the sound scared him more than anything else she had done that day.

"Mama?"

"Hush, Serapio. You ask too many questions. Silence will be your greatest ally now."

The needle pierced his eyelid, but he was only distantly aware of it. He could feel the stitches sealing his eyes shut, the pull and lift of the thread through his skin. The panic that had failed to rise earlier swelled up larger now, made him twitch in his chair, made the wounds on his back pull and sting, but the cords held him tight and the drugs kept his muscles lax.

A sudden pounding at the door made them both jump.

"Open the door!" a voice yelled, loud enough to shake the walls. "If you've touched that boy, I'll have your head, I swear it!"

It was his father. The boy thought to cry out to him, to let him know that he was okay. That the crow god's will must be followed, that he wanted this, that his mother would never hurt him.

She returned to her work, ignoring his father and his threats. "Almost done now."

"Saaya, please!" pleaded his father, voice breaking.

"Is he crying?" the boy asked, concerned.

"Shhh." The corner of his left eye tugged tight as she tied off the last knot.

Her lips pressed briefly to his forehead, and she ran a gentle hand through his hair.

"A child in a foreign place to a foreign man," she murmured, and Serapio knew she was talking to herself. "I've done everything required. Even this."

Even this was what he had suffered today, he knew it. And for the first time, a tendril of doubt crept through his belly.

"Who, Mama? Who asked you to do this?" There was still so much he didn't understand, that she hadn't told him.

She cleared her throat, and he felt the air shift as she stood. "I must go now, Serapio. You must carry on, but it is time for me to join the ancestors."

"Don't leave me!"

She bent her head and whispered in his ear. A secret name. His true name. He trembled.

And then she was moving away, her footfalls heading swiftly toward the open terrace. Running. Running to where? There was only the terrace that ended in the open sky.

And he knew she was running so she could fly.

"Mama!" he screamed. "No!"

He struggled to open his eyes, but the stitches held, and his lids did not budge. He thought to claw at his face, but the cords held him tight and the drink made time feel strange.

"Son!" his father screamed. Something huge hit the door, and the wood splintered. The door was coming down.

"Mama!" Serapio cried. "Come back!"

But his begging did no good. His mother was gone.

CHAPTER 2

City of Cuecola

Year 325 of the Sun

(20 Days before Convergence)

A Teek out of water swims in wine.

—Teek saying

The early-dawn fruit sellers walked the streets of Cuecola, enticements to purchase the day's brews ringing from their lips. Their voices flowed through the narrow streets and wide avenues alike, past the modest oval-shaped, thatch-roofed homes of the common citizens and up through the more lavish multistoried stone mansions of the merchant lords. They wove around the jaguar-headed stelae that guarded the great four-sided pyramids and across the well-worn royal ball court that sat empty in the predawn darkness. Across tombs and market squares and places of ceremony and out past the city walls, they filled the morning with their cries. Until even Xiala, blissfully unconscious until moments before, heard them.

"Somebody please shut them up," she muttered, cheek flat against the cold dirt floor on which she had slept. "They're giving me a headache." She waited, and when no one acknowledged her, she asked again, a little louder.

For answer, someone kicked her in the ribs. Not hard, but enough to make her grunt and crack an eye open to see who had done it.

"You shut up," the culprit said. It was a skinny woman twice her age with a drag to the left side of her face and an ominous scar across her neck. "You're making more noise than them."

"—mmm not," Xiala mumbled, giving the stranger her best glare. Dirt stuck to her lip. She dragged a hand across her mouth to wipe it away. Only then did she get a good look around at the room she was in: dark wet walls and a wooden-slatted door where an open entrance should have been. Too many women reeking of body odor and fermented cactus beer sprawled on the floor, a lucky few huddled under threadbare cotton blankets in the cold. Someone was softly weeping in a dark corner.

"Fuck," she said, sighing. "I'm in jail again."

The skinny woman, the one who had kicked her, cackled. She was missing teeth. The two front and another lower one. Xiala wondered if they'd rotted out or she had sold them. She looked like someone who might have sold them.

"This ain't a merchant lord's house," the woman said, grinning. "That's for sure."

"Thank the lesser gods for that, at least," she said, and meant it. She was no fan of merchant lords. In fact, it was working for a merchant lord that had landed her here, in an admittedly roundabout way. If Lord Pech hadn't tried to double-cross her, she wouldn't have had to throw him into the ocean. She hadn't stuck around to see if he was rescued or not, choosing instead to retreat to a cliffside cantina that looked much too seedy for someone like Lord Pech to frequent. Disgusted with the double-cross and her sour luck, she'd decided to drink. She would have decided to drink anyway, but it never hurt to have a good excuse.

Weary, she pushed herself to sitting. Too quickly, and her head spun, the price of her good excuses. Xiala gripped her skull with both hands, willing the world to steady. The skin on her knuckles pulled painfully, and she looked at her right hand to find them swollen and red. She must have hit someone, but for all the cacao in Cuecola, she couldn't remember who. The toothless woman laughed harder.

Shaking her sore hand out and pointedly ignoring her amused cellmate, Xiala got to her feet. She ran questing fingers over her clothes, taking stock of what she was missing. Her dagger, which was no surprise. Her small purse, also not surprising. But she still had the clothes on her back and the sandals on her feet, and she told herself to be grateful for that. There had been a time or two she had come out of a drunken night with less.

She stepped over the sleeping figures around her, not bothering to mouth apologies when she accidentally trod on a hand or kicked a turned back. Most of the women didn't notice, still sleeping or inebriated into oblivion. Xiala licked her dry, cracked lips. She wouldn't mind a drink right now herself. *No,* she told herself. *Didn't we just establish drinking is what landed you here to begin with? No more drink. And no more merchant lords.*

She threw that last one in for good measure, but she knew

neither resolution would hold for long. She was a sailor, after all, and sailors relied on both merchant lords and alcohol to survive.

She reached the slatted door and tentatively tested it to see if it would give. It didn't, so she pressed her face through the spaces between the bars, peering around the early-morning darkness. She faced a courtyard. The lack of light outside obscured the details, turning the building across from her into a rectangular stone block and the open space between them an empty hole. To her left and right stretched more cells, but she couldn't tell if they were occupied or not. Either way, she seemed to be the only soul awake. Except for the woman who had laughed at her, of course.

She could still hear the fruit sellers, but they were fainter now, having moved on. Instead, her ears filled with the rustle of the wind through the palms and the familiar cries of chachalacas waking in their nests. The air was scented with the lingering aroma of freshly pulped papaya, spindly night-bloomers, and over all of it, the salty tang of the sea.

The sea.

The very thought was a comfort. When she was on the sea, she was happiest. The problems of the land, of jails and lords, didn't exist. If she could get back on a ship, everything would be all right.

But first she had to get out of here.

"Guards!" she shouted, squinting into the darkness. She couldn't see anyone, but there had to be guards. She banged a flat hand against the slats. They didn't budge. She yelled again, but only the birds and the wind answered her. She needed something that would make some noise, that would draw attention. She had nothing on her but her clothes—black trousers that flared out to cleverly resemble the skirts that were more socially acceptable for Cuecolan women and a woven striped huipil, tied tight at her waist with a fringed scarf that trailed over one hip. None of it useful for making noise.

She tapped her foot against the ground, thinking. And rolled her eyes at the obvious solution. She slipped her left foot from its sandal and picked up the leather-soled shoe. She ran it across the slats, and it made a satisfying slapping sound.

"Guards!" she cried again, this time accompanied by the sound of leather striking the bars.

Annoyed voices rose behind her in disgruntled grumbling, but she kept at it, louder even.

Finally, a shadow detached itself from the wall two doors down. A woman in a guard uniform swaggered over, obviously in no hurry. Xiala ran her sandal across the slats with a heavier hand, willing the woman to speed. The guard's face came into view in the dim light, irritation making her eyes small and her mouth smaller. Once within reach, her hand darted out serpent fast and plucked the shoe from Xiala with a growl. "What do you think you're doing?"

"I'm getting your attention," Xiala said, raising her chin. "I'm ready to get out."

The guard scoffed. "You're not getting out."

Xiala frowned. "What do you mean? I've sobered up. I won't cause any trouble. You can let me go."

An ugly smirk spread the guard's mouth wide. "You're in until the tupile decides what to do with you."

"What to do with me?" Worry slipped down Xiala's spine. Her memory of the night before was hazy at best. She assumed she'd been picked up on the street and dropped here to sleep off the drink. She wasn't proud of it, but it wouldn't be the first time and likely not the last. But this guard was insinuating there was more to her circumstances than public intoxication and a poorly thrown punch. Maybe Pech had squealed. She stifled a rising dismay.

"You must let me out," she said, deciding to go for bravado. "I've got a ship waiting for me."

The guard barked a desultory laugh. "Oh, a ship? You a sailor, then? No, no, a captain? Wait, a merchant lord himself! One of the House of Seven." She guffawed loudly.

Xiala flushed. It did sound ridiculous, but the truth was often ridiculous. "Captain," Xiala said, trying to sound imperious, "and if I don't show at port to sail, my lord will be vexed. And you'll be sorry!"

"I guess I'll just have to be sorry. Until then . . ." She tucked Xiala's shoe under her arm and turned to go.

"Hey!" she shouted. "Give me my sandal!"

"You'll get your shoe when the tupile comes," the guard tossed over her shoulder as she walked away. "And keep it down, or I'll have you beaten!"

Xiala watched her until she'd melted back into the shadows. She shuddered, noticing the chill for the first time. She hunched forward, seeking a little warmth. But there was no warmth here. She finally gave up and shuffled back through the maze of sleeping women on the floor, a now-shoeless foot the only thing to show for her troubles. She found an empty spot against a wall and slumped down, arms across her knees and head down, nothing to do but wait.

• • • • •

She didn't wait long.

Within the hour, noise and movement outside the cell had her lifting her head to get a better look. A few of the women who had been asleep before were up, and they moved toward the barred door to see what was going on. Whatever they saw had them hurrying back to flop on the floor and feign sleep, no doubt to avoid whatever was coming. Xiala craned her neck, unafraid. The only thing she feared was not getting back to a ship.

A man came into view. He was middle-aged, thick and solid, his hair a black bowl around a heavily jowled face and hard eyes. He wore a sash that marked him as a tupile, the constable of the jail. Xiala's stomach sank. He did not look like a man of mercy.

And then another man stepped into view. A handsome man, tall and well built, neither too thin like the toothless woman nor thick like the tupile. Elegant strands of silver twisted through his black hair, which he wore long and tied back in a nobleman's high bun. He was dressed in white, a knee-length loincloth and one-shouldered cape that showed a muscular and well-tended physique. The cloth was rough and lacking in embroidery or adornment, a rejection of current trends. It spoke of modesty and devotion, but the conceit was belied by the collar of jade at his neck and the wealth of jewels in his ears and on his wrists. Even in this rotten jail, he glowed, exuding charm and confidence. And, above all, wealth.

A merchant lord for sure, a son of the noble class most likely, and one of the House of Seven if she had to guess.

Xiala hated his guts on principle.

As if sensing her regard, and likely her disgust, the lord looked up from his quiet conversation with the tupile. His gaze met hers, and he smiled. But it was a serpent's smile, pleasing enough to one who doesn't know fangs and venom lurk just out of sight.

"That's her," said the merchant lord with a slight nod in her direction.

Part of her wanted to shrink back from his notice, but more of her wanted out, and he looked like freedom. She stood tall, dusting the prison dirt from her clothes as best she could and doing her damnedest to look like she didn't belong in jail.

The tupile frowned, gaze cutting to Xiala and then back to the man. "The charges are serious, Lord Balam," he said in a low voice, thick with anxiety. "I cannot look the other way. We are, after all, a society of laws that apply equally to all, noble and common."

"Of course we are," Lord Balam replied, "and you are only doing your job. But perhaps I can smooth the way." He pressed something into the tupile's hand that Xiala could not see.

The heavier man clenched the object in his palm.

Balam turned the full weight of his dazzling gaze on the tupile. "I understand you are concerned," he said, taking the man's hands firmly between his own. "And I will see her punished. But if she is already in service to me, a sentence of slavery is not feasible."

"Hers are not crimes that result in slavery, Lord," the tupile sputtered. "These are capital offenses."

Xiala choked. Mother waters. She wasn't actually trying to kill Pech when she'd thrown him into the sea. It wasn't her fault he couldn't swim.

"Drunkenness," the tupile continued, "public lewdness, entering the home of another without invitation. An accusation of adultery with a wom—"

Oh. Not Pech. Not Pech at all.

It started to come back to her now. Her memory of arriving at the rowdy cantina was true enough. There was even the remembrance of her first drink. And her second, the sting of anise against her tongue. And there was the woman, flowers in her long hair, her huipil baring her shoulders. They had laughed together and danced and . . . all seven hells. Now she remembered. They had gone to the woman's house, and it was all going so well until the husband came home. Xiala vaguely recalled punching the man in the face, which explained her hand, but it was only because he was blocking the door and screaming at her. The rest was a blur. He must have had her arrested. And now here she was. Facing a death sentence.

She should have been scared of the tupile and his laws and his unjust justice, but she was not. She knew how Cuecola worked. A lord had taken interest in her, which meant she was as good as sprung. But sprung for what? A rich man didn't notice someone like her unless he wanted something.

The two men concluded their transaction, and the guard was told to unlock the cell door and usher Xiala forward.

She started to speak, but Lord Balam, her unasked-for savior, cut his gaze to her. For a moment he stared, his eyes widening. She lifted her chin, a dare. His gaze fell to her feet.

"Where is her other shoe?" he asked.

The female guard shuffled forward and handed it over with a muttered explanation, and Xiala had to work to suppress a wild desire to gloat.

Soon enough, he was leading her out of the courtyard with its collection of prison cells, and she breathed a deep sigh of relief. She was free.

She thought about bolting immediately, but she had no idea where they were. The neighborhood was unfamiliar, if typical of the countryside. The scent of eggs and corn cakes cooking flavored the air, and she was sure she could still smell the citrus fruit vendors' wares, although she hadn't spotted one. Her stomach growled. She couldn't remember when she'd last eaten, and she was ravenously hungry. But she shoved her hunger down. If she wanted to eat, she would have to ask this Balam for the funds to do it with, and she would not. Not until she knew what he wanted.

"Who—?" she started.

"You made me come to Kuharan," Balam said, interrupting her. He had a pleasant melodic voice and he said the words lightly, as if teasing a friend. "I do not enjoy Kuharan."

"Who are you? And what in all the hells is a Kuharan?"

He lifted a hand to gesture around him. "This is Kuharan. We're just outside the city in a small farming community. Do you not remember coming here?" The look he gave her, knowing full well her answer was no, made her flush hot. "Be lucky you did," he said. "I don't know that I could have bribed a city official as easily as I did this country one." His lips quirked up. "She must have been very beautiful."

Xiala flushed even hotter. "She was," she said defiantly.

"The things we do for beautiful women," he said with a knowing sigh.

She held her retort. She didn't believe for a moment this man next to her had done anything foolish for a beautiful woman, or a beautiful man for that matter. Lord Balam looked much too controlled to be swayed by something as simple as pleasures of the flesh.

"Perhaps you did not know such love is forbidden here?" he asked smoothly.

Xiala spat. "For a city this size, you would think there wouldn't be quite so many uptight prigs."

"Ah, but we aren't in the city." He sighed, as if burdened. "But even in the city proper . . ." He left the thought unfinished, but Xiala knew the answer. "Is it different where you come from?" he asked, voice innocent. "Among the Teek?"

"Where are your people?" she asked, changing the subject. Where she came from and who she loved were none of his business.

He tilted his head. "People?"

"Servants. A palanquin. I thought lords like you didn't have feet."

He laughed. "I prefer to walk, and Kuharan is not so far for a morning walk."

It was a lie. She guessed that he had come alone because he didn't want anyone to know he was here. But why? She still didn't know why he had come for her, or how he had even found her.

"You still haven't told me who you are."

"My name is Balam. Lord Balam of the House of Seven, Merchant Lord of Cuecola, Patron of the Crescent Sea, White Jaguar by Birthright."

They all had titles like that, and his meant as little as the ones she'd heard before. "Am I supposed to care?"

"Well, I was hoping it would impress you," he said dryly. "It would save us some time." He smiled that smile again, or maybe he had never stopped smiling. "I know who you are, after all." He paused to make eye contact so his meaning couldn't be missed. "*What* you are."

Of course he did. He'd come all the way to this place he hated to bail her out of jail. He had to know what she was.

"What is it you want, Lord of . . . Cats, was it?" she asked. "Rich men don't talk to me unless they want something. And they certainly don't bribe tupiles to get it."

"We could start with a bit of respect," he said mildly, "but that seems unlikely."

"Highly." She decided to get the basics out of the way. "Just so you know, I'm not selling my bones."

Balam startled. "Your bones?"

She tried to gauge whether he was faking his surprise. He had said he knew what she was, which meant he knew she was Teek. Some men collected Teek bones as good-luck charms. A finger bone might bring you auspicious weather or a strong wind. Catch a Teek and carve her throat bone out, and it would guarantee a good catch in deep waters, they said. She thumbed the missing top joint of the little finger on her left hand. It was her own fault she'd lost the pinkie. She'd had too much to drink and trusted the wrong man, a pretty one with eyes like wet earth after a spring rain and hands that had slipped between her legs and made her . . . well, never mind that. Now she kept a dagger on her belt that seemed enough to ward off treasure seekers. The dagger she'd lost at some point last night, either left behind by accident or confiscated by the jail. Well, perhaps that was for the better. She wasn't much for daggers. Hers was mostly for show, since if it ever came down to losing a body part again, she'd Sing her way out of trouble. Assuming she was sober enough to conjure her voice. People got discouraged by a dagger, but they got downright murderous if they thought you were trying to magic them with your Song.

"Eyes, then?" she asked, challenge in her voice. "I saw you staring."

Some Teek had eyes the crystal blue of the brightest waters, some the storm gray of gales, but the rarest of Teek had eyes like hers: a kaleidoscope of jewel colors, shifting like sunlight in shallow water. A man in a port she couldn't remember now once told her the nobles of Tova collected Teek eyes like hers to wear around their fingers like jewels. She had Sung that bastard down to sleep without hesitation. No harm done beyond not waking up in time to make muster on the dock the next day. Which no doubt led to missed work, missed wages. A small harm, then. But deserved.

"No bones, no eyes," Balam said with a theatrical shudder. "I have a job for you, Captain. I hear you might be in need of one."

"Lord Pech. That's how you found me?"

He nodded.

Of course all the lords talked. Which meant her job prospects were shrinking by the second. Not only would she be a dangerous Teek, she'd be a Teek with a temper.

"What kind of cargo?"

"The human kind."

"Slaves?" She shook her head. She was desperate but not that desperate. "I don't move people."

"Not slaves." He made a face like the idea was distasteful, but she wasn't convinced. The lords of Cuecola were not above the slave trade.

"Then who?"

He wagged a finger. "The question should be to where."

He was avoiding an answer, but she let it pass for the moment. "To where, then?" she asked.

"Tova."

She had never been there, but she knew of it. Everyone did. It was called the Jewel of the Continent and the Holy City and the City of the Sky Made. It was a cliff city high in the clouds, the legendary birthplace of the Sky Made clans and the home of the Sun Priest and the Watchers whose duty it was to keep the calendar and wrestle order from chaos. Tova was the religious heart of the Meridian continent, just as Cuecola was its commercial capital and Hokaia its military center.

She visualized the map of the Meridian in her head. It was a land mass whose populations centered around a crescent-shaped swoop of coastline with Cuecola at the bottom tail of the C, the mouth of the river Tovasheh, the gateway to Tova, at the top left corner of that C, and Hokaia at the far top edge of the C in a parallel line north-south from Cuecola. There were other cities and settlements on the continent, but none as large or as powerful as the three great cities that bordered the Crescent.

"It's a long way," she said, "and a dangerous route for this late in the year. The Crescent Sea is known for its late-autumn storms. Shipkillers, they call them. Waves three times as tall as a tall man. Winds to howl down the heavens. And rain. Flood rains."

Tova could be reached by land, but the fastest way was around the Crescent by ship and then upriver by barge or foot. Most ships had already put into dock for the off-season or were running short voyages that kept them glued to the coast. Her disastrous outing with Lord Pech was supposed to be her last for the year.

"You must be there in twenty days."

"Twenty days? No. That's impossible this time of year. More likely thirty to account for bad luck and bad weather, assuming you could even find a captain stupid enough to take you up on it."

"But it can be done?"

"I just said it was impossible."

"But if the seas were calm and weather favored you, and my stupid captain was brave enough to take to the open water rather than hugging the coast?"

Bones and pretty eyes were one thing, but this was where her power lay, and now she understood why he'd come for her. "My Song doesn't work like that. I can't do anything about the weather."

"But you can calm the seas, and it is said that your kind do not fear the open water."

"My *kind*?" She laced that with the disdain it deserved, but Balam was unbothered.

"Teek, of course."

She rolled her eyes to the stars. Why try to educate those who cared not to learn?

"It must be twenty days," he insisted. "Or else there is no deal."

They had passed the city wall and entered Cuecola proper. This part of town was more familiar. They walked a long wide avenue that Xiala recognized as running between the homes of the House of Seven before dead-ending into the docks and, finally, the sea.

"And what exactly is the deal you're offering?"

"A ship, with a full commission of cargo and crew," he said, "provided you continue to work for me. I will give you ten per-cent of whatever profits are made from the ship trade, in ad-dition to a basic living salary and a room in one of my houses when you are at port in Cuecola. However, if you leave my employment before the term is complete, the ship stays with me and you forfeit anything you have earned as payment."

"How long is the term?"

"Twelve years."

Twelve years. Twelve years was a long time under the thumb of any lord. Still, she could amass a tidy bundle in twelve years if his ship and cargo were as fine as she thought they might be. She could retire at thirty-nine, a well-off woman. The idea of not having to scramble for jobs, of not having to grovel to another lord or convince a doubting crew she was worth more than eyeballs and pinkie fingers.

"How do I know you aren't a bastard like Pech?"

He smiled. "Oh, I am a bastard, but I am a fair one. You will not regret your employment."

"So I work for you, and after twelve years you give me a fortune."

"Your earned payment," he acknowledged.

"And if I leave before the term is up?"

"You get nothing."

She chewed at her chapped bottom lip. "Can I be fired?"

"Only for a breach of morals."

She barked a laugh. A faint smile, a genuine smile, tugged at the corner of his mouth.

"Twenty percent," she challenged.

He came to a stop, forcing her to stand still with him. The street was busy enough the foot traffic had to veer around them like water around an isle, but no one dared question a lord of the House of Seven. If he wished to stand in the middle of the street and have a conversation with a woman in pants who reeked faintly of alcohol and piss, that was his prerogative.

"I would think, Captain," he said, his tone matter-of-fact, "that you would be glad for any employment right now that might remove you from Cuecola for a while. Time away may help a certain tupile forget about your capital crimes. Do not think it will be easy to hire on to another ship, after what you did to Pech. He was livid, you know. That alone would have you thrown in jail, never mind all the rest."

"Fifteen."

"Twelve, but if you continue to challenge me, it will be eight."

He waited for her reply, and when none came, he said, "Then we have a deal."

"One more thing."

His mouth tightened, and she said quickly, "A bath. I smell."

He relaxed. "There's a bathhouse near the docks. It can be arranged, but you must be quick."

Quick was fine, as long as it happened. "And fresh clothing."

"Captain, do I look like a laundress?"

She eyed the stalls around them. Most clothing was sewn to order and took weeks to deliver. "I'll launder my own clothes at the bathhouse, then," she conceded. They wouldn't have time to dry, but spending time on ships had accustomed her to being at the very least damp most of the time.

"Now, tell me who I'm taking to Tova," she said.

"A single Obregi man," he said lightly. "Blinded. Scarred. Some kind of religious affliction, as I understand it. Harmless." The last he said too quickly, as if he was hiding something.

"Usually," Xiala said carefully, "when someone describes a man as harmless, he ends up being a villain."

Balam turned his focus to her, the sudden intensity in his dark eyes making her breath catch in her throat. She instinctively reached for her Song the way another woman would reach for a weapon. She no longer had a dagger at her waist, but even if she had, her Song would have come first.

Balam narrowed his eyes, considering. As if he knew she had armed herself. As if he approved. After a moment he turned from her and continued down to the docks.

"Let us hope you are wrong, Captain," he said over his shoulder, "for both our sakes."

CHAPTER 3

CITY OF TOVA (COYOTE'S MAW)
YEAR 325 OF THE SUN
(THE DAY OF CONVERGENCE)

It is declared that each of the great peoples who had entered into agreement here shall once a year send four children of the age of twelve from within their territory to serve under the Sun Priest in the city of Tova and reside in the celestial tower for a period of no less than sixteen years upon which they may return home should they choose; the exception being that the child be designated the head of their society whereby they shall serve another sixteen years; the exception being the child be designated the Sun Priest, whereby they shall serve unto death.

—"On the Replenishment of the Watchers,"
from the signing of the Treaty of Hokaia and the
investiture of the Sun Priest, Year 1 of the Sun

Naranpa was not dead, even though the witch Zataya thought her so. She could not move her limbs or open her eyes, and her breath came out in an almost imperceptible wheeze, but she could hear and more so *feel* everything that was happening to her.

She felt the apprentices' hands, two girls who strained and heaved as they dragged her from the river. She heard Zataya order them to build up the fire, and then she breathed in the smoke the witch fanned from the flames. She screamed without sound at the hot, thick drip of blood against her naked chest, and then at Zataya's command to her apprentices to spread the blood evenly over Naranpa's supine form. And as the witch covered her with a blanket, pausing only to pry her mouth open and place a salt rock under her tongue, Naranpa wept unnoticed tears.

Naranpa had been a child once. Long before she joined the priesthood, before she learned to read the course of the sun and command Sky Made queens, she had been a beggar in the poor district of Tova called Coyote's Maw. Often when the streets were quiet before the evening crowd of gamblers, tourists, and pleasure seekers arrived in the Maw, Naranpa had sat on the westernmost ledge of the top level of the district and peered out over the dizzying distance that separated her home from the wealthier neighborhoods. Looking out over the city, she had dreamed. Of crossing the woven suspension bridges that swayed like spidersilk in the gentle canyon breezes and allowed free travel among all the districts but hers. Of exploring the wide roads and stately adobe brick homes, some four and five stories high, not as a servant like her mother but as someone who belonged there. And brashest of all, of being a scholar in the celestial tower in the district of Otsa.

She was only ten, then, her destiny far from decided. She had not yet learned she was poor and people like her only went to the celestial tower as servants, or that once you were poor, people hated you for it even when you weren't poor anymore.

She remembered a summer night she sat with her family around the cooking coals they shared with their neighbors, talking about how she wished to study the stars. In the Sky Made districts, the scions ate on great communal terraces where kitchens produced food for hundreds, but in the Maw, people kindled small dugout fires in the street where they roasted ground cornmeal or buried whole ears of corn in hot ash to bake overnight.

At her words, her mother had exchanged a mysterious glance with her father, and he had nodded.

"It is good fortune that you would talk of studying the stars tonight, Nara," her mother said, her voice high with excitement. "I spoke to the matron I serve, and she remembered you and how smart you are and how well you learn, and she has agreed to sponsor you at the celestial tower."

Naranpa felt dizzy. "I'm going to be a scholar-priest?" She knew there were other disciplines one could learn at the tower—healing, writing and history, even the art of death— but all she had ever wanted was to study the sun and moon and the movement of the stars.

Her father laughed. "Oh, no, little one. They would never let you study there. You are to work. You will serve the priests. Help cook their meals, wash their vestments, clean their floors."

Her stomach dropped in disappointment.

"But . . ." Her mother gave her father a long look. "Perhaps you will learn something if you listen closely. A servant can learn a lot through observation if she is quiet."

"Then I will be quiet," she vowed solemnly. "And I will learn everything!"

"That's not fair," her younger brother, Denaochi, protested. "Why does she get to go and not me?"

"Who wants to be a priest when you could be one of the Sky Made scions?" her other brother, Akel, asked.

Naranpa bit her lip. Being Sky Made *was* exciting. Water Strider was her favorite clan, and its matron was the one her mother served. It ruled the district of Titidi, which was closest to the Maw. She could see the curving edges of its cliffs when she gazed across the narrow canyon that divided them, its great sky-blue banners cascading down the sides of adobe buildings between dripping green vines and colorful tendrils of starburst flowers. She could even see trees there. Trees! The Maw had no trees. Titidi was a garden of impossible green and growth, with a waterfall that ran right through it like a living street before tumbling to the river that bisected Tova below. When her mother talked of it, she imagined Titidi was something out of a story, a place she could only hear about but never touch. But now . . .

"What clan would you be, Akel?" she asked.

"Why would anyone want to be anything but Golden Eagle?" Denaochi interrupted. "Everyone knows they are the most powerful of the four clans."

"Not if we go to war!" Akel countered.

"You want to ride on the back of a water insect when we go to war?" He lifted his sharp chin. "I'll be on the back of an eagle, shitting down on you!"

"Not a Water Strider, a Winged Serpent!"

"Same difference."

Akel lunged at his little brother, but Denaochi easily dodged his half-hearted blow.

"What's this talk of war?" their father said, rough anger coloring his voice. "Tova does not war. We have been at peace for three hundred years, since the priesthood united us."

"Akel's the one who wants to fight. I want to rule!" Denaochi's face was so smug Naranpa could only laugh.

"Boys don't rule in Tova," Akel countered. "Besides, all you could ever rule is the sewer pile. You and your shitting birds. I'm going to the war college in Hokaia with the scions where I'll learn to fight."

"Enough!" their father muttered. "You don't know what you're talking about, either of you. Do I have fools for sons? Dreaming of being lords and warriors? You'll be lucky to find work in the mines or in the fields in the east." He snorted. "The war college is not for the likes of you, Akel. If war comes, you would be nothing but fodder, or worse, a sacrifice on a foreign altar where the Sun Priest has not brought enlightenment. And you, Ochi . . ." He turned his gaze to the younger boy. "Akel's right. The only place you'll ever rule is right here in the Maw, and there's nothing here worth reigning over but trash."

"Jeyma," her mother chided her husband. "They're only children."

"They are too old for nonsense." He glared at his brood, one by one. "Remember well. You're no Sky Made scions, and you never will be. Get those thoughts out of your head or court misery the rest of your life."

Silence fell across the small family in the wake of her father's reprimand. Her mother said nothing, but Naranpa could see her disapproval clear enough in the set of her jaw, the look in her eyes.

"When I go to the celestial tower in Otsa, I will bring you all to visit me," Naranpa offered, trying to soothe the mood, "and you can ride an eagle, Ochi. And you a winged serpent, Akel. But not to war. Just for fun!"

"I said enough fool talk," her father grumbled, sounding more tired than angry. "You too, Nara. No more."

Her promise to her brothers had not come to fruition, of course. Not only because the riders of the great Sky Made clans' beasts were lords even among the scions and specially chosen from their clans to train for years before they were allowed mounts, but also because by the time Naranpa did leave her home and move to Otsa to become not just a servant, although she had been that, and not just a dedicant, although she was that, too, but the Sun Priest, its highest honor . . . by that time, her older brother was dead and her younger brother dead in spirit. She was not sure of her parents' final fates, but she assumed them dead, too. She had never gone back to find out.

Because her father had been right. The truth was that as much as she loved the city, the city did not love her back. It had little use for a Maw beggar girl; some use for a clever servant who caught the attention of the aging and eccentric Sun Priest; more use for an unlikely dedicant who had an uncanny ability to read the stars and outshine her society classmates; and a final and blistering use for an idealistic young Sun Priest who thought she could make a change to her beloved city but instead only made enemies.

Again and again, Tova forced her to earn its regard, and she had done so every time. She comforted herself with the fact that she had not done it for glory, or for power, but for the worst reason of all.

Faith. Faith in this place she called her home.

But, she thought as she lay under the witch's blanket plagued by memories of her childhood and her foolish fantasies, blood drying on her skin and salt burning her mouth, *faith is not going to save me now.*

CHAPTER 4

CITY OF TOVA

YEAR 325 OF THE SUN

(20 DAYS BEFORE CONVERGENCE)

It is declared that all roads both on Earth and in Sky converge at the Celestial Tower in Tova. It is declared to be the sacred duty of the Watchers of the Tower to maintain the Balance between what is above us and what is below. It is they who shall study the patterns of Sun and Moon and prophesy accordingly; they who shall ensure that the Rain falls and the Maize grows; they who shall raise up Reason and Science and labor to cast down the bloodthirsty gods of old. If they fail in their Task, all know that War may come again, and the people will suffer. But the Watchers will suffer worst of all, for they will be the first to Die.

—"On the Responsibility of the Watchers,"
from the signing of the Treaty of Hokaia and the
investiture of the Sun Priest, Year 1 of the Sun

Naranpa had forced the priesthood to gather at the foot of the bridge to Odo at sunrise, and no one was happy about it.

She could hear the grumbling and the foul-mouthed cursing, unseemly for such a gathering. Someone was complaining that there was no hot breakfast, and how were they supposed to walk the length of the city with no hot breakfast? She wanted to smack them. Or at least yell at them to toughen up. The Shuttering was supposed to begin tomorrow, twenty days of fasting and penance to prepare the way for the return of the sun upon the winter solstice. How did these dedicants think they would survive Shuttering if they were whining about not getting breakfast?

"It will be a wonder the sun wants to return at all with all this complaining," she said under her breath, loud enough for immediate company to hear, but no one else.

To be fair, the morning had dawned bitter cold, a sure sign the winter solstice was only days away. Priests and dedicants alike had donned fur cloaks and wool leggings in addition to their priestly vestments. They had even traded sandals for cured-hide boots. Even so, Naranpa had no doubt that by the end of the day, they would all be frozen as solid as one of the icicles that dangled from the top of the celestial tower.

Still not a reason to complain. There was nobility in suffering. It built character. Or at least she hoped it did. She supposed they would all find out soon enough.

"This procession is a fine idea, Naranpa," Haisan said good-naturedly as he joined Naranpa at the head of the gathered group. "Let us hope for a good showing from the Sky Made for the Day of Shuttering."

"Your mask, Haisan," Naranpa reminded the old priest. At least *he* was trying. He was ta dissa—the head of the historical records society—which made him a scholar and respected, but he was sometimes forgetful about the practical things.

"Oh!" Haisan patted the pockets of his robe, becoming increasingly distressed, until he finally reached under the folds of the great bearskin he wore and produced a black mask, tiny pinpricks of stars dotting the forehead and cheeks. With a small embarrassed smile, he pulled it over his face.

She cast a quick glance at her other two priestly companions. Abah, who was seegi and head of the healing society, and Iktan who was tsiyo, a knife, and head of that society. Both were masked and waiting, Abah in her white mantle and matching dress and furs and Iktan in a mask of solid red and a long skirt, both the color of sunset and the brightness of new blood.

Naranpa was hawaa, head of the oracle society. Her own mask was the sun, as vividly yellow as the belted dress she wore under her fur-lined dawn cloak. The mask was a mosaic made of long thin bars of gold, complemented by slim fingers of hammered metal radiating out like sunlight from shoulder to shoulder. She wore it with honor, always, but today with a sense of dread, too.

"I still don't see why we have to do this," Abah said, leaning close to whisper to Iktan, but Naranpa heard her all the same. Abah was young, the youngest of all four of them. She had risen to the head of her society when her mentor had unexpectedly died last spring. Naranpa had risen a few months after her for the same reason, but she was at least fifteen years older than the girl. Which meant at least a dozen years more experience, even if Abah had been granted her status before her.

"We do this to show the city that the priesthood is still here," Naranpa said, her face still forward. She didn't turn to see, and couldn't have said for certain because of her mask, but she was sure Abah was shooting murderous looks at her back.

"They know we're here, Nara," the younger woman replied, a note of irritation in her voice. "They pay tithes, don't they? Make offerings on holy days? Send their young from across the Meridian continent to train for the priesthood?"

"And they resent it." Now she did turn to face the other priest. "I want to show them we are not some shriveled-up old penitents in a tower, but a living breathing part of this city. That we are accessible. That we care."

"Oh," Haisan said, alarmed. "Is that wise? I mean, it's very radical, Naranpa. The priesthood has never paraded itself for the city like this. They come to us, not vice versa. Frankly, things seem to be working fine the way they are."

"You just said this was a good idea, Haisan," Naranpa reminded him gently.

"Oh, yes. Well, a morning walk. The rest, I'm not so sure."

"I'm sure," Abah said through chattering teeth. "And I say, why change what is not broken?"

But it is broken! Naranpa wanted to protest. Else, why fewer and fewer dedicants at their door each year despite the treaty requirements? Why fewer and fewer calls to draw star charts for births and deaths and weddings? Why the rumors of unsanctioned magic in the lower quarters of the city? The growth of cultists to the old gods that they could never quite eradicate? Why did it only seem like the elites of the Sky Made bothered with the priesthood anymore at all, and even their respect seemed sporadic and self-serving?

"We voted on this, Abah," she said, "and you agreed."

The younger woman huffed. "That was weeks ago. I had no idea it would be this cold." She tilted her head toward Naranpa, a sly motion even with her face hidden behind her mask. "If I'm honest, I agreed on a whim, Nara. An indulgence, even, for your sake. I've always thought this procession a terrible idea."

"Of course you did," Naranpa said smoothly, not taking the seegi's bait. "But it's too late to withdraw now. Look, here's the drum and smoke."

Abah muttered something unkind that Naranpa couldn't quite hear. She let it go. She had won despite what Abah might say now, and she allowed herself to savor the victory. It had not been an easy thing to rally the priesthood's societies to process through the city. She was determined to enjoy it while she could.

The drummer, a woman dressed in the pale blue of first light, stepped forward to set the rhythm. The man beside her, also wearing the same blue, lit the cedar and coaxed it to smoking. Naranpa breathed a sigh of relief as they led them away.

The four priests walked in a horizontal line behind the drum and smoke with their dedicants, counting forty-eight for each, trailing in single-file lines behind them like the tails of falling stars.

As they crossed the bridge into Odo, Naranpa marveled at the view of her beloved city. Tova at dawn was always a sight to behold. Its sheer cliffs were wreathed in mist and its famed woven bridges blanketed in frost, the dawn light making everything glow, ethereal and otherworldly. Behind her she knew the celestial tower stood, ever vigilant, its six stories rising from a small freestanding mesa separated from the rest of the city by bridges. In it lived the priests, dedicants, and a small contingent of live-in servants. It also included a library of maps and paper scrolls, a terrace where they all ate meals together, and, on the rooftop, a large circular observatory open to the night sky.

Home, she thought. A home she loved, even if she wasn't always sure she belonged. But that was the Maw talking, making her feel unworthy. The voice in her head that reminded her that she was the only Sun Priest in recorded memory who was not from a Sky Made clan. Because while any child of the Treaty lands was welcome at the tower, the heads of the societies traditionally came from the Sky Made clans of Tova. Her mentor, Kiutue, had raised her up as his successor with no small controversy. But there was no rule against her beyond tradition, so it was allowed, but it was not liked.

Under such circumstances, the smart thing to do would have been to keep her head down, follow convention to a fault, and live out her appointment in comfort. But she did not believe the priesthood had the luxury of her inattention. Kiutue had been content for the position to become more ceremonial than managerial, and the power the seat had once held had drained to the other societies. Unfortunately, none of the other societies was much concerned with the world outside the tower. The dedicant Naranpa had watched as the priesthood became more disconnected from the city with each passing year. It was a sorry fate for an institution that had once been the great unifying force on the continent. She would not be idle while her beloved priesthood eroded further under her watch.

As she turned back to the road, she caught sight of a dedicant who had the bridge railing in a death grip. Rather than sway with the motion of the bridge, the dedicant was fighting it on locked knees.

That one is going to make themselves ill, Naranpa thought.

"Lead on," she whispered to Haisan as she slowed her pace to let the other priests pass.

"Where are you going?" Haisan asked, alarmed.

"I'll only be a moment. Just . . ." She motioned him forward, and he did as he was told. Good old Haisan. At least she could always rely on his ability to follow orders. Abah watched her, no doubt curious, and Iktan didn't acknowledge her, but she knew xir eyes were on her anyway. She fell into step beside the dedicant, who looked up in surprise at their new companion.

"S-s-sun Priest?" the dedicant stuttered out through chattering teeth and a face gone pale with fear. A thin line of sweat blossomed at their temples despite the cold.

"The bridges are sturdy," Naranpa said reassuringly. "We won't fall."

"Oh, yes. I-I know. Tovan engineers are the best in the world. B-but . . . so many people crossing at the same time." The dedicant glanced back. "Is it smart to walk all at once? I mean, even great things fail."

"These bridges have never failed," Naranpa assured them. She didn't know if that was true, but now did not seem like the time to quibble. She studied the dedicant. The curl in their hair and the wide set of their eyes suggested they were from the southern part of the continent, but people moved around. Married as they wished. It was best not to presume, even when the dedicant had the audacity to question the permanence of Tovan structures.

"Where do you come from?" Naranpa asked.

"My apologies, Sun Priest. I'm from a small village, nothing you've heard of. It is south of here, along a branch of the river Tovasheh we call the Little Seduu, 'the little old man,' for the way its back bends." The dedicant flushed, as if embarrassed by their provincialism. "I'm meant to study healing and bring it back to my village."

"What is your name?"

"Kwaya."

"Commendable, Kwaya. Not all are meant to stay in the tower forever. Did you know 'seduu' is similar to the Tovan 'sedoh'?"

"Yes, Sun Priest. We are not so different, although . . ." They hesitated, and then continued in a rush. "I'll never understand how you Tovans live like this. My home is in the flatlands, and it seems much more practical to build there. There's a perfectly good river below us," they said, without looking beneath their feet. "Why not build the city there?"

"It once was, at least to hear the historians tell it. Some of the original dwellings are still in use in the district of Titidi." And the Maw, but she didn't mention that. "But our ancestors built among the cliffs to keep us safe from yours, I believe," Naranpa said with a patient smile. "We were farmers, and the southerners in the flatlands were raiders of farmers. Besides, we wanted to be closer to the heavens." She waved a hand around them.

The dedicant made a small horrified sound. "I'm so sorry. About the raids, I mean."

"I assure you all is forgiven." Although even as she said it, she remembered her father cursing flatlanders as thieves and uncivilized. Ancient prejudices died hard, even in a city united.

The dedicant looked dubious.

"Do not forget that in the celestial tower, we turn our eyes to the sky. Our duty is to study the patterns of the heavens so that they can be replicated on earth."

"But that is hawaa society," the dedicant protested. "I'm only a seegi."

"Do not healers look to the skies as well to understand the ailments of their patients?"

"Yes, of course," Kwaya agreed hastily. "I only meant—"

The sway of the bridge ceased as their feet touched Odo. Kwaya exhaled a long fraught breath. Naranpa patted their arm in sympathy, and they gave her a relieved nod. Only five more bridges to go today. She hoped the dedicant would survive.

"Everything well?" Haisan asked worriedly as she rejoined the priests in the front of the procession. Naranpa knew how much he hated any deviation in the order of things.

"Fine," she assured him. "Only a dedicant who needed a distraction."

Haisan frowned and glared back from where she had come. "That one is one of Abah's dedicants. You should have let Abah comfort them."

"It's fine, Haisan. The societies assign us our responsibilities, not our hearts. I saw a dedicant in need. That's all."

"But—"

"Enough. I'll comfort whom I wish. Now, pay attention. We are coming into Odo proper."

Odo was a sad and eerie place. It was the oldest of the Sky Made districts of the city of Tova, and it was the home of clan Carrion Crow. Carrion Crow were one of the original clans to live in the city in the clouds, but their ascendancy had long passed. Now the other clans held the majority of the power in the city, and Odo was tolerated, often pitied. They were a lesson in what happened when one defied the Watchers, and all took heed. In many ways Odo seemed of the city yet not part of it. Tolerated but not loved, which Naranpa understood more than she would have liked.

The bridge deposited them two stories down from the main throughway, and they had to walk up a flight of narrow and well-worn stone stairs to reach the district proper. Once they reached the top, the home of Carrion Crow stood before them. The district was known for the soft volcanic rock from which its earliest homes had been built. When Carrion Crow first claimed the high cliffs, the buildings had been carved into the original walls, and here and there as they walked down the main road, Naranpa still caught sight of these ancient structures hiding down the side alleys or slipped between more recent buildings. Most homes now were made from irregular bricks quarried and fashioned from the same type of volcanic rock but brought in from outside of Tova. And homes now were finished with wood, either charred to match the black bricks or, on more expensive homes and shop fronts, painted a bright crimson red. And everywhere the crow motif, the distinctive crow skull, was woven on the banners hung from walls and carved into the lintels over doorways.

People stood outside their black buildings, lining the streets to watch them pass. Most wore a variation of the common dress of Tova. Woven skirts for all genders or long loincloths that hung to calf length for men, with leggings in the winter, without in warmer weather. Many, the wealthier of the clans especially, wore belts that signified their rank in the clan. String belts were the most common, and then hides and fur that were often beaded elaborately, and then, for the matron and those of the Great House, aprons and cloaks fashioned from black feathers or black jaguar skin, tanned and shined to beauty. The weather was biting, so most wore capes of fur or hide as well. Others had braved the cold to show bodies carved with the haahan that the Crow clan bore on their skin.

"Black buildings and black looks," Haisan murmured beside her, too low for all but the four priests to hear. "It does not bode well to start our day."

"Of course it does," Naranpa corrected him in the same low whisper. "Do not our ancestors teach that all exist in dualities, scholar? Earth and sky, summer and winter? And among the clans, the brightness of Golden Eagle must be balanced by the shadow of Carrion Crow? The fire of Winged Serpent against Water Strider?"

"True," he admitted with a resigned sigh. "And yet I find Odo disquieting."

"They do not like us here," Abah said.

She was right, of course. They both were.

"Does that surprise you?" Naranpa asked. "They blame us for the Night of Knives. Another wound that we must repair."

"I need not repair anything," Abah protested. "I was not alive back then so have no responsibility for the Night of Knives. I don't know why they hate me."

"None of us was alive," Naranpa said, "save Haisan, and him likely a child. But alive or not, we bear the burden." *And we all reap the benefit*, she thought, but thought it best not to utter something so controversial aloud.

The priesthood had thought the Night of Knives a necessity at the time, a brutal rout of the heresy growing in Odo. Calling for the Night of Knives had been Kiutue's predecessor's doing and, Naranpa guessed, one of the reasons Kiutue himself strove to diminish the power of his own position. He had never admitted it to Naranpa, but it was easy enough to see. Living through it as a young man haunted him. Hundreds had died at the hands of the tsiyo. They had been citizens of Tova, Sky Made scions of what was one of the sacred clans. And yet they had been treated as enemies of the priesthood and slaughtered without mercy. The Night of Knives was a wound that festered in the city, a blight on its heart, and it had altered Tova in ways that still reverberated.

But the ugly truth was that the brutality had had the desired effect. It had humbled Carrion Crow, setting the clan back generations and driving the worship of their old god underground. Until recently, at least, when rumors of the cult's resurgence had been heard.

"Ah, here now! We approach the Great House," Haisan said as they reached a wide avenue that branched to the south. "Let us see if the clan matron greets us or not."

The first test, Naranpa thought. *If Carrion Crow doesn't come to acknowledge our procession, it will be a humiliation and a sure sign that we are in fact enemies.* But to Naranpa's great relief, the matron of Carrion Crow waited before them.

Yatliza was tall and painfully thin. She wore a long black sheath dress of panther skin. A lustrous cape of crow feathers fell elegantly from her shoulders to the ground, and around her neck, a collar of rare red macaw feathers framed a regal face. Her hair was loose down her back and adorned with bits of mica that caught the morning light. For a moment Naranpa felt that old intimidation of the Sky Made stir in her once again. How could you look upon a woman like this and not think her better than you, something that came from another world, perhaps the stars themselves?

But you were chosen, Naranpa reminded herself. *The Sky Made clans may be composed of queens, but Kiutue believed you were the future of the Watchers. Without you, there is no peace and their queendoms crumble. Do not forget!*

But it was hard to remember, painful even. She could almost feel the other priests judging her. Haisan's concern that she was disturbing the order of thing, Abah's thinly veiled disdain, Iktan . . . well, Iktan was her friend and would not judge her, but she sometimes wondered if xe thought she was in over her head but would not say it.

A few rote words of welcome and honor were exchanged, Naranpa managed it well enough, she thought, and then the procession was on its way again, headed to the next district.

Eagerly, they crossed the short bridge into Kun and left the black buildings and black looks of Odo behind.

By then the sun had risen in earnest and the morning frost had all but disappeared, making for a crisp but not miserable morning. As if sensing their western neighbors had not given the priestly procession an enthusiastic welcome, the district of Kun and clan Winged Serpent came out in earnest. The moment their feet left the bridge, a great cheer rose from the gathered crowd. Haisan made an approving sound, and Abah laughed, delighted. Naranpa felt a surge of gratitude and returned the appreciative nods of her fellow priests. Perhaps now they would think her idea not so foolish after all.

She turned to Iktan, but xe was silent behind xir mask. All around them, citizens shouted their support of the priesthood, waving green ribbons or dancing in rhythm to their processional drum, tiny bells jingling at their knees. It was a festival after Odo's funeral march.

"This is excessive," Iktan whispered at her side. She startled. Xe rarely spoke in public.

"What?" she asked over the din of singing and cheers.

"The Shuttering is a solemn day, not a day of celebration. Carrion Crow was a bit dour, yes, but they were more proper than this. What are they doing?"

She shrugged, annoyed at xir words. "Perhaps they're just happy to see us, grateful for our service."

"What service is that, Nara?"

"Was not Kiutue born Winged Serpent before he joined the celestial tower?" She meant it as proof of a shared history, but she could tell immediately Iktan took it poorly.

"We're meant to set aside such relationships once we join the tower," xe said, voice dark. "We are not to show favor to our birth clans, and they are not to remember us. Else we invite corruption. Our duty is to the heavens, is it not? They, unlike humans, are constant. Inviolable." The last word dripped with sarcasm.

"Not now, Iktan. Please." She was used to xir cynicism, but today was turning into a triumphant day. Couldn't she relish it for just a little while?

She turned her attention away from xir and back to the crowd intent on enjoying herself, but some of the pleasure at the clan's greeting had faded, and her old worries returned.

The matron of Winged Serpent had come down from their Great House to greet them in the road. Her name was Peyana. She was elegant, just as Yatliza had been, but Peyana had a vibrancy to her, a liveliness the Carrion Crow matron lacked. She wore a dress of iridescent winged serpent scales for the occasion that undulated like a living skin as she walked. Around her shoulders was a robe of bright green and blue feathers with bits of red and yellow threaded in. Her hair was coiled into two horns atop her head, and jade dripped like green flames from her ears.

After Naranpa and Peyana exchanged the ceremonial greeting, the procession did not stay long in Kun. Soon they had the bridge to Sun Rock at their feet.

"Do we not walk the whole district?" Abah asked.

"Kun is the largest district of Tova and stretches far down the cliffside," Haisan answered before Naranpa could reply. "No need to walk the whole thing. It would take most of the day! And if we crossed the river there, we would enter the northern half of the city in the Eastern districts, which is all farmland. There is certainly no need to walk there. And the only way back toward the Sky Made districts is through the Maw." He shuddered theatrically.

"We'll cross the Tovasheh to Titidi by way of Sun Rock," Naranpa added. "Then we can walk Titidi and Tsay and back across to Otsa by sunset." She ignored Haisan's insult of the Maw.

Sun Rock was a two-hundred-foot-high freestanding mesa in the center of the city. Below and around its walls rushed the Tovasheh river, the life-giving artery of Tova. No clans ruled here on the Rock, and it was only ever populated on ceremonial days and when the Speakers Council met.

The bridge crossing was the longest of their journey but otherwise uneventful. Naranpa wondered how the dedicant from the southern lowlands was faring but didn't inquire. The day was starting to wear on her, and she was ready to rest. Perhaps she could slip her boots off and rub her feet, if Abah wasn't looking and judging her impropriety.

Sun Rock felt empty and abandoned after the pageantry of Odo and Kun. Twenty paces from the bridge landing, the ground dropped away to reveal a great open-air circle dug out of the ground. It was shaped like the roundhouses of the clans' Great Houses but open to the stars, much like the rooftop observatory of the celestial tower. Benches lined its steep stairs all around, and as they passed the eastern entrance, Naranpa called a halt.

She heard the sighs of relief from the dedicants behind her. She took the first steps down into the amphitheater, and everyone followed, spreading out along the benches and calling for water from the servants.

A handful of servants who had trailed the entourage brought forward baskets full of corn cakes, venison, and flasks of water and began to distribute lunch. Naranpa watched the woman who had led the procession with her drum massage her hands before accepting water from a girl in a brown servant's robe.

Another servant wearing brown approached Naranpa, and she absently reached inside the basket he proffered. She missed entirely the knife he pulled from his sleeve until the flash of the obsidian blade caught her eye as it moved toward her chest. She cried out, but she was too late.

Suddenly she was being pulled backward, tumbling off the stone bench. Her head struck the bench behind her, and shock radiated through her body. Her vision blurred, and she flailed instinctively, trying to fight off whatever or whoever she was certain was going to stab her. But her hands hit only air, and by the time she had calmed enough to see what had happened, she realized Iktan had been the one to pull her back.

And xe had taken her place.

And xe had xir own knife buried deep in the servant-in-brown's neck.

Naranpa could do nothing but gape.

Until someone screamed, one of the dedicants. And then Naranpa was scrambling to her feet. Hands reached to help her up. She got to standing just as Iktan lowered the would-be assassin to the ground.

"Search them," the tsiyo called tersely, and it took a moment for Naranpa to realize xe was talking to two society dedicants. The other servants had dropped their baskets and raised their hands wide from their bodies, proclaiming their innocence, as the tsiyo-to-be moved among them, efficiently searching baskets and seeking more weapons.

"Skies and stars," Abah whispered, grasping Naranpa's arm. "Are you all right?"

Naranpa clawed at her mask, ripping it off. Removing one's mask was a thing not done in public, but she couldn't breathe, and there was no one to see but her own people. No, not only her own people. Someone had infiltrated their group and tried to kill her.

"Who was he?" she cried, striding over to Iktan and the dead man.

"You shouldn't have killed him so quickly," Haisan murmured as he approached, too. "Now we cannot ask him who he was."

"Or why he did this!" Abah said breathlessly just behind Naranpa's shoulder.

Naranpa glanced back at the girl. She had taken off her mask, too, and her face was flushed with excitement. Naranpa had a sudden urge to slap her but quelled it quickly. Abah was young, she reminded herself. And foolish, despite her rise to power.

"There's no need to ask," Iktan said in a quiet, measured voice. Xe had just killed a man, had just saved her life, but already xe was as calm as if they were out on a leisurely stroll. The tsiyo leaned down to tear away the man's robe, exposing his lower neck and chest.

Naranpa gasped.

There, carved into his body and dyed red, was the mark they had seen all morning, on banners and above doors: the skull of Carrion Crow.

CHAPTER 5

City of Tova

Year 325 of the Sun

(20 Days before Convergence)

Seek the pattern in all things.

—*The Manual of the Sun Priest*

The rest of the procession around the city passed in a blur. Titidi was a district of citizens in blue garb and measured celebration, and Tsay was much the same, only gold and concerned with eagles instead of insects. Naranpa didn't care about any of it. This was supposed to be a day of honoring the priesthood, an acknowledgment of their importance and power. *Her* power, and the beginnings of the Sun Priest's return to prominence within the tower. But now Naranpa could not calm her pulse, and every noise made her jump, her eyes searching the crowd for someone who wanted her dead.

Iktan had stayed behind on Sun Rock with a tsiyo dedicant to investigate her would-be assassination. Another tsiyo had donned Iktan's red mask and continued in xir stead.

"Is that wise?" Haisan had asked, when Iktan first proposed it. "Tradition would have us—"

"Not be murdered in our own city?" xe asked, amused.

That had silenced the scholar, but Naranpa had pulled her friend aside where they could talk privately.

"What do you think?" she asked xir.

"I think you should be careful and refrain from judgment."

She frowned. "What does that mean?"

"Nothing more than what I said. Let me and mine do our work, and I will come to you in your rooms before full moonrise to tell you what I have learned."

"Iktan . . ." She hesitated. She felt dizzy, off-balance. She knew her reforms were unpopular with the traditionalists, and Carrion Crow certainly had no love for the celestial tower, but an assassination? In all her plans for the future, she had not foreseen it.

She forced herself to breathe deeply. She would not be afraid, but she would be careful. "Do you think it safe for me to continue?"

Iktan tilted xir head, studying her. Dark eyes bored into her, the scrutiny so personal that she flushed. "Yes."

She squared her shoulders. "All right. I'll finish."

And so she had. But when the last bridge came into view, this one glowing in the sunset instead of the sunrise, and leading home to Otsa, she wanted to cry. She was grateful for the mask that she again wore, happy it covered her face and what must be her frightened-rabbit expression.

Tradition dictated that the doors of the celestial tower be symbolically locked at sunset to begin the Shuttering, as acknowledgment that the priests would stay sequestered until the solstice. Naranpa had never felt so glad to hear the boom of those mighty wooden doors closing. For twenty days, the outside world would remain out and her would-be assassins would remain outside with it.

"A vigorous day!" Haisan exclaimed behind her, and she startled so hard she almost fell. Skies, she had to calm down. "Shall we meet for Conclave when the moon is at its zenith to discuss the protocol for Shuttering?" he asked.

She looked around at the milling crowd. Nervous energy thrummed through the air, the excitement of her almost murder too much for the tower inhabitants to bear. "Of course. I suggest we all rest before then so we will be at our best for Conclave."

Haisan nodded, muttering a *yes, yes*, and the rest of the crowd slowly started to disperse, wandering off to their rooms or leaving in search of their last meal on the terrace before the rationing started for Shuttering. Naranpa had sworn them all to secrecy at Sun Rock, but she had no doubt the gossip would spread.

She flagged down a passing servant and asked them to have some of the strong dark tea she liked brought to her room. She knew she should eat while she still could, but she didn't have the appetite.

Once the servant was gone, she climbed the steps to the fourth floor of the tower and her rooms. She hadn't thought to have them searched for intruders before she was standing in front of her door, and suddenly she didn't want to enter. Rational thought told her no one would dare transgress the celestial tower. She was safe here.

And yet . . .

No! She would not cower. She threw the door open, marching boldly into the room, and almost fainted.

Iktan sat languid as a cat on a bench by her bed.

"Dramatic," xe murmured.

"Skies!" She pressed a hand to her chest. "Skies!" she cursed again. "You could have frightened me to death, Iktan. Do not do that."

Xe shrugged, clearly unrepentant. "You are young and healthy. Surely your heart can take it."

"You do not know what my heart can take," she quipped, irritated by xir dismissive attitude. And immediately regretted it.

Iktan raised an eyebrow.

"That is not what I meant," she said, sighing, "but that much is true, too." They had been lovers as dedicants, not unusual among the priests since most joined the tower when they were deep in the throes of puberty. But their affair had been mostly two fumbling teens exploring each other's bodies and still unsure what to do with them. When Iktan had been elevated to Priest of Knives, Naranpa had ended the affair for her own reasons. Iktan had taken her rebuff in stride, simply acquiescing to her wishes and never expressing how xe felt about it either way. And surprisingly, they had remained friends. She had a fondness for xir, and she always would, but she had to admit xe was also very much a killer with a killer's emotional aptitude, and that she found disquieting.

"Tell me what you found," she said.

Iktan was about to speak when a knock came at the door. Xe was up off the bench, a knife drawn from somewhere quicker than her eye could follow.

"No, stop!" She held up her hand. "It's fine. I asked for tea. It's just a servant."

"Did not a servant try to kill you earlier?"

She paused, eyes wide. "But that wasn't a real servant," she protested. She had assumed the infiltration had happened during their walk through Odo. It had not occurred to her that perhaps the assassin had been hiding in the tower this whole time. "Was he truly one of ours?"

Another polite knock, and Iktan opened the door, knife tucked discreetly up a sleeve. The servant, a girl Naranpa recognized, entered with a tray, and the scent of yaupon filled the room. She crossed to a table and set the tray down.

"Thank you, Deeya," Naranpa said. Deeya bowed once before leaving, never aware that Iktan was poised to bury a knife in her throat. Naranpa rubbed at her forehead, feeling the weight of the day. And then Iktan was there pouring her a cup of tea and offering it to her, hand outstretched, just as quickly as xe had bared a knife.

It was so like xir, such a surprising act of care moments after a willingness to violence, that she could only accept it and be grateful for xir presence.

Iktan returned to the bench. "The servant on the Rock was not one of ours," xe said as if they had never been interrupted. "And he certainly seemed to be Carrion Crow."

"And yet I hear hesitation in your voice." She sipped from her tea. "Who else wishes the Sun Priest dead as much as the

Crows? Perhaps another clan? Or maybe the progressives who prefer the Sun Priest weakened, or the traditionalists who think me a populist do-gooder, or someone else entirely that I'm not considering. A foreign city that chafes at the Watchers' authority? Tell me who my enemies are, Iktan, so at least I know who will put the knife in my back." She said it lightly, but her hands were shaking when she set her cup down.

"Perhaps you have many enemies, Nara. Perhaps you have just one. I don't know yet."

Xe was right. She was getting ahead of herself. "So what do you know?"

"The haahan at the base of the man's throat was new. Carrion Crow carve up their children at the onset of puberty or shortly thereafter. And tend to be excessive about it. Backs, arms."

"Yes, I know." She thought of the elaborate designs she had spied on Yatliza's skin earlier that day. "An outward sign of their mourning for those lost on the Night of Knives, so they never forget." It goaded her, goaded the Watchers and the tsiyo in particular, but what could they do about it? After such atrocities as the priesthood had committed, the least they could do was tolerate the Crows' grieving.

"This man was close to twenty-five years of age, give or take, but his haahan could not have been more than a few months old. And there was only one."

"So he's from somewhere else, a new convert to the crow god?"

"It's possible."

"Which means the rumors are true. The cultists are growing." The priesthood knew the cult around the ancient god of Carrion Crow still existed in pockets of fanaticism, but the general consensus was that such cultists were awaiting their god's rebirth, and until that impossibility came to fruition, they were generally more annoyance than danger.

Iktan said, "I have been keeping an eye on the cultists, and they do nothing more than meet, pray to a dead god, and feed the occasionally starving orphan. They are not a threat."

"You say that with the assassin's blood still coloring your sleeve?"

Iktan lifted an arm. The cuff of xir red robe was stained a deeper shade than the rest and stiffening. Xe shrugged, unimpressed. "I still believe it is possible that he was sent by someone who would like us to think he was Carrion Crow. If he had succeeded, the outcry would be enough that no one would believe the cultists were innocent."

Naranpa closed her eyes. If Iktan thought it might be subterfuge, then she must consider it. It wasn't that she was naive, but . . . oh, perhaps she was naive. She hadn't been the head of her society long enough to achieve Iktan's coating of cynicism.

"Kiutue certainly left me a mess," she murmured. "The Sun Priest weakened, the cultists empowered, the societies at odds. But even he could not have foreseen this."

"Nara."

"Yes?" she asked, eyes still closed, chin resting on her chest.

"There have been others." It was a quiet admission, but it threw her even further off-balance. She lifted her head, eyes wide, pulse suddenly racing, as if the danger was in the room with her.

"What?"

"One other, anyway. I took care of it."

"You . . ." She crossed her arms over her stomach as a low anger bubbled in her gut. "And you didn't tell me?"

"I was hoping I would not have to."

"Iktan." She fought to keep her voice steady, her nerves from fraying. "Carrion Crow?"

Silence.

"And you let me walk through Odo today?"

"If I thought you were in danger, I would have—"

"But I *was* in danger!" She made herself take a deep breath.

"I was not convinced."

"But you are now?"

Xe shrugged, a small lift of one shoulder, but it was the most doubt she had ever seen xir show. Iktan might not admit it to her, but the assassination attempt today had rattled xir.

Naranpa spoke calmly, rationally, but her voice held disappointment. "I know the others think I should be no more than a figurehead, but I did not count you among that number. I am not a child you have to keep secrets from. I need you especially, tsiyo, to have faith in me."

Xe said nothing, and xir face, that damn lovely face, was impassive.

"Go," she said, weary.

"You need me."

"Of course I need you." She sighed, annoyed because xe

had made her admit it aloud and because it was all too true. "But right now I need to think. And sleep. I haven't slept for thirty-six hours, and we have Conclave at high moon. How can I convince the Watchers to take me seriously when it seems I must persuade you, too?"

Iktan uncurled from the bench and walked to the door. Xe paused, a hand against the frame. "Let me take care of this, too, Naranpa. It is not a matter of persuasion but of duty. Mine, not yours."

She wanted to acquiesce, but she could not. Xe had always made her feel safe, but there was a fine line between protected and coddled, and hiding things from her only made her feel weak. And there was one thing she had to know. "Did you not tell me because we were . . . we used to . . . you don't believe me capable?"

Xe cocked xir head, tiny lines of confusion marring xir forehead. "You have never done anything to make me think you cannot perform your duties."

"Yes, but . . ." She pressed a hand to her neck, frustrated. Well, perhaps xe did not think less of her because they had once been intimate, but for one reason or another, xe certainly considered her a child. Or maybe she was being unfair, letting her own insecurities lead her. "Does anyone else know about the first attempt?"

"Only my own dedicants."

"So they knew when I did not?"

"As I explained—"

She held up a hand. "No, Iktan. When you keep things from me, it undermines my authority, and I am trying to assert some authority despite the fact that Kiutue left me little to work with. Do you understand?"

"Of course," xe murmured. "Anything else?" Xir words were normal enough, but Naranpa sensed a thread of annoyance underneath.

"No." She ran a tired hand across her face. Waved her once lover and now personal knife toward the door. "But don't do anything without consulting me. Can you promise me that? Then I'll see you at Conclave."

"I would not miss it for all the stars in the sky," xe said, and that time she caught the contempt plain enough. "Truly."

CHAPTER 6

CITY OF CUECOLA
YEAR 325 OF THE SUN
(20 DAYS BEFORE CONVERGENCE)

The sailors of Cuecola are the finest on the Meridian continent and therefore the known world. I had had occasion to sail upon a dozen different ships throughout my travels around the Crescent Sea and never did I doubt their strength and endurance or the savvy of the captain. It is through their labor that Cuecola grows in wealth and stature every day and the riches of the world collect in their coffers. The Cuecola sailor is truly their greatest asset.

—*A Commissioned Report of My Travels
to the Seven Merchant Lords of Cuecola,*
by Jutik, a Traveler from Barach

It had all started so well.

Balam had led her through the city and down to the docks where they had found the bathhouse he promised. She'd wanted to linger in the steam, but he had insisted that time was of the essence, so she'd scraped the dirt from her skin and washed her long hair with yucca and crushed lavender, rinsed her clothes and beat the damp from them against heated rocks, and decided that it would have to do. At least she no longer smelled of a night in jail.

The docks themselves stretched across marshland and inlets of seawater. All around her stilted reed paths ran like bridges across the increasingly deep waters where long flat-bottomed canoes that could accommodate twenty men or more were tethered to broad wooden docks. Crews hauled ashore bales of quetzal feathers in bright blues and reds, vats of rich brown honey, and mounds of salt and turquoise, the last trade of the year. Laughter and the sound of labor filled the air, and for the first time that day, Xiala had relaxed. This was her place, her people. Not even among her own Teek did she feel this at home. Commerce, work, the smell of the ocean. This was where she belonged.

They approached a particularly fine ship. A canoe likely a hundred fifty paces long and twenty paces across, with a cavernous reed-covered awning in the center that would keep the crew and cargo protected from the sun and winds of the open sea. Human figures moved about on the ship, securing goods and preparing the vessel to sail. Experience and her Teek eyesight allowed her to count the number of paddles on the side of the ship and, from that estimation, the size of her crew. At least twenty, but the ship could hold fifty bodies. She grinned. That was a lot of ship. She could already see the possibilities once this Tova run was done. With a ship like that, she could haul enough freight up and down the coast that in twelve years she was going to be very rich indeed.

Then she had met her crew, and it had all gone to hell.

"These are Pech's men," she murmured to Balam as she finally caught a full view of the workers. Well, not all of them. But there were five or six of the twenty whose faces were familiar, men she had done the last run up the coast with.

Balam smiled that way he had been smiling all morning. "Just like you, they were freshly out of work and the only crew I could find willing on such short notice. I had to pay handsomely for their services, but they are competent and, as you yourself know, experienced. They know the route to Tova—"

"—along the shoreline," she said, cutting him off. "I thought we discussed taking to the open sea."

"We did."

"They won't like it." She thrust a chin toward a short, stocky man in a white workman's skirt. "See him? That's Callo. I don't trust him or anyone he's vouched for." She unconsciously rubbed her thumb across her missing pinkie joint. It's not that she thought these men would hurt her, hunt her for her bones or anything. After all, she had sailed with them before just days ago, and they'd given her no trouble. Except for that last day when Pech had come to the docks accusing her of sabotaging her own cargo. She had tried to explain that it was not her fault the quetzal feathers had molted, the honey had gone bad, and the salt had gotten wet. There was a leak in the ship, because all ships leaked at one point or another, and she had failed to notice in time to save her cargo. But she was sure the crew had something to do with that. She had taken on a new man in Huecha, a friend of Callo's who came vouched for but had made the sign to ward off evil when he'd seen her eyes. She'd chosen to ignore it, trusted that Callo wouldn't let someone dangerous on her ship, and part of her still believed that people could separate their personal prejudices and get the job done. She had been wrong.

She hadn't noticed until Pech came aboard to inspect the cargo and found the ruined mess. She could have made an excuse, blamed the new man, called him out for suspected sabotage. But she hadn't had the chance to even consider it. Pech had made up his mind already. He'd taken one look at her face, her eyes, to be exact, and declared her a half-Teek bitch. A saboteur herself, and up to no good.

"Why would I sabotage my own cargo?" she'd asked, incredulous.

"Why do Teek do anything?" he'd shot back at her. "Half-human means half-animal, and who knows why animals like you do what they do? Spite? Evil? Jealousy?"

"Jealousy?" She'd laughed, loudly and with gusto, and let her face show what she thought of piddling Lord Pech. In retrospect, maybe she shouldn't have. He'd backhanded her, knuckles slicing across her cheek, and she'd shown him just what a half-Teek bitch could do.

He'd come up sputtering twenty feet out in the open harbor, yelling for someone to save him, and in the next breath, called for someone to have her arrested. She'd thrown another wave over his head and into his gullet just to shut him up. But she was no killer, and she'd let the waves push him to shallow water. And then she'd left her ship, her cargo, and her payment behind to go find a cantina and a beautiful woman and, eventually, a jail cell.

And then Lord Balam. And here.

Balam motioned Callo over with a wave, and the first mate dropped the rope he had been coiling and lumbered over. He was a short man, the same height as Xiala but twice as wide, and muscles bulged on his well-worked arms. His hair was black, tied back in a simple knot high on the back of his head. A white cloth headband circled his broad forehead, and he wiped sweat from eyes that Xiala thought of as wistful. He always looked sad to her, like life had not lived up to his expectations and he mourned the injustice. Callo might not have done the sabotage outright, but it was his man who had, she was sure, which made him partly responsible.

"My friend, whom I am paying well," Balam said to the first mate, "you know our captain, yes? And there won't be a problem, will there?"

Callo's puppy eyes rolled across her, and he shrugged. "She's a good captain for a . . ."

Xiala snorted and crossed her arms over her chest. "For a woman? For a Teek?" she supplied. "Say it, Callo."

He stared at her a moment before lowering his gaze. "Women don't belong on boats. That's what the old ones say. They are cold and draw the storms. But then, you're not a woman, are you? A female, maybe, but not a woman."

"Mother waters, is that what you whisper about me? That I'm not even human?" She balled her hands into fists and reached for her Song. It came to her like a dark swirl rising up from the depths of a whirlpool and rested ready on her tongue. It occurred to her that using her Song might prove him right, but in the moment, she didn't care.

"Now, now," Balam said in alarm, his eyes on her. "No need for that."

She glanced at him, again surprised that he seemed to sense when she called her magic. He gave her that same smile. Lord Balam was more than he appeared, too. She wasn't sure what, a sorcerer or a diviner, perhaps. Someone sensitive to magic.

Callo was not, and did not seem to notice how close he was to catching her wrath. "It's no insult," he said with an indifferent shrug. "Just a fact. I sailed with you before, didn't I? Maybe a fishwoman is better on the sea than a human woman. Don't take it so bad."

"Ah, there you have it!" Balam beamed. "Not an insult. A compliment . . . in its own way. So . . ."

"But your friend . . . ?" She had forgotten his name, had only called him Huecha because of the town he hailed from. "He sabotaged Pech's ship, you know he did. Cost me wages and reputation."

"Ah." Callo sighed. "He was no good. Cost me wages, too. That's on my honor. We and the others took care of him."

Xiala hadn't expected an admission of guilt. It was enough to slow her anger. She let her Song slip back down her throat unused, but she kept it close and ready, just in case.

"And there you have it," Balam said, clapping his hands together merrily. "All is well, lost wages are recompensed on a new adventure, and this voyage can continue as we planned."

"Maybe not yet," Callo said, his flat-pan voice raised slightly. "Looks like we have company." He motioned with his chin back toward the docks, over Xiala's shoulder.

She and Balam turned. Striding toward them, looking righteously furious, was Lord Pech. He was accompanied by a dozen soldiers with shields and spears, and by his side, wringing his hands, was the tupile from Xiala's jail. Pech wore a loincloth and hip skirt with matching shoulder cape like Balam's, but Pech's skirt and cape were notched at the hem and dyed red, decorated with elaborate circles of gold. He wore a feathered headdress, the kind that sat low across his forehead and covered his ears with flaps. Feathers plumed from the top in rare reds and yellows. Jewels glittered on his neck and arms and even his ankles. It was an ostentatious display of wealth, and it made Xiala convinced the man was definitely compensating for some other lack.

"Seven hells," Balam murmured, the first expletive Xiala had heard from his cultured lips. "He must have had me followed to Kuharan." He chuckled, amused. "That sly dog." He turned back to Xiala and Callo. "I suggest you board the ship and make ready to sail. And quickly, too."

Callo nodded sharply and hurried back to the men, shouting orders.

"And you?" Xiala asked.

Balam raised a well-groomed eyebrow and gave her a dubious look. "Me? Are you concerned about me?"

"Only that you stay alive long enough to pay me."

His face relaxed as if her concern had made him uncomfortable and her retort was more familiar territory. "You live a much more tenuous life than I, Xiala of the Teek. I can handle Pech."

She started to protest that Pech had shown up with armed men and Balam might not be able to talk his way out of that, especially considering the bribe he'd paid the tupile, but she remembered that feeling she'd had that her new lord was more than he seemed. In her brief time spent with Pech, she knew he was exactly and only what he appeared to be. Pech's banality was no match for Balam, despite the tupile and the small household army that came following at his heels.

"Good luck, then," she said, and when Balam said nothing more, she turned and climbed across the plank that linked the dock to the ship and dropped down into the dugout canoe.

"Take that, too," Balam called over his shoulder, indicating the plank she had crossed. "If Pech and his men want to reach you, they'll have to swim."

She did as he instructed and pulled the walkway aboard the ship after her.

"Now then." Balam squared his handsome shoulders. "Get that Obregi to Tova, Captain Xiala. I am relying on you. It is an old obligation I have, a promise made that must be fulfilled, and I am counting on you to be my agent in this."

"And the goods?" She glanced at the stores already stacked under the reed overhang in the center of the ship. "The salt and feathers, the cacao beans and jade?"

"Make me wealth, of course, but it is the Obregi that concerns me most."

"Why?" she asked, but Balam was already striding away, going forward to meet Pech before he made it onto the pier.

She would not have felt the bird watching her if she hadn't been holding her Song low in her throat. The creature was too prescient, too focused. It was unnatural. She whistled sharply, her Song threaded through her breath to create a pitch too high for humans to hear, to send it on its way.

Instead, a vision flashed in front of her. A face. That of a young man, smiling. Teeth stained red and something like a bird skull carved into his skin at the base of his throat. His hair as black as a crow's wings, curling back from a handsome face. He wore a cloth tied around his eyes, but he raised his head as if he had seen her, too. And then he was gone.

Strange. Visions were not one of her gifts, and she knew no men who looked like that. But she would think about that later. She had more pressing worries on her mind.

Callo had whipped the men into movement, and already they were falling into place, ten on each side picking up their paddles, Callo at the bow as watch to guide them out. She strode down the middle of the ship past the reed-covered cabin in the center and between the rows of men with paddles raised. She silenced conversation as she passed. She could feel the eyes on her, the murmurs of "captain," and she realized she had a reputation among the sailors and not all of it was bad. By the time she took her place at the stern of the ship, hands on the tiller, she was smiling.

She spared one last glance at the shore and caught sight of Pech. He looked livid, stomping his feet and shouting something she couldn't hear. But Balam had his arms spread and was blocking Pech and his men from the pier, and that's all she needed to know.

"All drop!" she shouted, and as one, the crew dipped their paddles into the water. "Count two . . . and away!"

"Lead out!" cried Callo from his place, and the canoe moved. "One. Two. One. Two."

The men echoed him with precision. "One. Two." And again.

"Good and steady," she said.

There was outraged clamor from land, but she ignored it. Already they were moving, sleek and easy through the water on the strength of the paddlers, and as Cuecola became smaller and smaller behind them, so did her cares. She'd have to properly introduce herself to the crew later, once they were well gone, and share the news that they would break for open water once she'd mapped their course. But all in all, it was not a bad end to a morning that had started in jail.

She laughed, loud and brash, as saltwater sprayed from the paddles and wet her face. Maybe being Teek was lucky after all.

CHAPTER 7

CITY OF CUECOLA

YEAR 325 OF THE SUN

(20 DAYS BEFORE CONVERGENCE)

The crows that flock around the Great House have a sense of cooperation and fair play. I have noticed that they will work together both with their own and even with a creature unlike themselves to achieve an end. But beware, the crow is also a trickster and will take the greater share of the reward, too, if he thinks he is able.

—From *Observations on Crows*, by Saaya, age thirteen

Serapio had arrived at the Cuecola harbor before sunrise. Lord Balam had insisted on bringing him early to the ship, so they had woken well before dawn, breakfasted on unfamiliar foods, and come to the harbor.

Serapio did not mind it. He had been in Cuecola for two days, newly arrived from Obregi, but he had waited ten years to be on a ship to Tova and had no desire to linger in the foreign city that under a layer of fragrant black copal smelled of blood, hot stone, the sweat of laboring men, and sour ambition.

In truth, his journey had begun the day he was blinded. That had also been the day of his mother's death. Both had happened under a swallowed sun, and his journey would end under much the same sky in a brief twenty days—ten years and uncountable miles from where it had begun in Obregi.

The ten years in Obregi without his mother had not been easy. Many of them were marked by his father's benign neglect, and those that were not had instead been informed by the intentional cruelty of his tutors. Love, after his mother's death, was not a thing he knew.

But he did have something that others lacked, something he would have willingly traded for love had the bargain ever been offered. He had purpose.

"A man with a destiny is a man who fears nothing," he whispered to himself.

He had said the same to Lord Balam. When the pilgrims who had brought him from Obregi to Cuecola had dropped him at Balam's doorstep, the lord had inquired about his past and his tutors and, of course, his mother. Serapio had told him as much as he thought prudent and kept the rest to himself. He did not think Balam truly wanted to know about the horrors of his childhood or what he had endured to arrive at this point. A morbid curiosity did not justify an inquiry into his pain after all, and pain it was. But Serapio did not dwell on it. In twenty days, none of the brutalities of his childhood would matter.

But first he had to get to Tova.

An hour after Balam had left him on the ship, he had heard the crew arrive. They had readied the craft all morning, their tread heavy and their voices loud as they dragged large things across the wooden deck and tended to the ship's hull. Once he had heard a sailor with a thick unfamiliar accent ask another about the "priest in the hut," but his companion had quickly hushed him and told him that was "Balam's business and none of ours." Serapio had determined he must be the priest in the hut and frowned at the misnomer. But otherwise, the morning had been pleasant. No one had bothered him, and he found himself appreciating the almost company of the men. His previous travel companions had been pilgrims who had sworn a vow of silence.

Around midday he heard more than just the banter of sailors preparing for a voyage. There was a confrontation of some kind on the docks, a handful of voices raised in argument. One he recognized as Lord Balam's.

Concerned, Serapio pulled a small skin bag from around his neck and opened it. He licked the pad of his index finger and dipped it inside. Star pollen clung like shattered light to his wet skin in a fine sheen of silver dust. He pressed his finger against his tongue and sucked it clean. It had a slightly bitter taste, sharp and acrid.

The effect of the drug was almost immediate. Dark light infused his body, rushing through his bloodstream and opening his mind like a night-blooming flower opening to the moon. He threw his mind out and found a willing host. The crow launched from the tree, climbing skyward, until Serapio could see everything as if from above.

There below him in dock was his ship with the crew. They had all stopped in their work and were facing landward, looking at the pier. They leaned against upright oars or sat on the edge of the railing, as if watching a play.

Serapio urged the bird farther.

Men stood arguing, Lord Balam among them. The others he did not know. One was stout and sweating through his woven shirt despite the mild weather, a sash of office tight across his middle. Another man was bare-chested and bejeweled, with a tail of gray hair peeking from below a short box-shaped headdress. His attire marked him as a man of wealth, but he was otherwise plain.

The crow turned back toward the boat. And Serapio saw her.

She was striking, hair the color of plums that trailed to her waist in thick coils. Skin brown and smooth and face wide and attractive, but her mouth was flattened to a thin line in what looked like rage, and something roiled from her body that pulsed with energy, wound and waiting. It was so real, so alive, he could almost hear it. A song like the echo caught in a seashell one of his tutors had brought him from his coastal travels, or the shimmer of a rainbow after a summer rain, tangled between the hills of the valley where he grew up.

He sent his host circling closer, curious to know more.

The woman turned, tilting her head up to look at his crow. Serapio caught a glimpse of her eyes. White sclera, but her irises were a swirl of colors, like various paints stirred in a pot. *Teek*, he thought, *just like from the children's stories*, before she whistled sharply.

His crow pulled up at the sound, squawking a sharp retort. A flap of black feathers and a cry of surprise, and Serapio was expelled from his host. He rocked back in the chair, gasping. He pressed a hand to his ear. It was wet. He dabbed at it gingerly and touched the liquid to the tip of his tongue. Blood. Somehow she had not only thrown him from the crow but had followed his connection back and made him bleed.

He laughed, breathless with surprise. He had never felt anything like it.

He forced his breathing to slow, but his mind was still bright with possibility. How had she done that? Cast him out of his own creature? It was a useful thing to know, if only to make sure it never happened again.

He wiped his face clean with the edge of his black robe and adjusted the blindfold that covered the stitched flesh that sealed his eyes shut.

More shouting, but this time is was an all clear, and men were hauling ropes aboard while paddles dipped into the sea. They were moving. The star pollen was still in his veins, and he thought about seeking out another crow so he could watch the great ship leave Cuecola, so he could glimpse the path before him, but he decided against it. There would be plenty of time in the coming days to see the sea and get to know the crew. And the captain.

CHAPTER 8

It is said that crows can remember the faces of men who hurt them and do not forgive. They will carry a grudge against their tormentor until their deaths and pass on their resentment to their children. It is how they survive.

—From *Observations on Crows*, by Saaya, age thirteen

The boy sat cross-legged on the wide stone terrace, his thin body nestled among the crows. There were at least a dozen of the large black birds around him, pecking and squawking and turning their heads this way and that. One perched on a bony knee, another on his jutting shoulder. Three fought for place on his outstretched arm, eating scraps from his cupped hand.

He murmured words to them, bare whispers of his own loneliness, apologies of how little food he had to share with them intermixed with confessions of his own gnawing hunger, soft inquiries about the larger world outside his room and what it was like. The crows answered, telling him of how the snow was growing deep on the nearby mountains and how the cold winds rattled through their nests and how the sun weakened and the nights lengthened.

He held his free hand out as a large, broad-chested crow with a notched beak and a sleek sheen of feathers dropped something that glinted in the morning sun into the boy's palm. The boy ran a thumb across it, feeling for the shape and size of it. He hefted it a few times in his hand and smiled. Pleased with the gift, he added it to the small pile of treasures he had already collected that morning.

"Is it always this way?" a voice asked from behind him.

The boy stiffened. A stranger had spoken. He didn't receive many visitors. In fact, besides his father's weekly visits, he rarely had any company at all beyond the servants and the guard who stood outside his door.

"Yes," said a second voice.

The boy tensed, nostrils flaring. That voice he recognized.

"He prefers to sit outside with the birds," the second voice continued, something bitter in the tone. "I thought to forbid it after—"

"No, don't. Do nothing," the stranger said quickly. "I'll talk to him now. Alone."

"I cannot leave you alone with . . . the boy."

The boy. Not *my son.* Serapio's fist clenched, anger and shame warring inside him. His father left him alone all the time. Why would now make any difference?

"Lord Marcal," said the stranger, voice patient, "I am here to help your son. Do you not trust that?"

"I'm not worried you will hurt him," his father said, voice dropped to a whisper that he no doubt thought Serapio couldn't hear. "I am concerned he will hurt you. He is . . . unnatural."

"He is a child."

"Fourteen. Not so young. And perhaps you don't understand. Loss of sight is not his only affliction . . ."

"I understand enough. Now, let me work."

His father hesitated and then said, "I will leave a guard by the door. Call for him should you need anything. I'll be back after my duties to check on you."

"It won't be necessary."

"I . . . well, if you are sure . . ."

"Quite."

And then there were steps, hurried, like his father couldn't wait to be gone. Which left the stranger here alone with him.

"Hello, Serapio."

A crow pecked at his hand. He dug into his pocket and pulled out another handful of crumbs. The bird squawked happily. It was joined immediately by its compatriots, and the food quickly disappeared.

"Who are you?" the boy asked.

"I'm here to help you."

"I don't think you can help me."

The man chuckled. It was not a kind sound. He imagined the man standing in the doorway that led out to the terrace, leaning against the frame, studying him. The man set Serapio on edge, which made his birds fuss and flap.

"Are you another healer?" Serapio asked. "Someone come to poke and prod at my eyes?"

"Oh, I'm not here to help you see again," the man said. "I

suspect that would be a waste of time. You're going to have to let that hope go, boy."

Serapio cocked his head, curious. No one had said that to him before. Spoken so plainly about his fate. It was always platitudes and false comforts which inevitably led to whispered incredulity that his own mother had "ruined" him and what a monster she must have been.

"I don't have false hope," he countered quietly.

"Of course you do," the man said, patiently. "Life is a series of false hopes. We all have misplaced hopes until we learn better. I did."

"What do you want?"

"I'm here to prepare you for your destiny."

"I already know my destiny." He pulled more food from his pocket, and the notched-beak crow landed on his palm. He knew it was him by the weight of him, the particular sound of his hungry caw.

A pause from the stranger, and Serapio knew he must be considering his words. "Tell me."

"I'm meant to be reborn a crow."

"And then?"

No one had ever asked "and then?" They all just assumed him mentally ill, head full of fanciful delusions of flying or escaping his maiming.

"They speak to me, you know," the boy said.

"Not surprising. They know one of their own. And what do they tell you?"

"Mostly crow things. Of pleasant hunting grounds and the joy of flight. Of family and lost things, too."

"You must know something about that last bit." It was the first note of sympathy that Serapio had heard from the man.

He nodded.

"What else do they tell you?"

"That I'm one of them. That just like their great ancestor, I have swallowed the shadow of the sun. They call me Grandfather Crow sometimes, although I am not so old."

"An ancestor, eh?"

He lifted a knobby shoulder in a shrug.

"What else do they call you, Serapio?"

He hesitated. "When my skin is too cold, Nightbringer. Or Suneater, sometimes, when I'm angry. They say that my body is cold, but my anger is hot."

"All this you have learned from the crows?" He sounded surprised, like he had not expected that.

"They are my friends. I have earned their trust."

"And what did your mother call you?"

Serapio twisted from where he sat on the stones to face the stranger. "Did my mother send you?" he asked.

"Your mother is dead." The man's voice was flat and unsympathetic, a man making a statement of fact. "But yes, she did send me, after a fashion. Arranged for me and two others to come should her work succeed."

"You mean me," Serapio said. "I am my mother's work."

"What did she tell you?"

"That I would be a god."

The stranger was silent for so long Serapio thought he might have left undetected.

"You are a strange one," he remarked, finally. "Come in. I have something here for you."

Serapio heard the man's footsteps retreating into the room. He considered ignoring the command to follow, but his curiosity got the better of him. He whispered a farewell to his friends, stood to dust off his hands and pants, and made his way to the bench he knew to be just inside the door. He took a seat.

"Take this." Something pressed against his knee, and Serapio grasped it. It was rough bark and thick, as long as his hand and as wide. He flattened his other palm against it.

"A tree branch?"

"And now this."

Something else at his knee. He took it, feeling a handle and a wide blade, blunt and tapered on the end. "A knife?"

"A chisel. I'm going to teach you how to carve."

"Why?"

"It is only a tool, a means to an end. Now, when was the last time you used your hands?"

"I just used them to pick up this chisel and wood."

A sharp blow struck his cheek. He cried out, collapsing to the floor. The crows outside shrieked. He raised a trembling hand to his face. It came away wet with blood, a thin slice of skin ripped free from the kiss of some weapon he didn't know. It stung where the flesh was exposed to air. Rage bubbled up inside him, not cold at all, and he opened his mouth to call his crows.

"Bring them down on me, and I'll strike them, too. I don't want to hurt them, or you, Serapio, but you will respect me. Do you understand?"

Serapio snapped his jaw shut. To hit him was one thing. He would not risk his friends.

"Let's start again," the man said. "Wood and chisel."

Serapio fought back tears and tried to ignore his bleeding cheek. He weighed the raw wood in his hand and the chisel in the other. He thought of throwing them at the man. But then what? Where would he run to avoid another blow? And his birds. The man might hurt his birds.

"Stop feeling sorry for yourself," the man said. "I can smell your self-pity from here. Do as I say, and we'll get along fine. I'll only hit you when you need it. I am reasonable, after all."

Serapio didn't answer.

Quick steps, and Serapio knew another blow was coming. He shied back as the man's hand gripped him by the hair, pulled him to his knees.

"You talk about destiny," he hissed, "but are unwilling to suffer to achieve it? You won't get to Tova if you are afraid, Serapio. I will make your mind strong, hone your ability to endure pain, if you let me. Or do you wish to stay on this terrace and rot with these keepers of yours?"

The stranger shook him, making his head bob back and forth like a reed in the wind. "I will suffer!" Serapio cried, voice high and frightened.

The man released him, and Serapio collapsed forward. He caught himself on hands and knees, breathing hard, wood and chisel still gripped between fingers and palm.

He heard the man cross the room and settle back on the far bench. His voice came from a distance. "Describe the wood to me. Tell me what you feel."

Serapio took a deep steadying breath. Pushed himself to sitting and turned the wood between his fingers, against his palm. "It feels rough," he ventured, fighting to keep his voice steady.

"More than that," the man coaxed. "Concentrate. Use your fingers and your mind."

"Rough," Serapio repeated, and then, "Pitted. Jagged along here, the left side, and knotted just below where my thumb is." He ran the edge of his thumbnail along the knot.

"Better," the man said. "Now, feel for the creature already inside the block. It's there, hiding, waiting for you to bring it forth." A rustle of clothing as the man leaned closer. "Can you do it, Serapio? Can you find the creature inside the wood?"

"Yes." He ran the chisel along the groove he had mapped with his fingernail, imagining a crow in his mind. Small head, large beak, curving breast, and feathered wings. He dug the chisel into the wood, but it slipped, thrusting under his fingernail instead. He cried out in pain and drew his hand back. Stuck the finger in his mouth and sucked.

"Make the pain your friend, Serapio," the man urged. "Learn to appreciate it the way you might a lover. Let it become the thing you crave most."

Serapio knew nothing personally about what lovers did, but he had heard the servants fucking in the room next to his often enough. He did know he wanted nothing to do with suffering and pain. Is that what this man was here to teach him? He didn't want it, but if it meant he would become what his mother wanted him to, he would endure.

"Now," his tutor said, "tell me again about the wood. Use different words this time."

Serapio did.

Time passed. The room grew colder as the sun set, and servants came to light the wall lamps and offer them supper. The man ate but instructed Serapio to keep working since he had not yet earned the right to eat.

Only when the night servants came to ready Serapio's bed did the man say, "It's time for me to leave."

"Are you coming back?" Serapio asked, unsure if he wanted the man to stay or if he wanted him gone forever.

"Yes. I keep my promises." He clamped a hand on Serapio's shoulder and squeezed hard enough for his thin bones to shift painfully under his shirt. "Next time I come, you can call me Paadeh. We'll be friends yet."

Serapio knew instinctively that this was a lie. Paadeh did not like him. He wasn't sure why, but he knew it as well as he knew his name. He might be here to honor a promise that he had made to his mother long ago, he might be here to teach him pain so that he could fulfill his destiny, but they would never be friends.

After his new tutor had left, Serapio held his hand to his cheek for a long time, thinking. The blood had dried in a hardened line that flaked off when he tugged at it.

The pain had startled him, but he had already begun to forgive it, make it his friend as Paadeh had said.

He worked on his wooden sculpture long into the night. He fell asleep, hunched forward on his bench. Clutched in his hand was the beginning of a crow. Not wholly formed, just the outline of what it would become, but it was being born nonetheless.

CHAPTER 9

My observations of the Priesthood of Watchers are that they have become a shell of what they once were. It is an irony of the age that the scientific advances the Watchers once forced upon the masses to quiet the worship of the old gods have now become so commonplace as to begin to make them obsolete. No one denies that they once held center on the Meridian continent and kept us at peace for three centuries, but I suspect that it is only tradition and nostalgia from whence their power flows now. They claim to read the skies, but their work seems mostly a novelty for the upper class. They issue rain predictions, but could not an astute farmer read the soil for himself? Shrewd eyes might turn to the trade cities of the Crescent Sea to find their future. Whether the cities of the Crescent Sea should continue to pay tithe to the Sun Priest is a topic worthy of discussion among the Seven Lords.

> —*A Commissioned Report of My Travels*
> *to the Seven Merchant Lords of Cuecola,*
> by Jutik, a Traveler from Barach

The Conclave had passed into its second hour when Naranpa noticed Iktan slip in through the eastern door. Xe made xir way around the back of the circular room, passing behind the healers to join the tsiyo dedicants on the southern side of the circle. Xe slid into an empty space on a stone bench, as quiet and unnoticed as a shadow after dark.

Naranpa would not have recognized xir if she did not know what to look for, had not realized twenty minutes into Haisan's droning lecture on Shuttering etiquette that the person sitting in Iktan's place, wearing the red mask and covered from head to toe by a formless red robe, was not Iktan at all.

An impostor, she thought, *just like during the end of the procession earlier.* And the impostor sat just as still and just as silent as Iktan always did, so unless they spoke, which Iktan rarely did, why would anyone even suspect? Which made her wonder how often Iktan practiced this deception, and how often xe wasn't actually in the room when everyone thought xe was.

She watched Iktan, the real Iktan, blend in with the dedicants in attendance, dutifully seated behind the fake priest.

"And so we will meet on the solstice to break our Shuttering," Haisan was saying, "at dusk on Sun Rock. And this year, the solstice will be marked by the rarest of celestial occurrences. As the year divides into old and new, so also will the earth, sun, and moon align in the Convergence. Over our very heads, we will witness order move to chaos and back to order again. So it is with the heavens, so it will be with Tova. We will bear witness to the cycle of evil rising in darkness to be battled back by goodness and light when the sun prevails."

It was a stirring speech, and the dedicants and priests stomped their feet in polite approval.

Where had xe been? she wondered. She had expressly told xir not to do anything without her say-so, but trust Iktan to interpret that request in the narrowest fashion possible.

"Sun Priest, if you would like to address the Conclave."

Well, maybe that was ungenerous. Perhaps xe was investigating. Following a lead or something. Wasn't that what people did when there was a crime? Or an attempted crime, at least?

"Sun Priest?"

An attempted murder, she should say. It wasn't simply a crime.

"Naranpa!"

She blinked. Everyone was staring at her. The other three priests (well, Iktan's impostor), the dedicants, even the servants who stood in waiting around the edges of the circular room.

She cleared her throat, desperately trying to recall what Haisan had been speaking of, but nothing came to mind.

"My apologies," she said. "Could you repeat that?"

Haisan's face fell. "Which part?"

"Ah . . . just the last part will do."

Haisan flushed, clearly distressed. "I-I suppose I could start with—"

"Nara, are you unwell?" Abah asked, leaning forward.

She was seated directly across from her on the western side of the circle, concern etched on her pretty face.

Naranpa bristled at Abah's use of her nickname. She'd noticed the woman using it earlier, too. It was a name she most definitely did not have permission to use.

"I'm . . ." She stopped. She had thought to be dismissive of Abah's concern, correct her familiarity, but that was not her way. One did not lead through criticism. She rose to her feet. "Actually, thank you for asking, Abah. Now that you mention it, I do have something I'd like to discuss with the Conclave. As most of you know, there was an attempt on my life today."

She paused dramatically. Not a single gasp of surprise. Well, the rumor wheel had indeed been turning. "The attempted assassin bore the marks of one of the Sky Made clans."

Again, no reaction from the gathering, so they must all know of which clan she spoke.

She continued, "This happened because to so many we have become faceless bureaucrats, not true servants of the people. We do our duty to chart the stars, but we are also called to mold our world to better mirror the heavens. Order from chaos, good"—she looked at Haisan, finally remembering something he'd said—"good from evil. But that is not accomplished simply in prayer but in practice. It is well and good that we Shutter ourselves to prepare for the sun to return, but what of ministry to the people? Healers accessible not only to the Sky Made but to all? Knowledge of the heavens shared with the common citizen?"

"There are civil institutions for all of that," Haisan said. "It is the Sky Made's duty to—"

"But couldn't it be ours, too? Why do we cede so much to the Sky Made?"

"We do not meddle in worldly politics."

"I'm not talking about meddling," she said, frustration

clenching her fists. Why was she not more eloquent when she needed to be?

"Then what *are* you talking about?" Abah asked.

"I just want . . ." *I want us to not become irrelevant.*

"Nara . . ." Abah stood, and all attention turned her way.

Naranpa winced at that damn nickname. Did the woman do it on purpose? She must.

"It is understandable that you are shaken by the events of the day," the healer continued. "They were terrible! I am still shaken, and it didn't even happen to me!" She paused, her delicate features flushed with remembered horrors of something that didn't even happen to her. "So if you need to rest, we can certainly continue this Conclave without you. Perhaps one of your dedicants can stand in for you? Perhaps Eche?"

Naranpa glanced briefly at the dedicant named Eche who was seated to her right. He was one of her favored pupils, handsome if a bit vacuous at times, but his star charts were admirably accurate. She had been leaning toward officially naming him as her successor, as he was the obvious choice. Only recently, he had been late to study, and last week he had challenged some of her weather predictions. Nothing serious, but it had surprised her. Seeing him now, smiling at Abah and then looking back at her as if expecting her to concede to the seegi's suggestion, his recent behavior changes suddenly made sense.

Abah was fucking him. Naranpa could see it, plain as the moon bright overhead. Which was fine, generally, but not if she was influencing him unduly.

"That won't be necessary," she said crisply. "I am able to continue. I would just like the gathered parties to consider my—"

"But Nara," Abah said, interrupting her, "this attack against you, I think it's worth acknowledging that it might be compromising."

Naranpa's brows knit. "What?"

"This talk you make, of reforms and people and breaking our long-held and sacred traditions? Well, isn't it possible that someone is trying to kill you for it? And if that's the case, then maybe you should relinquish the Sun seat. For your own safety."

Naranpa blinked, shocked. Had Abah just suggested that she abdicate? Hand over the Sun Priest duties to someone else *for her own good*? The Sun Priest served unto death. To voluntarily give up her place? It was not done.

"I am loath to admit it," Haisan said, speaking from his seat in the north, "but Abah may have a point."

Naranpa turned her surprised gaze to the old man. "You think I deserve to die for my reforms?"

"Heavens, no. What I meant—"

"Don't you have some unsavory connections to Coyote's Maw?" Abah cut in smoothly.

Naranpa turned back to the woman, her shock morphing to panic. Two thoughts flared hot in her mind. What was Abah doing? And how did she know? "I don't know what you mean."

"I'm sorry, Nara," Abah said, her face the picture of concerned sympathy. "I don't mean to bring up unpleasant memories, or remind you of difficult times, but your brother? The one who's still alive? Isn't he a criminal in Coyote's Maw? And wasn't your other brother murdered? I hadn't considered it before, but isn't it also possible that what happened today . . . and before . . . is related to your family?"

Abah knew of the previous assassination attempt? Did that mean she had a spy among the tsiyo dedicants, too? And now to name it in open Conclave. Iktan would answer for that.

"Both my brothers are dead," Naranpa said flatly, struggling to keep her voice from betraying her emotions. Her hands she could not soothe, so she crossed her arms and stuck them in the sleeves of her robe.

"Well, we know that's not true," Abah countered, stone in her voice.

"It is true to me." Her voice was cold, but rage boiled close to the surface, throwing off her calm. Bringing up her family? The Maw? It was anathema. The past was the past, and family connections forsaken for divine ones, as Iktan had rightly reminded her only yesterday.

"Ah, perhaps we have strayed from the topic at hand," Haisan cut in, voice placating.

Naranpa fumed. Oh, *now* they had gone too far?

"I don't think—" Naranpa started.

"We can speak freely in the circle, can we not?" Abah asked, voice rising. "We are all siblings here, and none of us a criminal."

"Oh, fuck off, Abah!" she snapped.

"Naranpa!" Haisan cautioned sharply.

Naranpa bit back a scream. She understood intellectually that Abah had lured her into this fight, she could see it as plain as the summer sun. She knew that Abah, despite her youth, fell squarely into the traditionalists' camp, but this personal attack was beyond the pale.

Worse, somehow Naranpa had let herself be outmaneuvered by a nineteen-year-old. It burned.

She looked across the circle to Iktan. The real Iktan, two rows behind the impostor. *Say something!* she thought angrily. But hadn't she asked xir not to interfere, to let her fight her own fights? And if xe spoke now, everyone would know xe had deceived them. No, she was on her own. And she had to reclaim some of her dignity before she dug herself in any deeper.

"My sincere apologies," she said, inclining her head toward Abah. "It seems that today's events have in fact unsettled me. Haisan, if you've said all you need tonight, let us conclude this meeting and meet again tomorrow to continue."

A commotion by the eastern door drew their attention. They all turned, even Abah, who had to crane her neck to see.

A servant, breathing hard and sweating as if they had run up the stairs.

"What is it?" Naranpa barked, temper well frayed despite what felt like a momentous display of self-control. "Why have you disturbed the Conclave?"

"My apologies, Sun Priest," the girl said, panting. "But there is news. Tragic news! The matron of Carrion Crow, Matron Yatliza?"

"Yes?" Naranpa thought of the thin woman in the black dress earlier that day, dignified yet morose. "What about her?"

The servant hesitated.

"Say it, girl," Haisan prompted.

"My apologies for bearing dark news," she said, "but Yatliza Carrion Crow is dead!"

CHAPTER 10

CITY OF TOVA

YEAR 325 OF THE SUN

(19 DAYS BEFORE CONVERGENCE)

Just as Cuecola values the sacred power of seven, so do the Tovans esteem the number four. This can be seen in both the Sky Made clans, numbering four, and the priestly societies of the Watchers, also four. The Watcher societies are healer, assassin, historian, and oracle, with oracle holding the highest seat in the hierarchy. I have heard that it is forbidden for the oracle to divine their own fate, but that seems unlikely. What use is a power to read the heavens if it cannot be turned to your own benefit?

—*A Commissioned Report of My Travels*
to the Seven Merchant Lords of Cuecola,
by Jutik, a Traveler from Barach

Murmurs of shock rippled through the crowd, and even Abah looked stunned. A matron murdered? Surely not, and on the same day an attempt was made on the Sun Priest's life? It was impossible to see this as a coincidence.

But mostly Naranpa thought of a great aching hole in the heart of Carrion Crow. Their matron dead, one of the four seats of civil leadership vacant. Unrest was bound to follow. The cultists would latch on to it as a sign of something nefarious, likely blame the tower. The rest of the Sky Made must act, and act quickly, to assure the people that things would continue as normal, that whoever had done this would be brought to justice.

And the priesthood must help facilitate it.

"Dedicants are dismissed," Naranpa said, seizing control of the meeting. "Priests, if you will stay. And you, too," she said, singling out the servant who had brought the news.

It took a moment, but the dedicants complied, voices still raised in chattering disbelief. Haisan approached, joined by Abah, who to her surprise did not argue at Naranpa's taking control of the Conclave. Iktan, who had used the cover of the dedicants' departure to take the mask from xir impostor and hold it in xir hands, as if xe had been wearing it moments ago, joined them.

"How was she murdered?" Naranpa asked the servant.

"M-murdered?"

"Yes. Who killed her? Do we know?"

"N-no, Sun Priest. I mean . . . no. She wasn't murdered."

Naranpa stared, dumbfounded. "I'm sorry, what?"

"The messenger from Carrion Crow said that she was found dead in her bed. No one said she was murdered."

Naranpa breathed a long, audible sigh, some of her spirit escaping along with her breath, she was sure. Did she feel relief that there was not another assassin loose in the city? Or was it frustration that for a moment she was sure that with Yatliza's murder, she would be able to convince her fellow priests that Abah and her nasty implications about her family were completely out of line? Both, she realized.

"Tell us everything you know," Iktan said to the servant. "From the beginning."

The girl gulped noisily, clearly nervous, but stuttered out her story anyway.

Naranpa only half-listened. She knew she should be paying attention, but really, if the woman had died in her sleep, what was the point? The city would mourn, and she, as Sun Priest, would have to lead that mourning. The funeral alone would require days to prepare, and a star chart for the dead to be divined, but Haisan would find the right songs to sing in eulogy, and Eche, her protégé, who apparently wanted so badly to lead, well, she would have plenty of work for him, too.

The girl wound down with a breathy sob, and Abah, nodding compassionately, hugged her before walking her to the door.

Once Abah was back, she asked, "What do we do?" She wrung her hands, looking genuinely distraught.

"We prepare a funeral," Naranpa said.

"But the Shuttering—" Haisan started.

"Oh, fuck the Shuttering," Iktan countered, clearly exasperated. "Mortify yourself for the dead woman, mortify yourself for the sun. What's the difference?"

"You speak blasphemy!" Haisan exclaimed.

"Yes, I do. And what will you do about it?"

"Enough!" Naranpa shouted. "Both of you." She took a

deep breath. "We need to work together." She looked around the loose circle they had formed, and when no one countered her, she continued, "We will have a state funeral in four days, as is proper. Exceptions to the rules that govern the priest-hood during Shuttering will just have to be made."

"And what of the governance of Carrion Crow?" Abah asked quietly. "Who will keep them from rioting?"

"Does she not have a daughter?" Iktan asked.

"A son and a daughter," Haisan agreed. "The daughter here in the Great House in Kun and the son, as I understand it, three years in Hokaia training to become her Shield."

"At the war college?" Naranpa asked, curious. "Is he a beast rider, too?"

"Yes, I believe so."

A man of war, then, although it had been a misnomer for the past hundred years to call the school at Hokaia a war col-lege. It still taught strategy and hand-to-hand combat, but it had not trained the continent's young to be generals of armies for a century. Under the Hokaia Treaty, the Sky Made were meant to send a limited number of their scions to train at the war college in the ways of warfare, but it was considered mostly ceremonial since the clans had not gone to war since the Treaty was signed more than three hundred years ago. The scions who went used their training to become armed escorts and bodyguards, those they called Shield, to the pow-erful matrons in their respective clans. Protectors more than soldiers, but still considered formidable.

"You will have to anoint the daughter, Nara," Iktan said. "We can arrange the ceremony to happen after the funeral."

"An inauspicious time," Haisan complained. "Your disregard for tradition is already controversial, Naranpa. To hold an investiture for a new matron days before the solstice while we are still Shuttered will not be popular."

She rubbed a hand over her forehead. Investing any new matron was one of the oldest duties of the Sun Priest. "What would you have me do?"

"Wait until after the solstice," Haisan urged.

"And leave the seat of matron empty?" Abah protested. "Carrion Crow without a ruler? The Speakers Council without its required four?"

"Only for a brief time."

"Twenty days," Abah countered. "Enough time for certain factions to gain traction while the Speakers Council is hobbled."

"Nineteen," Iktan corrected unhelpfully. "The sun will rise soon."

"Even if I waited to anoint the new matron," Naranpa said, "we cannot assume it would be her daughter. The surviving council members will want their say."

"And the heavens will have to bless her," Haisan said.

"We can make the heavens bless whomever we want," Iktan said.

Haisan drew in a choked breath. "Enough with your heresy, tsiyo! Stop this talk, or leave!"

"I will say who leaves," Naranpa growled, "and neither one of you is so lucky. But truly, Iktan, stop provoking him."

"I am simply advocating for the priesthood to take a more direct manner in deciding rulership of the city. Isn't that what you have been asking for, Nara? A more hands-on approach?"

"Not like that. Our opinions do not matter. We interpret the stars—"

"With our opinions. It is the same."

"It is not."

"And what if the Speakers Council suggests someone else besides the daughter to rule, hmm? What then? Will you look to your star charts and challenge them?"

That brought her up short. She was already on very thin ice with the traditionalists. Would she dare cross them so openly? She opened her mouth to answer, but nothing came to mind.

"Iktan's example is a sophistication," Haisan said dismissively. "The Council would never raise someone whom Carrion Crow did not approve of. Why would they?"

"But what if they did?" Iktan argued.

"They won't!"

The two bickered on, Iktan in an unusually combative mood and Haisan taking all the bait offered.

Naranpa rubbed her thumb and pointer finger along her temples and looked up at the night sky. Already the eastern horizon was starting to pale, just as Iktan had said. She would need to meet with the surviving matrons of the clans to inform them of funeral obligations. She would also propose Iktan's idea of letting Yatliza's daughter succeed her mother immediately. That did indeed seem the most reasonable solution. And, after the Shuttering and the solstice, when the sun was returning and the timing more favorable, if the Speakers Council wanted someone else to rule Carrion Crow, they could all discuss it.

"Haisan," she said, cutting off whatever the man had been saying, "can you work with Eche to start funeral preparations? Which songs to sing in eulogy? The order of the ceremony?"

He blinked, surprised at her command. "I can."

"Good. I'm going to call for a Speakers Council meeting."

"At Sun Rock?" Iktan asked.

It was the usual place, but returning to the location of her attempted murder so soon did not tempt. And now she had the perfect excuse.

"No, let them come here. We are Shuttered, after all. They aren't. They can come to us this time."

"I'll attend with you," Abah offered.

"No." Naranpa had already anticipated her request and had a serviceable answer for that, too. "The citizens of Tova will need your healing after such a trying day. I want you and your dedicants to be available at Sun Rock to receive them."

"What?" Her eyes were laughably wide in shock.

"You heard me. Go minister, Abah. To the masses. Soothe our city in its time of need."

She crossed her arms like a tantrumming child. "Don't be ridiculous."

Naranpa raised an eyebrow. "Is it ridiculous to care for our people? Were you not just saying that someone needed to comfort Carrion Crow?"

Abah opened her mouth to protest and closed it shut just as quickly. Naranpa suppressed a smile.

"Fine," the Priest of Succor snapped.

"I'll come with you to meet the clan matrons," Iktan said.

Naranpa shook her head. "No."

Speaking the word hurt. She wanted Iktan to accompany her. Xe would be a comfort at her side, and bringing a tsiyo would certainly remind the clans that the Sun Priest was more than a figurehead. She was convinced that the assassin had come from the ranks of Carrion Crow's cultists, but she wasn't ready to accuse anyone outright, particularly with their matron newly dead. Their meeting should be focused on the funeral and succession, not the attempt against her life. Nevertheless, perhaps she could manage to discuss both.

She squeezed her eyes shut. Was she being stubborn for no reason? She trusted Iktan. Of course she did. But she didn't want to appear to depend on xir so much. She needed to do this by herself, perhaps to prove to herself that she could.

"I will handle the matrons alone." She looked at the others. "You know your tasks. Let them be done."

• • • • •

Iktan caught up to her as she was approaching her rooms. One moment she was alone, the next xe was there.

"That was well done."

"I wondered when you would show up," she said, not slowing her pace. "I'm surprised you let me walk this far unaccompanied."

"You were not unaccompanied. I had one of my tsiyos watching you."

She had been joking. The truth both pleased and angered her. She wasn't ungrateful. But if she wasn't safe in her own home . . .

"But you still cannot trust Abah."

"I admit I am surprised she agreed to minister to the public."

"As am I," Iktan admitted. "But she must see some personal benefit in it to acquiesce so easily."

She stopped, turning to Iktan. "How do you think she knew of Ochi?" She was still flabbergasted the girl had brought up her brother. How had she even discovered that he was alive? Naranpa told everyone he was dead, and he was to her. The only person who knew she had a brother who was not only very much alive but also the head of a successful crime syndicate in the Maw was standing next to her.

"It would not be so hard to find out if one went looking," Iktan said dismissively. Xe resumed walking, and she reluctantly followed.

They reached the entrance to her rooms. She paused, leaning against the door. "Isn't it strange, though? For her to know?" She didn't believe it was Iktan who had told Abah of Ochi, but she also didn't believe her connections to the Maw and to her last living relative would be as easy to discover as Iktan suggested. Naranpa had been thorough when she had destroyed her past. If someone had gone resurrecting it, maybe Iktan's first suspicions that the attempt against her life had nothing to do with Carrion Crow might have merit. But she had walked the streets of Odo today, felt the menace rolling from its people all aimed at the priesthood. Having felt that, seen that, and knowing this was the second attempt by someone bearing haahan, it was difficult to entertain some Maw connection. In her experience, often the simplest answer was the correct one.

"What are you thinking, Nara?"

She ran an absent hand through her hair, letting her fingers twist in the strands that had come loose from her coiled buns. "She bested me today at Conclave. Made me look like a fool."

"Not so badly. You recovered."

"She should be censured for the way she spoke to me. But if I raise it, it will seem petty. It might *be* petty."

"Then we find another way."

Her vexation gave way to alarm. "I don't think I like the sound of that." Abah was a pain in her side, but she was still a member of the priesthood, still sacred. "Iktan, please tell me you don't mean . . ."

Xir look was baleful. "Despite your belief that I am some kind of monster, Nara, I do not solve all my problems with murder."

"Fine, fine," she said, waving xir outrage away. "I apologize. What do you suggest I . . ."

Her words drifted off as she frowned, noticing something. A scratch on Iktan's neck, low and just beneath the collar. It looked red and raw and had not been there before the Conclave.

"What happened to your neck?" she asked.

Xe tilted xir head, effectively hiding the scratch. "It's nothing."

"It looks like it hurts. Have you cleaned it? I have water and willow bark in my room." She straightened. "Perhaps you should—"

"I said it is nothing, Nara. I'll treat it when we're done here."

Suspicions blossomed in her mind. "Where were you during the Conclave? I saw you come in late."

Xe turned dark eyes to her. Xir gaze was always so direct, so intimate. It made her shiver. "No."

She flinched. Despite their occasional bickering, they never shut each other out like that. "What business could you have when I told you to do nothing until I—"

"It did not concern you, Nara." And the heat xe pushed into xir voice, the sly emphasis on *you*, made xir intent clear.

She inhaled sharply in disbelief. Iktan had lovers. Of course xe had lovers. Xe was clever, sensual, beautiful, and dangerous. What person wouldn't thrill at xir attention? But xe had always been discreet enough not to throw it in her face. And certainly not to show up with love marks on xir neck for the world to see. A sour spike of jealousy shot through her gut, and she did not like it.

"Eche I understand. But you? Led around by your genitals? I thought you had better sense." It was a low blow, purposefully cruel, and she regretted it the moment it left her lips.

Iktan said nothing, instead staring at someone in the middle distance over her shoulder, not meeting her eyes but not turning away.

And she knew the conversation was over.

Frustrated, she pushed her shoulder against her bedroom door. Before she could fully open it, Iktan slipped in. She followed, watching xir check the corners, the privy, the alcove where she hung her robes. Xe even ran a hand under her bedding, checking for she wasn't sure what. Even when Iktan was mad at her, which xe clearly was, xe would not leave her in danger. Only when xe seemed satisfied that no one was lying in wait to kill her did xe return to the door.

Xe was going to leave without saying goodbye, and before she could stop herself, she called: "Iktan."

Xe paused, halfway gone already.

She wanted to ask xir to stay, to share her bed, if only for a few hours so she knew she wasn't alone. And to stake her claim, she admitted, to someone she no longer had any claim to. She had no right to ask such a thing, but she desperately wanted to. She had been so strong for so long, and now with the events of the day, she wanted to be weak, if only for a moment. But she would not allow herself even that. So she settled for "Good night."

"It's almost dawn, Naranpa."

"Of course," she corrected.

"I'll leave a tsiyo at your door. Take them with you to the meeting. It's a small thing I ask. For your safety, Sun Priest."

Not for love, she thought bitterly. *Not even for friendship. But because it is your duty, Priest of Knives.*

"Yes. Of course." It felt silly to argue over such a small thing, and she realized she wanted xir gone.

And when xe was gone, she realized she wanted xir to come back.

CHAPTER 11

THE CRESCENT SEA

YEAR 325 OF THE SUN

(20 DAYS BEFORE CONVERGENCE)

Only a foolish Teek speaks when she could Sing.

—Teek saying

They had been at sea pulling strong for a good six hours along the coast when Xiala told Callo to lift paddle and bring the ship to shore.

"There's a cay not far from here," she said. "You know it?"

"Lost Moth. I know it."

"We'll dock there to sup. Give the crew a night onshore while we can."

"While we can?" Callo asked, sounding surprised. "We're making for Tova, Lord Balam said. It's coastline all the way around."

She could have kicked herself for the slip, but it was time to let the crew know her plans to take to open water.

"And all hands, Callo," she said, not answering his question. "No one stays behind. I need to have a talk with my

113

crew." She started to walk away and paused. "Who's in charge of the galley?"

"Patu. You know him."

"I do," she confirmed. Patu was a terrible sailor. He tired easily and was prone to seasickness, but he was a brilliant cook. He had a nose for good fish that rivaled Xiala's own without the Teek senses to help. And he'd once made a dish with chunks of watermelon, papaya, and fresh seabird eggs that she still thought about at least once a week. But he was in high demand. Every crew wanted Patu. "How'd you convince him to join up?"

"Not me. Lord Balam."

"Ah." It seemed Lord Cat could buy anything, but this time she wasn't complaining.

She left Callo shouting orders at the crew and went in search of Patu. The ship was large, one of the biggest she'd ever commanded, but it was still small enough that she found Patu easily, huddled under the thatch looking miserable.

"I'm on break," he said defensively as she approached. If Callo always looked a bit disappointed at the hand life had dealt him, Patu looked downright affronted. The man was slope-shouldered and round-bottomed, and he wore his hair cut in a blunt bang across a face with eyes too big and a chin too weak. He wore the same white skirt and sandals as the other men, but he also had a thick rough blanket wrapped around his upper body like he was cold.

"Patu," she greeted him. "It is good to see you."

He gave her a miserable nod.

"Seasick?"

He shook his head. "Came in on a ship from Huluuc last night. It was raining the whole voyage. Damn near drowned us, we couldn't bail the water fast enough." He coughed wetly into his arm. "But this"—he gestured to his body and the blanket wrapped around it—"is nothing to worry about. I have a chill is all."

Xiala frowned. She didn't like the idea of having a sick man on her ship, great cook or not. Illness had a way of taking over, and out in the middle of the sea, there was no outrunning a cough that burrowed into your lungs and kept you from keeping food down.

"Callo approved me," Patu said hastily at her disapproving look. "Just a rain cough. I swear to the deep. I wouldn't take a commission if it was worse. I don't need the pay."

She relaxed a bit at that. He probably didn't.

"We're pulling into shore in less than an hour. Nice sandbar I remember from coming this way."

Patu leaned over to look past her shoulder at the coastline. He studied the limited landscape for a moment. "Lost Moth. Sure, I know it. Docked there once with another crew out of Sutal. Nice sand. Driftwood for making a fire. Fresh water across on the mainland."

"That's right. Can you cook us a meal, then? I want the crew well fed tonight."

"Lord Balam provided the food. I didn't get to choose." He sounded morose. "Said we had to sail today, no time to go to the market." He stopped long enough for another round of wet coughing, and Xiala waited him out. "But he gave me an inventory. I imagine it's all maize. Enough for cold porridge in the morning, maybe a flatbread for supper with a little salted fish. Standard fare." He pulled a sheet of bark paper from a bag on his belt and unfolded it. Someone had marked it well in ink, pictures and hash lines by each. Xiala could not read the picture language of the Cuecolans, so she waited for Patu to tell her what was on the list.

The man let out a sigh. "So there's maize." He gave her a look that conveyed his lack of surprise. "In balls for flatbread and porridge, of course. But also fruit. Papaya, melon, and lime. Salted fish, maybe more than one kind." He straightened, wide eyes getting wider. "Fowl soaked in vinegar, musk hog dried and cooked, mangrove oysters . . ." He smiled. "I do believe Lord Balam has given us some of his private food stores."

Xiala patted a much-cheered Patu on the shoulder. "Good, then. Make us a meal. A feast. Well, perhaps not too heavy, but the things that won't last as long. Fruit and oysters, yes? Maybe there's some balché on that list?"

Patu grinned. "There's better than that. There's a crate of xtabentún."

The anise and honey drink she'd had so much of the night before that she'd ended up in jail. Part of her wanted some desperately. But the rest of her, the captain part of her, knew better. "Ah, let's hold that. First day, after all."

"Of course." The man stood, clearly refreshed. "I better get started. Callo's got us almost to shore."

Xiala looked, but she didn't have to. She could tell they were getting closer to land by the rocking of the canoe under her feet, the feel of the swell that changed as the waters shallowed. But she didn't explain, only nodded in agreement and started to walk back to her place at the helm.

She stopped in front of the door to the single enclosed space on the ship. Most of their cargo was in wooden crates or wrapped in woven fiber cloth and stacked beneath the thatched reed roof, but there was this small room, probably no more than ten paces square. Big enough for a bench and a bed and a scribe's table, perhaps. Usually it was used as a captain's quarters or for a cargo too precious to trust to the open sea air. On this voyage the precious cargo was a man. A man who hadn't shown his face in the six-odd hours they'd been on the water.

Xiala wondered why not. Balam had said the man was blinded and scarred. A religious recluse of some kind. Some old and wrinkled monk, she assumed, from some obscure Obregi order she cared less than nothing about. She inevitably didn't get along with religious types. Always so dour with their prayers and their morality that they felt the need to force upon others. And never did their theologies have room for her, be it her Teek heritage that proved to be the abomination, her fondness for drink, or her sexual preferences. The more she thought about some old pruned-up Obregi in there, no doubt ready to press her to conform in the name of his gods, the more annoyed she became. Until she was feeling ready to throw him overboard on principle, promise to Balam or not.

Stop it! she told herself. *He is not here to sit in judgment of you. He is your guest. Your only job is to deliver him to Tova.*

And so she would. Although she had to admit she was curious. She had not met many Obregi in her travels. The country was deep in the high southern mountains and did not produce many sailors or have cause to participate in much sea trade. Even though she had met people from dozens of cities and places on the Meridian continent, Obregi was a landlocked mystery.

She decided she would introduce herself, see to his comforts should he need anything, and keep matters professional and polite. It was her duty, after all.

She reached her hand out to push the door open, but before she completed the act, a shout went up from Callo. She felt the gentle thump of the hull against soft sand. They were on land.

She sighed and withdrew her hand. The Obregi would have to wait.

• • • • •

She was the last one off the ship. Callo had led the crew of two dozen to the sandbar. It was a wide, gently sloping cay perhaps an eighth of a mile long and fifteen paces wide, set off from the mainland shore by half the length of the ship itself. The water was shallow enough to be a chest-high walk at low tide and an easy swim at high. The water on the ocean side went from drop-off to sand in a matter of seconds, making it a perfect place to anchor. Easy to get the canoe back in water deep enough to row without the aid of a dock.

Patu had been busy. The crew sat on the ground crowded around blankets spread with the wealth and variety of food Balam had provided them. Patu's corn cakes were there, cooked over a pit fire with bits of squash. Oysters had been cracked open and drizzled with melted avocado and pepper seeds, and there was a plate heaped with fish, their dead eyes and orange scales glimmering in the fire.

Someone had popped the lid off a clay barrel of balché. A cleaned bowl-shaped seashell was being dipped in the barrel, filled with the milky alcoholic drink, and passed around. Laughter and low peaceful talk filled the air, the sound of a crew who had worked a hard day under the sun and were being rewarded for it. They would have more hard days ahead of them, but for now, in the cool darkness in front of a fire and a spread of food fit for a merchant lord, all was proper and right.

"Captain," a voice called to her as her feet touched the sand. "Come join us."

A solid cheer went up from the crew. She slipped off her sandals to dig her toes into the still-warm sand. The balché shell was filled and passed her way, and she tipped the bowl back, draining the cup in one long swallow. Another cheer and a laugh, and someone called out, "Teek!"

She grinned and gave a small bow, which elicited more laughter. A few of these men she'd drunk under the table in times past.

She passed the shell back to the man who had handed it to her and dropped down in front of the blanket piled with food, folding her legs beneath her. Patu offered her an oyster and a small black blade that was no longer than her maimed pinkie finger. She used the blade to pry the meat out and sucked it down, the pepper seeds burning her mouth in a pleasant way. She used the same small blade to fillet a fish, a quick and practiced slice that bared the spine. She tossed the guts and dug her fingers in to pull flesh from delicate bone. It was delicious.

The conversation flowed easily around her. Stories of the day and how far they'd come and what good weather it was for storm season and how it was because their captain was Teek and good luck, and through all of it she ate and smiled and worried about what she would say once all had full bellies and the balché had run out. Would all this camaraderie vanish, all this goodwill disappear like it never was? Would she still be good luck, or would she be a curse, a bad omen, when the waves rose and the rain fell, as they undoubtedly would before they reached Tova?

She held off telling them just a bit longer, basking in the moment as the sun settled behind the horizon and the moon rose to take its place. And then she held off a bit more as one of the crew, Loob was his name, regaled them with a story of a swimming jaguar that chased him across a river and up a tree until he had been rescued. He turned his back to show the scar as proof, a place where claws had gouged a chunk from his flesh.

"My house cat has done worse," another man, Baat, said.

"Hells, your wife did worse to me," Xiala added, and Loob was the first to laugh.

"Loob's wife is from Tova," Callo said. "That's where we're headed. Maybe you can bring her back something from her homeland."

"Do you mean Loob or the captain?" Baat asked.

More raucous laughter that Xiala joined in. She motioned for someone to pass her the balché shell, and she drank deep again. And then she was ready.

She stood and waited for their attention to turn her way.

"Let's talk about Tova," she said. The fire on the edge of their gathering flared as the driftwood Patu had used to make it shifted, sending small orange sparks into the light breeze. The air smelled of cooking spices and ocean, and the waves lapped a soft rhythm behind her. She cleared her throat and did her best to make eye contact with each man as she spoke. "Lord Balam hired us all on, gave us our commissions for the voyage. And he's paying us well," she said, gesturing around at the remnants of the feast. "In cacao and food."

A cheer went up. "To Lord Balam!"

"To Lord Balam," the rest called back.

"To Lord Balam," Xiala agreed. "Who has tasked us with a difficult mission. Difficult, but not impossible."

Most cheered at that. They knew they were sailing in storm season and expected some challenges, but others, those sailors with more experience, understood she was leading them somewhere and exchanged uneasy looks, not sure they were going to like what was coming next.

"We're set for Tova," she said, "but Balam needs us there in twenty days. Nineteen now, when the sun rises."

A small moment of shock followed by protests of outrage. "It's too far!" someone shouted. "It's thirty days, maybe more if the seas are choppy or a storm comes in and we're forced to wait it out on land."

"I told him that," she said.

Loob scratched at his head. "The only way to make it in nineteen days is to sail the open water. And to row double shifts."

A groan went up.

"We don't have enough crew to row double," Baat said. "We already ran double today, and my back is aching."

"Shoulders, too," someone added.

"The men would be hard pressed to keep it up for twenty days," Callo agreed.

"But it can be done," she said, over them all. "I told Balam that with this crew, these men, it could be done."

They paused, unsure how to process her words, appreciating the compliment, but not liking what it implied.

"And I'll be there," she added. "I'll be there to calm the waters, to make sure your luck holds."

Her meaning was obvious, and they sat with it, absorbing what amounted to a promise to keep the seas friendly for them. Which was foolish, a lie, even, although they didn't know it. She had her Song and her Teek power to calm or agitate the sea, but she wouldn't be able to do much if a ship-killer hit. But what else could she say to convince them? Anything else, and she'd lose her crew before she'd started.

After a few moments of quiet grumbling, Callo raised his hand.

"Speak," she said.

"When I speak, I will speak for the crew," he said.

When no one gainsaid him, Xiala said, "You will."

He stood and rubbed his chin. Two dozen pairs of eyes moved from her to him, waiting. Xiala held her breath. Callo had seemed genuinely remorseful over Huecha's treachery, but he'd also admitted he thought she was part fish. She realized now his superstition might work in her favor.

"I've sailed the open sea before," he said, his words slow

and measured, "but not this time of year. This time of year, careful men stay in port and grow fat."

"Poloc's already fat," someone said, which earned him a push from the man next to him, likely Poloc.

"But we are better than careful men," Callo said, ignoring the teasing. "We are brave. I say we do it, not just because Balam has paid us all well, but for the adventure."

"I want to be alive to enjoy my riches," a voice called from the far end near the fire. "Can't do that if a shipkiller gets me and makes me food for the fishes."

"You heard the captain," Loob said. "She'll keep the storms away."

"Smooth sailing across the Crescent Sea! A story to tell," Poloc said, a note of awe in his voice.

"Our captain can do it," Callo agreed, which made Xiala blink in surprise.

"We'll be legendary!" That was Baat.

Xiala exhaled, but her shoulders stayed tense around her ears, and she folded her hands behind her back to hide the fact that they were shaking. Callo's support had been unexpected but gratifying, and the way the other men had fallen in line behind him was both good and bad. Good on this day because it went in her favor, but she wondered what would happen if she and Callo came to differences. Which way would the crew split? A shudder of foreboding rolled across her already tense shoulders. She hoped she never had to find out.

"Teek!" Loob shouted. "Teek! Teek!" And then someone else joined him. And then Callo and Poloc and Patu and Baat, too, until everyone was chanting, "Teek! Teek! Teek!" like her heritage was a talisman that would keep them all alive. Dread curled in her belly, knowing it was her own fault for suggesting the truth in their superstition. Part of her regretted it, but another part exulted in their acceptance, no matter how precarious.

"The crossing will be hard, but my Song will get us there safely. And, as Callo said, we might see wonders." She looked at Baat. "Become legends."

"Tail to tip, straight across to the Tovasheh river in nineteen days!" Loob marveled.

"Sixteen," Xiala corrected. "It's three days upriver, so that gives us sixteen days to reach the river mouth."

Stunned silence, and for a moment she thought she might have lost them. But Baat yelled, "All hells, we'll make it in ten!"

"Nine!"

"Seven!"

"We'll be there tomorrow by supper!"

And then they were laughing and passing the balché around again.

Xiala motioned Callo over. He came, plaintive eyes wary.

"My thanks, Callo."

He shrugged. "I meant it enough. And I need the pay." He looked down. "And it's not a lie I told, is it? You'll get us there, Teek."

She bristled at the name but only nodded. Nothing but confidence would do now.

"Make sure the balché runs dry in another half hour whether the barrel is empty or not. It's going to be a long day tomorrow, and they'll need their stamina. There's a fresh-water chultun not too far in on the mainland."

"I know it," Callo said.

"Send two of your most sober men to fill as many water pots as they can."

"And firewood? There wasn't much here to gather."

"No wood. We'll only eat cold and burn resin on the open water."

"Aye."

"I'll stay with the ship tonight. You stay here bunked with the crew, enjoy land while it's under your feet." She cared little for a few extra hours on land, but sleeping on the ship had a more practical purpose. A drink and meal shared was good leadership, but she was still a woman and the only woman among two dozen men. She was a hedonist at heart, never shy about loving men or women or any other gender, but she drew the line with her crew. She had a rule to never mix business with pleasure, and it served her well. Best to sleep on the ship to avoid even the hint of availability. Besides, she liked the gentle rocking of the waves under her head. She worried about Callo forming a stronger bond with the crew in her absence, but that could not be helped. She would have to trust her first mate.

"All right. Then up before dawn tomorrow, and we—Callo?"

Her first mate's face had gone pale in the firelight, eyes huge and staring at something behind her shoulder. Her senses prickled in alarm. The voices of the crew quieted. And she turned to see what stood between her and her ship.

CHAPTER 12

THE CRESCENT SEA
YEAR 325 OF THE SUN
(20 DAYS BEFORE CONVERGENCE)

Crows are highly sociable creatures. They form family units with mothers and fathers and even siblings. I have seen the solitary crow, but even they might gather with another to look for food or ward off a predator. I once saw a crow befriend a kitten and protect it with its own life.

—From *Observations on Crows*, by Saaya, age thirteen

The distant sounds of voices and laughter called to him. The crew had been a constant companion throughout the day, the measured count of their strokes a meditation, the bawdy songs they sang to keep rhythm as they sliced through the waters his entertainment. It was a pleasant way to pass time, something new and unusual.

He was used to spending most of his time alone, but that did not mean that once he had the choice of joining the others, he did not want it, it did not beckon. And then he heard them chanting "Teek! Teek!" and his curiosity got the best of him.

He thought to call on his crows and let them tell him what there was to see, but the truth was that a secondhand experience would not be satisfying. He wanted to know what was beyond this small room—put shape and size and person to the sailors' voices, and to the ocean and the island, and especially to the Teek woman, the captain.

He stood and smoothed the wrinkles from his robe. He had not removed his boots or any other item of clothing, save the strip of black cloth he wore tied around his eyes. He didn't need it, of course. The flesh of his eyelids had long ago sealed shut like a healed wound around the gut his mother had threaded through them a decade ago, but covering his eyes seemed to comfort others, so for their sake he wore it.

Even with the cloth on, he could still see some. A little in the normal way if the light was bright against his eyelids, but he also had his other senses, touch and taste and smell, that his tutors had honed to impressive performance. It was not magic, but countless hours of practice. Practice told him where a person was standing from the movement of the air around them. Practice taught him to listen to a person's breathing and whether it was steady with calm or short and panicked with lies. Practice had taught him the myriad smells of bodies and rain and heat and what they said about a person and the weather and the time of day.

And of course, he had his birds that let him borrow their eyes when he took the star pollen.

And he had something else. The crow god.

But none of it replaced what he ached for most.

The company of people.

Their laughter, the easy camaraderie. No one was easy around him, although he wished them to be, and beyond his tutors, he had never had anything that resembled friends except his crows. So he bound the cloth around his head for the sake of others. Before he left the room, he pulled his cowl up over his head, too, an extra precaution.

He moved silently, the low creak of the canoe on gentle waves the only sound. He marveled that people could build such a ship and have it withstand the power of the sea. It seemed only wood and resin and wild faith to him, but he was a man who knew wild faith, so perhaps it was not so strange after all.

It took him some time to locate the plank the crew had left for crossing to shore, but once he found it through touch and remembering where it had been when he boarded, he crossed easily enough.

The sand under his feet was packed and solid. He pushed his way up a small rise toward the voices, listening to what his new environment could teach him. First there was the lap of water against land, a different sound from both the roar of waves in the harbor and the staccato slapping of smaller waves against the canoe. Then the voices of the crew all made distinct by variation in accent and tone. He could determine personality, mood, sometimes origin, although he wished he had heard more foreigners speak during his time in Obregi to better place them on his map.

The voices were low, both in register and in location. Some lively but most dulled with fatigue and drink. They seemed to be at the bottom of a hill or closer to the ground.

He imagined the crew spread out along the ground at the dip of the hill somewhat below him. A breeze danced through the night sky, carrying the scent of spices and oils and what he had recently learned was fish. There was also a slightly sour undertone that he guessed emanated from the drink the men consumed. Shadows danced on the corner of his vision, suggesting that there must be a low fire nearby, the smell of smoke confirming it.

Another voice joined the talk, a feminine one. Authoritative, and used to directing men. That must be the captain. Her voice came back to him on the breeze, as if she was standing with her back turned to him. And there was the first mate he knew was named Callo, his distinctive cadence easy to recognize.

He listened for a while longer, enjoying the scene before him, until silence fell, and he knew they had seen him.

"*Beex gala'ee,*" he greeted them, employing his limited Cuecolan. He smiled in an attempt to reassure them of his benevolent motives, but that only made the shadowed figure nearest flinch. Ah, his teeth. He had forgotten. He closed his mouth.

"It's the Obregi," someone murmured, and the word circulated through the crew on tongues both curious and wary.

"My lord," a female voice said, not scared but definitely cautious. "We are honored to receive you." It was the shadowy shape that had flinched, the captain. Serapio inhaled, taking in her scent. It was white salt warmed on dark skin. Azure water, deep and endless. Power, bright and furious.

Magic.

He breathed her in, half-giddy. Who was she? What was she?

The figure next to her moved. Tossed something toward Serapio. Instinct had him calling shadow to his fingers before he realized whatever it was had fallen to the sandy shore well short of him. He released his power immediately, but the feeling of it lingered around him, a dark vibration in the air.

A small gasp of irritation from the woman. "Callo!" Her voice was sharp with reprimand. "Don't be an idiot. Get *our guest* something to eat," she said, emphasis plain, a reminder to the first mate to keep his manners.

Callo. Serapio memorized his scent, too. Salt, yes, but wet and clotted, more like human sweat than the clear summery smell of the captain. And there was the sour drink, even more than what he caught from the captain. And . . . something acrid. Confusion, perhaps. Something that smelled of deceit and indecision, conflict and fear. Callo was to be watched.

He heard hesitation, then dragging steps as Callo moved back toward the fire.

Serapio realized he was indeed hungry. He had gone without food before, for days sometimes when his father had forgotten him or when his tutors thought hunger would teach him a necessary lesson, so he was used to the empty feeling, the knot in his belly. But he was pleased when Callo came back. The man paused a few paces away and proffered the bowl in his outstretched hands, as if he feared getting too close.

"Oh, mother waters," the woman cursed, grabbing the bowl from the man and closing the distance between them. "Here." She thrust the food at him. He took it. "And with my apologies. But . . ." She sighed, sounded burdened and embarrassed. "Best you eat on the ship, eh? You've got the crew spooked, and they're superstitious enough without someone like you showing up in the moonlight like a specter." She pulled gently at his arm. She wanted him to follow her.

He allowed her to lead him back the way he had come.

Once on board, he reached a hand in to feel the contents of his bowl. All unfamiliar except for the imperfectly round cakes he assumed to be corn. He pulled a long scale-covered creature out and held it up.

"A fish?"

"The Cuecolans call them shushu. These have been smoked."

"Smoked" meant nothing to him in particular. He was not a gourmand by any stretch of the imagination. Food, when it came, was simply a necessity to keep him functioning. He took no delight in flavor and method and texture. He held the fish to his mouth and bit into its side. Scales cut his lips and the roof of his mouth. Alarmed, he ran his tongue over his bruised flesh.

"You like them?" she asked, humor in her voice.

"Yes, I think. But they are difficult to eat."

She snorted. "Your Cuecolan is terrible. You speak Trade?"

"Yes."

"Let us talk in Trade, then. So, Obregi has no seas?"

He shook his head no. The fish was strange but good, and now that he was eating, he was ravenous.

She laughed a small, relieved laugh. "You're just a man, then."

He paused, the fish already halfway to his mouth. It was a statement she had made, not a question, so he said nothing and let her assumption go unremarked. He took another bite.

"The way you came up out of nowhere just now, I thought

for a minute . . ." Her words drifted off. "You see strange things at sea sometimes. A black bird that turns into a man in a black robe would not be the strangest."

"What would be?" he asked, curious.

"Women with fish tails and a voice that can change a man's will," she said, and her tone told him that she was making fun of herself.

He took another fish, this time biting off the head instead of starting on the side.

"Seven hells," she said, laughing. "Has no one taught you to eat a fish?"

The thing was slick in his mouth, the bones trying their best to slide between his teeth. "No."

She tapped his arm. "Give it to me."

He handed it over as he swallowed the bit in his mouth.

"Sit," she commanded, and he followed her quick steps over to the paddle benches. Whatever she did, she did fast, and then she handed him back the fish. "I've cut it in two. Watch for the bones. They can stick in the throat. But the white flesh is good. Eat that part first."

"White flesh?" he asked.

"My mistake," she said, sounding apologetic. "Just pick the meat from the bone. Can you do that?"

"Of couse." It took him a moment to figure it out by touch, but soon he was using his fingers to pry the flesh free. It was soft and melted against his tongue. So much tastier than the scales and bones.

"Here."

She handed him something else. It was one of the shell

creatures that had been in the bowl with the corn cakes and fish. She had opened the shell, and it sat in two pieces in his hand, just like the fish had. He reached in with his fingers.

"No," she said. "You suck an oyster down. No hands. Just your mouth."

He held the shell to his lips and sucked. The oyster slid down his throat in a salty wash. It was even better than the fish and easier to eat.

"Another," she said, and he took a second oyster. He could feel her eyes on him, watching. Deciding.

After his fifth oyster, he held up his hand to say no more. He reached inside the bowl that sat on the bench between them and took a corn cake. He broke it in half, the crumbs falling between his fingers, and offered her a piece. After a moment she took it.

"My name is Xiala, but you can call me Captain," she said, chewing.

"I am Serapio."

"You can see." It was another non-question.

"Shapes, shadows, and light. Movement. The rest is scent, taste, touch." He did not tell her about the crows or about his god.

"You're good at it."

"Better than most that are not blind."

"And the cloth on your eyes, it's just for show?"

"No. And yes."

She made a sound like she understood. "I had a dagger like that." She took another bite, chewing loudly. "You scare the crew."

"I know."

"They're good enough men, strong. But I'm in a particular situation."

He said nothing, only waited. Finally, she seemed to make a decision. "You know what I am?"

"The captain?"

The canoe creaked as she leaned back against the ledge. "Good," she said, a grin evident in her voice, "but I mean the other thing."

"Teek."

"That one. They're scared of that, too."

"I heard them chanting for you."

"Aye," she acknowledged. "But two days ago some of those men were happy to blame my being Teek for turning the salt bad."

"What changed?"

"Not sure. Balam? Cacao in their hands? A belly full of good food?"

"Callo?"

"Him, too."

"So it could change back."

"You are a smart man, Obregi."

"Observant."

She laughed at that, as if he had told a great joke, and perhaps he had. "Tomorrow you come out in the daylight. Wear a white skirt like the other men, not these black robes, let them see you. But . . ." She hesitated. "Keep your eyes covered, yeah? Sometimes it is best not to tell them everything at once."

"I don't have a workman's skirt."

"I'll give you one. There's clean ones in the storage under the awning."

He thought about it. She was trying to show the men he was harmless, a man just like them. It was a lie, but he understood the necessity of it. "All right."

"Good." She stood up. "They'll sleep on shore tonight and you in your room. I'll be here on the ship, just outside your door, so if one of them gets the notion to come drown you in the middle of the night, I'll be here to protect you."

He thought of the crew—their songs, the camaraderie that he envied. He would not kill them if he didn't have to, but if they impeded his mission, they would die. She would, too, although he did not enjoy that thought.

"Who protects you?" he asked, not doubting her abilities but curious to hear her answer.

It was brash, much like the captain herself.

"The sea herself," she said. "I am her daughter, and when I'm with my mother"—she exhaled gustily—"nobody fucks with her children."

CHAPTER 13

The Obregi Mountains

Year 319 of the Sun

(6 Years before Convergence)

> Violence should only be used in defense, and even then, it corrupts. If you must kill your enemy, do it quickly and be done. To linger only invites humiliation of both the victim and the self, and there is no honor there.
>
> — *On the Philosophy of War*, taught at the Hokaia War College

"These are very beautiful," the stranger said as she entered the boy's room. Her voice was low, rough, and had an accent Serapio had never heard before. Her footfalls were light and quick, and she carried something that she tapped against the stone floor in rhythm with her steps. "When Paadeh sent for me, he said you were talented, but I did not realize I was to train an artist."

Serapio paused. Despite her flattery, something about the woman felt threatening, although he wasn't sure what. He set his current carving down on his workbench. It was the same bench that Paadeh had first brought to his room two years ago. He slipped the chisel into his trouser pocket. It was not much of a weapon, but it was enough to dig into a throat or to sink into vulnerable flesh if he had to.

"Who are you?" he asked.

"You should be able to figure out the answer to that, crow son," she said from across the room. He heard her pick up a carving from a shelf, presumably to admire it. Movement broke the line of light streaming in from the window as she tossed the piece up in the air and caught it again. He heard the wood slap dully against the flesh of her palm. "In fact, you should have expected me."

"Please," he said, voice strained. "Each of my carvings represents many hours of work. Does Marcal know you're here?"

She snorted, but he heard the tap of wood being set back on the shelf.

"Your father thinks I've come to teach you how to use a staff to see."

He cocked his head. "Have you?"

She exhaled, sounding annoyed. "After a fashion."

She was being evasive on purpose, he could tell. The slight tic in her enunciation, the way her voice seemed to come from a distance, as if she wasn't looking directly at him. He did not exactly fear the woman in his room, but something about her boldness, the way she spoke, kept him wary. He no longer had a guard or servants coming and going to care for him, and he was acutely aware that he was alone with a stranger whom he had not invited in. But she claimed that Paadeh had sent her. Did she know Paadeh was dead?

"Did you make all of these?"

He knew she must be talking about the small menagerie of wooden animal carvings he had meticulously arranged on the shelf along the far wall. "Yes."

"And this trunk, too? The one on the table under the window?"

It was his triumph, an ornately carved trunk of rosewood, the lid a map of the Meridian continent hewn in meticulous detail. Paadeh had made him build it, insisting that Serapio learn geography and knowing the only way to do it right was to create the map on his own as only he could. His tutor had whipped his hands when he'd gotten something wrong and made him start again. Each city, road, sea, and mountain was to scale, his fingers committing to memory the lay of the continent better than any traditional map might have taught him, each mountain range and sea colored with his blood and sweat.

"Yes, I made the trunk."

She was quiet, as if studying his art, studying him.

"You may call me Eedi," she said, moving closer. Her footfalls ended abruptly. She fully blocked the little light that came into his room from the windows, increasing the shadows around him. He felt the weight of her gaze, heard the *tap, tap* of whatever she was holding against the floor. A staff, he realized.

"I am your second tutor," she said, "and I am here to serve."

He felt movement. Had she bowed to him?

"As Paadeh served?"

"Where is that old bastard?" she asked.

"I learned all I could from him," he said. "He said he would not come again." It was a lie, but he did not trust her enough to tell her the truth.

She was quiet, and his hand tightened on his chisel, ready.

Finally, she spoke. "Good. It is best you do not get attached to any of us, crow son. We are here to teach you the things you will need, but we are not your friends."

"Paadeh said pain was my only friend."

"He would," she said, and he could almost see her eye roll. "But it's overkill, isn't it? There's nothing good in the fate Saaya set for you. No friends, either, but the rest is . . . well, Paadeh always did like to turn philosophical."

"I have a higher purpose."

"Paadeh told you, eh?"

"The crows did. And my mother."

Quiet, and then, "Paadeh sent a letter saying that you were a strange one. You talk to the birds? I don't remember that being part of Saaya's workings."

They are my friends. "Do you come from Odo, like Paadeh did?"

"Did?" She held on to that past tense, and Serapio realized his mistake, but she continued smoothly. "Is that what he told you? Odo? No, boy, neither of us is from Odo, although he's closer. He was from Tova city, at least, although somewhere called Coyote's Maw. You know it?"

He shook his head.

"I hail from the war college at Hokaia. Surely you know it." She sounded proud, but there was a hint of something else there, too. Bitterness, perhaps.

He had heard of Hokaia, but only in stories, tales of the city on the mighty river a thousand miles north, the place where the peoples of the continent signed their peace treaty, the place where the Meridian continent sent its children to train in the arts of war in hopes that one never happened again. And he knew what that likely made her. "You're a spearmaiden."

"I used to be a spearmaiden," the woman said, that bitterness he detected before blossoming to resentment. "Now I am the trainer of spearmaidens. And blind boys, it seems."

He thought perhaps she was trying to anger him, but he was long past rising to every provocation, especially ones that were the truth. Besides, she interested him. "If you are from Hokaia, how can you be here to serve me, a crow son?"

"Ah," she said. "The reach of your god is long, and some of us chafe against the Sun Priest's influence. Your people and mine are united in purpose if not blood, and for that, I have pledged my life. Plus, your mother was a persuasive bitch." She laughed fondly.

"Did you love her?" he asked suddenly. A hunch, but something about the spearmaiden's voice made him think it.

"We all loved her," she said, sounding startled, "and hated her, too. But mostly, we admired her."

"Is that why you're here?"

"Let's just say that there are those in Hokaia who wish Tova and the celestial tower reformed."

The way she said the last word sounded like she meant an entirely different word from *reformed*. "Reformation is your purpose?"

She made a *tsk*ing sound with her tongue. "Clever, crow son, but just as Paadeh could not reveal your true purpose, neither can I. It is not our place and not your time. But patience. When Powageh comes all will be told."

"I know my true purpose already," he said automatically. "Who is Powageh?"

"Did I not just say to be patient?"

"Will he be the one to return me to Tova?"

He remembered enough from what his mother had told him and learned enough from his two years with Paadeh to know that whatever purpose they meant for him, it would happen in Tova, in the seat of Carrion Crow. And now this woman had linked it to the celestial tower.

He filed every bit of knowledge away, willing himself to the patience that Eedi exhorted. Paadeh had taught him that, too. Taught him to trust in this process of becoming, knowing just as he shaped the wood, so his tutors would shape him. But for what?

"Are you ready to begin?" she asked.

He thought of what she had said about being there to teach him to use the staff but also not. "Begin what?"

Something struck him in the arm, hard. He cried out in surprise. It hit him again, and he realized it was the thing she had been tapping on the floor—staff, spear, or something else. He felt the small rush of air as she moved to strike him a third time. He whipped his hand out, shoving the shaft away before it could hit him again.

"Good," she said, her voice evaluating. "Your reaction time is slow, but reflexes are good once you get started.

Your sense of space is excellent. Now, what about your instincts?"

Five long strides, and she was across the room. Something crashed to the floor.

Serapio stood immediately. "What are you doing?"

Another crash, and Serapio knew Eedi was razing his shelf, knocking his carefully carved animals to the ground.

"Stop!" he cried. He took two steps forward and rammed his knee into his workbench. In his haste he had forgotten it was there. He cursed, a word he'd learned from Paadeh.

Eedi laughed. "Well, you swear like a soldier. Let's see if we can make you fight like one."

Another crash, wood dropped against stone to splinter apart. His stomach lurched. He had to stop her. He felt his way around the bench, leg throbbing, and took the nineteen remaining strides to the shelf. Ignoring her, he reached out and ran a hand along the place where his forest creations normally sat. It was empty. He cursed again and went to his knees, feeling the stone floor. His hand closed on an object, and after a moment of exploration, he recognized it as his crow. It was still whole. The first object he'd ever carved. He slipped it into the pocket opposite his chisel. He felt for more objects and retrieved a rabbit, a squirrel, and a fox. Six in all that he clutched against his chest as he rose. One by one he placed them back on the shelf, except for the crow, which he left in his pocket. He could feel Eedi behind him, watching, weighing.

"What kind of training is this?" he asked, angry.

"I'll just knock them down again," she said, flippant.

"Don't!" His breath was short, panicked.

Movement, and he heard something else fall farther along the shelf. "You'll have to stop me."

"I can't see!" he shouted, all his calmness, his hard-won control, slipping in the face of the destruction of the things he had made, the things he loved.

"No shit, crow son. But you don't need to." She had moved, somewhere by the door. He turned, following her voice. His heart stuttered. She was near the table by the window, the one where his carved trunk with the map of the Meridian continent sat.

"Don't touch it!" he screamed. He had suffered for the map, bled for it. He would not let her destroy it.

She spit the words one by one: "Come. Stop. Me."

He rushed her, arms outstretched, knowing his folly even as he did it but having no choice. It was seven strides compensated for with speed, but she easily sidestepped him. He slammed shoulder-first against the stone wall, his hip grazing the table. Pain radiated down his arm until his fingers tingled. He cried out and braced a hand on the table, feeling desperately for his trunk. He exhaled in relief to find it there, untouched from what he could tell.

"Well, at least you still have your balls," she said, critically. "Now what?"

She had moved again, back to the shelf. He forced himself to calm down, to think. He wasn't going to physically overpower her this way, flailing ridiculously, tripping over his own feet. He had to outthink her.

His hand roved the table, searching for something of use. His fingers closed on something slick on one side, rough on the other. A mirror, circular with a slate backing. He recognized it as something his mother had used for divination. It had been sitting on the table, four years forgotten.

Her image flooded his mind, a beautiful creature under a cascade of black hair, calling him over to peer into the mirror that led to another place, a dark canvas that allowed his mother to see things others could not. A gateway into shadow.

Shadow was his to control. He knew it instinctively as if the thing he had stolen from the sun awoke with his need, the power that he had earned through blood and loss. He pressed his open palm against the reflective side of the mirror and concentrated. He thought of winter's kiss against the fresh cuts of his haahan, of the burn of the sun as it seared away his vision, of ice and snow and shadow. He could feel the shadow rising to his hand, a dark power for him to command.

"Well?" Eedi asked, sounding bored. "Do something, or the next thing I break is your bones."

Serapio's left hand closed around the wooden crow in his pocket. In his right was whatever had come from the mirror, a roiling icy smoke boiling around his fingertips.

He thrust the mirror forward, willing the smoke to fly. She cried out. He knew that her eyes had followed his movement and that the mirror had released its icy shadow.

He yanked the wooden crow from his pocket, aimed for where he thought Eedi's head should be, and threw it as hard as he could.

She grunted as it struck. Her spear clattered to the floor.

Serapio rushed forward, retracing his path, and this time he connected. Their bodies collided. She went down hard on her back, him on top.

Quick as lightning, he wrenched the chisel from his pocket and swung at where he thought her face should be. But she had already moved, or he had miscalculated. The blade skidded against the stone floor, jangling the bones in his arm. His fingers spasmed in pain.

Not waiting, he clawed to his left, seeking her eyes. She caught his hand, holding it back. But he was strong, two years of woodworking lacing his hands and forearms with muscle. He broke her hold, raking a hand across her cheek, close enough for his fingernail to catch her eyelid.

She screamed in agony. He pushed harder.

"Enough!" she cried out, voice a spike of pain.

But it wasn't enough. His rage told him it would never be enough. He screamed, a half-formed sound, and doubled his efforts.

The punch to his nose knocked him back. Bright lights flashed in his head, and he rolled away. Another punch to the side of his head, as if for good measure, and he rolled farther.

"You fucking villain!" she shouted, panting. The noise was near the floor, like she was splayed out on her back. Her breathing was heavy, her words cruel, but her voice sounded elated. "What the fuck did you do?"

"I didn't want you to break my map," he said, lying beside her, struggling to get his own words out around the adrenaline racing through his body.

"My fucking eye!" she cried, stumbling to her feet. "You tried to tear out my fucking eye!"

"I didn't succeed?"

"Fuck you!"

And she was stumbling for the door, shouting for a healer. He laughed, he couldn't help it. It had felt good to strike back, to stop her. He did not like her breaking the things he loved.

"Villain," he mouthed, liking the sound of it, the weight of the word on his bloodied lip. If protecting his crows made him a villain, then a villain he would be.

• • • • •

He wasn't sure how long he lay there before she came back. Part of him was surprised she had returned at all. He had all but convinced himself that he was done with tutors, that he did not need them anymore. But he recognized her steps, the tap of her staff, and breathed a quiet sigh of relief that she had not left him.

"The mirror?" she asked from somewhere above him and to his right. He expected her to be angry with him, but her voice was calm, interested. "Where did you learn to do that?"

"I . . ." He thought about his hand resting on the mirror, the vision of his mother, and the knowledge that he could call on the darkness to help him. "What exactly did it do?"

"You threw a shadow, crow son," she said, and now he heard something in her voice, a reverence. "You loosed a stream of darkness right at my face. It was like being blinded."

"Blinded," he said, voice silky with sarcasm. "I seriously doubt that."

She barked a laugh and came closer. She kicked him in the arm. Lightly, only enough to get his attention. "I'm helping you up. Take my hand."

He stuck his arm out, and two hands grasped him, wrenching him to his feet.

"How's your eye?" he asked, curious but not remorseful.

"The healer said it isn't permanently damaged, but it hurts like seven hells." He caught a bare thread of admiration in her voice. "Just know that if I was really trying to kill you, you would have already been dead ten times over before you launched your attack."

"So you say."

"Shall we go again?"

"No," he said, choking on a half-laugh. "My jaw aches. And I bit my tongue." He frowned, the obvious coming together slowly in his rattled brain. "Is that what you're here for? To teach me how to fight?"

"Ah, so you're not completely devoid of sense. Yes, to fight. Paadeh trained the mind, I train the body. But I know nothing about this shadow magic. That's Powageh's shit. He was always the mystic among us."

"My third tutor," he said, remembering the name. He hesitated and then asked. "And when will Powageh come?"

"Don't know. Not my business. This"—she bent to pick up something and shoved it against his chest—"is my business."

He wrapped his hands around it. It was the staff. Or spear. Or simply a very long piece of . . .

"Is this bone?" he asked. He ran a hand along the smooth surface. It was porous and yielded when he pressed his thumb against it. "It's not wood." That he was sure of.

"Bone it is," Eedi admitted. "A true master spearmaiden's weapon, harvested from the ice fields north of Hokaia and reinforced with blood magic. You can't have it because it's mine, but I'll teach you to use it. As both a weapon and a seeing aid. And then you can make your own."

She picked something else up and touched it against his hand. He took it. It was his crow, the one he had thrown at her. It was still unbroken.

"Shall we begin?"

CHAPTER 14

City of Tova

Year 325 of the Sun

(18 Days before Convergence)

> Truly the Sky Made clans are the best of Tovan society. Graceful and stately, they remind me of our own Seven Lords of the Seven Houses. I have inquired as to whether my host among the Sky Made might wish to visit Cuecola and was told that they already lived at the center of the universe and need not travel outside it. I found such an answer ill informed but kept such thoughts to myself.
>
> —*A Commissioned Report of My Travels*
> *to the Seven Merchant Lords of Cuecola,*
> by Jutik, a Traveler from Barach

To Naranpa's surprise, all of the Sky Made matrons, including Yatliza's daughter, agreed to meet at the celestial tower. She expected Golden Eagle to balk at the very least, because Nuuma always preferred to have her way, but all sent back messages that they would meet her an hour before sunset.

She arranged for the meeting to take place in the observatory at the top of the tower, the same space where they held the Conclave. The walls of the circular room displayed the sacred mosaic that depicted the Treaty of Hokaia and the investiture of the Sun Priest. Along the southern wall lay the jaguar of Cuecola crushed and bleeding from its mouth, nose, eyes, and ears, vivid red tiles meant to represent blood. The east depicted the fishwoman of the Teek, her head cut from her body and only slightly less gory than the dead jaguar. The spear of Hokaia was the simplest of all, a long bone spear broken into pieces and cast down on the ground. And finally, in the east, the only intact city totem—the sun of Tova. It was in ascension, rising to rest atop a great golden throne. And surrounding the foot of the throne were the totems of the four clans: crow, eagle, winged serpent, and water strider.

In the center of the room on stone pillars rested the drum and the sacred bundle of cedar branches that had been used in their procession the previous day, the power of above and below endowed within them.

All of them, the mosaic with its unsubtle history and the objects in the center, were reminders of the dominion of the priesthood. The Sky Made may hold the civil power in Tova, but they were nothing compared to the celestial authority that the tower commanded over the whole of the Meridian continent.

She took her seat on the bench in the east. She had brought in four other seats, spare and wooden, and arranged them in a fan shape radiating out from her in a semicircle. They were simple stools used by dedicants. Another not-so-subtle reminder of who held the power here. She had thought about forcing the matrons to sit on the floor but decided that bordered on insult, and she had not reclaimed enough of the Sun Priest's former mandate to risk it. The stools walked a fine line as it was, but an acceptable one.

Now there was nothing to do but wait.

She watched the light move down the far wall, clocking the passage of time as late afternoon moved toward evening. When the sun had all but disappeared and the sun clock told her that all that was left of daylight was minutes and not hours, she realized no one was coming.

She sat, staring at her feet, unsure what to do. They had said they would attend. Had something happened? Another calamity befallen the city while she sat at the top of her tower and waited?

She forced herself to stand, her legs unsteady under her ornate yellow vestments. Her mind felt blank, at a loss for what she was to do next.

Go downstairs, she told herself. *Send runners to find out if there was an accident. A bridge collapse. Another death.*

It was all unlikely.

What was likely was the simplest solution. Someone had interfered.

Abah.

That thought finally made her move.

She had passed through the eastern door and down to the fifth floor before she encountered a servant. She recognized him and called him by name.

"Leaya, has something happened?" she asked. "Why have the matrons not arrived?"

"They arrived an hour ago, Sun Priest."

"Where are they? I left orders for them to be brought to the observatory immediately upon arrival."

Leaya frowned. "No, Sun Priest. The other priest said your orders had changed and they were to be brought to the terrace."

"What other priest?"

"The seegi. She told us you were in prayer for the dead matron and you weren't to be disturbed. So we didn't disturb you. Is . . . did we misunderstand?"

Naranpa ground her teeth in frustration, her suspicions confirmed. And worst of all, Naranpa had walked right into it.

"No," she told the boy. "You did fine. Are they still here? On the terrace?"

"Last I saw, Sun Priest. Eche had us bring them refreshments, even though he did not partake because of the Shuttering."

"How pious of him," she muttered.

"Yes, Sun Priest."

She glared at the boy, but he didn't understand and certainly didn't deserve to be the target of her ire. "You may go. And thank you. You did well." She managed a smile.

Naranpa leaned against the nearby wall, staring at nothing. Night had fallen in earnest, and she could see other servants in brown making their way up the stairs, lighting the resin lamps in their sconces as they climbed. The longer she stood here, the more likely she was to miss the matrons entirely.

She wasn't sure what to do. She wanted to barge into the meeting and reassert her presence, humiliate Eche and Abah if she was there. But Abah had already outsmarted her twice that day. There was no guarantee that Abah had not already made a contingency plan should she appear. And for all she wanted to hurt Eche and Abah, she did not want to do anything that might make the priesthood look weak or confused to the Sky Made. Abah may not understand that they needed to present a unified face to the city's leadership, but she did.

For the first time, Nara felt like she had truly misplayed her hand. Yesterday had started out with so much promise, but between then and now, she had taken a beating.

Yesterday before the procession, she had thought herself well on her way to restoring the glory of the Sun Priest. Now she was teetering on the edge of the cliff, looking at a long fall back to where Kiutue had left her if she didn't find a way to regain control and quickly. But whom could she trust? Her ego wouldn't allow her to ask Iktan for help, particularly after her discovery that xe was sleeping with someone that wasn't her. Plus, xe was keeping secrets, and as much as she hated to admit it, it gave her pause. Haisan was the eldest, and wise. But she knew he thought her only marginally competent. And Abah clearly was out to replace her with Naranpa's own protégé.

Stars and sky, how had she gotten so lost in such a short period of time? But it wasn't so short, was it? Her mission had always been a gamble. She had loved her old mentor, and he had become a father to her in many ways, but he had allowed the hawaa's power to be claimed by other societies, leaving what was once the most essential role in the priesthood a shell of what it had been before him, now more symbolic than functional. Naranpa had set out to seize some of that power back, not for herself but because she believed that the priesthood could be better, do better, for not only the city but the entire continent. But she was beginning to admit that she had underestimated how much the game was rigged against her.

Well, there was nothing to do now but face the consequences and try to recoup her losses in the next round. And if there was no next round and it all went up in flames, then so be it.

She straightened the cuffs of her yellow robes and smoothed a hand down the wide skirt before squaring her shoulders and marching to the terrace.

· · · · ·

She spotted Eche first. He was facing away from her so did not see her enter the terrace. He was resplendent in the Sun Priest's raiment, an ankle-length skirt of deep yellow, embroidered at the hem, and overlapping wrap with darker yellow sunbursts. He wore the same cloak she did. His was the original, the one her mentor had worn, meant for broader shoulders and a taller body. Hers had been remade new to fit her smaller, more feminine stature. Both were the white of dawn at the shoulders and back, progressing to a deep star-dusted black by the time it reached the knees. He wasn't wearing the Sun Priest's mask—small miracle. She would not have put it past Abah to sneak into her room and steal it, considering everything else she had done. But Eche did have his thick black hair tied back in a club with yellow string, and his fresh face was smiling, no doubt.

He was chatting with Nuuma, the matron of Golden Eagle. Naranpa watched as Eche said something that made Nuuma laugh and touch a hand lightly to his arm. Needless to say, Nuuma had never touched her with that kind of familiarity. And why would she? They weren't friends, Naranpa had never said anything particularly witty to her, and she wasn't even Sky Made.

It occurred to her that Eche came from the Golden Eagle clan, and Nuuma, now well into her forties, had probably known him since he was born. Watched him grow into a fine young man and join the priesthood to rise to his rightful stature. Skies, she was probably proud of him.

And now that she thought of it, Abah was Golden Eagle–born, too. No wonder they wanted her out. She didn't belong the way they did. For all she knew, they were all related.

"Feeling better?" asked a voice from behind her.

She turned to find Ieyoue, matron of Water Strider, behind her. Ieyoue had traded her clan blues for a long dress of mourning white, and around her shoulders hung a black-and-white skunk-fur short cloak. It was a touch flamboyant, like the woman herself. Around her wrist she wore a red ribbon, a sign of respect for Carrion Crow's loss. It was a well-orchestrated ensemble. Respectful but not conservative. Sad but not needlessly so. Naranpa had always found her to be the shrewdest of the matrons.

"I am, thank you," she said quickly. She glanced over her shoulder to see Eche still talking to Nuuma Golden Eagle. "What did Eche tell you?" She hoped her inquiry sounded innocent enough.

"That the strain of the day had caught up with you and that you had asked him to take your place. I thought it strange, since you were the one who had sent the invitations to begin with, but then he told us of the assassination attempt on Sun Rock. Skies, it must have been terrible." She said it all well enough, the right touch of concern, a hint of true outrage. But Naranpa could see her brown eyes were eager, searching her face for some sign of conflict or subterfuge.

Ieyoue could make an admirable ally or a dangerous foe. Unfortunately, she didn't know the woman well enough to know which, and she was entirely out of trust.

"It was terrible," she agreed, putting some of the fright of the moment into her voice. "But the Knives handled it. He never got close," she lied. *Did you send him?* she wondered suddenly. *If not, do you know who did?*

"Well, I for one am glad to hear you are well, Naranpa. Eche did an admirable job paying Yatliza proper respects. I think the funeral he and Haisan planned will be appreciated by all. But . . ." She hesitated, leaning in. "He *is* quite young."

"Barely twenty-five," she agreed.

"He will make a fine Sun Priest one day," Ieyoue continued. "But today is not that day." The Water Strider matron widened her eyes meaningfully. "I hope I haven't offended you. I know he is your chosen successor, after all."

"Not yet," Naranpa corrected. "There are other dedicants who may be a better choice. One day."

Ieyoue made a show of thinking about it.

"Well, you would know who best serves the Watchers." She looked pointedly at the two behind Naranpa. "Seems that it may be difficult to tell the difference between yellow and gold for some, and those of us who are neither would prefer to keep the colors separate. Such a clash can ruin one's entire ensemble. Wouldn't you agree?"

Naranpa could have kissed her, but instead she only allowed her lips to curve in a small smile. "I find a splash of blue or green can do wonders."

"Or perhaps one need not use color at all."

"There truly are so many options."

Ieyoue nodded sagely. "I had only stepped out to pay my respects to Haisan. He's in the archives working on what will certainly be a very long speech extolling Yatliza's merits." She gestured back to the terrace. "Did you mean to come in?"

"No," Naranpa said, making a spur-of-the-moment decision. She realized now that the matrons already knew that Eche had usurped her, and Water Strider, at least, did not approve. She was equally sure that Nuuma was thrilled, and she would work out the balance with Winged Serpent and Carrion Crow another day. For now, this was enough.

"Give my regards to the other matrons, if Eche has not already. And I will see you at the funeral."

"Of course," Ieyoue said. "I am glad we had this chance to talk. It was, as always, illuminating."

They exchanged polite bows and Ieyoue went back to the terrace while Naranpa went the other way. Only when she was halfway down the hall on her way back to her rooms did she realize Ieyoue had made a joke.

CHAPTER 15

Lose one child to war and receive four generations of peace.

—Words inscribed over the war college at Hokaia

The news of his mother's death came to Okoa on the back of a great crow. He was in the war college training field just west of the aviary, the spread of the larger campus laid out behind him, when he spied the corvid's approach, its black wings catching the afternoon sunlight. He always marveled at these creatures his clan claimed as their namesake. Its wings seemed not enough to support its weight, never mind the rider on its back. But Okoa knew from his own experience that their patron crows could do just that and travel the miles east from Tova to the flat green grasslands of Hokaia in a fraction of the time it took to cross the same distance on boat or foot.

Okoa placed his training spear in the rack and used the edge of his cotton shirt to rub the sweat from his eyes. He had hoped to get another hour of practice in before night drove him inside, but he knew that rider and whatever message he brought was meant for him. Practice would have to wait.

Eyes still on the approaching rider, he jogged toward the aviary. It was nothing like the great aviaries of Tova. Those were proper aeries, great stables high in the cliffs around the city. Each Sky Made clan had one, save Water Strider, who kept their namesake beasts in a cave system closer to the Tovasheh river. But Golden Eagle, Winged Serpent, and Carrion Crow preferred to be close to the sky.

The war college accommodated the riders of Tova's Sky Made clans as best they could on the wide flat plains of Hokaia by constructing large wooden holding pens. The pens were laid out in a series of circles, each one two acres in diameter, with hitching posts, feeding troughs, and high open fences that served as walls. Plenty of room for the beasts to land but not to stay for any length of time in any kind of comfort. After all, Tova's Sky Made scions were accommodated in Hokaia, as were all who came to study the ancient arts of warcraft, but no one wanted the Tovans to get too comfortable bringing their creatures there, most of all the native Hokaians.

Some enterprising students had hung clan banners by the gates to each pen, likely brought from home. First was the crow's-head skull on a field of red, next the outline of an eagle in flight against a sheet of gold, then the sticklike insect on blue, and finally the green twist of a winged serpent. Okoa headed to the red banner. Once inside the pen, he looked up, hand shading his eyes from the setting sun, to watch the crow and rider land.

He grinned as the bird hovered briefly above him. Its talons were large enough to crush his head as if it were no more than a melon. It flexed them as if in greeting before it dropped to the grass beside him. A great gust of breath poured from its mouth, smelling like the corpse of some animal it had eaten during the journey, and it shook its massive head, feathered mane glossy from care. It let out an ear-blasting squawk, and Okoa laughed.

"Well met, Kutssah," he said, patting the beak that the bird offered up. Seeing the creature made him miss his own mount terribly. His own Benundah would be five years old come spring, a great blue-black beauty Okoa had cared for since her hatching. But Benundah had not made the journey with him to Hokaia. There was nowhere for the bird to stay long-term, and it would be unkind to separate her from her kin for the years Okoa spent here, so far from Tova.

"Ho, Cousin!" a voice called from the beast's back. "Stop making Kutssah soft!"

"Ho, Chaiya," Okoa answered, his smile spreading even wider. "Kutssah is a warrior, like her rider. No amount of petting will change that. Isn't that right, Kutssah?" He rubbed the crow's beak again until she nudged his hand, contented.

"Soft!" his cousin repeated, laughing as he slid from his mount. He was tall and broad-shouldered, same as Okoa, muscles thick on his arms and shoulders from handling his mount and war training. He pulled his feathered helmet from his head and shook out his hair. His hair was more sun-lightened brown than Okoa's midnight black, and he wore it tied back from his face in a series of intricate interlocking twists. Okoa preferred the Hokaia style of wearing two matching braids tight against the head and trailing down his back, a sound fighting style and better than the looser styles popular in Tova. But beyond the small differences, the cousins could pass as brothers. Square-jawed, broad-faced, with a touch of sensuality around the lips and mischief in the high arching eyebrows.

Chaiya's panther-hide riding trousers were stained from heavy wear, as were his hide armor and the edges of the high-collared shirt that showed around his unshaven neck. It was a familiar uniform, one Okoa himself had worn before and ached to wear again.

He liked Hokaia, appreciated the education he was receiving here in strategy, leadership, and hand-to-hand combat. He was honored that it had been he who was chosen to attend the war college after Chaiya. But he had lingered at the school too long, a year past when he should have returned, and he was ready to go home. He wanted to see the cliffs of Tova again, to walk its bridges and wander its streets that ran through the clouds. He wanted to see his mother again, and perhaps even his sister. And he wanted to see Benundah.

"What brings you to Hokaia?" he asked.

"It is good to see you again," Chaiya said, pulling him into an embrace. His cousin's armor had acquired a thin sheen of ice from his time in the sky, and it chilled Okoa where it touched his skin.

A shudder rocked Chaiya's body. Okoa untangled himself from Chaiya's heavy arms, alarmed. He searched his normally steady cousin's face. "What is it? Why are you weeping? Skies, what has happened?"

Chaiya was the toughest of all their brood. Stone-faced and impossible to upset. Loyal to the clan above all else, a soldier in a city that did not particularly require or appreciate soldiers beyond the ceremonial. But Okoa had always appreciated him, always admired him. He had molded himself after his older cousin, wanting nothing more than to follow in his footsteps and become one of the matron's Shield when Chaiya retired. The tears running down Chaiya's broad cheeks frightened him like nothing else could.

"Is it Benundah?" he asked. "Has something happened to her?"

Chaiya swiped at his eyes with the back of a leather-covered hand. "No, Okoa," he said with a wry chuckle, "it's not Benundah. She is fine, although she misses you."

Okoa felt relief, but it was short-lived. Benundah was well, but if not his crow, then what? Something had upset his normally unflappable cousin. "What then?"

Chaiya took another deep breath and seemed to settle himself. "Can I leave Kutssah here? We should talk inside."

"Of course. I have forgotten my manners. There should be food in the mess."

"And something to drink to take the chill off."

"Tea, but nothing stronger. At least not officially. But I am sure I can find us a bottle of xtabentún somewhere."

Chaiya smiled as he secured Kutssah to a hitching post in the pen. "I'm not a student anymore. I'm not worried about getting caught with forbidden drink."

Okoa flushed, feeling like a teenager again. "Of course not."

"Never mind," Chaiya said, waving a hand. "I've brought my own." He gestured with the rug saddle that he'd lifted off Kutssah's back. Attached was a leather sack, and after he'd laid the saddle across a nearby bench, he reached into the bag and extracted a pile of fabric. He unfolded it to reveal a clay flask.

"Ten years since I've walked these grounds," the older man said, his voice wistful with melancholy. He unstopped the flask and took a long drink. "I didn't think I'd ever come back. But Kutssah is swift, and I volunteered to bring you the news." He proffered the flask toward Okoa.

"What news?" Okoa asked, taking a deep drink. At first, the alcohol was sweet on his tongue like summer fruit, but it had a long tail that burned down his throat like chipped glass. He coughed and handed the flask back.

Chaiya slipped the flask into a holster on his belt. He took off his gloves and slid them in beside the flask. "Inside," he said, motioning Okoa forward through the cedar gate. "I'll explain it all once we're good and drunk."

· · · · ·

"Dead?" Okoa repeated. He wasn't sure how many times he had said the word, wasn't even sure he knew what the word meant anymore. But every time he said it, Chaiya, who was sitting across from him, big hands wrapped around a cup, nodded and said nothing.

"Are you sure?" Okoa asked.

They had found an unoccupied table and two stools in the far corner of the common eating room; two bowls of berry-sweetened toasted knotweed and accompanying marshelder bread sat before them, Chaiya's empty. Around them swirled the noise and energy of the hundred cadets and officers whom the war college fed and housed, but Okoa felt like he and Chaiya were utterly alone, tucked in some bubble of space and time that existed outside of Hokaia and the reality he had always known.

"Are you sure?" he asked again.

And once again, his cousin nodded.

"How?"

"Suicide, Cousin," Chaiya said gently. "But we've told the Sky Made Council and the priests that she died in her sleep."

"Why?"

"Your sister thought it best. She worried there would be a scandal."

"But . . ."

"She jumped off the terrace of her private rooms in the Great House. I guarded her door that night myself and no one entered. There's no other way she could have ended up in the Tovasheh. Her body washed down the river, and the monks who live below found her body."

"The monks." Okoa knew of them. A sacred order that lived far east on the banks of the Tovasheh and subsisted off whatever they pulled from the river. Sometimes that was a body, which they carefully cleaned and wrapped and reported upriver for payment. Most bodies that ended up in the Tovasheh were from accidents. The cliffs of Tova were known to claim their share of victims. Drunkards who went over the edge after a night of carousing in the Maw, foolish teenagers who dared each other to climb impossible rock faces, and, occasionally, a suicide. There was no shame in it, particularly among the elderly or the very ill. Only grief, potential lost, and those left behind.

"But my mother was none of those things," Okoa said.

"None of what things?"

Okoa looked up from the mug he had filled with whatever was in the flask. It was now empty, but Okoa clung to it anyway, like an anchor. His cousin was weeping again, silent tears running down his cheeks, but his own face was dry. He wasn't sure why.

"My mother wasn't ill or old. She was in her prime. Why? Why would she jump?"

"I don't know. These last years have been hard on her, Okoa. With you gone and the cultists gaining power. She confided in me many times that she was tired."

Okoa flinched. "Was this my fault?"

"I didn't mean to suggest that."

"No, I should have been there," Okoa said, voice barely above a whisper. "I should have helped her. Instead I lingered here too long, playing war games."

"No, Okoa." Chaiya's voice was firm. "You are a man. Your place, your honor, was here. Yatliza had me as her Shield, so what could you have done? It was your sister's duty to ease your mother's burdens, not yours. She is the one who will rule after your mother, so she is the one whose responsibility it was to care for her."

"Esa is not me," he said flatly, citing the obvious but meaning much more. He remembered his sister as striving, obsessed with Sky Made politics and prone to gossip and fretting about fashion. It did not surprise him that her first concern upon learning about their mother's death was to cover up her suicide to avoid scandal.

"She's matured since last you saw her, Okoa. She will never

have your warmth, will never be the people's favorite the way you are," he said, and Okoa flushed at the compliment, "but she is a good woman. She will be a good matron."

Chaiya was probably right. The last time he and Esa had spent any time together they were teenagers. He had certainly changed, so why not her? Strange to think he was twenty and she twenty-two and about to lead the clan.

"Will you stay on as the captain of Esa's Shield?"

"No," Chaiya said, voice heavy. "I failed your mother. It would be shameful for me to stay on. Besides, Esa has asked for you to become her captain."

"Of course." Okoa pushed back from the table, limbs jittery, restless. He knew the time for him to take Chaiya's position would come eventually, but he had imagined it happening decades from now.

"I'll need to come back for the funeral." He turned to Chaiya. "There will be a funeral, won't there?"

"A citywide funeral, three days hence, upon our return."

"Good. That's good." He paced back and forth, trying to grasp the facts. His mother. She was gone. Truly gone. And now he had to go home and serve his sister.

"We will arrange to have your things sent home," Chaiya said. "They'll come by boat down the river and along the coast, all the way back to Tova."

"It will take months."

"It can't be helped. You and I will ride Kutssah back to Tova tomorrow morning. We'll return in time for the funeral."

"Good." Okoa swiveled on the ball of his foot and turned back the other way. He stopped in front of Chaiya. "Then I guess that's it." It was an awkward thing to say, wholly inadequate, but he had never lost a mother before and was unsure what one said at these times. For a moment, he did wish Esa was here. For all her ambition and obsession with propriety, she was still his big sister. She would know what to say.

"Sit, Cousin," Chaiya said. "There's one more thing."

Okoa stopped his pacing. He didn't sit but folded his arms across his chest and leaned against the wall behind him. "Go on."

Chaiya reached into the fold of his shirt and withdrew a sheet of slim yellowed paper. It had been folded and sealed with the glyph his mother had used to sign her name to official documents. He handed it to Okoa.

"What is this?" Bark paper was rare in Tova, imported from Cuecola. The process for making it was laborious and lengthy. Most paper was kept by the celestial tower for its records and star charts, but the Sky Made clans each had a store of its own for civic matters.

"Yatliza entrusted it to me upon your birth."

"My mother gave this to you when I was born? How could that be? You must have been a child."

"I was thirteen. A child, but not much of one. I had received my first egg, hatched Kutssah, and if you recall, my mother had already died."

Okoa remembered now. He did not recall Chaiya's mother because Okoa had not yet been born when his aunt died, but he realized this letter was probably meant to be held in trust to her. In her absence the letter had gone to her only child, Chaiya. And now it came to him.

"What should I do with this?" he asked, looking at Chaiya for guidance.

"Open it. Read it."

Okoa held the paper to his chest. It was his mother's last words, but they were words that had been written twenty years ago and not meant to be read until this day. What had his mother thought to write upon the birth of her son? Words of love, no doubt. Of the future. Perhaps simply an echo of the star chart that all Sky Made had drawn by the priests upon birthdays and funerals.

"Should I open it now?"

"If you like." Chaiya's eyes watched him, and Okoa felt a sudden shiver of foreboding. He trusted his cousin with his life. But something, a feeling he couldn't name, told him to wait.

He tucked the paper into his shirt, his pulse spiking with anxiety. "I think I'd like to read it first alone. You understand."

Chaiya's eyes narrowed, more in hurt than suspicion. He stood abruptly.

"Of course," he said smoothly. "You are right not to trust me."

"I-I'm sorry, Cousin. I do trust you, of course I do. But I just need to read this alone." He couldn't explain his sudden discomfort, but he knew to trust his instincts, and his instincts were telling him Chaiya was not telling him something. Not lying, but not being honest, either.

Chaiya's anger softened in understanding. He grasped Okoa by the shoulder, shaking him roughly, a gesture of camaraderie. "I'll bunk with Kutssah out in the open air tonight. Meet me at first light in the aviary. We have a long flight back to Tova, and with Kutssah carrying us both, we will move slower."

"Can she bear both our weights? We are not small men."

"Of course, Cousin. I would not have come all this way if she could not." He smiled, showing red-stained teeth.

Teeth like a predator, Okoa thought. And stained as if for ceremony. Or battle. Which didn't help his calm.

Chaiya embraced him in farewell. Okoa wondered if the older man could hear his elevated heart rate.

"Tomorrow, then," Chaiya said.

"Yes," Okoa agreed. "Tomorrow. First light."

Once he was sure Chaiya was well on his way back to the aviary, he left the mess, taking the back way and weaving through the high-grass fields until he arrived at the barracks. It was only a few hours past sunset, although it felt like it couldn't possibly be the same day Chaiya had arrived. Hadn't weeks passed? Years?

All the other cadets were still at the evening meal, so he quietly crawled onto his straw sleeping mat. He pulled a small box from his nearby belongings, struck flint, and lit resin to cast a weak light, enough for him to read by.

The seal broke cleanly. In all those years, Chaiya had not tampered with the letter or tried to read it. He felt a pang of guilt. Perhaps he was misjudging his cousin, being unfair. But Okoa had not imagined that glimpse of Chaiya's face as he left that was considering, calculating, and completely sober.

He carefully unfolded the paper, which had gone cracked and stiff in the intervening years. On the paper was a single symbol. Okoa's eyes widened.

He had been wrong. These were not words of love or sentiment, things said from a mother to a son upon his birth. These words were a warning. A prediction.

He ran a finger over the ink.

On the paper was a single glyph: the glyph of life with a diagonal line breaking the symbol in half, shattering "life."

It could be interpreted in a number of ways—a life ending, a life changed or cut short or cut in half. And it was most likely meant as a warning for the child Okoa, a reading of the stars upon his birth, a warning about his possible fate.

But Okoa didn't think so.

For him, the glyph was clear.

His mother had been murdered.

CHAPTER 16

THE CRESCENT SEA
YEAR 325 OF THE SUN
(19 DAYS BEFORE CONVERGENCE)

> Impress a man today, and he'll expect you to impress him
> tomorrow, too.
>
> —Teek saying

Xiala's morning had gone well enough. She had risen early
to chart their course for the day, the sun indicating the eastern horizon at her back. Every captain of a vessel had a way
to map their course, most using the methods they learned
under the apprenticeship of other captains. These captains
were from Cuecola or the coastal cities along the Crescent
Sea. But Xiala used the way her mother and aunts had taught
her, the Teek way to read the sea, as ancient and true as the
ocean herself. It was part instinct, part memorization, and all
observation. Not so much looking as knowing what to look
for. She was confident she could find her way to anywhere on
land across the open water within a dozen square miles.

Dawn was the most important time of the day for navigating, when the sun squatted on the horizon. With the sun low, its line of light stretched long and narrow along the water, an easy path west to follow. Once east and west were marked, she knew north was to her right and south to her left.

As the sun climbed in the sky, its path of light would widen, too diffused to be the sole source of determining direction. So Xiala studied the waves, too. Their shape and swell pattern and the path they followed toward the shore. And she noted the wind, and from where it came, and marked that direction. She looked for seabirds leaving the shore to fish in the deep atolls, and later she would mark their paths home and she would know which way land was.

All of this she did, holding the details in her memory, knowing that keeping track of these markers throughout the day would keep them alive, and losing track of them would mean death. When she was satisfied that she had plotted their course north-northwest toward the Tovasheh and there were enough ways to know where northwest was once land had slipped from view, she called for the first shift to drop paddle.

Callo echoed her command from the bow, and the men shouted it back to them both. And they were away, pulsing through the waters, headed for open sea.

The men were in surprisingly good spirits. Xiala's gamble on the feast and good sleep on the cay having paid off. They came back that morning with smiles and happy greetings, hauling Patu's cooking supplies and newly filled pots of fresh water. The mood was bright with anticipation of a new day that felt full of the promise of adventure, so infectious that Xiala couldn't help but feel some of their optimism, too.

She had expected someone to mention Serapio's strange appearance last night, but no one did. Perhaps they were willing to ignore it, or pretend like it never happened, to keep the peace.

When she had first turned to face Serapio, she would have sworn a great black bird hovered above him, its head blocking the moon and its wings flaring out as wide as the ship behind it. It had chilled her to the bone, sent a primal fear screaming through her brain that had made her forget to call her Song. If that bird had wanted to reach down and rip her limb from limb with its massive black beak, she would have stood there with her mouth hanging open and let it.

And if the bird wasn't enough to terrorize, there was the man himself. The black robe like a shroud, the bandage over his eyes, the red-stained teeth. He was a nightmare vision, something out of a children's cautionary tale.

But then the Obregi had spoken, and all her fear evaporated on the tide of his stilted Cuecolan and his awkward hello. It was as if a veil had been lifted, and suddenly she could see he was young and strangely eager and, above all, human. She was about to invite him to join the crew when Callo threw the ward against evil, and Xiala realized the veil may not have lifted for everyone. She'd hustled the Obregi to the ship as fast as she could after that, sat with him through a brief but surprisingly pleasant meal, and finally ushered him off to bed with an understanding between them. The suggestion for him to dress as the others and join the crew on deck the next day had been an impulsive one. A hope that perhaps without the nightmare trappings to distract them, the crew would see what she saw, which was a strange man, most assuredly, but only a man.

She had been wrong.

Serapio appeared just as the sun breached the horizon in full, and it was as if the sun, upon seeing him there, hesitated. Shadows fell across the ship without clouds to prompt them and the wind that had been barely a breeze moments ago picked up in earnest. It rattled the reed awning and sent chop against the hull violently enough that Xiala had to spread her feet to stay standing. Others were not so lucky. Poloc slid across the rowing bench, arms flailing. Baat, who was sitting between Poloc and the wall of the canoe, tilted seaward, hitting rough up against the rail, barely avoiding going overboard.

Then the world seemed to hiccup, and the sun found its course again and everything was as it had been—light, no shadows, no wind—except the waters still beat against the wooden panels starboard. Proof she had not imagined it.

Serapio had done as she had advised. He wore a thigh-length laborer's skirt wrapped around his waist, held in place by a string belt. His hair, which had been hidden by the cowl last night, was the black of a starless night and fell to his spare shoulders in a windswept mass. He still wore the cloth over his eyes, as she had suggested. But she had not thought to ask what the rest of his body looked like.

Scarred, Balam had said. And she had conveniently forgotten, perhaps too charmed by his strange manner.

But scarred he was.

Someone none-too-skilled had taken a knife to his upper body and carved. On his bare chest was the bird she had seen last night, but in skeletal relief with gaping eyeholes and a sharp beak that pointed down toward his stomach. It was a crow's skull that started at the dip in his throat and covered his chest. It had been recently outlined in red dye, which made it stand out even more. Arching across his back were great wings, the feathers painstakingly detailed. They, too, had been outlined with red dye. There were other scars, too, on his arms and legs, each of them suggesting flight in some way.

"Mother waters," Xiala murmured. If she had had any doubts about seeing that great spectral crow above him last night, they died immediately. And then she remembered another crow, one that hovered above her with preternatural intelligence, and she knew his was the face she had seen on the pier before they set sail. He had something to do with that crow that had watched her, although she wasn't sure how. She rubbed at her arms, suddenly chilled despite the warmth of the morning.

The crew had fallen silent. She didn't know if they had seen the same vision that she had last night, but certainly this would not allay their superstitions. She stepped forward, unsure what she would say or do, but knowing she had to do something.

"Odo Sedoh."

It was Loob who had spoken. Xiala turned to him. He was sitting on a row bench facing Serapio, his eyes wide.

"What?" she asked.

Loob looked to her and then around at the crew. "Odo Sedoh." His voice was breathy with awe. "The grandfather crow." He turned to Serapio. "You say you are Obregi, but this I recognize from Tova. My wife is from Tova. Not Crow clan." He shook his head adamantly, as if such a thing was unthinkable. "But I know it. The Odo. The Crows. That's you." He pointed at Serapio.

Serapio had turned his head toward Loob when he started talking, listening but still standing just outside the small shack where he slept, as if ready to make a retreat should he need to.

"That is I," he said.

Some of the men were muttering, words that sounded angry, but Loob cut them off.

"No, you don't understand!" he said loudly, coming to his feet. "If the Odo Sedoh travels with us, if we are taking the Odo Sedoh to Tova"—he nodded vigorously as if the truth of their mission had just occurred to him—"then we are blessed. We travel with a god's favor to the Holy City."

"Not my god," Patu said, and Xiala was surprised to hear him speak. She had never taken him for being a religious man, or even one of the more superstitious ones like Callo.

"Your only god is your stomach," someone said. It was Baat, Loob's friend. "What do you know of gods?"

Patu was staring at Serapio, arms crossed and chin jutting forward like a petulant child. "I give my offerings to the jaguar god. The Cuecolans do not know this crow god."

"We aren't in Cuecola," Baat said, sounding exasperated. "Besides, your jaguar god has been dead three hundred years. It's blasphemy to talk of jaguar gods these days."

"Baat's right," Poloc said. "Cuecola pays tithe to the Sun Priest, does it not?"

"And not all of us are Cuecolan," Loob added.

"What does it mean?" Callo asked. The others turned to him. He had walked up between the row benches from the bow of the ship. His eyes were fixed on Serapio, and his jaw was tight. "To worship this god. What does it mean? Blood? Fire? What does this crow desire?"

"It doesn't matter what it desires," Xiala said. The crew turned toward her. "What matters is that we take this man to Tova as we promised. As Lord Balam paid us to do. And then we are done."

"Are you a Watcher?" someone asked.

Serapio visibly shuddered as if the suggestion offended him.

"He is a blessing," Loob answered. "I tell you now. Between the Teek and the Odo Sedoh, we are surely favored!" He slapped Baat on the shoulder, laughing. Baat grunted good-naturedly and turned to his paddle, the matter settled for him.

Xiala took a chance. "All right, then," she said, clapping her hands together sharply. "Everyone has now seen, so back to work. All to row. We have a sea to cross."

That seemed to break the spell, and the crew took back up their paddles. Callo still stared, but now it was at her, not Serapio. She cocked her head. *Problem?*

His eyes flickered, jaw still tight. She waited for him to say something, but he turned his back to her and went back to the bow without another word. She waited until he was past the reed awning and out of her direct line of sight before walking over to Serapio.

He turned his head to her as she approached.

"You did not tell me about this last night," she said once

she was before him, voice cast too low for the crew to hear. She gestured to his body.

"About what?"

"Your . . . scars."

"You did not ask."

"Ah." She clicked her teeth, irritated. Maybe it was her fault, in part. She had asked him to come out and bare his skin. But he could have told her what they would see, should have told her. "You're lucky Loob recognized your scars."

"We call them haahan."

"Whatever you call them, that could have gone a different way."

He pursed his lips, as if contemplating her words. "I don't think so."

"No? Is that one of your secrets, too? Telling the future?"

Some emotion rippled through his body. "No," he said flatly.

She frowned. Had her words meant something more than she thought? She reined in her anger. It had all gone well in the end, perhaps even better than she could have hoped for, thanks to Loob and his wife. And Serapio was still their honored guest.

"My apologies if I insulted you," she said. "I made a mistake asking you to come to the deck. I won't do it again."

He sighed heavily, sounding disappointed. "As you wish it." He turned to go.

"Wait." She reached out and grabbed his upper arm. His skin was cool, the haahan strangely tactile and sensual under her fingers. A thrill trilled through her body, as if she had stuck her hand in ice and found it did not freeze as much as soothe.

He looked back at her, waiting, clearly unaware of the effect touching his bare skin had had on her. She quickly dropped her hand.

"I will have someone bring you supper. In your room," she added hastily.

He stared at her a long moment, or at least it felt like he was staring. She didn't know what his eyes did beneath that rag. Or if he even had eyes, despite his assurances last night that he had some command of his vision. She suspected there was something more to that, too.

"Of course, Captain," he finally said. "Whatever makes you and the crew comfortable."

• • • • •

The day went on without incident. Xiala still navigated, keeping her watch on wind, wave, and sun, but her thoughts kept returning to Serapio. She had to admit that he fascinated her. He had an otherworldliness about him, much like herself. She could practically touch the magic rolling off him, and it made her wonder who he was. What he was. Someone had asked if he was a Watcher, but she suspected they meant to ask if he was a priest of some kind, but she thought he was not. Well, not exactly. He was something else, though, something tied in flesh and spirit to his god.

Even so, she wasn't convinced his presence was a blessing. But certainly Loob's enthusiasm for the Obregi-now-Tovan was. Most of the crew seemed to have warmed to the idea that Serapio was, if not a good thing, at least not a curse. Even Callo stayed quiet about it, although she might have preferred him to make more of a scene, so she knew at least he was speaking his mind. This keeping his thoughts to himself was worrisome, but she would not push him just yet. He need not like Serapio's being on the ship, only tolerate it.

As evening began to approach and the crew broke for a meal, Xiala ordered Loob to take Serapio some of the porridge and salted fish Patu had laid out for supper. Loob was thrilled to do it, saying it was an honor and he would surely be blessed now.

"Do you think the Odo Sedoh will speak to me?" he asked her, sounding breathless.

"What?"

"Just a few words, nothing special."

"I . . ." Xiala shrugged. "Why not?"

Loob grinned and hurried off, fish and porridge in hand.

Xiala watched him go, thoughtful.

She let the men linger over their meal while she called to Callo to join her at the helm.

"What is it?" he asked, not hostile but certainly lacking the warmth he'd had for her the night before. The man and his moods baffled her. She was tired of trying to guess if he was friend or foe. It was essential to know him, to anticipate him, and to keep him on her side. If only he didn't make it so difficult.

"There's something I want to show you," she said. She had thought about it all day, particularly in the wake of Serapio's dramatic appearance on deck, and had come to a decision.

He eyed her, all morose suspicion, but she only smiled. She motioned him to join her on the captain's bench. He hesitated.

"I won't bite you," she said. "You're not my type."

His face darkened at that, and she reminded herself not to tease him. Another man like Loob or Baat might laugh, but as far as she could tell, Callo had no sense of humor.

"Sit," she said again, this time with more command in her voice. And he sat, keeping a distance between them, so much that his left buttock hung off the edge of the bench.

She suppressed a comment.

Xiala said, "You told me last night that the men rowing through the night would be too taxing."

"Aye," Callo acknowledged slowly. "They could manage for a day or two perhaps, but a week or more? They'll wear out. But if no one rows, we'll be adrift, no more than a piece of rotted wood thrown into the sea."

"Propulsion, to hold direction."

"Aye."

She lifted her hand. "I have a solution. A Teek solution."

He sucked at his lip, watching her.

"Tonight I paddle," she said.

Callo glanced back at the men huddled under the awning, their paddles resting unmanned against empty benches while they ate. "How?"

"I can't do it every night," she said. "I must sleep, too. And it will not move us at the rate the men can achieve as twenty, when I am only one. But it is what I will give to this journey. For us all."

She stood, turning away from him, from the men under the awning with their bowls of food, and faced the water. Faced her mother. Not the woman who gave birth to her, but the sea, her true mother. The true mother of all her kind.

She opened her mouth.

And she Sang.

The notes started somewhere deep in her chest. They rose through her throat, tripped delicately across her tongue, and flowed from her lips like the sounds of the ocean itself. She had picked a simple Song, one from her childhood, a gentle call to the sea, asking it to keep her safe and take her to distant shores. She improvised as she Sang, reminding the sea that they were kin, that the waves were her brothers and the salty brine her sister. That the animals that lived below the surface and swam the waters were her cousins, and that family helped family.

And her mother responded. Almost unnoticeable at first, but then they were moving. Callo gripped the side of the canoe, eyes wide in awe.

She Sang more, letting the Song build. Louder, but still gentle. A petition, not a command. And when she felt secure that they were on their way and the sea would continue to move them north-northwest as she requested, she let her voice trail off with an outro of gratitude.

It was done. She swayed on her feet. Dropped heavily to the bench. She floated somewhere between exhaustion and exultation. She rarely let herself use her Song, and she had never Sung quite like that. The melody she had pulled from her past, and the words she had improvised, but what drove the Song was the emotion of it, the sincerity of her belief. And for a few moments, she had let herself believe entirely.

She turned back to Callo only to find the whole crew standing beside him, watching her. Her heart sped up, and she braced herself. It was one thing to have a Teek captain, another to have her use her magic, even if it was for your benefit. She didn't wholly trust the crew to accept it, despite how well they had handled all the other strange events of the voyage.

But there was no anger, no fear.

Just reverent faces, even Callo's.

She said, "I promised you the Tovasheh in sixteen days. You give everything you have, and I will give everything I have. That is the deal."

"Teek," Callo said, respect, finally, in his voice.

"Teek," the crew echoed with the same wonder.

She grinned. Gave them a small nod of acknowledgment.

"Now rest," she said, waving them away with a tired hand. "Don't waste my work. My Song will push us forward until sunrise, and then some of you bastards will have to row."

"I'll take first shift," Loob offered happily.

"Aye," said Baat. "I'll join him." Others added their voices.

She nodded, pleased. Her eyes roamed over the crew. One face missing. Patu. Where was her cook? Perhaps still not feeling well, but a thin trickle of worry wormed down her spine. Of all of them, he had resented Serapio the most. But surely Patu would never take matters into his own hands. But then, where was he?

She was about to call for him when she spied the man, huddled well under the reed awning, wrapped in a striped blanket, and looking miserable. She had imagined the worst, Patu a potential murderer, when he was only ill. She whispered an apology to the sailor in her mind for thinking him capable of such deeds.

"Patu!" she called. "You rest both shifts. Someone cover his time on the paddle, and you'll have extra cacao in your purse come end of the voyage."

A man with a steep sloping forehead and hair shaved high above his ears offered.

"My thanks, Atan," she said, remembering his name.

It had been a risk, using her power like that, but she had decided that if she could not have Callo's friendship, she would have his respect. She would have all of their respect. For as long as she could.

CHAPTER 17

The Crescent Sea

Year 325 of the Sun

(19 Days before Convergence)

> My uncle allowed me to accompany him to the aviary today.
> It was a rare treat since only the riders are usually allowed,
> but his mount Paida has found a mate and would be leaving
> for their rookery soon. He told me crows mate for life, and
> I thought that impractical and said so. He laughed and ex-
> plained that they are sexually promiscuous but loyal to their
> mates and that the two are different. I asked him if crows fell
> in love, and he assured me they did not.
>
> —From *Observations on Crows*, by Saaya, age thirteen

The man who called himself Loob had brought Serapio his
dinner. Loob had a light lilting accent and talked incessantly.
He also seemed to be very much in awe of the Odo Sedoh.
It was an interesting encounter. Serapio was used to being
hated, feared even, but not respected. He wasn't sure how he
felt about it. It made their brief conversation awkward, and
Serapio was glad when the man left.

He felt Xiala's Song before he heard it, a building of energy like a shift in the very atmosphere. Not unlike the way a late-afternoon storm would build over the valley during summer and release the gentle rain all at once.

He listened as the notes wove around him. He recognized them for the magic they were. He felt vast energy moving, being redirected. But it was different from what he did when he called shadow. Then he dropped barriers, submitted himself to the shadow inside him, letting some of it emerge.

Xiala's Song was an invitation. An invitation extended to an external power to join with her. Nevertheless, the potential was immense and made him wary, but not afraid. It wasn't meant for him.

· · · · ·

He waited until he could hear the men snoring, some soft-breathed, almost silent, others with great lumbering snorts that suggested exhaustion. But once he was sure they were all asleep, he tied the cloth around his eyes and left his shed.

It was easy to remember the way back to the captain's bench, but he took his time, feeling his way in case the crew had moved cargo into his path unknowingly. But the path was clear, and he found her where he had expected to, exultant and smelling of power.

"Obregi," she said, greeting him.

He had been quiet, so he was surprised that she had heard him.

"I hear everything on my ship," she said, her voice joyful, teasing. "Especially after I Sing. Is that what you were wondering?"

"Yes."

He heard her shift her weight on the bench. She yawned loudly and made a sound like bones cracking. "What is it you want?"

"Surely you realize I am Tovan now."

She grunted, sounding unconvinced. "Both, I think. I think you're holding space for both in there."

"The way you do for Teek?"

"Ah, but tonight I am all Teek, I think." She laughed, delighted.

Her mood was infectious, and he found himself wanting to smile. He did not, but he considered it. "May I join you?"

"Please."

He felt the bench at his left calf, exactly where he remembered it being from the previous night, and he touched a hand to the wood. It was damp with seawater but worn smooth with use. He sat down gingerly, feeling the moisture seep through his clothing. It was cold, and a bit clammy, but the night itself was mild, a late-summer night that had not yet succumbed to the winter.

They sat together, he silent and she humming softly, a song that seemed to consist mostly of chorus, something easy and catchy. He hummed a bit, too, following along.

She cut off abruptly. More silence until she said, "Do you know that song?"

"No," he admitted. "I was copying you."

"Copy— . . . was I singing?" He heard her moving again, feet coming down off the rail.

"I'm sorry. Did I offend?"

"No," she said. "Only surprise. It is a Teek lullaby. For you to know it would have been quite strange." She laughed, and he realized he was beginning to enjoy her laugh. "I didn't even realize I was humming."

"It's the same song you sang at sunset."

"I . . . yes, after a fashion."

"It was beautiful. They talk of the power of Teek Song in the stories but never of their beauty."

She made a sound in her throat, mildly disapproving. "What stories?"

"In Obregi there are stories of all the places on the Meridian continent. The coastal cities of which Cuecola is the greatest, Tova the Holy City, and all the inland river cities like Hokaia and Barach."

He could hear her lean forward, the scratch of fabric as she rested her elbows across her knees. "What do they say of the Teek in Obregi?"

"That they live in a great floating city on the edges of the world that no sailor can find. All who have searched have never been seen again."

Her breath was soft, steady, but it hitched nervously when she asked, "And what happens to these sailors who are lost?"

"Some say they simply sail too far out to sea and cannot find their way back. Others say they find the islands of the Teek, but the lands and their inhabitants are so beautiful they choose to stay and never return to Meridian."

"Flatterers," she murmured.

"And others say . . ." He hesitated, suddenly aware the next part of the story was none too kind.

"Go on," she urged.

"Others say any sailor who finds the islands is seduced . . . and then eaten in a great feast."

A pocket of silence when he was sure he had misspoken, but then she huffed an amused laugh. "Eaten. I like that. Keeps the cowards away." She clapped her hands together and laughed again. "What else do they say?"

He hesitated, and continued. "The stories tell of a Teek princess."

"Oh, well, that was your first mistake," she said, voice expansive. "The Teek have no princesses. No queens, either."

"And no men? The stories said that, too."

"And I came from a fish egg," she said, her sarcasm thick. "What else?"

He recognized that she hadn't answered his question, and that a bit of nervousness had come back into her voice. She was hiding something. He could tell by the lift at the ends of her sentences, the way she tapped her heel. He was curious to know her secret, but he was enjoying the conversation too much to push. "That you ride on the backs of manatees."

"We do that," she said solemnly, before bursting into another laugh. She sounded relieved. "But we ask permission first. We call them our siblings. We would never ride our siblings without asking first."

He understood she had made a bawdy joke and let the side of his mouth lift in a half-smile. He was rewarded when she said, "Ah, so you do have a sense of humor."

"There's something I want to know," he asked, ignoring her jibe.

"What, that the stories don't tell you?"

"The stories are too limited to ask the right question."

"And what is the question?"

"How do you navigate at night, with no hint of the horizon? How do you know we are still headed to Tova when everywhere you look, it is the same?"

She was quiet, but he felt the energy thrumming from her, remnants of the Song she had Sung to the sea. It had something to do with that, he knew. Some part of her magic.

"It is a Teek secret," she finally said. "It is why I am a captain despite their superstition." He felt her fling her arm out toward the crew behind him. "And despite the fact that I am a woman and young and all the things they cannot tolerate on land."

"Yet they revere here on the sea."

Her breath caught, like he had surprised her. "Yes."

"Will you teach me?" he asked.

He could feel her eyes on him. Studying. Assessing.

"You're blind," she said, like he was ignoring the obvious. Her voice was apologetic.

Now he let himself smile, knowing his red teeth flashed in the moonlight. "A woman who knows the waves by the way they move beneath her feet and the wind by the way it kisses her neck wonders how the blind man might learn about the sea?"

"But these are stars . . ."

He leaned forward, pressing a hand against her leg and moving close enough that he felt her startled huff of breath against his cheek. Her magic scented the air. "Did you not hear, Xiala, that I am grandfather crow? You may study the stars, but I am made of the shadow between stars. Tell me what you see, and I will understand it."

He felt her heartbeat quicken, her breathing accelerate. From fear or simply because he was so near, he wasn't sure, but he didn't move away.

She cleared her throat. "All right, then," she said, voice trembling slightly. "Give me your hands."

He held both hands out, palms up. He felt her fingers against his right palm, tentative at first. But as she spoke, her touch steadied, became surer.

"You told me the stories your people tell of mine," she said, "but let me tell you what we say of ourselves. We are Teek, which means 'the people,' and our ways are Teek, and our islands Teek. Do you understand?"

"That all is the same," he said, understanding immediately. "There is no difference between yourselves and the land."

He could almost feel her smile. "Good."

"And the water?"

"Ah . . ." Her breath was soft with reverence. "We call the water Al-Teek. Our mother. Constant, life-giving, sustaining."

He followed a hunch, thinking of how she had spoken about the stars. "And the sky is your father?"

"No," she said flatly. "Teek do not have fathers."

He frowned, confused, but did not ask the obvious question, sure he would only get another quip about fish eggs.

"We call the sky her lover," she corrected. "Fickle, ever-changing, sometimes cold and sometimes very hot, indeed." She ran her finger along the lines of his palm in a way that made him shiver. She laughed, low and suggestive, and for a moment he was caught off guard by the lust it roused in him, an emotion so rare as to feel foreign. His face felt hot, and he shifted on the bench.

He felt her pause as if registering his response before she continued, her finger still pressed against his bare skin, her breath mingling with his. "We are a floating nation, not moored to land. That is why we cannot be found unless we want to be found. And since we travel the tides, we learn to read the night sky with our mother's milk." Her finger moved again, this time tracing a circle against his open hands. "The sky is a dome. The sun rises here"—she pressed a point near his right thumb—"and sets here." He thought to tell her that being blind did not make him unaware of where the sun rose and set; he had watched it rise and fall for twelve years, and after that, he could feel its heat against his skin and knew from which direction it came, but she was still talking, still tracing her finger over his palm, so he let her continue. She drew another point, a straight light across to his left. "North is here, south here." She made a small popping sound with her lips, as if releasing a secret that lingered on them. "Now you hold the sky in your hands."

He knew it was a metaphor, but it did feel like she had shaped something in his palms. He cupped it carefully, thinking of how precious it was.

"But direction is not enough," she continued. "You are correct that at night without the sun, the horizon becomes useless."

"So you navigate by the stars," he said, remembering her earlier comment.

"Yes, and no. The stars move, rising, traveling, and falling just as the sun does. But if you divide your map"—she rubbed her thumbs across his hands, starting in the center and then moving east-west and then north-south—"into four quadrants, and those four quadrants again until you have sixteen, you have a map that will allow you to track the stars. When a constellation rises in the house of the water beetle here"—she touched his hand just below the eastern horizon she had marked on his thumb—"it will set here." She ran her finger diagonally across, ending just above the western horizon she had marked opposite. "So if I set my course with the water beetle constellation at my back and watch it all night, keeping the ship steady toward the same house opposite, I can guide us with no sun."

"Spatial awareness. You sail the same way a blind man moves."

"Is that so?"

"Yes." His attention caught on a detail. "This name for the house, you call it water beetle?"

"We do."

"And the others?"

"The other sky houses? Black bird, white bird, water snake."

"Like the four Sky Made clans of Tova. The names are almost the same."

She was dismissive when she said, "For the Teek, these are not real houses, not real clans. There are no giant creatures like the ones in Tova, just ways to remember the movement of the heavenly bodies through the sky."

"But there must be a connection," he pressed. "In Tova, it is taught that the ancestors came from the stars and settled on the continent. What do the Teek teach?"

He could tell by the way she leaned away from him, the heat of her body leaving his space and her breath no longer warm against his face, that she wasn't interested in finding the similarities between Teek and Tovan.

She answered, but her voice was reluctant, "That we crawled from the sea, the offspring of a great manatee." She paused, and then added, "Like I said: siblings."

Another joke; at least he thought it was.

"I think I prefer the sky," he said bluntly.

"As would a man like you, made of star shadow and dedicated to a crow."

He grinned. He wanted to tell her his story, share something about himself and Obregi, or perhaps his mother and Tova. Well, what he knew of Tova from her stories, anyway. He wanted Xiala to know something of him, the way he felt he now knew something of her. But his mother's voice stopped him. *You will have many enemies. Silence is your greatest ally.* And there were the voices of his tutors, reminding him that no one was his friend. So he held himself back.

"Thank you." He could say that much and mean it.

"You're welcome." She sounded surprised, but pleased. He had done well, he thought, to ask her to share. And now he would have another story, another place, to keep him company during his own vigil.

"What will you do tonight?" he asked.

"Stay up and watch the stars. Keep us steady until the next shift of paddlers starts near dawn and they have the sun to show their way."

"Will you sleep?"

"Only then."

"I can keep you company. I slept much of the day and am not tired." It felt daring to offer to stay, but he remembered the feel of her skin against his and wanted her to hold his hand again. And her voice was soothing after spending so many hours with only the banter of the crew through the wall to keep him company.

He heard her slide to her right, the rub of her clothes across the wooden bench, and she tapped her hand on the newly empty space as invitation. He reached out to find his way and then moved his body across to sit next to hers. Their legs touched through the fabric, and her shoulder pressed against his. Around him he could feel the movement of the ship as her magic entreated the waves to press them forward, hear their soft rocking against the canoe. This close, she smelled of salt and sea and magic, yes, but also of clean sweat and the oil she used on her hair and skin. The air had cooled considerably, but her body was warm next to his.

"Tell me more of the Teek."

"What is there to tell?"

"Another story."

"What kind of story?"

"I do not know any stories save the one about the princess. I do not want to hear a lie."

"All stories are lies." She exhaled dramatically. "You have a lot to learn for some crow grandpa."

He wanted to tell her she was wrong. All stories were true, in their own way. But instead he said, "I have not experienced much of the world. All I know are its stories. Will you tell me more of yours?"

And to his surprise, she did. Perhaps not the most important ones, or the most secret, but she did tell him Teek stories. Of the manatee that gave birth to her people. Of how the great reefs came to be, and how the fish got their stripes, and why one never tried to catch a crab on a full moon.

He relished each one, careful not to interrupt but eager with questions when she was done. And he became more adept at following her jokes. He found Teek humor centered around body functions and nudity and being caught in an awkward situation by one's female relatives. There were also jokes at mainlanders' expense, usually a sailor who had had too much to drink or sometimes not enough to drink, and people who could not swim died in prodigious numbers. He did not tell her he could not swim.

As the night went on, she took occasional breaks to walk the length of the ship, presumably to check for problems that might arise in the dark. He would count her steps and wait for her to settle back next to him, and soon enough, she would be telling him another tale. When Xiala told him that the moon was setting and he should retire for the day, he was surprised by how quickly the night had passed.

"Will you sleep now?" he asked.

"Once the sun rises and I've set our direction for the day," she confirmed.

"Would you like to share my room?" He meant it only as an invitation to escape the sun, but he realized that it sounded like he was offering her much more as soon as he'd said it.

Before she could answer, he heard footsteps approaching, and a now-familiar voice.

"Captain?"

"Callo." She stood quickly, knocking her knee against his. She stepped forward to meet her first mate.

And then the two sailors were conferring about wind and weather and other things that were not in his purview. He pushed himself to his feet, pressing past the two with a soft apology, and made his way back to his room without incident.

Once inside he took off his blindfold and stretched out on the reed mat that was his bed. The ship rocked gently below him. Voices, sleepy and low, filtered through his walls as Callo roused the crew for first shift.

Serapio smiled, content. He traced his finger over one half of the sky that Xiala had drawn on his opposite hand, again and again, until he fell asleep.

CHAPTER 18

CITY OF TOVA

YEAR 325 OF THE SUN

(13 DAYS BEFORE CONVERGENCE)

> There will always be those who urge you to war. Interrogate
> their objective. If you find that it is peace, then consider war
> as a means to an end; if their end is only more war, send
> them away.
>
> —*On the Philosophy of War,* taught at the Hokaia War College

Okoa haunted the halls of the Great House in Odo, his mood
as black as the banners that decorated its ash-gray walls. His
mother's funeral was to begin at noon on Sun Rock, which
meant he had an entire morning free with nothing to do but
brood and pace. He had already argued with his sister about
his attire. She wanted him in a long tunic of funeral white,
which was proper, but he preferred the panther hide of his
uniform, which was also proper after a fashion.

"Why must you always have your way?" she had yelled at
him. An accusation that seemed ridiculous as Esa had three
servants weaving bits of mica through her artfully distressed

hair. Their reunion had been cordial at best. They had immediately fallen into the same familiar behaviors of their childhood, her resenting her brother's freedom and he, annoyed by her demands.

"Mother would not have cared what I wore," he countered.

"Mother is dead," she said flatly.

"Died in her bed, was it, Sister?"

"That again? Of course people will find out she was in the river eventually, but honestly, Okoa, I wasn't ready to answer the questions that would follow. The curious, the morbid. I only lied to buy us some time."

"Us?"

"Yes, because like it or not, you are part of this family."

"What are you talking about?" he said, incredulous. "This family is everything to me."

"Well, you weren't here, were you? You graduated the war college last year and yet you stayed, doing what exactly? You never said. I had to deal with Mother's death alone."

His jaw clenched, his guilt heavy. He didn't mention the many aunts and cousins who were here in the Great House and undoubtedly had helped Esa handle the shock of their mother's death, because that's not what his sister had meant, anyway. "That's unfair, Esa. Mother wanted me at Hokaia."

"She wanted you to train and return home."

"To what? I could not ascend to Shield while Chaiya was still captain."

"You could have done something else."

"Become one of the scions who spend their time in the Maw at the gambling tables? Or in the pleasure houses?

There was nothing for me here. I stayed away for the good of our family."

"Did you? I'm not sure, Brother."

And the arch way she spoke, the way she could always find exactly the right thing to say to dig under his skin, make him feel shame for finding joy in the thing he loved when he should only feel obligation. He slammed a fist against the wall, hard enough for the pain to throb through his bones and make him grind his teeth. But it felt good. Solid. A physical pain to match the emotional.

"Are you done?" she asked, disdainful but with a small quake of fear in her voice, as if his violence had been aimed at her. It was too much. He fled her room and her judgments.

What are you doing? he thought to himself as he stalked down the hall. *She's not just your sister anymore, she's the matron of Carrion Crow. And you're the captain of her Shield. Best start acting the part.*

He flexed his fists as he walked, fingers still numb from punching the wall. Frustration and grief warred within him. He had not forgotten the message his mother had left him. The single glyph inked on bark paper, the warning of a life cut short. It had to mean she was murdered, and this farce of a funeral was meaningless. The Sky Made clans would gather to mourn her death in a matter of hours, while one or more among them were responsible for putting her in that river.

He had not confessed his suspicions to Esa, not even to Chaiya, who Okoa would have sworn was the most trustworthy of them all before Hokaia. Instead he had kept his secret near his heart and nurtured it with distrust and rage for the past three days. And then he had taken it out on his sister like a spoiled child.

Servants and relatives alike scattered before him as he made his way up the wide stone steps to the aviary. It was an open-air stable at the highest point in Odo, accessible only through the Great House and separated from the land surrounding Tova by a narrow crevasse that promised a drop too deep to measure into the darkness below. He had always loved the aviary, and since he had returned from Hokaia, it had become his refuge.

Unlike some of the other Sky Made clans, Carrion Crow did not cage their beasts. Confinement went against some unassailable principle that was never articulated but well understood by the clan, and more important, the crows wouldn't have tolerated it. Theirs was a partnership between human and corvid, a willing agreement to serve each other. Okoa liked it that way. He would no more try to control Benundah than his own heart.

As if sensing his thought, his mount let out a bright staccato greeting at his arrival. Immediately his mind eased, and he felt a deep abiding calm take the place of his anger. He grinned, his first smile of the day, and he returned her salutation with a gentle ruffle of her glossy head. He reached into a bag he kept at his waist and pulled out a handful of grubs.

Benundah pecked the wriggling creatures from his hand to swallow them whole.

"You're the only sane one here, Benundah," he murmured, threading gloved fingers through her wings. "I don't know how I'm going to get through this day." He considered saddling the great bird, climbing on her back, and flying far away.

Forget the funeral and his obligations. He would go back to Hokaia, or to the far north where there were no cities, or perhaps even to one of the great port cities of the Crescent Sea. What a sight he would be on Benundah's back. The thought made him happy, if only temporarily.

In truth, he would go nowhere. Tova was his home and Carrion Crow his responsibility. He had a duty to his people, and he would not run from it, no matter how tempting the idea was on a day like today. They had suffered so much, lost so many. The Night of Knives still haunted the families of the Crow, including his own. His mother had lost her grandmother and most of the family of that generation to it, and she wasn't unique. Whole generations gone in one night's massacre.

He shivered at the memories and thought of the haahan carved into his arms and back, hidden under a layer of clothing.

"We will have our justice," he said quietly. He wasn't sure how or when, but the Sky Made would answer for the complicity, and the celestial tower would be made to bend. Maybe not by him, but surely his children or their children. He had no doubt that it would happen. It was justice, and justice always prevailed.

"Lord?"

Okoa turned. One of the stablemen, a stocky older man in a loose shirt and pants and carrying a rake, approached him.

"Ashk," he greeted the man. Ashk he knew well. He had been a stable hand since he was a child, tended to two generations of great crows born to the clan.

Ashk dipped his head. "I thought that was you, Lord Okoa."

Okoa embraced the man. "It is me. I wish I was returning in happier times . . ."

"Yes, yes." The older man sighed. "It is a terrible thing."

Okoa pressed a hand to Ashk's upper arm and squeezed. "How are you managing? And the other stable hands?"

"Oh, we are fine, my lord. Sad, of course. Heartbroken. Your mother was always kind. Bringing us into the household, treating us like family."

Okoa knew many of the Sky Made hired servants from the Dry Earth districts but did not allow them to live in their districts, even when it made sense. The birds in the aviary needed constant care, particularly since they came and went at their leisure. It was practical for the stable hands to live within the Great House, close to the birds. Tovan society was strictly hierarchical, but an allowance had been made for the crows.

"How has Benundah fared in my absence?" he asked.

"Oh, she missed you," Ashk assured him, "but she's an independent sort. Will you ride her today to the funeral?"

"No. It is expected to snow, and the wind currents through the canyon are unpredictable when storms roll in. I wouldn't want to endanger her."

"So everyone is grounded?"

"That's right."

Benundah nudged Okoa with her black beak, and he laughed. "I have her favorite treat, but I hope you brought her a meal."

"Aye," Ashk said, lifting the handled pot he held with both hands. He walked to the trough that ran the length of the open stall and emptied its contents. Okoa caught sight of insects, chopped-up fruits that must have been taken from the dry storage this time of year, and a rainbow of corn kernels.

"A feast," he remarked.

"She deserves it. But . . ." The old man hesitated. "I came for another reason, Lord." He dipped his head again.

Okoa tensed, his senses on alert again.

"Go on," he said warily. Did Ashk know something about his mother's death? Something he could only approach Okoa about now?

"You've heard of the Odohaa?"

Okoa grimaced. "The cultists?" he asked, deflated. He was a fool to have gotten his hopes up, if only for a moment.

Okoa had never asked about the stable hand's religious leanings, and why would he? But now he was beginning to suspect that he was talking to a believer.

"Yes, I know them. I've even attended a meeting or two."

It was a small thing to confess. Most Carrion Crow scions of a certain age had been to at least one Odohaa ceremony, either out of curiosity or on a dare. And many people had a relative, an older aunt or cousin, who claimed membership in the group. They were a fact of life in Odo, even if the rest of Tova and the Watchers in the tower thought them cowed into submission.

Ashk grinned at Okoa's confession, showing a mouthful of uneven gray teeth that had once been stained red. "They say a storm is coming. And soon. That the Odo Sedoh will return."

Okoa nodded. They had been saying that all his life. Vengeance for the Night of Knives. Honor and pride once again for the clan.

"They sent me," Ashk said, leaning conspiratorially close. "Told me to invite you to their next meeting. It will be tonight, after the funeral."

Okoa shook his head, thinking quick. "I'll likely be in mourning with my family." It was custom to cover oneself in ash and sit vigil until the next morning, so he was not lying, but he was certainly glad for the convenient excuse.

Ashk pressed something into his hand. It was a crow feather. Someone had written with chalk on one side. "Here is the house where we meet. Come tonight if you can. If not, another time. There will always be an Odohaa there to welcome you, Lord Okoa."

The man made to leave, but Okoa stopped him. "Who asked you to come to me? And why me? What do the Odohaa want from me?"

Ashk's eyes were shining with tears, clearly overcome with some emotion. So much that Okoa took an involuntary step back.

"The storm is coming, Lord, and we want you to teach us."

Okoa wanted justice for his clan, but joining with the cultists was not the way. They were fanatics, men and women convinced that if they only prayed hard enough, they could raise a god who had been dead for a thousand years. If he had learned anything at Hokaia, it was that justice came though the actions of humans holding wrongdoers to account, not through some vague divine retribution and certainly not through violence.

He pressed the feather back into the man's hand. "I can't help you. You've got the wrong man. I want nothing to do with the Odohaa or their reborn god."

He turned sharply on his heel and left the aviary before Ashk could say anything else.

• • • • •

The storm is coming, and we want you to teach us. Okoa turned the phrase over again and again in his mind as he and his myriad relatives and the citizens of Odo processed to Sun Rock to send his mother on her way into death. *The storm is coming, and we want you to teach us. The storm is coming, and we want you to teach us.*

"Stars, Okoa! The least you could do is pay attention. We are going to our mother's funeral, after all."

Okoa shook himself to attention. He had been lost in thought and had accidentally stepped on Esa's hem. She had worn a dress in proper mourning white that dragged on the ground, picking up a layer of dirt as they walked through the street. If she had truly aspired to the customary, she would have gone barefoot, but flurries had begun to fall an hour ago, and the air cut at the skin like pinpricks made of ice. Again, custom would have them bare-armed, a display of haahan appropriate in a time of grief. But Esa wore a thick fur coat of some poor white animal, and the rest of his relatives, cousins and aunts and uncles, who trailed behind their new matron and her Shield, did much the same, only with less panache.

"Apologies, Sister," he murmured.

"I see you chose to wear your blacks after all," she said, voice dry. She arched an eyebrow at his leathers. Not only had he kept his uniform on, but he'd topped it with a cloak of crow feathers made from Benundah's own shed. He'd sewn it himself and kept it oiled and well preserved. It was the first time he had donned it in years, and it felt good to have it on his shoulders once again.

And I see you chose to pick at me like a hungry gull, he thought, but held his tongue. He might have said it aloud to Esa even as recently as this morning, but he understood now that she was targeting him for the smallest slight in order to distract herself from what lay ahead of them. He had been ungenerous before to judge her. They were both grieving, after all.

"What do you know of the Odohaa?" he asked instead.

She hesitated, no doubt expecting him to argue with her, but she answered his question. "They have done a lot for the people."

That surprised him. "When I left, they were mostly underground. Focused on ceremonies to resurrect the crow god."

"They still are in private, but no one's foolish enough to stand in the streets calling for the Crow God Reborn anymore, and certainly there's no talk of usurping the Watchers or the Sun Priest. No one wants another Night of Knives. So they've turned their public attention to charity, mostly. Feeding children, caring for widows. That sort of thing."

"Militia training?"

Her mouth turned down. "I haven't heard anything about that."

"I spoke to a cultist today, someone I know. He asked me to train them to war."

She frowned, thinking. "Armed rebellion?" she asked.

"Even with a hundred fighters, two hundred, they could not challenge the tower as long as it had the support of the other clans." His fingers wove through the obsidian cloak clasp at his neck as he thought. "How many call themselves Carrion Crow?"

"Somewhere around two thousand, but that includes children and elders who could not fight."

He mulled it over. Even five hundred might be enough, but . . . No. War was not the answer. "It doesn't matter. It would take years to train them to take on the Knives, and it would be another slaughter along the way. And to what end? We bring down the priesthood and replace it with Odohaa?"

"It worries me that they came to you," Esa said. "I've wondered when they'd make their move. Mother was too lenient with them."

"What do you mean?"

"Their numbers have increased since you've been gone. It's no secret that she indulged them. Let them do as they pleased even if it endangered us all."

"And you mean to change that?" He asked it cautiously, careful not to give away any of his own feelings on the matter.

"When things quiet after the solstice, and I am officially invested as matron of the clan, I'll have you use the Shield to bring them back in line, perhaps thin their numbers a bit. They've become too bold. You just said so yourself. Best we stop this nonsense before they do something that will land all of Odo's heads on a chopping block. Again."

An involuntary chill shuddered through his body. Surely that could never happen again. This time, the other Sky Made clans would rise in Carrion Crow's defense. This time, the Watchers would not condone the slaughter of so many innocents to destroy a fanatical few.

But to use the Shield to restrain their own people, as Esa suggested? He didn't condone that, either. It felt like the kind of betrayal that a body like Carrion Crow would not recover from.

They had reached the bridge to Sun Rock. Beyond it, he caught the dull glint of gold and blue, the soft gloss of green through the flurrying snow. The other clans were already there and in place. Which meant that at the center of the circle, beyond his sight, was the Sun Priest. She would be standing there now in her mask of hammered gold, her tsiyos—killers all—surrounding her.

"You didn't paint your face?"

Esa's face was coated with ash and thick red streaks ran below her eyes like tears.

"I didn't have time."

"Too busy brooding?" Her lips curled in affection.

"I . . ." He shrugged.

She sighed. "Come here, Brother."

He stepped closer and she drew a finger through the red on her own face, glazing her fingertip. "Close your eyes." He did, and she painted three lines on his face from forehead to cheek, over his eyelids, two on the left and one on the right.

He opened his eyes to find her studying him approvingly.

"Better?" he asked.

"Better." Her smile turned grim. She squared her shoulders. "Now let's go show them what it means to be a Crow."

CHAPTER 19

CITY OF TOVA

YEAR 325 OF THE SUN

(13 DAYS BEFORE CONVERGENCE)

> Above all things, the Sun Priest must unite what is above to what is below. He must mirror the perfect order of the heavens to contain the disorder of the earth. Only when these are aligned can there be balance, and without balance, surely the world will tip into chaos.
>
> —*The Manual of the Sun Priest*

The air around Naranpa simmered even though the snow had been falling steadily for a while. What had started as morning flurries had become a true fall. It turned the world to white, as if the sky itself mourned the Crow matron. The noise of the crowd gathered on Sun Rock was dampened to an impatient rumble as those gathered waited for Carrion Crow to appear.

They were late, of course. But that was their prerogative, and it would have been unseemly for another clan to arrive after them. To avoid such a social transgression, they came late.

Naranpa didn't mind. She had so much on her mind that the funeral was a welcome distraction, an embrace of her official duties that she relished. She was back in her yellow vestments, day cape, and sun mask. Slipping that mask on had felt like a warm wash of summer air even in the heart of a snowstorm. She felt her power close, the wonder of the universe and the wheel of the sky at her fingertips. It was almost enough to make her believe in the old ways and the old gods. If someone asked her now, she could divine their future from the lay of the stars as easily as she drew breath.

She wished that power allowed her to divine her own future, or the future of any of the priests. But it was forbidden, and that was one rule she would not break. Not because she respected the rules so much, although she did. But because she did not want to know.

Her gaze traveled to Abah. The seegi priest stood fidgeting beside her in her mask and vestments. She had said nothing to Naranpa these past days since her trickery at the matrons meeting, and Naranpa had returned the favor. No doubt the young woman was waiting for Naranpa to accuse her, call her out in Conclave or at the very least to the four societies. But Naranpa found that she preferred to let Abah squirm. *Let her wait and wonder what I have planned for her*, she thought. *Perhaps that will keep her busy.*

There was a risk in that. Abah could escalate. But Naranpa had not been entirely idle. She had left Abah to stew, but Eche she had demoted down to the lowliest of dedicants. He was no longer in line to succeed her, was not even here on the Rock with the rest of the celestial tower. Instead he had stayed behind to scribe records that Haisan had told her a while ago were decaying. It was difficult, hand-cramping work usually left for first-year dedicants, and now it was all Eche's.

He had taken to the punishment without a word of protest. She knew this thing between them was not over yet. He had powerful advocates, Nuuma Golden Eagle particularly. But he also had made enemies, not just in the tower but in the clans. She felt it was enough to clip his ambition until after the Shuttering was over and she could formulate a better solution.

Thoughts of the Shuttering made her stomach growl. She was, as were all the priests, fasting in anticipation of the solstice. They were limited to a small meal in the morning and one before bed. In between they were only meant to consume water and yaupon tea, which often had emetic qualities when consumed in large quantities. The priesthood stayed inside and in contemplation during the Shuttering for a reason. Being out and active for this necessary but unfortunately timed funeral was trying for everyone.

She looked over at Haisan, just to her right. He had remembered his mask this time, but he looked to be suffering the worst of them all—the lack of sustenance, the weather, and his age combining to no doubt make the old priest miserable. He was buried deep in his bear cloak and instead of standing was seated on a portable stool, head bowed and hands deep in the folds of his sleeves. She thought he might be napping. Well, no one would blame him. He had done the most work in preparation for the funeral. Prepared the songs that Naranpa would recite, reviewed from records the steps of the ceremony needed to send the matron on to the Sky Made ancestors in the proper fashion.

Iktan was at her immediate side, silent in xir blood-red mask. Xe had not spoken to her since their last encounter, either. In fact, she was sure xe had been avoiding her. Oh, there was always a tsiyo at her side, or rather, hovering somewhere close. Xe would never let a personal disagreement compromise her safety.

The truth was, she was ready for their feud to end. She had overstepped, made a crude remark meant to hurt, and obviously hit her mark. She needed to apologize and made herself a promise to do that as soon as this funeral business was done.

"Finally," Abah huffed. "I'm freezing my tits off!"

Speaking of crude. Naranpa gave Abah a skeptical look, but the seegi just huffed and turned her shoulder to her. Mildly amused, Naranpa tapped Haisan awake. "Carrion Crow is coming," she told him, as he roused himself to attention.

She turned her focus to the bridge from Odo. Skies, did they make an impression.

The children of the Crow materialized out of the snowstorm like white-clad spirits. They flowed into the open-air roundhouse, filling the benches that had been left empty for them. Most Sky Made had brought twenty, thirty representatives at the most. But Carrion Crow had brought ten times that. They dominated the Rock, and Naranpa felt Iktan move closer to her side, as if sensing her disquiet. She did not mind xir presence.

Six figures came forward bearing the body of the fallen matron. She was shrouded in red and sat on a bed of black feathers that were as long as a human, obviously taken from their great corvids. They placed the body on the low platform twenty paces in front of Naranpa and the rest of the priests and rearranged the feathers so they covered her body like a second shroud. Around her were objects to accompany her into the next life between the stars—a drinking cup and eating utensils, jewelry of obsidian and jade and turquoise, an extra pair of sandals.

Once the body was in place and the bearers had retreated, Yatliza's two children stepped forward. Naranpa recognized the white-clad daughter. She was tall and willowy like her mother had been, and mica glittered in her fall of tangled dark hair. Her narrow face was painted with ash and carmine, making her doelike eyes even more prominent. She placed something on her mother's chest that Naranpa couldn't quite make out, no doubt an object of personal affection.

The son stepped forward next. He was the only one among them who still wore Carrion Crow black, a sleek uniform of panther hide under an impressive cloak of feathers. His long black hair was parted down the center and braided in two rows tight against his head, the loose ends tied with ribbon and dyed red where they trailed past his shoulders. He cut a striking figure, handsome and muscular and possessing the grace of a warrior.

He bent to place a folded paper on his mother's chest. As he straightened, he looked up and met Naranpa's eyes.

Fire and fury. That's what blazed through his dark gaze. So hot it almost burned her. Skies and stars, the hate. She felt it like standing too close to a fire.

Iktan tensed beside her; xe had noticed, too.

In that moment she fully believed Carrion Crow had sent an assassin to end her life.

And then the son was stepping back to join his sister, and it was Naranpa's turn to approach the corpse. Her hand shook as she placed a scroll of bark paper on the pyre. It was the star map she had divined for the mother so that she may find her way home among the stars and dwell with the ancestors of the Sky Made.

And then there was nothing left to do but begin the ceremony.

It went well enough. Two hours of songs and prayers that left Naranpa's throat sore and her voice almost gone. Haisan had sung parts of the eulogy song, and Abah, who had a sweet voice that belied her viperous nature, sang a song of healing that had many in the gathering wiping tears from their eyes. Naranpa closed the funeral with a dedication to the sun that did not go over particularly well with some of the Carrion Crow clan. She could feel more than see the restless wave that rolled through the Crows in white, and she was positive she heard a few call out, "Odohaa!"

There must be cultists in the crowd, she thought to herself. *Of course there are. Dozens. No, more.* She had thought the popularity of the Odohaa, the Breath of the Crow, as they called themselves, was small, but perhaps she had been wrong. Iktan would know how many there were. Xe would have been keeping an eye on them, surely.

Later that night, members of Carrion Crow would return to take the body and the burial items to be interred somewhere private in Odo while something of the woman would be burned to hasten her return to the stars. The other Sky Made clans and the priesthood would not be present for that. The public part of the funeral was over.

The snow had turned to an icy rain, and the top of Sun Rock was a winter-locked world. A chilling wind blew across the open mesa. There was no protection here from the elements, no roofs to huddle under or trees or other structures to temper the breeze. No one wanted to linger.

The clans began the procession back to their respective districts over the woven suspension bridges. The bridges had iced over and become treacherous during the ceremony. People were forced to move slowly, and with the biting wind and ever-darkening sky, no one was particularly patient. There were more than a few shouts to slow down, and a small scuffle broke out at the base of the bridge to Titidi. Naranpa craned her neck to see if she could see the cause, but there were too many people between her and the bridge to see.

There was no direct bridge to Otsa and the celestial tower. The priesthood could cross into Odo with Carrion Crow or into Tsay with Golden Eagle. They'd come through Tsay, and tradition would have them return through Odo, but Naranpa could not fathom it. She wanted to believe she and the others would be safe in Odo, but tonight of all nights it seemed like tempting fate. Instead, they had decided to return the way they came, although after the stunt that Abah and Eche had pulled, Tsay did not sound particularly attractive, either.

For the second time in as many outings, she realized she was not safe in her own city.

"Stand back, Crow."

Naranpa turned at the sound of Iktan's voice. She was startled to see Yatliza's son, the warrior who had looked at her with such hatred, no more than a few paces behind her. Iktan had stepped between them, blocking the man, who had been only a few steps away from reaching out and touching her.

She flinched back before she could regain her composure, grateful once again for the mask that hid her face.

"I only meant to pay my respects, Knife," the man said, his words as sharp as the sleeting ice falling around them. If she thought the look he had given her was hateful, the glare he aimed at Iktan was pure loathing.

"It's fine," she said, willing her voice to steady. She pressed a firm hand to Iktan's back, a request for xir to let her pass. Xe glanced back at her, barely taking xir gaze from the Crow, before shifting a fraction to the side. Still close enough to interfere if she needed xir.

The man briefly dipped his chin, pressing a hand to his heart. "My name is Okoa Carrion Crow. I am captain of the Shield. I am . . . was the son of Yatliza, matron of our clan. I wanted to meet you."

Naranpa mirrored his bow. "It is a welcome honor to meet you, son of Yatliza. I know your mother thought highly of you."

His eyes widened briefly in surprise. "Did you speak to my mother often?" His voice had more than a touch of disbelief.

"Not often," she admitted. "But we had occasion to see each other. She was proud of your time at the war college and the care you took with your beast. Benundah, was it?"

Okoa blinked.

Naranpa smiled. She had not remembered the great crow's

name until that very minute and had not remembered the son's name at all until he had introduced himself. But it was worth it to see his expression.

"You honored my mother well today," he said. "I will not forget it."

Naranpa hesitated, and, because she might not get another chance to say it, blurted, "The Watchers are not your enemy, Okoa. I know we have failed the Crow clan in the past, but we are different now. We will make things right."

"Naranpa," Iktan warned beside her.

Okoa studied her, dark eyes probing. But she was hidden behind her mask, with little of her to see. She thought of removing it so he could see her face, recognize that she was sincere.

"You are not the same Sun Priest I knew before I left for Hokaia," he said. "You are . . . unexpected."

Warmth that belied the wintry day spread through her. She reached out a hand, meaning to grip his forearm in a gesture of respect.

Okoa reached out, too.

Someone jostled Okoa from behind. She couldn't see how it happened and later would remember only the milling crowd and the bodies all in white save his, but the next thing she knew, Iktan was there, obsidian knife between them, and Okoa had shifted directions, arm thrown wide to strike her or to block Iktan or perhaps stop himself from falling on the slippery ground. The black knife sliced Okoa's jaw. A spray of red splattered across Naranpa's golden mask, and then there was screaming and someone was pulling her away and Iktan's dedicant tsiyos were rushing past her to join the fray.

It was the assassination attempt all over again, except this time she was sure it was a misunderstanding.

"Let me go!" she cried, struggling to break free of whoever held her. The arms around her didn't move, so she threw all her might behind a jabbing elbow to the belly. The person let out a gust of shock and released her. But she had been dragged too far away, and there were too many people between her and Iktan and Okoa to get back now.

"Naranpa!"

She turned as someone cried her name. It was Ieyoue Water Strider. "Hurry! We must get you away."

"But he wasn't trying to hurt me," she tried to explain. She wasn't sure how much Ieyoue had seen, if what she was saying even made sense. She guessed it didn't from the look the matron gave her.

"The crowd is turning into a riot," the woman said. "It's not safe for any of us, but definitely not you."

"But I've got to explain."

"Nara!" Ieyoue said, exasperated. She grabbed Naranpa by the shoulders and turned her back to face the way she'd come.

Blood. Enough to turn the snow red. Churned by men fighting with hands and knives and complicated by people desperately trying to flee across the narrow bridges that could only accommodate two abreast and less in the ice.

"Skies," she whispered, shocked.

"Now!" And this time when Ieyoue pulled her away, she followed. Across the bridge to Titidi, the Water Strider clan making way for their matron and the Sun Priest.

Naranpa lost sight of the rest of the Watchers, letting Ieyoue lead her through the streets of the district and to the Great House. Glimpses of water gardens and canals wearing a fine coating of frost were incongruously peaceful after the rush and horror of the riot.

Once they were inside, Ieyoue had her wrapped in blankets and sitting in her offices, a hot beverage in her hand, before Naranpa could process what had happened.

"Get the Sun Priest something to eat," the matron commanded a nearby servant.

"No," Naranpa protested softly. "I'm fasting."

"Surely you can break your fast for now. You need food to fight the shock."

"I . . ." But she didn't have the will to fight about it.

Ieyoue nodded, sending the servant away to fetch a plate.

"May I?" She reached behind Naranpa's head to release the mask's clasp. She pulled it from her face. "Now, drink. The tea will help."

Naranpa looked at her golden mask, now streaked with Carrion Crow blood. "Do you think they're dead?"

"Who, Nara?"

Iktan, she thought first. And then the son, Okoa. But her lips could form neither name.

"Someone's definitely dead," Ieyoue said gently. "We will wait a few hours to return you to the tower and sort out who."

CHAPTER 20

THE CRESCENT SEA

YEAR 325 OF THE SUN

(12 DAYS BEFORE CONVERGENCE)

The sea has no mercy, even for a Teek.

—Teek saying

The storm didn't strike until well into the next week. Seven days of clear skies, favorable winds, and steady progress through the endless blue were more than Xiala had hoped for, and every morning that dawned clear, she gave thanks to her mother, the sea. But experience warned her that the weather wouldn't hold, and she had never been wrong before.

After an increasingly cloudy night that obscured the stars and left her with her ear pressed to the floor of the canoe, listening to the way the waves moved around them to determine direction, she knew a storm was hours away and not days. When the morning dawned a fiery red, she cursed her fickle father above. Serapio had kept watch with her, and he asked what was wrong.

"Red skies mean rain," she said, "and skies that red mean a whole fucking lot of it."

227

"Is it beautiful?" he asked.

She laughed, low and skeptical. "Beautiful enough to kill you."

His lips ticked up, but he said nothing.

Ever since that first night when she had used her Song to give the crew a break, Serapio had shown up once the moon was high and the crew was mostly asleep and sat vigil with her. She had indulged him at first, amused by his enthusiasm for her stories and, admittedly, flattered by his attention and unusual curiosity. But by the fourth evening, she realized that she was impatiently glancing toward his shed, wondering when he would come out. She had already thought of a handful of stories to tell him that night, knowing that he would like best the one about the seabird that flew a thousand miles to save its hatchling.

"Look at you, Xiala," she whispered to herself with a wry shake of her head. "You like him. The blind foreigner who doesn't say much. Well, you always do like the strange ones."

Which wasn't true. She usually liked the pretty ones, the easy ones she could leave in port the next day and not feel bad about. But there was something about his quiet presence beside her night after night, something intentional about the way he sat next to her, his hands folded in his lap. Or if she was telling a particularly enthralling story, the way he would absently trace a finger over his palm, circling an invisible line on his skin. She took pleasure in his proximity, the kiss of his breath against her skin, the smell of distant smoke that lingered on his clothes.

He was peculiar, though. There was no denying that. But she no longer felt uneasy in his company or saw giant crows around his head. She was willing to chalk his awkwardness up to being a foreigner, and a sheltered one at that. How could one know anything about the world, about people and the way they interacted, if one had grown up isolated in the mountains like he had?

She'd gotten that much out of him, but she wanted to know more about those mountains and everything else about his homeland, but he was tight-lipped. "A man is like a clam," her mother had once told her. "Let him open on his own, and he will give you a pearl."

Her aunt had scoffed, arguing that it was best to crack them open right away to find out if inside there was only sand and no pearl at all, and that's why the Teek had no use for them. But that wasn't entirely right, and Xiala had known that even at a young age. True, there were no men in their society. She had told Serapio that sailors simply did not find their floating islands very often. But the truth was that some did; they just didn't live long enough to tell anyone else about it. And she, a Teek a long way from home, would not be explaining the murderous habits of her kinfolk anytime soon. She considered it a cultural peculiarity and no one's business but the Teek's.

So she simply enjoyed their nights up talking and watching the stars and listening to the sea, knowing it would end soon enough.

And now, with a storm coming in looking like a shipkiller, they all might have a little less time to enjoy one another's company.

"We'll have to dump some of the weight," she told Callo, once Serapio had returned to his room and she and her first mate were giving orders to the men to prepare.

"Lord Balam won't like it," he said.

"Lord Balam will truly not give a fuck if it means we survive."

Callo eyed her skeptically, as if to say a rich man always cared about losing his wealth, but she remembered what he'd said to her on the dock in Cuecola. Serapio was the only treasure on this ship that mattered.

"Dump the heavier stuff," she said, pointing to the wooden crates. "There, and there. And it will make more room for the crew under the awning when they rest."

"And the bladders?" He meant the flotation bladders that they would tie to the bow and stern to keep the ship from sinking.

"Fill them now so they are ready," she said. "And the paddle ones, too." They had more bladders to tie to the paddles. They would secure those to the sides of the boat and stretch them out over the water to make the canoe wider and more stable. "After the bladders are in place, set four men on bailing duty, and as soon as the rain starts, they start bailing."

Callo nodded. "Anything else?"

"Everyone works in threes. Men tied together, too, and hitched to something immovable on the ship." Tying men together gave them a fighting chance of being rescued if they went overboard, but it also meant that if the ship went down, the men tied to it went down with it. Of course, on the open sea, it didn't matter. They all understood that if the ship sank today, there was no rescue.

"I'll have Patu walk the seams again," Callo offered. "There's resin left enough to seal any leaks."

"Do it," she said, eyes on the horizon. "And hurry. We don't have much time." She chewed at her lip, thinking. Hoping to all seven hells that she hadn't forgotten anything and trusting Callo to remind her if she had.

All morning, Xiala kept the men at paddles, moving forward at double time, doing their best to angle away from the beast that they could not outrun. She watched the sky grow dense and heavy with water, her eyes cast westward watching the far-off lightning that inched closer by the hour.

Callo came to her after high sun. "The men are asking why we're preparing for the storm when you said you'd Sing us safe to shore." His voice held a note of accusation, and she was surprised it had taken him so long to ask.

"And not you?"

He lifted one shoulder. "Maybe you can Sing down a spring squall, but this one's big as a mountain range. More." He gestured toward the horizon. "What's a Teek to that monster?"

He was right, but she bristled nonetheless. She liked it better when he'd had faith in her.

"A Teek is always something," she said, her pride smarting. "Let me do what I can."

"What you can, then." One sharp nod, and he was lumbering away, and Xiala was left wondering why she'd said that. He was right. There was nothing she could do. But she could try, couldn't she?

She looked over at her crew. They were bent to their tasks, most working furiously, with the occasional furtive glance her way. Tension thickened the air, bad as any pressure leading the storm, and she knew how she could help.

She took a few deep breaths to clear her own nerves and thought of the first thunderstorm she'd lived through as a child. The whole village had gathered under one roof, better to be together in case mudslides hit or flooding took a house. And the grandmothers of the village had Sung for them all, sweet soothing Songs of better days and kinder seas. Songs of soft beds and no worries and waiting arms, and it had worked. Everyone had calmed and made it through that storm together. The next morning they'd come out to find palm trees torn apart as if by the hands of giants and roofs blown clear away, fields flooded to ruin, and strange creatures washed up on the shore. But no one had died, and that was what mattered; the rest could be rebuilt.

She Sang that Song now, a Song of comfort and ease, and even as the men bent to their tasks, their shoulders loosened. They exchanged smiles more often and encouraged one another with generous words. Thunder cracked, still far away, and someone, Atan, shouted defiance. The rest laughed, and Loob patted him on his broad shoulders.

She caught Callo's eye and nodded. He nodded back.

And it was something after all.

The storm struck full in the late afternoon, clouds black with thunder rolling overhead punctuated by sharp crackling lightning that streaked across the sky in blinding flashes. The direction of the wind shifted with a fury forcing the ship off course like a child flicking a bug across a pond. Xiala marked the change and which way was north-northwest in hopes that they'd be able to find it again, and the rain came in great horizontal sheets that stung like spine needles against skin. And then the real fight began.

"Bailmen!" she shouted from her place at the stern. She hunched in her cowl, trying to keep the painful downpour off her face as best she could. Every article of clothing had been immediately soaked, toes to head, and it clung wet and cold to her body, as if the summer of a few days ago was a memory so distant it was as improbable as one of Serapio's tales.

The ship rolled with the waves, and the bailmen took turns keeping the ship from being overwhelmed. Callo stayed tied to the bow as lookout and Xiala to the stern, and they all prayed to whatever beings they thought protected them.

The rogue wave hit an hour later, a monster grown twice as high as its companions, which were already clawing up the sides of the canoe, doing their damnedest to get over. Xiala saw it coming and screamed a single note at it, more instinct than aid, but it did no good and the wave barreled down over the ship.

She flung herself against the deck, wrapped her arms around the bench leg, and held on. Her stomach dropped as the ship pitched, the water shoving her head down so hard she saw stars when her temple struck the floor. Then she was being lifted, her body suddenly weightless. Her shoulders burned as the water dragged at her, promising to pull her out to sea. But she didn't go, and soon she was huddled by the bench again, with the wind lashing and the waves slapping the ship, but not actively trying to kill her.

As soon as she and the ship had righted themselves, she screamed for another bail team. She wasn't sure if her voice could be heard over the storm, but three men lashed together ventured out from the poor shelter of the reed awning, heads ducked and buckets in hand. The lead man crossed the width of the ship to tie himself to the far side and joined the other team already bailing the ankle-deep water.

She checked the flotation bladder at her back, knowing Callo would be doing the same for the bow. Once sure it was still secure, she turned to the bladdered paddles that were doubling as outrigging. She spied a loose one, the sac torn free and dangling and the shaft rattling against the side of the ship, dangerously close to breaking free.

"Paddle loose!" she cried. "Starboard, back quarter. Somebody secure it!"

There was shuffling under the reed awning. Finally, a man crawled out on his hands and knees. She thought it was Loob, but in the sheeting rain, she couldn't be sure. He was tied to another man, likely Baat, who followed him but kept the rope slack between them. A third man was their anchor, just outside the awning. Xiala squinted through the rain. Their anchor wasn't tied down, and his rope had unspooled from his middle, where it was quickly slipping from his hands.

She opened her mouth to scream at the man to tie down, but before she could speak, the ship tilted violently, a wave coming up under them. The bow veered. The bailmen tumbled hard to the deck like bits of debris in a hurricane. The distressed paddle broke free, flying out into the open water like a loosed bird.

Loob lunged for it. Baat stumbled, Loob's momentum pulling him forward.

And then it happened. They both went overboard.

One minute there, the next gone. The anchor who had failed to tie down was scrambling on all fours to keep himself from following.

Instinctively, Xiala dragged her securing rope down over her hips. It pooled at her feet.

And she was running, no time to think about what she was doing.

"Man overboard!" she screamed as she leaped onto the bench, braced a foot on the railing, and dove headfirst into the water.

The sea was darkness, vast and alive, and it swallowed her whole like she was no more than the smallest minnow. She dove deeper, past the surface tumble and rain, eyes seeking her lost men. She could feel her eyes change, her Teek eyelids coming down to keep the water out, the shape changing to let in more light, the field of her vision expanding.

She spotted Baat first, kicking and struggling toward the surface but steadily sinking anyway. She spied Loob below him, hanging on the rope like a weight. Dead, her brain told her, but she corrected that to unconscious. But it made no difference to Baat whether the rock dragging him to the seafloor was dead or simply unconscious.

She pushed toward him, arms slicing through the water like blades, legs together kicking as one. Came up on him fast, knocking into his shoulder to get his attention.

He struck out, panicked, fist hitting her in the temple, before he realized someone was trying to help him. His eyes went wide, and she wondered what he saw. What he thought he saw. Her waist-length hair a black cloud around her, her multicolored eyes rounder and wider than any human's. It was fear on his face, and not just because he was drowning.

She reached for the dagger on Baat's belt and pulled it free. He paddled back from her, terrified. She ignored him and kicked down, past his churning legs. She grasped the rope and hacked at it until it frayed and broke. Released from Loob's weight, Baat shot up toward the surface. She watched him rise, not knowing if he would make it to the ship, but at least she had given him a chance.

As Baat shrank away, she realized Loob, on the other end of the rope in her hand, was pulling her down now. She kicked hard, dragging him up. But her progress was too slow like this. If he was still alive, he needed air, and she needed both arms to get him to the surface. She looped the frayed rope around her upper chest. Once her arms were free, she swam.

But the body at the end of the rope was dead weight.

She pumped her legs and used her whole body to move forward, but it wasn't enough. And her air was running out, too, even with the extra time that being Teek had bought her. Her head ached where Baat had hit her, and her limbs were tiring. She needed more. She needed her Song.

But to Sing, she needed air.

Tears of frustration fell from her eyes, washed away immediately by the salty water. She could cut Loob loose, call him dead when she found him, and maybe not be wrong. But she remembered his wife from Tova and how he had been the first to defend Serapio, and she was his captain, and she would not let him drown when she could save him.

She opened her mouth and let the water rush in. At first it choked her, dizzying and terrible. But she forced herself to think of her Song, of the way it came from deep inside her, more than simply air and pressure and vocal cords. She screamed, a desperate prayer to her mother not to kill her, to let her live and this man, too, and please, please, please.

And then she was surging upward. Cutting through the water as easily as if she was sunlight through kelp and born to it. She searched for the hull of the canoe, a disturbingly small speck on the endless surface, and angled toward it. Kick, reach, sing, pray. Again and again, until she bumped up against the ship. Her ship.

She thrust an arm up, slamming her palm against the wood as hard as she could. She heard muffled shouts and knew she had been spotted. Seconds later, she was being heaved up and over the side of the ship. She opened her mouth to suck in the precious air but found that she didn't need it. It didn't make sense, but she dismissed the moment as shock.

Arms were laying her on the deck and someone untangling the rope from her chest, and she could see them dragging Loob up behind her, still a dead weight. They were hitting his back and trying to force the water from his lungs, but he was still, his face slack and gray. She closed her eyes. She had taken too long; he was dead.

She shivered, frozen through. Asked through chattering teeth for a blanket. She was too tired to lift her head, but she pried her eyes open again to see where her crew was, where those gentle hands had gone. But all she saw was Callo, standing a dozen paces away, eyes steady on her.

"Callo," she whispered. "Cold."

But her first mate didn't move. No one helped her.

She tried to push herself to sitting, tried to pull her legs up under her, but they wouldn't move. Why wouldn't her legs move? Something crashed against the benches, heavy and wet, and she glimpsed scales, black and shimmering iridescent in the rain. Her mind tried to make sense of it, but she couldn't.

She managed to rise up on her elbows. Her crew stood around her, frozen, staring. Accusing. She could almost smell the fear in the air, acrid and animal. And directed at her.

Her chest tightened. Her eyes met Callo's.

"Teek," he said. A curse, this. An abomination.

Something struck her hard across the back of her head, and her world went black, darker than the depths of the sea.

CHAPTER 21

THE CRESCENT SEA
YEAR 325 OF THE SUN
(11 DAYS BEFORE CONVERGENCE)

> There is a boy here, a son of one of the matron's own Shields.
> I will not call him by name but know that he is mean and bul-
> lies the smaller children when no adults are there to see. Tana
> once told me he even bullied the crows. Today he fell from the
> cliffs and is dead. Mother told the boy's parents that it was
> an accident, but Akel whispered to me that he saw the crows
> harry the boy off the ledge. I suspect it was no accident and
> nothing but the crow's own justice.
>
> —From *Observations on Crows*, by Saaya, age thirteen

Xiala woke, still in darkness and stretched out on the floor.
She was still on the ship, that she knew immediately from the
soft rocking of the waves.

Soft rocking of the waves. Which meant the storm had
passed. Which meant they had survived.

She opened her eyes, cringing at the pain in her head, and
looked around. She was inside, which was why it was dark.

Light filtered through the wood pole walls and reed roof, which meant it was daylight. Thoughts came slowly, but she determined that she was in the shed she had come to think of as Serapio's room.

Serapio. There he was, sitting so close she could touch the edge of his robe if she stretched out her hand. His back was against the wall and his neck tilted. He looked to be sleeping, but his body held a tension that belied rest, arms locked at his sides and body jerking in small convulsions as she watched. If she had to describe him, she would say that he was caught in a nightmare.

Around his neck hung a leather pouch, tiny shards of glimmering powder caught in the drawstring at the narrow opening. They looked like shattered light.

His face was illuminated by the slanting daylight. Jaw slack, mouth slightly open, and eyes uncovered. From here he looked like he had simply closed his eyes in sleep, lashes resting across high-boned cheeks. Smooth skin. Full lips. Hair in a soft curl that cascaded to his shoulders.

I guess I fall for the pretty ones after all, she thought to herself.

She wondered if she should wake him. He didn't look comfortable, but she didn't know if he would welcome her intrusion. Why was she in his room, anyway?

She tried to remember what had happened during the storm. She remembered Loob and Baat overboard. And Loob dead, gray-faced, with eyes staring at nothing. And Callo's face, the revulsion evident in the curve of his lip, the narrowing of his eyes. And the smell of fear, and . . . fish scales. Black and iridescent. Beautiful but wrong.

She shook her head, trying to make sense of the jumble of memories, but all it did was make her head ache worse. She rubbed a hand over the back of her skull, sure she'd find a bump under her mass of salt-soaked hair.

She pushed herself to her feet, her legs wobbly like she'd been swimming all day and forgotten how to walk. The room was small, she hadn't realized how small. She walked to the door, careful not to wake Serapio, and tugged on the rope pull. It didn't budge. She yanked again, harder. Nothing, and she had a flashback to being in the jail cell in Kuharan, and a half dozen other jail cells before that.

I'm a prisoner, she thought suddenly. *They've locked me in here.*

She didn't know what exactly had happened on the deck in the heart of the storm to make her crew lock her up, but she had that same feeling she had upon waking up after a night of being blackout drunk.

I'm sober! she wanted to scream. *Whatever it was, it's over. Let me out!*

"Let me out!" she cried loudly, banging a fist against the door. Another flash of memory rocked her back. Another jail cell, this one on her home island, her mother weeping outside, her auntie cursing her name. Panic welled up in her chest, and she heaved, fighting for breath, fighting back tears.

A voice outside, one of the crew, and she yelled again. But the voice was moving away, not closer.

"I'm the fucking captain!" she screamed.

"They know that."

She whirled to find Serapio facing her, expression alert.

"What?"

"I said—"

"I know what you said! I meant why? Why am I in here?" She pushed down the anxiety threatening to overwhelm her and turned to rattle the door again, this time peering through the small spaces between the thin wooden poles. Her stomach dropped. "And why are there crates blocking the door?"

"To keep you inside."

"Why? Why would they need to block off the door? It's not like . . ." Her headache swelled again, and she tried to shake it off, pull out those memories that refused to coalesce into more than flashes. *It's not like I killed anyone!* she wanted to scream, but the truth was she wasn't sure what had happened.

"Loob didn't survive," he said.

She swallowed, some of her anger and confusion giving way to sorrow. "I know. I . . . I tried."

"Baat is blaming you. Saying you cut the rope between them, and if you hadn't done it, they both could have made it to the surface."

The tick of sorrow morphed into disbelief. "Loob was dragging him down, flailing his arms in a fucking panic. If I hadn't cut him loose, Baat would be dead, too!"

Serapio was silent for a moment before saying, "That makes sense. But it is not what Baat thinks. Or the others."

"The others . . . how do they know? How do *you* know?"

"I can hear them."

That pulled her up short. Quieted her, and she pressed an ear to the wall to see if she could hear anything. Voices talking, no, arguing, but she couldn't make out any words.

"My hearing is better than yours," he said.

"By magic?"

"No. By necessity. I am better trained." He tapped a finger against his right eyelid, a reminder of his blindness.

She gave up on the door. Serapio had calmed her, keeping her present and not lost to bad memories. She would get out; it was only a matter of time. And if he was here with her, the wait would be tolerable.

She looked around. Nowhere to sit in this damn tiny room except on the bench next to Serapio.

"Mind if I sit?"

He straightened, reaching up to tuck the pouch back under his robe and run his hands through his hair, brushing it back from his face. "Be my guest."

She grinned, a small twinkle of joy. His attempt at grooming was for her, she was sure of it. And she liked it.

She dropped down on the bench next to him, tucking her legs beside her. She leaned back, resting her head against the wooden slats behind her, and cursed softly. What had happened? What had she done? A familiar shame rolled through her body. Usually that feeling came after a night of drinking. She hadn't had a drop, so why the fractured memories, why the feeling that she'd ruined something precious?

"Do my eyes uncovered bother you?" Serapio asked. His voice was quiet, almost hesitant. It was the first bit of uncertainty he'd shown since that night on the cay.

"Not at all," she said, and meant it. This close, she could see now the jagged raised edge of flesh, a keloid scar at the lash line. Whatever had happened to his eyes, it had healed smoothly, not that terrible at all. Not terrible enough to always keep covered, unless he was ashamed.

"Does my nakedness bother you?" she asked.

He flushed. "You're naked?"

"Very much so."

He laughed, breathy and incredulous. "I've never sat next to a naked woman before," he admitted. "Or at least, one who told me she was naked."

"We'll have to work on that, my friend," she said, grinning. But of course, he couldn't see her smile. But maybe he sensed it anyway, because he grinned back, red-stained teeth and all.

"Would you like my blanket?" he asked.

"I'd prefer some clothes if you have them," she admitted. "Perhaps you have an extremely out-of-fashion black robe you can spare?"

"Are my clothes that terrible?"

"For a crow man, no. For the rest of us . . ."

He grinned a little wider, and despite her dire circumstances, she felt something untwist inside her. *He doesn't judge me*, she thought, as the loosening in her chest manifested in tears. She pressed the meat of her palms to her eyes. She didn't realize the sense of relief that would come with simply being accepted.

"I have pants and a shirt," he offered, standing. "But I cannot promise they are any more fashionable or any less black than my robes." He made his way over to a small chest in the corner behind the door. He opened it smoothly, hand moving inerrantly to neatly folded clothes in the top drawer. He brought them back and handed them to her. They were pale cotton, soft, almost luxurious, and thick enough to keep out the cold.

"Perfect," she said, grateful. "And off-white. Not black at all."

"Oh," he said, surprised. "I assumed."

She slid off the bench, taking her new clothes with her. She had never been the modest type. She came from a culture that lived on islands and in the water. Clothes were for protection from the elements and occasionally to show status, but generally, Teek weren't big on covering up for any supposed moral reasons. Cuecolans and, frankly, all the mainlanders were much too uptight about nudity, so even if Serapio could have seen her, she would have done the same. *No*, she thought with a wicked grin, *if he could see me, I'd put a little more flirt into it.*

She chuckled under her breath, surprised at how much better she was feeling. Here she was, locked up for who knew what reason, memory a failed mess, and at least one crewman dead, and she was thinking about sex. Well, life-threatening circumstances did that to people, didn't they? She'd heard that somewhere, and it sounded plausible enough.

"How do they fit?" he asked.

She held out an arm. The sleeve fell well past her fingers, and it was much the same with the pants length. At least the waist generally fit.

"Made for an Obregi giant," she teased, "but they'll do."

She hopped back to her place on the bench, elbows propped on her crossed knees. "Can you hear them now? What they're saying?"

He lifted a hand, asking for her silence. They both listened. She could tell they were still arguing, but beyond that, their voices were just a roar of distant wind.

After a moment, Serapio nodded.

"Well?" she asked.

"The crew and first mate are debating whether it would be sufficient to cut your tongue out so you can't Sing and enslave them, or if they need to slit your throat entirely and take their chances on the sea without you."

She stared at him in shock, heart thumping in her ears.

"Someone is making the case that your bones are worth a lot of cacao. No need to waste those."

She rubbed at her throat, and the missing digit on her pinkie throbbed.

"That's Baat," he added. "He seems to be the most outspoken advocate for your immediate demise."

"Wonderful," she muttered, feeling light-headed.

"Are you all right?"

She looked up at him. His face was drawn in concern, eyebrows bunched and lips pressed together tightly.

"Seven hells," she spit, some of her shock giving way to anger. "I saved that bastard's life. I should have let him drown."

"Yes," Serapio agreed. "It would have been better for you had he drowned. Wait . . ." He lifted his hand again, listening. After a moment, he said, a note of surprise in his voice, "Callo appears to be cautioning the crew to patience. He doesn't want to make any decisions until they're within sight of land. They might need you after all. Although . . ."

Dread curled in her belly. "What?"

"Patu seems to think we're both bad luck and they should slaughter us now and take their chances." He laughed, light and amused. "I don't recall doing anything to earn that kind of vitriol."

"And I did?"

He cocked his head toward her, as if listening to her now. For what, she wasn't sure, but she was suddenly aware of her breathing and the beat of her heart. And the rustle of her pants legs as they brushed against each other.

"Do you really not remember what happened when they brought you to this room?" he asked finally. "Do you really not know?"

"Know what?" she asked, voice innocent but brain thinking of that moment when she left the water and couldn't breathe.

"Xiala," he said, voice soft, not with reprimand but with wonder, "when they brought you here, you did not have the legs of a human. Or the throat . . . or eyes."

Eyes, she knew. She always had Teek eyes. But the rest . . . She pressed a hand to her throat. *Gills!* popped into her mind. Again, the memory teased her, refused to resolve, but she remembered the glint of scales, something huge and black flopping on the deck.

Her tail.

"Mother waters," she breathed, heavy with shock.

She wanted to ask him how he knew, what he had heard or seen when he could not see, but she knew it didn't matter. She had heard of it happening, like the legends and stories she had shared with him these past nights. Teek in extreme danger who had transformed to another nature, becoming a true child of the sea.

"Xiala . . ." he repeated, softer still.

"I don't remember," she said, picking her words carefully. A feeling she couldn't quite name filled her heart. Pride, awe, but also terror. "But I *know*."

• • • • •

They kept them in the room for two days, letting them out once in the morning and once in the evening to take care of toilet needs. Xiala's guards had thick cotton stuffed in their ears but they stuck a rag in her mouth anyway as a precaution, and because she'd cursed them out using turns of phrase that made even the hardened sailors blush. They took Serapio out under similar guard but didn't bother with a gag since he didn't speak or Sing. Xiala contemplated taking the rag out of her mouth, but what good would it do? They'd just put it back, likely tying it tight to her head. She decided that she could be patient, wait to see how this mutiny played out. She would bide her time, wait until they needed her and came begging for her to steer them to land. Then she would decide whether to let them live or Sing them to the bottom of the sea.

She felt the canoe change course during the first night, the shift in wave pattern making a different sound against the hull. Too subtle for most sailors to notice, but she was Teek and had napped in tidepools as an infant. She guessed they were following the sun by day and under a clear sky, navigating by the brightest north star. Blunt, unsophisticated, but likely to get them to shore if they weren't picky about where they landed. Nowhere near the mouth of the Tovasheh, that was for sure, unless by foolish luck.

By her count they were down to nine days. Nine days to get Serapio to Tova. Which for her had become a lesser worry than simply keeping herself and Serapio alive.

Serapio himself didn't seem concerned with their course. She thought he would, but after that initial amusement at finding out Patu wanted him dead, he didn't mention it. He seemed tolerant of his confinement, as if this state was not unfamiliar to him. And, to be fair, it was not wholly unfamiliar to her, jail being an old but unwelcome friend. But she had never been imprisoned for this long and in quite this close quarters.

On the third day, as they shared a single corn cake someone had shoved under the door, Serapio snapped to attention.

"What is it?" she asked, sensing the danger.

He held up a hand, listening. Made his way to the wall and pressed an ear against the wood.

"Patu's dead."

She stared at him. "Did you . . . ?" She wasn't sure he could do such a thing while locked in this room, but she remembered how casually he had agreed that she should have let Baat drown.

"No," he said, a small smile lifting his lips. "As much as it would have pleased me. Callo believes it was the illness he carried."

"Shit."

Perhaps Serapio did not understand the dangers of illness on a ship, but she did. She was on her feet, stuffing the last of her breakfast into her mouth. She hurried to the corner and pressed an ear to the wall. She'd found this was the best place for eavesdropping, although all she ever caught was a word here or there. But she had learned to identify voices without seeing their speakers, and that helped some.

Cries and a great splash.

"They've thrown his body overboard," Serapio narrated.

"I got that much."

"He had a . . ." He shook his head. "I'm not sure of the Cuecolan word. A rough knot? A rough . . . bump? All over his body."

"A rash." Her voice was tight. "Callo should have never let him on the ship."

"Will it spread? Kill everyone?"

So he did understand. She listened some more, but the voices were too jumbled to decipher. "Maybe," she said, voice grim and bitter. "We can always hope."

"You assume we would be immune."

She glanced over at him. "If it's catching, no doubt we all already have it. At least those bastards will go down with us." She sauntered over to the bench and sat in the spot she now thought of as her own.

"You seem pleased," he said. "Tell me why."

She had long given up on how exactly he could tell such things. Could he hear the shift in her gait? Smell the satisfaction rolling off her like a perfume? She had no idea, but he was right. She was pleased.

"I give it a half hour and they'll be coming to us, asking for help."

"Help?"

"People like us are always hated until they need us—isn't that always the way?"

He tilted his head to the side as he sometimes did, as if it helped him hear. "Not a half hour. They're coming for you now."

He said it in a rush and then pulled his leather pouch free, dipped a finger in, and stuck it in his mouth, sucking the delicate crystal powder off his skin. He'd done it twice before, once every day while they'd been in here together, and she'd not asked him what it was, but now she did.

"What is that stuff? Medicine?"

"Medicine," he agreed, repeating her word. "After a fashion."

"It is for your eyes?"

"Yes. Again, not the way you mean it, though."

He pressed his back against the wall, and she knew he was going to do that thing again, where he seemed to go into a trance. She had thought it a nightmare the first time she saw him but understood it now as more like a willing unconsciousness, a time when his mind went somewhere else far from this room. But to what end, she still didn't know.

"When they take you, Xiala, stall them. Help is on the way."

"You misunderstand, Serapio," she said, confident. "They need my help now. They won't hurt me."

But he was already gone to wherever he went when he ate that powder that resembled broken moonlight on the open water.

The door banged open, and she turned, grinning. Three men crowded into the room, two grabbing her arms and one sticking a cloth down her throat.

"Hey, careful," she mumbled around the filthy fabric.

They dragged her out onto the deck into weak watery daylight. A wall of gray clouds as big as an island hid the sun, and below the clouds, a mirror of seawater so flat she could skip a stone across it. She took it all in with a glance. The water was too still, the sky too unreadable. They'd cut too far south and hit the early-winter doldrums.

Land fuckers, she thought to herself. *Rank amateurs. Novices, fucking farmers, indwellers.* She laughed around her rag.

The two crewmen holding her arms forced her onto a bench, which was a shade nicer than making her kneel, she supposed. Callo sat across from her, eyes wary. He studied her, his perpetually wistful face even more so.

"Patu's dead," he said, big brown eyes searching hers. "Two men sick and unable to row, and soon maybe more."

She widened her eyes theatrically, hoping he read her lack of empathy.

He sighed and rubbed a hand over his face. And to think she'd thought marginally kind things about that face. Well, he could go to all seven hells now.

"We're stuck here, Xiala," he said. "We could row out, but without the wind to tell me which way, I could be sending us in circles. You know the stories of the doldrums. Men get lost in them. Die in them. And we've got sick men. We need land, and we need it fast."

She rolled her eyes.

"You can help us!" one of the crew said from behind Callo. Her first mate—no, he was just a mutinous bastard now—waved him quiet.

She tried to talk through the gag, but it came out a mumble.

Callo sighed. "I'll take it out, but no Singing, or Baat slits your throat." He looked up at someone behind her, just off her shoulder, and she felt the cold press of a blade against her neck. Rage welled up in her chest, not fear. *Fuckers!*

Callo reached over and removed the gag.

"Fuck you, you rank traitorous—"

He stuffed the cloth back in her mouth. She growled around it, eyes flaring in rage.

Casually, he leaned forward and slapped her. An open hand across her cheek, so hard her head spun, and she was stunned to silence. The rage in her became something hot, molten. He had touched her. Not just touched. Hit.

Oh, he was going to die. She just wasn't sure how or when. She let that sentiment show in the look she gave him, and he leaned back.

"Please, Xiala!" he said, voice rough with something that sounded like desperation. "I don't want to hurt you anymore. I want . . ."

"I say we gut her like the fish she is," Baat said, the blade back against her neck.

"Shut up," Callo snapped. "Don't you understand what's happened to us? Where we are?" He wiped his palm across his sweating forehead.

Xiala's eyes narrowed. Callo didn't have any rough bumps, as Serapio had called them, but he was perspiring more than normal for an overcast morning, and he did look gray under his brown skin. Was he already ill with Patu's disease?

"We'll try again, right? I'll take the gag out, and you'll talk nicely. Not this swearing. Agreed?"

The rage was still there, simmering, and the sting of his hand against her skin lingered, but she was focused now. She wouldn't waste her chance. She had to be smart.

She nodded.

He sighed, and reached out a second time and removed the gag. This time, she kept her mouth shut.

Callo watched her, waiting. Baat pressed the blade closer, and she felt the prick of the obsidian and a trickle of blood drip down her neck.

"Calm," Callo said, either to her or to Baat or to both.

"What do you want?" she asked, and her voice only shook a little.

"Get us out of here, and once we see land, we let you go. Separate ways, no hard feelings."

She would have laughed had she not been worried Baat would cut an artery.

"After what you've done to me? Mutinied? Taken my ship? My fucking ship!"

"Xiala," he said, sounding resigned. "You promised."

"I did not fucking promise you anything!"

He started to lift the rag again.

"Okay, okay," she said quickly. "No more ranting. I . . . I'll talk."

He looked at her, long and thoughtful. "Lord Balam—" he started.

"Gave me this ship," she said, voice as calm and dead as the waters around them. "He made me captain. You think he won't have you hanged for mutiny, you're wrong."

Callo exhaled, dipping his chin, eyes on the deck between his feet.

"You're dead, Callo," she hissed. "You were dead as soon as you locked me in that room. If Patu's sickness hasn't already gotten you, Cuecola justice will."

"Stop."

"Some of you may get out alive," she said, pitching her voice to the crew. "Tell them Callo made you do it, that the mutiny was his idea."

He looked up, his eyes narrowed. "I fought to keep you alive. They wanted to kill you as soon as Loob died."

"You did it for yourself, not me. You know I had to cut that rope to save this asshole." She rolled her eyes upward to indicate Baat. "Pretty sure Loob was dead when I got to him, and this one"—again she gestured toward Baat—"panicked. Probably kicked his friend in the head on the way down. Killed him himself . . ." She trailed off, the truth dawning as she said the words.

"Kill her now," Baat said, pressing the blade deeper into her skin. It didn't hurt as much as sting where the air hit the wound, but the blood felt plentiful, too plentiful, as it started to pool in her collarbone and stain her borrowed shirt.

"Hold." Callo raised a hand for Baat, eyes still on her. "Is that it, then? We all die together?"

"I'm not dying, you traitorous shit. Did you already forget why you locked me in that room? I can swim."

He stood. Paced away from her, hands behind his back, shoulders tense.

"What are we waiting for, Captain?" Baat growled. "Let me gut this Teek."

How quickly he had turned against her. She remembered him at the feast on Little Moth, joining in her joke about Loob's wife.

"What are you so scared of?" she asked.

"Shut your dirty mouth."

"Are you scared of me, or are you scared because you know what I said about you panicking was true? That you're the one who killed Loob, not me."

"I said, shut the fuck up!" He pushed the knife deeper into her neck, and this time something inside her throat gave. She cried out, and it came out a gurgle. Her heart thundered, her pulse so loud in her ears that Callo's protests on her behalf came to her as a distant roar, like waves crashing against a faraway shore. She was choking on her own blood.

"Xiala!"

Her name was a thunderclap, a sound that saturated the air. A single word that seemed to fill the space around them, freezing Baat as he withdrew the blade, stopping Callo as if encased in stone, and immobilizing the rest of the crew just as they were turning to see who or what had spoken.

It was Serapio who had shouted her name. He stood just outside their shared prison door.

Xiala could see him plainly. It was the same as that first time he had appeared on the deck, although this time he wore his black robe. The world seemed to shudder, as if it recognized him and feared what it saw. The sun, hidden behind the clouds, seemed to dim even further, as if cowering from an old enemy, and the wind, which had been nonexistent moments before, rose up screaming across the deck, tossing Xiala's hair around her face.

Then the world blinked and righted itself. All but the sun. It was completely gone.

The sky had become a black wall. A living, undulating, screeching wall of feathers and claws and beaks that was descending on them like a nightmare.

The first crow struck Baat. Quick and sharp as an oyster blade, a deep slash that ripped his scalp away. She watched him drop, feeling light and strangely detached. *I've lost a lot of blood*, she thought absently, as the birds fell upon them.

Men jolted back to life, screaming as birds ripped flesh from cheeks and plucked eyes from sockets. She watched a black-feathered body use its beak to tear Callo's lips from his face. Watched as he dropped dead in front of her as heavy as a felled log. Watched as the birds took his eyes, and his ears, and continued to rip apart the rest of his body.

She looked away, tears leaking from her own eyes. She had wanted to kill the bastard, hadn't she? But mother waters, not like this.

Her eyelids drooped closed, and she tumbled from the bench.

She didn't know how long it had lasted when the screaming finally stopped. She thought perhaps she had lost consciousness for a while, her body's small mercy granted to her to survive the whirlwind of death.

Her lids fluttered open.

Serapio hadn't moved. His robe flared around him like black wings, and the crows he had called, from where she couldn't fathom, came to him as if to their master. They flowed around his form in a tight spiral, round and round, until they broke and surged upward. They seemed to shatter across the sky in bands of shadow, radiating from his body like the feathered rays of a black sun.

Serapio's face was radiant, caught in ecstasy, his broad smile showing teeth red enough to match the blood that soaked the deck.

She wanted to say something, call to him. But her throat didn't want to work.

He seemed to sense her there, reaching for him.

When he spoke, his voice was the sound of a thousand beating wings.

"I am not the sea," he said, "but I have children, too."

CHAPTER 22

City of Tova

Year 325 of the Sun

(12 Days before Convergence)

The costliest mistake one can make is to underestimate one's opponent through low expectations.

—*On the Philosophy of War,* taught at the Hokaia War College

It took a day for the streets of Tova to settle. All the Sky Made clans called their personal guards to service to disperse crowds and enforce a curfew. Those who were caught loitering or out on the street without demonstrable business were detained and escorted home. Tova did not possess a civil police force, only individual clan militias and makeshift jail cells meant for temporary use. The most common punishments among the tight-knit Sky Made clans were banishment and, for lesser crimes, a system of restitution to make the injured party whole. Things were different in the Maw, where crime bosses ruled the streets, but the system, even there, worked much the same. Restitution, banishment, and, for the truly horrendous, a quick and merciful death.

"My guard will escort you back to the tower," Ieyoue offered to a restless Naranpa. She had been confined to Water Strider's Great House for almost a full twenty-four hours with no news of what had happened. Ieyoue had sent word to the tower that she, Naranpa, was well and safe, but they had not sent news back.

"Thank you for all you've done," she said to the matron. "I and the Watchers will not forget it."

Ieyoue took the declaration in stride, no doubt tallying the favor for later use, but Naranpa didn't mind. She was grateful.

She returned to the tower in a blue hooded robe, her priestly raiment and mask hidden in a nondescript bag she carried on her back. The great doors were barred, for Shuttering or because of the riots, and she had to petition the tsiyo at the door for entry. The girl recognized her, small miracles, and let her pass. The main room was empty, as were the stairs, and she made her way back through the tower in eerie silence. She stopped at the terrace, but it was empty. The only place left was the observatory.

She hurried to the roof to find her people engaged in debate. Her eyes searched the room, looking for one face.

There xe was, arguing about something with Haisan, and the banality of it, the two of them at each other's throat as they always were, brought a sob of relief to her lips. They both turned at the sound.

"Nara!" Iktan called, and xe was at her side, pulling her into an embrace. It was a rare show of public affection and one that likely made her look weak, but she didn't care. Xir arms were strong and solid, and the warmth of xir body against hers meant xe was very much alive.

"You're alive," she murmured.

"Yes, I'm fine. It is hard to kill me, Nara. You should know that."

"I do," she said, laughing. "And I'm grateful for it."

They broke their embrace, and Nara looked around the room, cheeks flushed and tears in her eyes. "My apologies for interrupting."

"It's no interruption," Haisan said with a gentle smile. "We are glad to see you well."

"Let me take you to your rooms to rest," Iktan said.

"No, you are in Conclave. I'll join you. I feel like I've been gone an eternity."

"We were just finishing," Abah said, her mouth curved in an indulgent smile. "Let Iktan care for you. You've had such a difficult time, Nara. I can send a healer later if you like."

"That's not necessary," Iktan said, dark eyes cutting to the seegi. Abah only smiled wider. *Like a cat who ate the bird*, Naranpa thought.

"What's happened?" she asked, suspicious.

"I'll explain later," Iktan whispered close to her ear. Xe turned Naranpa toward the exit.

Naranpa frowned. She had obviously missed something important, but she wasn't sure what. But Iktan's hand was firm against her back, so she let xir lead her away. Once they were back in her rooms, she asked, "What's happened, Iktan? Abah looked much too satisfied."

"I've asked them to send you up some tea."

"I don't need tea. I need to know why you were in Conclave."

"Nevertheless." A knock on the door, and moments later xe returned with a tray holding a clay pot and two short cups. Xe set the tray down and poured her a cup.

The smell of lavender, fragrant and soothing, filled the room. She smiled despite herself. Tea did sound wonderful. She took the cup when offered. Let it warm her hands before she took a tentative sip. It was too hot to enjoy. "Now, tell me what you were discussing."

"Nothing important."

"It looked important. Important enough for you and Hai-san to argue about it." Of course, they would argue about the color of a spring sky, but she didn't mention that.

Iktan licked nervously at xir lips, a gesture she had never seen from xir before. "We were discussing retaliation."

She almost dropped her mug. "For what? Against whom?"

"He was going to harm you. Harm the Sun Priest. Something public must be done, and swiftly."

Her hands were shaking too badly to hold her cup. She set the tea down on the table beside her.

"Who?"

"Okoa Carrion Crow."

She had expected it, had known it would be him. She was relieved he was still alive. She thought they had connected, if only for a moment, and perhaps that meant that the tower could begin to heal the wound between it and the clan. But this had only rent the wound wide open.

"He wasn't going to harm me. It was a misunderstanding. Someone pushed him on the ice. Did you not see?"

Iktan frowned. "He meant to strike you."

"No . . ." She stood, pacing across the room. "No, Iktan. He had complimented me. He was only going to thank me."

She could feel Iktan's mood shift, the caregiver replaced by the exasperated commander of her guard.

"They want you dead. How many more times must they try before you believe it?"

"You told me the assassin on the Day of Shuttering may not have been Carrion Crow."

"I said not to rush to conclusions. But now it seems clear enough."

"Does it? I don't know . . ."

"Have we traded places now?" xe scoffed. "You convincing me Carrion Crow is innocent?"

"I don't think Okoa meant to harm me."

"Because he's young and handsome?"

"What? No. No! He's ten years too young for me and more interested in birds than women. I have absolutely no—" She laughed, incredulous. "Skies, are you jealous, Iktan?"

"Not jealous," xe said. Iktan touched a hand to her face, cupping her cheek. "I thought you were dead, Nara. That I had failed you."

"Oh." She let herself relax. "No. You didn't fail me. I'm fine."

She kissed the edge of xir hand, and then came up on her toes to kiss xir lips. It was a familiar gesture born of old habits and rebirthed by her exhaustion. The minute she did it, she regretted it. But the damage had been done.

"Nara . . ." Iktan gently pushed her away.

"Oh." Her voice was fluttery. She pressed a hand to her

chest. "I-I'm sorry. I wasn't thinking. I'm just . . ." She exhaled. "I'm sorry."

"There's something else I need to tell you."

"About your new lover? It's none of my business, really. I was out of line."

Xe frowned. "My . . . ? No. The Conclave was concerned you wouldn't agree to a public retaliation against Carrion Crow."

"And they were right. I won't."

"Any action the tower takes must be unanimous, as you are well aware. So . . . we voted."

Her stomach dropped. "Voted on what exactly?"

Xe looked apologetic. "Eche will take over your duties as Sun Priest until further notice, and Haisan and Abah will be at his side to ensure his success. Golden Eagle has already agreed to send in a contingent of household guards to bolster the tower's security until we can bring to justice the ones responsible for these attempts on your life and to aid the tsiyo in any future action against the Crows."

"What?" She turned, mouth open in shock.

"I know it is difficult to accept, and we did not come lightly to the decision."

"*We?* You agreed to this?"

"We all did."

She backed away, eyes wide. Looking for some escape. Not just from Iktan and this room but from this moment. Minutes ago she had been weeping with relief to be back in the tower and among those she thought of as her family. A contentious family, perhaps, but hers nonetheless.

Her back hit the wall behind her. Her hands were shaking, and she fought for air. The room spun.

"Breathe, Nara," Iktan said, voice concerned. Xe reached for her, and she pushed xir hard enough that xe stumbled.

"No! I . . ." Her voice trembled. "You cannot take this away from me!"

Iktan's black eyes were unhappy, but the set of xir jaw was uncompromising.

"We already have."

• • • • •

Xe left her there alone with a promise to have a servant bring her a meal later on and a tsiyo on the other side of the door. Ostensibly to guard her but undoubtedly to keep her inside her room.

She sat on the bench for hours, watching the sun move across the room. She realized her gambit to restore the Sun Priest's power had truly failed. In fact, she had somehow made things worse. *Perhaps you didn't want it badly enough, Nara*, she thought to herself. *Or perhaps you wanted it for the wrong reasons.* But that felt like a lie. Her motivations had been pure. She had only ever thought of how to grow the priesthood, how to raise up the people of Tova. And now the worst had come to pass. Talk of retaliation against Carrion Crow, allowing the Golden Eagle guard into the sacred tower.

"It is a path of destruction," she whispered to only herself. The priesthood had walked this path before and ruined countless lives. Perhaps Abah and Haisan and even Iktan could not see the damage that striking Carrion Crow would do, not only to the clan but to the city, to themselves.

But she could. She had lived side by side with Kiutue for years, had become his pupil and confidante. She knew only death came from death. But what could she do to stop it? She was locked in this damn room with no one on her side and no resources.

Unless.

It took her a day to decide, but once she had, it was not so difficult to obtain the things she needed. Most of them she already had in her room. Warm clothes, a woven belt she unraveled that would substitute for rope in an emergency, an old eating dagger that made a serviceable weapon, and her climbing shoes.

She waited to go until the sky was truly dark and the moon had not quite cleared the eastern mesa. She dressed warmly, thick leggings of woven cotton and a bulky formless jacket with a heavy cowl that covered her head and shadowed her face. She bound her breasts to flatten them and tied up her hair in a single topknot. She slipped thin climbing shoes on her feet, specially made from lambskin and cut to hug her toes individually. They were expensive and rare and were the tools the tsiyo used to scale walls. Iktan had gifted them to her long ago, a joke between them about her childhood spent climbing the intimidating cliffs of the Maw, but she had never had occasion to use them. She felt a pang of guilt that their first employment would be to defy her once friend, but she saw no other way.

She left by the window. As a young child she had loved

climbing the Maw and searching out tunnels and secret passages with her brothers. She was good at it—small, lightweight, and fearless. She remembered her brothers' lessons well: read your route, don't forget your feet, arms straight and legs bent. She repeated them to herself now and hoped it was as the old ones said: one never forgot how to climb.

She pulled herself through the window, the chill slapping her senses awake. The night was cold and quiet. She tasted snow in the air and knew it would come again by dawn to turn the stones around her to slick ice.

She balanced on her toes along the thin ledge, fingers gripping rough stone. The only light to guide her was the glow of a resin lamp she had left burning in her room. It was not enough; she would have to climb through the dark.

She cautiously ran a hand across the outside wall. The rock beneath her fingers was rough. She found a niche a few paces above her head for a handhold. She wedged her fingers in and pulled herself out and over, finding a place for her foot. She reached again and repeated the process, moving up a few arm's widths before switching directions and moving slowly down the wall. She was out now, exposed to the open air, and exhilaration thrummed through her body, her pulse loud in her ears. She moved slowly, methodically, nothing like her old self who had fearlessly scaled the Maw. But she did move, and she smiled grimly as she passed a row of narrow windows that marked the third floor. *Only two stories to go*, she told herself. *Nothing for a Maw brat.*

Wind caught at her clothes and hair, a gentle but insistent reminder that to fall now would mean broken bones at the least, death if she was unlucky. But she wasn't unlucky, and soon enough her feet touched solid ground.

Naranpa laughed breathlessly. Part of her, that part that was all too aware of her failures, couldn't believe she had done it. She dusted off her lightly scraped hands and shook her head. A swell of pride bubbled in her chest. It was a simple thing, but it felt good. She had had a problem and she solved it. It wasn't so hard. A manageable danger rather than the precipice of future decisions that lay ahead. A little risk on a rock wall was much more favorable than what she had to face next.

The bridges leading back and forth from Otsa were not guarded, so it was easy work to cross the grounds of the celestial tower and make her way across the bridge to Tsay. The streets were empty, the curfew still in effect as far as she knew, so her greatest worry was being spotted by a roving guard. She pulled her hood up and kept to the corners, picking alleys over wide thoroughfares as she worked her way toward Titidi.

It was a long hour before she crossed the bridge into Water Strider territory, and another two hours across the district, but she finally found herself standing cliffside in an open-air park looking across the canyon at the Maw. She wasn't sure how long she stared across at the place of her birth, her childhood, as a swirl of emotions warred within her. Coming here had been a desperate decision, one she felt compelled to make. But now, facing the place, knowing what came next, she hesitated. Was this folly? Surely. Would she even be welcomed? Recognized? All her doubts loomed large, but so did her desperation.

"There is only one way to know for sure," she murmured, and made herself move.

At the edge of the park the only transportation to and from the Maw from Tova proper waited. She had used it once, at thirteen, and had never looked back. Now, at thirty-three, she would use it again, unsure of what she would find on the other side.

Rather than an easily accessible bridge, the way across to the Maw was a gondola. Although the term *gondola* was generous. The transport was more of a platform, maybe thirty paces wide and twenty paces deep, made of wood and connected to a thick cable of ropes that arched overhead to attach to a similar pier on the other side of the crevasse. The crevasse itself was narrow, no more than fifty paces where the airlift crossed, but the drop was three, perhaps four, times that. All that separated her and the other passengers from certain death was a flimsy wooden waist-high rail.

She paid her toll in cacao from a small leather pouch tied to her belt and crowded onto the gondola with the other passengers. Most were Dry Earthers, people who lived in the Maw or the Eastern districts farther out. They had all no doubt spent the day as servants in the Sky Made houses and were now trudging their way home, something she had witnessed her mother do countless times. There were a handful of colorfully dressed scions of the Sky Made clans in their recognizable clan colors, obviously unfazed by the curfew. They were the loudest, shouting and laughing and passing clay bottles of imported xtabentún between them. They were undoubtedly headed to the Maw for the debauchery it offered, gambling houses and pleasure dens and enticements that the more respectable parts of the city banned.

Naranpa frowned at the scions. Fools lining other fools' purses. All for a taste of oblivion, be it found in drink or risk or between someone's willing thighs. Such things had never appealed to her, perhaps because she had grown up seeing the ruin it made of people's lives. Now, as the last person who could fit squeezed onto the gondola and she stood cheek to jowl with so many strangers, she felt it even more deeply. A pang of homesickness, not for the Maw but for her spacious and well-scrubbed rooms in the celestial tower, washed over her.

The gondola lurched forward, some inebriated scion screamed in delight, and Naranpa focused on maintaining her balance as she crossed into Coyote's Maw.

CHAPTER 23

CITY OF TOVA

YEAR 325 OF THE SUN

(13 DAYS BEFORE CONVERGENCE)

> Beware, beware the bitter Crow
> The Knives dealt them a bloody blow
> Crows hope to bring the Sun down low
> A plot that surely ends in woe.
>
> —Children's rhyme heard in Tova

It was chaos on Sun Rock. He had only meant to grip the Sun Priest's arm in respectful greeting, as unlikely as that had seemed at the time. But then someone had struck him from behind, and his foot had slipped, and that damned Knife was there, an open blade in their hand.

Okoa had flung an arm out, enough to throw the assassin's aim off and stop the knife from burrowing into his heart where the Knife was no doubt aiming, but the blade had still sliced across his jaw, opening him up. The pain had burned, shocking and immediate, and Okoa had screamed.

His scream had brought the Shield and the Knife and their

tsiyos, and before he could quite grasp what was happening, it had descended into violent chaos.

Chaiya was there, throwing Okoa out of the line of attack.

"To your matron!" he shouted. "Get her safe."

Okoa's instinct was to argue, to push his way back into the fight, but his training took over, and he ran back to his sister, calling two Shields to his side as he did.

Esa stood stunned mere paces from the sky bridge. She had been about to cross when the fight broke out.

"What is happening?" she shouted, alarmed.

"Home," Okoa commanded grimly.

"Oh, skies. Okoa! Your face!"

After the initial stinging pain, he'd forgotten about his injury.

"It's nothing," he said. "First we get you safe."

She nodded, smart enough to grasp the situation, and he and the two Shields with him surrounded her and pressed through the crowd on the icy bridge. After the second time Esa almost slipped on the treacherous crossing she paused to rip the hem of her overlong dress away. She had it half gone before Okoa drew his knife and quickly cut the rest. They continued, and after what felt like an hour, they crossed onto Odo soil.

"Take her to the Great House," he ordered the two men with him.

"What about you?" she asked, voice high with concern.

"I'm going back."

"Okoa! No! You're covered in blood."

He looked down. She was right. The blood from the wound had dripped from his jaw to cover his neck and chest.

Suddenly, he felt dizzy. The bridge swayed, and he wasn't sure if it was from the rush of people still crossing over or because his vision was failing.

"Esa," he murmured, unsteady.

"I've got him."

Okoa looked up to find a man standing beside him. A Crow in white, around Chaiya's age, his black hair cut in a straight bang and shaved to skin on the sides and shoulder-length in the back. Fresh red dye outlined the haahan on his bare chest. A cultist.

Okoa started to protest, but the man ducked under his arm and braced his body against his, slinging Okoa's arm over his shoulder.

"Take the matron to the Great House," he directed the Shield as if he was one of them. "I've got your captain. We'll follow behind."

The men nodded and hustled Esa away, who had no time to protest one way or the other.

Okoa swayed.

"I have you, crow son," the man said.

"Who are you?" Okoa asked, voice slurring. He really was dizzy. A thought occurred to him. Had the blade been poisoned? Oh, skies, that treacherous Knife.

"My name is Maaka. I am the one who sent Ashk." He grinned, his teeth so stained it filled the cracks in his lips and the lines at the edges of his mouth. "I've been wanting to meet you, Okoa."

Okoa tried to speak, but the words would not come. His vision faded to shadows and shapes. The last he remembered was Maaka dragging him down the street in the opposite direction of the Great House.

• • • • •

"Drink this."

Okoa pried sticky eyes open. He was on a bed. Fresh reeds on a raised shelf, blankets that smelled recently laundered. But the room was unfamiliar. There was a man holding out a cup to him.

Okoa grasped for some memory of the man. Maaka. From the bridge. Who had taken him from Esa.

His hand shot to his belt, only to find he was naked, a blanket modestly draped over his lower body. He struck, hand shooting forward to knock the cup from Maaka's hand, and then he was up on his feet, throwing a punch into Maaka's chest that had the man stumbling back, gasping for breath.

He didn't wait for him to recover. He bolted for the door. Ripped it open and pulled up short. Before him was only air, and a drop straight down into the Tovasheh.

"A sky room," he whispered to himself.

Maaka coughed behind him. Okoa looked back. He was dragging himself to his feet, hand to his chest. Okoa took two quick steps back and grasped the man by the nape of the woven shirt he wore. He hauled him over to the door, thrusting his upper body out into the open air.

"Talk, or I throw you out."

"Calm yourself, crow son!" Maaka cried. "Please. We mean you no harm. We saved your life!"

Okoa frowned. His memory was coming back in pieces. The fight at his mother's funeral. The Knife who opened up his jaw with what he was sure had been a poisoned blade. With the memories came the dizziness, too. He dragged Maaka back from the precipice and released him. He dropped heavily to the floor.

Okoa stumbled back to sit on the bed. "Where I am? And who is 'we'?"

Maaka rose on shaky feet and walked to the sky door. He shut the door tightly, throwing the lock, before turning to pick up the pieces of the clay cup that had shattered when Okoa knocked it from his hand. The water had spilled, and Okoa eyed it with regret. He was, in fact, very thirsty.

"You are in my house," the man said, voice shaking slightly. "Once I realized that you had been poisoned, I brought you here. My wife is a great healer, and I knew you had no time to spare." Maaka set the broken pottery in a small alcove next to a resin lantern.

"My apologies, then. I seem to have . . . overreacted."

Maaka waved Okoa's words away.

"It is I who should apologize. I should have realized you would wake up distraught." He gestured toward a door in the floor that Okoa had failed to notice. "Let us go downstairs. There are people I want you to meet."

"And water?" he asked, embarrassed.

"Of course."

The younger man stood and secured the blanket around his waist like a wrap skirt, tucking in the loose edge. "Thank you."

"It is my honor, Lord Okoa," Maaka said quietly. He pulled the door open and gestured for Okoa to go first. Okoa did, climbing down the ladder to find a room filled to bursting. Body heat hit him in a wave, and Okoa briefly thought of going back up to the sleeping room. There were at least two dozen people gathered below him. At his appearance, their conversation had halted and all faces had turned up to stare. He saw before him all ages. Elders whose skin had grown loose around their necks and arms, women with newborns on their hips, those whose hair was only beginning to gray.

He slowed but continued to the ground warily.

"Lord Okoa," Maaka said as he pulled the door closed above them and followed down the ladder, "I'd like you to meet the Odohaa."

They introduced themselves one by one, telling him their names and something of their families, and what his mother had meant to them, and how sorry they were that she had died. Maaka's wife had made him a place to sit, placed a jug of water at his side that he gulped from unabashedly, and plied him with food. She had said nothing about the broken cup, although by the looks of their home, they did not have a lot of possessions. Maaka had not said what he did for labor, but if his wife was a healer, she must do well. Which meant they likely gave all their wealth away. Esa had mentioned the Odohaa had focused on charity work in recent years, and here seemed to be one funding source for it.

After the last Odohaa member had introduced themselves, the room fell silent again. Okoa shifted, feeling uneasy despite the impeccable hospitality he had received. He knew it was time for him to speak, but he wasn't sure what they wanted to hear from him. He cleared his throat.

"Thank you to Maaka," he began, "and to Maaka's wife." He had heard so many names today, and the poison, or the antidote, seemed to make his thinking fuzzy. He could not remember her name, and he flushed, embarrassed at his poor manners.

Maaka's wife smiled. "You don't remember me, do you, Okoa? We played together as boys."

Okoa studied her face, trying to remember.

"My mother worked in the Great House. I was older than you, but we got along well, especially at stick games."

"Feyou," he said, placing her immediately. "But now you are a woman."

"I was always a woman," Feyou said. "I just needed some time to become who I am."

"Thank you for saving my life. And for the food."

She nodded. "You owe me a cup, Okoa. That was one of my best."

"My deepest apologies. I swear I will replace it."

"All right, Feyou, don't harass him," Maaka said, a hand on his wife's shoulder. "I didn't bring him here for that."

"Why did you bring me here?"

Maaka glanced out at the gathering and then back at Okoa. "Ashk told me that you refused our invitation outright. I was hoping that if you met us, if you saw who we are, you would not judge us so harshly. I know that among some, the Odohaa do not have the best reputation."

Okoa said nothing, and Maaka nodded, understanding.

"We are people who believe," Maaka continued, "and practice the same way as our ancestors practiced. We will not let the Sun Priest take that from us." His voice shook with passion. "But we also must counter violence with violence. We will not let them slaughter us again. We will fight, Lord Okoa, whether you help us or not."

Okoa rubbed at his head. The injury on his jaw pulled, and he touched it gingerly. Feyou had coated it with a poultice to draw out the poison, and it felt clammy against his skin.

"You do know the war college teaches peacekeeping?" he asked Maaka. "War college is a poor name for it."

Maaka crossed his arms. "I am not a fool. I have seen the Shield fight. And the way you attacked me when I woke you."

Okoa winced. "I did not mean that."

"No, Lord Okoa. It was good. You can teach us. And strategies against your enemies. They teach you that, do they not?"

Okoa thought of another tactic. "But where would you get weapons? You saw what the blade of one Knife can do to a man."

"We make our own knives," he said. "And Feyou can make a poison to rival anything the tower can brew."

"I cannot convince you this is folly, can I, Maaka? This is, how many? Thirty? Against the tower? Possibly the other Sky Made should we initiate the conflict. It's suicide."

Maaka grinned, and the people in the room echoed his amusement in friendly laughter. "This is just our war council. The Odohaa tuyon. They are here to meet you, to witness what you have to say. And then they will bring it back to their own houses to share."

Okoa did his best to hide his shock but was sure he failed. They had formed a war council? And appointed to it new mothers and stoop-backed elders? Skies, these people were truly insane if they thought they could take on the Knives and the clans and not be butchered.

Maaka tensed. "From the look on your face, I know you do not have faith, Lord Okoa Carrion Crow"—the rebuke was evident in the use of Okoa's clan name to remind him of who he was—"but we do. It is the most powerful thing we have."

Okoa accepted the scolding. He did not mean to insult them, but this was ludicrous. "Faith is well and good, Maaka," Okoa said, trying to gentle his words. "But it is easier you pray for the Crow God Reborn to appear than plan to fight the priesthood. Without a god to smooth your way, I can see no path forward for you."

Maaka straightened. "We are done waiting for our god to return," he said. "We will challenge the tower with or without your help, Lord Okoa, and with or without the crow god."

Okoa met the eyes of the faces that surrounded him. He saw determination. Ferocity. Pride. All the qualities he hoped for in expressions young and old. The last thing he wanted to do was leave them on their own to die.

"Very well," he said. "We will talk more—"

Excitement rippled through the crowd.

"—another day." He held up his hand to quiet them. "I am not saying I will help you. I am saying that I see you now and acknowledge that. So give me time to see what I can do."

"But the solstice Convergence comes soon!" someone called

from the crowd. "Prophecy says we must strike on the day of the solstice when the sun is weakest."

Okoa wasn't familiar with the prophecy the person was referencing, but he knew the solstice was too soon to form any kind of fighting force.

"Time," he repeated. "I will meet with you again soon, Maaka. But let me go home and see my sister. Let me consult my Shield and discover what wisdom we keep in the Great House about this prophecy. Then we will talk again."

Maaka looked at him, evaluating. Finally, he nodded. "Until that time, Lord Okoa. The Odohaa will hold you to your promise."

"I would expect nothing less. Now . . ." Okoa rested his hands on the blanket around his waist. "May I have my pants back?"

CHAPTER 24

CITY OF TOVA (COYOTE'S MAW)
YEAR 325 OF THE SUN
(12 DAYS BEFORE CONVERGENCE)

> Dry Earth for Dry Earthers. Sky Made go home!
>
> —Graffiti on the wall of a Maw establishment

The Coyote's Maw was a deep fissure in the earth that ran off the main canyon of Tova. It separated the Sky Made districts from the Dry Earth ones. The canyon was so narrow and so deep it received at most a few scant hours of indirect sunlight a day, sometimes less, depending on the time of year. And even that was limited to the top levels that catered to tourists and Sky Made who came to the Maw to play. Below that, it was perpetual darkness, the only light coming from resin lamps or pit fires.

Long before Naranpa was born, her ancestors had carved their homes into the sides of the fissure. Why there instead of sticking to the wider and more welcoming cliffsides that would become the Sky Made districts, she didn't know, despite what she'd said to the dedicant on the bridge on the Day of Shuttering. But she felt a profound irony in descending from a people who preferred perpetual shadow only to rise as the priest of the sun and fall again to nothing.

The top level of the Maw was the market, and the level below that public gaming and pleasure houses. The third level gave way to houses that were more like caves that stretched back into the solid rock. All of it was connected by ledges that served as a network of looping foot trails that curved sinuously along the walls of the fissure like lines of ribbon hugging the hem of a dress. They were connected by roads so thin that even the widest ones couldn't fit more than two people abreast and most of them fit only one. The roads themselves ran only the length of any given level. They were connected to each other by ladders for the human traffic and platforms, miniature versions of the gondola, for everything else. Naranpa had lived on the fifth level as a child and done most of her begging on levels one and two, but she knew the Maw stretched down all the way to the river.

She exited the gondola on the first level directly into the main market. The smell of cooking food hit her first. Rich and dense, the scent of cakes stuffed with corn and peppers and stews of squash, beans, and turkey wafting from the open doors of eating houses and the open pits and shared kitchens that characterized the district. Her mouth watered. She hadn't eaten such rich food since before the Shuttering, the simple but nourishing meal at Ieyoue's notwithstanding. And she had never been able to afford this kind of food when she lived in the Maw. But now she returned with a purse full of cacao, more Sky Made than Dry Earth, and she realized she could buy anything she wanted.

Looking around her, she saw the Maw had avoided a curfew. People filled the streets, some finishing their evening shopping under the glow of torchlight but most already out carousing for the evening's entertainment. Women in bright one-shouldered dresses that bared skin, despite the cold, and men in leggings and hip skirts adorned with colorful string and embroidery. Music poured from doorways, flute and drum and trumpet, accompanied by singing and the slap of dancing feet.

She didn't remember the Maw being this loud and alive, but perhaps her faulty memory was due to the more conservative and reserved life she had been living inside the celestial tower. Twenty-three years of dour penitence to ensure the return of the sun had soured her to such unrestrained celebration. Although she had to admit, it was joyful, primal. There was something about it that felt vital.

At first when she saw the red ribbon tied around a young woman's upper arm, she thought nothing of it, but as she traveled farther into the Maw and saw more and more people wearing the ribbon and shopfronts offering bunches of dried marigolds and white shells to burn incense in, she recognized it for what it was: the Maw was still grieving Yatliza's death. The Sky Made clans had put their mourning regalia aside after the funeral, but Dry Earth had not.

Naranpa had been raised on the old Dry Earth ways of mourning—turquoise for remembrance and corpse ash in your hair. But all she saw around her was marigolds and incense, just like in the Sky Made districts. It made her sad to see the Dry Earth ways forgotten, but then, who was she to speak? She had left that side of herself well behind. She would be a hypocrite to begrudge the people here their dried flowers when she wore Sun Priest robes day in and day out. Or, at least, she used to.

"A commemorative ribbon?"

Naranpa turned to find a woman, clearly a shopkeeper, asking. She held out a narrow band of red string. The same one that half the market was wearing. On a whim, Naranpa took it. She tied it to her arm and then reached into her bag to retrieve a handful of cacao for payment.

"Only one," the shopkeeper said with a smile as she plucked the desired number of beans from her palm.

"I'm looking for someone," Naranpa ventured. "Perhaps you can help me?"

The woman looked doubtful, but she glanced at Naranpa's plain but clearly expensive clothing and nodded.

"A local boss. He may go by Denaochi."

The woman had looked amused before, mildly indulgent, but now her expression went flat. "I don't want any trouble," she said, taking a step back.

Naranpa hastily reached into her bag and pulled out more cacao. "I don't, either. He's a . . . relative," she said, improvising. "And I'm visiting from out of town. My mother promised his mother that I'd call on him."

The shopkeeper gaped. "He's got a mother?" She made the sign to ward off evil. "No, sir. You seem kind enough, but I wouldn't go seeking him out." Her mouth seemed to twist, as if she purposefully was avoiding saying his name. "He's not who your family thinks he is."

Sir? It took a moment for Naranpa to remember how she was dressed. She grabbed the woman's hand before she could move away. She pressed the cacao into it. The shopkeeper's eyes widened. It was probably more than she made in a season.

"I promised."

Finally, the woman nodded. "Second level, gambling house called the Lupine. He's known to frequent it. Has his ringers fleecing gulls at the patol table." She flushed. "You go, and if he wants to be found, he'll find you."

Naranpa nodded.

"Don't mention my name, or this shop!" she added hastily. "I don't want his eye on me."

"Of course not," Naranpa murmured.

Now she had a lead, and a solid one at that. Iktan was right; it wasn't hard to find her brother if someone wanted to look. Had she really been that naive to think she was so severed from her past? The thought both comforted her and depressed her as she made her way down the winding path to the switchback that led to the second level.

She found the Lupine easily enough. A windowless roundhouse built into the cliff wall, only the front half of the circle visible from the street. On its whitewashed wall was the painting of the eponymous tiered purple desert flower. Patrons had to ascend a ladder to enter from a trapdoor in the roof, much like the ceremonial roundhouses of the districts, but this one in the Maw was decidedly secular. A large man squatted at the entrance, a war club resting in one meaty hand. He eyed Naranpa as she climbed the ladder.

Here was the test. The reason she had chosen to dress in a masculine style. She knew the gaming houses were often segregated and hoped she had made enough of an effort to pass.

As she reached the roof, she kept her head down and lifted her purse to show that it was heavy with cacao.

The man took in her disguise, and his mouth turned down, unimpressed. But then his gaze traveled to her full purse. With a half-hearted grunt, he opened the trapdoor to let her pass.

She peered inside but couldn't see much. A powerful waft of rich tobacco and fermented cactus beer hit her full force, and she swayed. She caught the big man grinning and steeled herself to the task at hand.

She took the ladder rungs one by one until her feet hit the stairs that circled the inside wall. She stopped a moment to orient herself. Below were male voices raised in conversation. Already there were crowds gathered at the gaming tables. Boys, and she suspected a fair number of girls dressed like boys, ran between tables, carrying food and drink and wagers back to the bosses. The bosses sat on a balcony overlooking the whole room hidden behind a cloud of smoke.

The balcony was where she would find her brother, but she wouldn't get up there without an invitation. She needed to draw some attention, and the best way to do that was to start winning. She knew the game favored in here and in every gambling house in Tova was patol. She hadn't played patol since she was a dedicant playing for chore duty, but she remembered the rules well enough. It was a game of luck, and risk, and she'd always had both on her side.

She took a deep breath, straightened her spine, and sauntered down the steps of the Lupine.

She had to pick a table, and one that answered to the right boss. But which would be her brother Denaochi's in this place? She weaved through the room, looking for something that would give it away. And then she spotted it, and knew it for her brother's domain immediately. A table marked by a rough drawing of an eagle hanging from a noose, its eyes turned into crude X marks. It was crass, and no doubt controversial, which sounded like Denaochi, too.

She picked the dead-eagle table closest to the center, the resin lamps bright around the board. Two men played, one pale-skinned and chestnut-haired, a foreigner, no doubt, likely from the trade cities to the north. Her old skills for spotting gulls came back to her as she sized him up. His clothes were a few seasons out of style. His hair was too long around the ears compared to the others in the hall. She guessed that he was a tourist, or a tradesman in town for some business, come to the gaming house to catch some local color. Naranpa imagined that the man had planned to drink a few rounds of beer, try his luck at the gaming tables, and, after losing a little cacao, probably head topside to a moderate but respectable travelers' inn to sleep off his adventure.

But that wasn't how he looked now. Sweat had gathered at his hairline, he tapped the fingers of his left hand nervously on the edge of the table, and his eyes kept darting between the board, the game pieces, and the dice as if they marked the difference between his life and death. And perhaps they did.

The other player was Tovan, brown-skinned and black-haired. Nose sharp and eyes slightly tilted, hands quick and competent with the dice like he played for a living. A professional, Naranpa noted. One of her brother's sure things, here to reel in the gulls and line his boss's coffers.

She moved closer to watch the inevitable, and when the foreign man groaned and swayed in his chair and the dark-haired man swept a hand across the table, she knew the gull had been properly fleeced.

She shuddered, revolted. For a moment she had been caught up in the thrill of it, the danger, just like the old days. But seeing the look on the man's face, the utter despair as the runners came and took what looked to be his last cacao, all she felt was pity.

"Who's next?" the winner asked. Murmurs circulated around the gathered crowd as spectators worked up the courage to become participants.

"I'll take the wager," she said quickly before someone could beat her to it, and before she could lose her nerve. She watched the man size her up, taking in the cost of her coat, her obviously pampered face and hands, even the way she moved as she took the seat across from him.

She met his eyes, and he gave her a lopsided grin, no doubt seeing through her basic disguise.

"Slumming it, scion?" he asked, his voice a low cocky drawl. "How much did you bribe the man up top to let you in?"

She heard a few laughs from the crowd.

"I'm Maw born and bred," she countered. "What's wrong? Are you scared I'll win?"

A few oohs and ahhs rippled around them. The player glanced up at the balcony. Naranpa followed his gaze. She stared into that nothing, long and pointed, and imagined her brother's shock at seeing her. Would he even recognize her?

Whatever the man across from her saw seemed to be satisfactory, and he gave a sharp nod to the runner who hovered at his elbow.

"Set the board," he commanded, and the young boy scurried to do his bidding. He set three small carved figures on the square table. The table itself was divided into sixteen quadrants called houses. Lines called rivers ran at the cardinal points. Naranpa examined each figure in turn before deciding on a small obsidian bison. Her opponent chose a turquoise antelope. Together, they placed their game pieces in the first house.

The runner took the third, unused figurine away and replaced it with a set of bone dice. Naranpa scooped them into her hand, shaking them against her palm. The rattle of the bones seemed loud in her ears. She remembered the words used to start the game, murmured, "May fate be revealed," and threw the dice, hitting them at a sharp angle against the table.

They spiked, just as they were supposed to, at a respectable seven. She moved her figurine accordingly, her opponent watching. Once her bison was in place, he picked up the dice, shook them quickly, and spiked them against the board. A fourteen. The crowd clapped. His first try, and he was two houses from completing a rotation.

Naranpa frowned. It was unlikely she would catch him. She had to play defensively. She picked up the dice. They were warm against her palm. She said a small prayer to the sun out of habit, although the game they played was an ancient Dry Earth one and the gods who ruled it had no truck with the sun. She threw.

Five!

Those among the crowd who understood the game gasped, and Naranpa grinned. Five wouldn't catch her opponent before he circled, but it would allow her to reverse direction and knock him from the board. She did so, to applause.

A rush of adrenaline made her flush. She understood why that gull had stayed and played his last cacao, why people went to the workhouse to cover debt run up at the table. Her earlier disgust evaporated in a wave of pleasure at her own win.

The dark-haired man across from her dipped his chin in acknowledgment as a runner swept in to clear the board and move the small pile of winnings to her side.

"Again?" the man asked.

She nodded vigorously and dug into her purse for her wager. But before she could pull her cacao out, a hand came down on the table. She looked up to find a young man blocking her. He looked Tovan, but his hair was bleached and dyed a brassy bright gold. Green stones dangled from his ears. *Crescent Sea fashions*, she thought to herself. *Cuecolan, then, perhaps.*

"Boss says take a break," the newcomer said to her opponent. The man slipped off his bench and vanished into the crowd without hesitation.

"Boss will see you," he said to her, his earrings swinging as he turned to her.

She started to protest that they'd only played one round and a proper game required twelve, but then she realized what she was doing. The whole point of playing had been to get her brother's attention, and she had.

She let her bag of cacao fall to her side, glanced briefly at the still-shadowed balcony, and stood to follow the golden-haired man.

CHAPTER 25

THE OBREGI MOUNTAINS

YEAR 320 OF THE SUN

(5 YEARS BEFORE CONVERGENCE)

> We have become a place of long weeping
> A house of scattered feathers
> There is no home for us between earth and sky.
>
> —From *Collected Lamentations from the Night of Knives*

It was Serapio's seventeenth birthday, and the Obregi sooth-sayer had come to divine his fate. He was outside, hiding under the great pine on the edge of the cliffside. The late-winter grass was brittle under his feet, but the first frost had not yet come. The ground still yielded under his heels as he rocked back and forth, but the icy breeze that sliced across his cheeks told him it was only a matter of time before Obregi would be hunker-ing down for a mountain winter, everything frozen solid.

"Where is he?" he heard the soothsayer complain, their high warbling voice echoing down from the terrace above. "I've come all this way. Does the boy not want to know his destiny?"

"The boy already knows his destiny," Serapio whispered to himself. "He only needs a way to fulfill it."

His father's voice cut across the field, as clear as if he was standing only a few paces away. "Find him!" he shouted. "And drag him back here if you must. I will not be defied!"

Serapio sighed and dropped down cross-legged under the tree. The day had turned frigid, and he pulled his wool cloak tighter around him. He settled his bone staff across his knees. It would be at least another hour until they thought to look for him outside.

He hoped Powageh found him first. The crows had told him that they had seen an old man traveling the roads alone, and while it could be anyone, he hoped it was his third and last tutor. After all, he was seventeen now. Surely it was time.

He sat for a while, listening to more shouting and scurrying, trying to feel the winter approaching.

A crunch of leaves behind him alerted him to a presence. His body tensed, but he immediately released it, keeping his shoulders and limbs loose like Eedi had taught him. He slid his staff down to his side, gripped the end, and listened. Another crunch, closer. Someone approaching and being careless at the noise they were making.

Powageh, as he had wished? Perhaps, but he could not be sure.

He considered whether to strike. Another step, and the stranger would be close enough that he could sweep them off their feet. Have them helpless on their back in seconds.

The leaves crunched again, and Serapio decided.

He moved, pivoting and rolling onto his hip and thrusting

his staff wide, sweeping the perimeter until he hit something solid. He shifted his grip to two hands and swung. A voice cried out, and he heard a body strike the ground. Serapio was on his feet, moving low, dagger out, when the stranger cried, "No, please! Spare me!"

The boy stopped. He could hear the stranger breathing hard, air moving too quickly through lungs that sounded feeble. Old. Serapio straightened and sheathed his blade, but he held the staff ready. He extended it until he hit flesh. He jabbed hard, and the stranger grunted, the staff digging into his stomach.

"Are you the old man the crows saw on the road?"

"Am I the . . . ?" They sounded bewildered, confused. "Perhaps? I-I-I do not know your crows." The stranger sounded ancient, a white-hair for sure. "And I am not a man, or a woman, for that matter. But I am old."

Serapio didn't understand what that meant, neither man nor woman, but he let it pass. It was not relevant.

"Is your name Powageh?"

A moment of hesitation, and then, "Powageh is my title, not my name. But yes, I am the third tutor to the crow god. Which"—the stranger chuckled, still short of breath—"must be you. Well met, Serapio."

The boy mused on that for a moment. It hadn't occurred to him that Paadeh and Eedi were not names but titles. Meaning he had never known their names in truth. It sat strange with him.

He circled back around to the easier question, the one that didn't make him feel like he had been deceived.

"If you are neither man nor woman, what are you?"

"A third gender, one I don't believe you acknowledge here in this little backwater country. I am bayeki. But what should concern you more is that I am a Watcher."

"A Tovan priest!" Serapio growled, and his hand slipped back to his dagger.

"I am not your enemy, Serapio," Powageh said. "Far from it."

"But you are from the celestial tower."

"I was. Past tense. Very, very past."

"And now?" he challenged.

"I am its enemy." The stranger sighed, as if the memory was a burden. "Once I was very much a part of the celestial tower, a member of the Society of Knives, even, sworn to defend the Sun Priest."

"My enemy."

"Both our enemies. We are united in our hatred."

"Why?"

Powageh hesitated. "Let us sit and talk properly, Serapio. Not with me on my back and your weapon in my belly. We haven't much time, but I will tell you everything I know." The stranger's voice caught with emotion. "We have kept you hidden for so long, as long as we dared, but the time draws near for you to be revealed."

• • • • •

They sat under the sheltering eaves of the great pine tree. Powageh had laid out a small lunch, foods brought from a hotter, waterier clime that Serapio did not know. Tiny salted fish, skinless and boneless, that slid quickly down his throat and left a salty wake behind. Nuts spiced with hot pepper that burned in his mouth. A strange spiky fruit that Powageh opened with a knife to reveal soft, juicy flesh. And, most astounding of all, a thick and creamy drink that started bitter on Serapio's tongue and blossomed to a pleasing peppery heat. He could only describe it as the taste of pleasure.

"It is kakau in the Cuecola language. They call it the drink of the gods," Powageh said, after Serapio's exclamation. "Fitting for you, crow son."

Serapio thought at first his new tutor was teasing him, but xir voice sounded completely sincere. The crows had come to join them, no doubt curious about the stranger, and Serapio fed them bits of the new food, but they only liked the drink. Typical.

"The Night of Knives," Powageh said as xe slurped from xir cup. "Did Saaya tell you of the Night of Knives?"

"When I was five," Serapio acknowledged. It was one of the first stories his mother had told him, and the one she told him most often after. "She told me that the Watchers led an army to slaughter all who followed the crow god. She said assassins murdered my grandmother and my cousins and aunts and uncles."

"Anything else? Nothing of a tsiyo turned to protector?"

Serapio frowned. "She did mention a young priest whom she found crying over the body of a child. The priest was covered in their own sick, begging for forgiveness."

"Yes, well . . ." Powageh sighed. "I suppose that's not inaccurate."

"She said the priest helped her escape the city and took her to sanctuary." He lifted his head toward Powageh. "Was that you?"

"It was. Many years ago." Xe cleared xir throat. "After we escaped, well, neither of us could go back, so we went to Cuecola, my birthplace. I had family there still, good family, and very wealthy. And a cousin who offered to employ me in his import-and-export business. For two years I worked for him on the docks, a boss at one of his warehouses. Your mother and I talked of marrying, but she was still very young. No older than you. But I was smitten with her, you understand, and indulged her tremendously."

"What does that mean?"

"Saaya was single-minded. Grief is one thing, obsession another. All she thought about was revenge against the celestial tower, death to the Sun Priest. It was all she wanted. More than a comfortable life, certainly more than me. And she recruited others to her cause. There was a Dry Earth Tovan, a master woodworker, who had emigrated to Cuecola and had a grudge against the priesthood; a disgraced spearmaiden driven from the war college at Hokaia for crimes of insubordination; my cousin, Balam, a proper and polished lord who found her just as enchanting as I did. He was the one who provided her the means to do it."

Balam. The name meant nothing to him. The wind rustled the pine, sending needles raining down around them. "Do what?"

"Balam had an affinity for divination and blood magic, which is not uncommon in Cuecola. But what made him special is that he had plenty of wealth to spend pursuing his interests. Soon he and Saaya were spending all their time together. I was jealous at first, oh, was I jealous. My cousin is quite charming."

"But you were wrong? They weren't lovers?"

"Oh, they were lovers," Powageh confessed ruefully. "But I did not find that out until much later. It's unimportant now. I'm old and the fires of jealousy have long banked within my heart."

"Then what?"

"Saaya told me that she and Balam were looking for a way to raise the crow god into human form using blood sacrifice."

Serapio shivered.

"Yes, I was horrified at first, too. And then intrigued. Blood magic is forbidden by the celestial tower, and all peoples of the Meridian have banned human sacrifice. It is considered uncivilized, barbaric."

"Dangerous," Serapio said, instinctively.

"Powerful," Powageh added, voice soft. "Too powerful for humans. Best we stick to sacrificing people the old ways, with wars and famine and despot rulers." Xir voice was thick with bitterness.

"What did you do?"

"I joined them," xe said simply.

"And the others joined, too?" Serapio asked, the story coming together in his mind. "Paadeh and Eedi? For common cause?"

Silence at first, and then a small laugh. "Yes, I suppose that's obvious now. Paadeh and Eedi were the other two schemers in our plan, but it was me she needed the most—the one with the gift of reading the stars, the trained priest who understood the movement of the heavens. I am ashamed to say it gave me joy, to usurp my cousin and his wealth in her hierarchy, but there it is."

"So what happened?" He had become enthralled by Powageh's story, the tale of his own making, his origin story.

"We still needed a vessel to contain the god, one that met some very specific and arcane specifications that Balam had found in an ancient glyph book, but Saaya had an answer for that, too."

"Which was . . . ?"

"You," he said. "I divined the next time and place where the crow god would be at the height of his power, Balam provided the funds to get your mother here, and Paadeh and Eedi promised to aid her in whatever way they could. She made us all swear blood oaths under a moonless sky. There are no bindings more powerful to your god."

"And my father? What role did he play in all this? Did he know?" He couldn't imagine it. He knew his father had once loved him, but after what his mother had done, his father had never recovered. Never accepted Serapio again. To hear Powageh describe his mother, he wondered if Marcal's problem was not Serapio's blindness but that he reminded his father too strongly of his lost wife.

Powageh's voice was apologetic. "Marcal was just the first acceptable Obregi to impregnate her. Wealthy enough to keep her in comfort, kind enough to protect her son once he was born. Your father was a means to an end."

Serapio pressed his lips together in displeasure. He had no love for his father, hated him and his condescension most days, but to hear him talked about like a fool, and his mother as a heartless temptress, bothered him. He wondered how much was Powageh's fabrication and how much the truth.

"Your mother was very beautiful," Powageh said, voice dreamy with remembrance. "Powerful. She burned with such a fierceness, Serapio. She swept people up in her presence. It was impossible to deny her what she wanted, and what she wanted was you."

"Not me," he countered. He remembered Powageh's words: *a vessel*.

His new tutor was silent for a moment. "You want me to reassure you that she loved you," xe said, voice low and not unkind, "but I cannot. The Saaya I knew was practical, set on vengeance and vengeance alone."

"I know she loved me," Serapio challenged, remembering the way his mother had touched his cheek, his hair. The love in her eyes as she had painted his teeth that first time, marked him with the knife. "No matter what her purpose was to begin with, I know she loved me in the end."

He could feel the weight of Powageh's gaze. It felt like pity. He didn't like it.

"Her death says otherwise. She was the human sacrifice, after all. The last link in the spell. Although . . ." Powageh's voice was thoughtful. "Perhaps it was her love for you that made her sorcery so effective in the end, Odo Sedoh."

"Odo Sedoh." He repeated the unfamiliar words. The wind caught them, tossed them through the branches of the trees, the crows cried out, seeming to speak the words back to him, and his whole body burst wide open.

As the words passed his lips, his limbs convulsed, power juddering through his bones. Cold flared inside him, freezing his blood. His skin tried to stretch, break and release the shadow that squatted inside him. He opened his mouth to scream, but no words came out. He fell over, heaving, tears of ice leaking from his eyes.

He could hear Powageh's distress faintly, indistinct noises in his ears, a hand reaching for him that he pushed aside.

"Don't. Touch," he managed. "Cold. And . . ." He panted, reaching, trying to understand. "W-w-wings?"

That was the feeling. Like wings were threatening to burst from his body, his human form ready to shatter to make way for something else entirely.

"Drink this," Powageh said, xir voice distant but urgent. Panicked. Xe held something, a clay vial, to Serapio's lips. "Drink it, Serapio. Now!"

He pried protesting lips open and let the old priest pour the liquid down his throat. He recognized the taste, even after all this time. The same drink his mother had given him on the night of the eclipse. Pale, milky poison. He swallowed, convulsing, and Powageh forced more in.

Slowly the tremors faded, his skin and muscles settled, his blood warmed to normal. He lay on his side in the winter grass, panting, shock rolling through his body like the rumble of snow loosed from the mountainside.

"What do they mean?" he finally said, gasping. "Those words. What do they mean?"

Powageh's voice was awestruck, wary. "It is the old name for the crow god, in the language of the people who became Carrion Crow. It is your true name and, obviously, not to be said lightly. At least by you."

Serapio nodded, knowing it was true. Knowing his name was power, and not the kind he could control. Knowing that uttering it was enough to unleash what was inside him.

"It is just as Saaya predicted," Powageh said. Xe chuckled softly, incredulously. "She did it. I cannot believe she did it."

What did she do?

Powageh grasped Serapio's arm and shook him hard. His teeth rattled in his head, his stomach protested around the unfamiliar foods he had consumed. He lay in the brittle grass, wrung out and helpless, shivering as the coming winter descended upon him and the old priest laughed.

"My boy," xe said, awe in xir voice, "you are more than simply a vessel. You are the weapon that will bring the Sun Priest and the Watchers to their knees."

CHAPTER 26

The Crescent Sea
Year 325 of the Sun
(9 Days before Convergence)

There are only two kinds of men: ones who betray you sooner
and ones who betray you later.

—Teek saying

Xiala wasn't sure how long she slept, but when she woke
up, it was night. She was back in Serapio's room, back on
the bedding on the floor, and she thought perhaps she had
dreamed it all. Baat's knife in her throat as she choked on her
own blood, Callo's gruesome end as his flesh was torn apart,
Serapio standing there in an unnatural wind like some dark
god made of feathers and blood and vengeance.

The wound on her throat throbbed. She pressed a hand
to the place where it burned and found a bandage, freshly
changed. She wasn't bleeding, but the wound still felt raw,
certainly real enough to prove that the slaughter of her crew
and all the rest of it was no dream.

She gingerly turned her head, hoping to find Serapio sitting on his bench like she had become so accustomed to, but she was alone.

She closed her eyes and let her mind drift. To golden sand beaches and children's unrestrained laughter. To women cleaning nets and mending thatch houses. To the smell of salt and sun and no man for a hundred miles.

Home.

Homesickness so profound it scared her, seized her heart. She wanted to go home.

But that wasn't an option.

Another vision filled her mind. Her mother, face dark as a thundercloud. Xiala, kneeling in a pool of blood not her own. The village elder, lips moving in a prayer turned curse as Xiala ran, tripping and stumbling, into the dark ocean, her tears mixing with the salt of the sea, as she swam for her life.

She drew her knees up and wrapped her arms around her legs and let tears silently flow from her eyes. After a while she fell back to sleep, but all that awaited her there were nightmares. Of blood not hers, and curses to flee, and, this time, black-winged birds.

· · · · ·

Next time she woke, she was glad for it. She forced herself up immediately, washed her face with a moistened cloth, and drank a few gulps of precious water. Then she remembered that her crew was dead and there was plenty of water for only two people, and she upended the clay flask, swallowing until it was empty.

She found him sitting on her captain's bench at stern, wrapped in his black robe, head down, forearms resting on bent knees, looking very human and very tired. She started to walk over and paused. Just to her right was the barrel of balché left over from the feast on Lost Moth. It had been shoved under a cloth tarp that had been blown ragged by the storm. She dragged off the remains of the tarp, grabbed the barrel, and walked over to sit across from the captain's bench.

Serapio didn't raise his head to acknowledge her, but he had to know she was there.

She thumbed the lid off the balché and tipped it back, letting some of the sour alcohol run down her throat. It hurt to swallow as the far-from-healed wound stretched, but the balché tasted so good that she didn't mind. After another swallow, she held the barrel out to Serapio, tapping it against his knee.

"The drink from before on the sand," he said quietly. "I recognize it. It smells terrible."

"The smell doesn't matter," she said patiently. "It's how it makes you feel afterward."

"It's alcoholic?"

"I hope so."

He shook his head. "I don't drink alcohol."

She sighed, the only icebreaker she knew thwarted. "Well, more for me, then." She tilted it back for another mouthful before setting the barrel on the bench beside her. She waited for him to say something, but he had fallen into silence again, a quiet that felt large, like he wished not to speak for a long time. Perhaps forever.

But already she was anxious. She had never been the one to let a conversational pause linger, always preferring to fill it when she could. But what should she say? Ask him if he spoke to birds and if he had meant for them to kill her crew? Inquire about his strange relationship with sudden eerie winds and disappearing suns? It all seemed preposterous and as unlikely as . . . well, as a woman who turned into a sea creature of legend. If she was honest, his apparent powers were no stranger than what had happened to her when she'd dived too deep to save Loob and the sea had transformed her. There was magic in the world, pure and simple, things she didn't understand. Best get used to it.

She chuckled under her breath.

He lifted his head now, a clear question on his face.

She grinned, remembered he couldn't see her, and said, "Here I was wondering what kind of unnatural creature you are, crow man, when I was abruptly reminded of my own peculiar nature." She shrugged and rolled a finger around the edge of the balché barrel. "I think they call that pot and fry pan alike or something."

His brow furrowed.

"Never mind," she said. "A Cuecolan saying. Something about how you and I are more the same than different."

Something in his shoulders relaxed, and a faint smile, just a lifting of lips, creased the corner of his mouth. "We are nothing alike, Xiala," he said, and there was enough regret in it, enough longing, that it didn't feel like an insult.

"You're not so special, Obregi," she said, but there was no heat to it.

Her gaze traveled around the ship, and she shivered. "All dead," she said, her voice soft with something between disbelief and regret. She took in the bloodstained canoe, the decimated cargo, the ominous creak of the ship on waves, flat and unkind. *Where have the bodies gone?* she thought to herself. *Did he remove them while I was unconscious? Throw them overboard? Or did the birds eat them all? Tendon and fat and muscle, picked down to bones.* She shook the macabre image from her head. Surely he had simply thrown them overboard.

When he spoke, his voice was a rumble, a dark beating of wings. "Men die."

She shivered and reached for the balché. "Yes, and thank you for assuring that it was not me. But . . ." Images came back unbidden. Callo's eyeless sockets, Baat's beak-shredded face. She shuddered and drank more, not caring that she was consuming too much too fast. "Perhaps next time you use a knife, yeah?"

Suddenly Serapio's hands were holding hers, warm and firm. She blinked. He had moved so fast. Had he always moved that fast, or was she already drunker than she realized? And then Serapio's face was inches from hers, so close his breath shivered across her lashes, making her blink. She thought passingly of how unerring his direction was even without seeing where she sat.

"I am sorry for your crew. They were never truly cruel to me, but they were going to kill you, and I could not let that happen."

Her heart fluttered, and heat kindled in her belly. Was he saying he cared for her? That her life mattered to him? So few people had ever cared whether she lived or died, only about what she could provide to them through her Teek talents. And a goodly half of those ended up actively wanting her dead by the time they parted ways. Was he different?

"They were indwelling bastards, all of them," she said with a shrug. "Even that fucking Callo." Her breath caught a little, and she quickly took another drink. "You did what you had to do."

They sat together for a while, neither speaking, but with Xiala steadily drinking. They were still in the doldrums—for how many days? she wondered. How long had she slept while he sat here on this flat, windless sea, waiting for her to wake up? Well, he had come to clean her wounds and give her water. She tried to remember how many times but couldn't. In fact, remembering anything at all was getting harder and harder the more balché made it down her throat. Just the way she liked it.

"Now what?" she asked, her voice slurring slightly.

He looked surprised at her question. "Tova by the Convergence," he said. "My plans have not altered."

"Sure, but . . ." She gestured expansively. "Look around, Ser. Even if I wanted to get you to Tova, I don't know where the hell it is."

His lips quirked up at the nickname, but he didn't correct her.

"There is the mouth of a great river that way," he said, lifting a hand to point slightly behind him and to the west.

"And how do you know that?"

He cocked his head. As if in response, a crow cawed out.

She turned to look behind her, too quickly, and it pulled at her wound. But there it was, a huge black body, perched on top of the shack she had been sleeping in. It spread its wings and yelled at her again, flapping for emphasis.

"Where did they all come from?" she asked, although there was only one bird on the roof.

"Land. I'd been talking to them since we left shore, but only began to rally them to us when they locked you in with me."

She imagined what that must have looked like. Hundreds of crows rising up and flying unerringly out to sea.

"Got it," she said, turning back to Serapio. "So they are like your eyes?"

"When they wish it."

"And your weapons?"

"Not my only one, but yes."

Not his only one? What other power was he hiding? She thought back to Lord Balam. Clearly she had not asked enough questions before taking on this commission.

"Okay, so your crow friends say the Tovasheh is that way. How many days?"

He pressed his lips together, thinking. "They are not always clear on the passage of time. But it should not matter. We go as quickly as we can and arrive in time for the Convergence."

"And how do we get there? I seem to have lost my crew. I don't suppose your birds can work a paddle?"

His brow creased. "No. But they have offered to make a wind . . ."

She had a vision of them arriving at port, a flock of black

birds gallantly pushing them to dock with their tiny beaks and flapping wings.

"Mother waters, no. Let me try with my Song first."

"Of course."

"But . . ." She lifted a finger. It swayed slightly before her. "I want to know why."

"Why what?"

"What's so special about Tova for you? And why must you be there by the Convergence? What is the Convergence, anyway? You keep saying that like I'm supposed to know what you're talking about." She sighed, big and gusty. "I'm done not asking questions. I want to know everything."

He was silent. Skies, the man could go silent with the best of them. She was about to concede that they were at a standstill, when he said, "A Convergence is a celestial alignment. A day when the sun, moon, and earth align, and the moon's shadow devours the sun."

"A black sun," she said, nodding. "That's what the Teek call it. They are rare."

"Rare, yes, but this one is the rarest of all. This Convergence will happen over Tova on the winter solstice when the sun is already vulnerable. A Convergence has not been seen in Tova in almost four hundred years, and never on the winter solstice. Truly, the sun's power will be at its weakest in a millennium."

"And why must you be there?" Even as she asked, she thought of the way the sun seemed to shudder when it first saw him, hide from him when he was in his power. Which sounded ridiculous, as she was deeply aware. But she had felt it; the sun feared him.

"I have a meeting I must keep on that day."

"With the sun?"

"With the sun's priest."

"Why?"

He didn't answer. Just pulled her hands to his mouth and pressed them against his warm lips. Her heartbeat quickened, and a mild tingle raced across the back of her neck, as if he had whispered something against her skin. She shivered, more pleasure than fear.

"Can you get us to Tova, Xiala?" he asked, voice low and fervent. "Can you call the sea with your Song and get us to the Tovasheh?"

"I . . ." She suddenly felt very drunk, as if the balché hit her all at once. And with the feeling of Serapio's lips lingering against her knuckles and his words still in her ears, she knew she was about to do something foolish. A small voice in her head reminded her that he was dangerous, and she knew little about him. But that wasn't true. She knew he had a sense of humor, although he hid it well, that he had never seen a naked woman, that he had nursed her wound back to health, and that, most of all, he had saved her life.

"I'll get us to the Tovasheh," she agreed.

And then, because of the balché and because of the shock and because she was grieving the loss of her crew—even superstitious Callo and murderous Baat and Patu's eggs and fruit—and because she'd been very much wanting to for almost a week, she leaned in, a matter of only a few feet, and kissed him.

He resisted at first, as if confused, and she wondered if he'd ever been kissed. But then his mouth softened and returned her interest. She climbed onto his lap, straddling his thighs, and kissed him some more. It felt good. His skin was cool, like a welcomed drink of cold water after a day's work in the summer sun. And he was clumsy, not fatally so but clearly inexperienced, and she liked that, liked that she had the upper hand, that his reaction was so very human. And he felt good and solid and real, his chest against hers, her arms around him, and as long as she was kissing him, she didn't have to think of impossible sea voyages and dead crewmen and swarms of black birds, just her and this man who she wasn't sure was a hero or a villain, but maybe she didn't have to know if only she could get his robe off and—

He stood abruptly, and she rose with him, legs wrapping around his waist.

"Xiala," he murmured, "I can't." He drew his mouth away. She leaned in, aching, not wanting this feeling to end, wanting just a little oblivion between the balché and two bodies, but he pulled back and turned his head.

"Fuck," she said, dropping her feet to the deck and her arms to her side.

"I can't."

She laughed, pretty sure he had taken her expletive literally. Her laugh turned into a hiccup and then a sigh. "Religious affliction?" she asked.

"What?"

"Nothing."

She stood there awkwardly, eyes downcast, the heat of embarrassment coloring her cheeks. Grateful that perhaps he couldn't see her. But who was she kidding? He was studying her. Listening to her heartbeat, sensing her growing mortification, smelling her arousal or whatever he did to read her so well without the benefit of sight. She thought seriously about having more balché to numb her embarrassment but decided against it, and then commended herself for her amazing feat of will.

"Tova," he said, urgent.

She glanced up. His hair was tousled from her hands, his lips slightly swollen from being pressed against hers. Definitely a man but perhaps a bit of a monster, too? The same could be said of her. And did it matter at all, these labels and categories, when it was just the two of them here, together?

"I'll get you to your meeting with the Sun Priest," she said finally. "I made a promise, after all."

He seemed satisfied by that. "Do you want to tell me a story?"

She squeezed her eyes shut, surprised at his request. "No, Serapio," she said, another laugh wanting to break free from the hurt place in her heart. "No stories tonight."

"All right. Shall I sit with you, anyway? While you Sing to the sea?"

She rubbed at her missing pinkie joint. He was dangerous, unfathomably attractive, and clearly on some single-minded mission that made him entirely unavailable. *Oh, Xiala*, she thought, *tell him to go away. Say no. Say. No.*

"Sure." She dropped to the captain's bench and patted the space next to her. "I've even got a story for you. About a doomed mermaid and the mysterious lover who rejects her. You'll like it. I swear."

CHAPTER 27

CITY OF TOVA (COYOTE'S MAW)
YEAR 325 OF THE SUN
(8 DAYS BEFORE CONVERGENCE)

> The people of Tova have a love for gameplay. It is manifested most in the varied gambling houses of Coyote's Maw, and in a very popular dice game called patol. Patol is as popular in Tova as the ball court is in Cuecola. I thought the game only an amusement at first, but my host informed me that the play itself was sacred. They consider it another way to unite earth to the heavens. I pointed out that it was most often played for cacao. He adamantly objected and explained the philosophy to me and with all due patience, but I failed to understand.
>
> —*A Commissioned Report of My Travels*
> *to the Seven Merchant Lords of Cuecola,*
> by Jutik, a Traveler from Barach

Naranpa thought the golden-haired man would lead her to the balcony where the bosses sat, but instead he took her farther into the gambling house, well past the half-circle walls that marked the front of the roundhouse. Slowly, the crowd thinned, patrons and runners and the smell of drink giving way to empty halls, the scent of earth, and semidarkness.

Resin lanterns were staggered along the floor to light the way. They glowed faintly, only enough to show one where their feet should go. They didn't ward off the foreboding growing inside her, and it did nothing to counter the reality of going farther underground. Adrenaline from the patol table still lingered in her veins, but now it was making her tired, disoriented, wary of every shadow. The ground sloped down, deeper into the heart of the Maw.

The man glanced over his shoulder once to check on her. She gave him a reassuring nod, but he had already turned away. She found herself struggling with the limited air. *Breathe like a Dry Earther*, she admonished herself. *The air is less here, so deep into the rock. So stop gulping like a spoiled Sky Made. Have you been away that long, Nara?*

"How much farther?" she finally asked, her voice thin.

"Not much farther."

She forced herself to concentrate and mark the route in her head, a thing she'd done hundreds of times as a child. Back then, it had been instinctual, but now she found it exceedingly difficult. Before long she couldn't remember which way they'd come, and she was quite sure she would not be able to find her way back alone.

This is on purpose, she thought, *to intimidate me. Remind me that I have no power here. That this place is not mine anymore.*

They came to an abrupt halt. "Here," he commanded.

She peered through the shadows. "Where?"

He gestured her forward, but she couldn't see anywhere to go until she looked down.

They stood at the lip of a hole. She saw now that there was a ladder protruding from the opening. Narrow wooden poles stretching up to her knees. She would have to sit with her feet dangling over the edge, reach forward until she was almost falling, and grab the poles.

"You want me to climb that?" she asked, disbelieving.

He nodded.

"Is there another way?" She thought of her adventure on the tower wall earlier. After all the walking to get to the Maw, she was already fatigued and dreaded scaling that wall again upon her return.

"I am instructed to tell you that the true Nara could climb anything."

She barked a laugh. "That was twenty years ago," she protested.

"Twenty-three," a voice called, so loud and clear she could have sworn the speaker was standing next to her. "Come down, Sister."

"Denaochi?"

"You've gone to all this trouble to find me," her brother said, amusement in his voice. "What's a few more steps?"

She looked at her guide, but he stood, implacable.

A game. Denaochi was playing a game with her. Fine. She would play.

She sat, grimacing at how hard it was to lower herself to the floor with any sense of dignity. She let herself fall forward and grabbed for the poles. Her whole body followed, too fast, and she slammed into the ladder, a curse on her lips. She scrambled until one foot was planted on the first rung. And then the other. The narrow rungs dug uncomfortably into her feet, her climbing shoes offering little protection.

The climb was shorter than she anticipated, a mere six steps down into the darkness. She could still see golden-hair above her, almost close enough to reach out and touch his foot if she'd been a bit taller. There was a tunnel to her right, the entrance just high enough that she didn't have to duck to go through. But she was short. Most people would have to bend their necks, perhaps even hunch their backs, to enter. *He makes them come to him humbled*, she thought.

She walked through, but just like the climb down, the passage was brief, and after only a handful of steps, the space opened wide.

She stood in a room bigger than most in the Maw. Certainly bigger than the two-room cave house she had grown up in. It was twenty paces across both ways, and resin lanterns hung from the ceiling well above her head and diffused soft light down into the room. It was spacious and well lit by Maw standards, but still small and claustrophobic to her acquired Sky Made sensibilities. There was a large table that served as a desk in the center of the room, and behind it stood a seat-backed chair of foreign import. A Tovan-style bench sat in front for guests. She sensed more than saw someone in the far corner of the room, seated on the floor. They were hidden in the shadows, clearly an observer, perhaps some kind of security. But she didn't have time to analyze it further as her little brother, and it could only be him, greeted her.

"Welcome, Sun Priest," he said, his tone wide and mocking. "I would have had a feast prepared, but I didn't know you were coming."

She ignored his jibe. She had expected as much, and likely deserved it. What she hadn't expected was the flood of emotions that threatened to overwhelm her. Her breath caught in her throat, and she blinked rapidly, fighting back sudden tears.

She hadn't seen him since he was six, but she would have recognized him anywhere. It was those eyes. Big and black and liquid, ringed by delicate lashes even now. Her mother had always said Denaochi had the prettiest eyes of them all. He had been a lovely child, but now, as an adult, she could see that much of that loveliness had long been driven out of him. He was lean now, the way the coyotes on the eastern plains were lean in winter. He looked hollowed out, a man of perpetual hunger. His black hair was greased back from his face and razored short above his ears. A long thick scar cut across one cheek from ear to nose, proof that someone had once come close to killing him. He wore a lip plug and matching jade earrings. Layers of jade, turquoise, and coral necklaces looped his corded neck over an elaborately embroidered shirt. An expensive mantle of porcupine quills splayed out across the back of his chair.

"Ochi," she said, opting to greet him by his childhood nickname.

He stared. "Are you crying, dear sister?"

"It is good to see you," she said, simply. "I have missed you."

He scoffed, but there was something rough in his voice. Grief of his own? She could only hope.

"Are we starting our reunion with lies, then?" he asked.

She flinched. Of course, he was bitter. He had every right. She had left at the first opportunity and never looked back. "I truly mean it. It has been too long."

"Twenty-three years by my count. I could possibly provide you with the exact day count, to the hour, if you like." He leaned forward, folding his hands on the desk before him. "But keeping calendars is your job, is it not, Priest?"

She made herself walk to the bench and sit across from him. This close, Naranpa noticed that he was missing three fingers on his right hand, two completely and one cut off at the second knuckle, and his hands themselves were riddled with burn scars, as if they had been held in a fire.

She suppressed a shudder. His eyes flickered, as if he had caught her gawking.

"Do you hate me, then?" she asked.

"Yes," he said, gaze meeting hers, "but I understand why you left us. I would have done the same had I been given the chance."

She closed her eyes. She had meant to come to her brother unbent, proud of her decision to get out and never look back, of her years of service to the priesthood. But she had been lying to herself, and all the shame of her abandonment overwhelmed her. "I am sorry I left you alone."

"Alone?" He slammed a hand against the desk so hard she jumped. Whoever, or whatever, sat in the shadowy corner behind him startled, too, letting loose a small chittering cry. It made the hair on Naranpa's neck rise. "You misunderstand, Sister. I was never alone."

"But . . . didn't they die?"

"They? You can't even bring yourself to say their names? Do you mean your forgotten family?"

She raised her head. "They were never forgotten!"

He wagged a finger at her. "See? I knew it. I told Mama that Nara would never forget us. Off to her fancy tower, a place among the Sky Made, but she was a good girl and would never forget her family. I kept telling her that on her deathbed, in fact, as the coughs rattled through her lungs and stole her away." His voice had grown cold. "And when a boss tossed Akel from the cliffs for skimming his winnings to pay for Mama's medicine, I told her that again. And when that same boss showed up at our door and demanded payment, and the only thing we had to pay with was me, I told her then, too. And when that first Sky Made scion offered more cacao than we'd seen in a year for one night with me in that pleasure house, I know for a fact that I whispered that to the pillow he held against my face."

A wave of nausea rolled over her. "You worked the pleasure houses?" Now her memories of what a beautiful boy he had been seemed sinister, tainted.

"Is that so shocking? The Maw makes all of us whores for the Sky Made."

Is that what he thought of the priesthood? Whores for the Sky Made?

"Not always by choice, I admit," he continued, his voice still dispassionate, as if simply catching up with an old friend. "And only until they realized that I had a taste for more violent bed play. For a while, that became my salvation, I'll not deny it, and I served my time in houses that catered to clients of particular taste, but then I met a man who paid my debt."

"To own you?"

"On the contrary," Denaochi said. "To set me free." He smiled, but it was a bitter thing, twisted and dark, and she knew for a fact that the benefactor, if that's what he had been, was dead by Denaochi's hand. No, this was not her sweet little brother anymore. The suffering she had left in her wake had formed him, warped him into who he was. Was this her fault? Her doing? Or would it have all happened the same with her there? Would she have been the one taken into the pleasure houses to pay Akel's debt instead? Would she be the murderer with blood on her hands?

Her brother straightened on a deep inhale, eyelids fluttering open and closed. "My apologies. My anger makes me lose myself. I was a child then, but that was a long time ago. Nevertheless, seeing you again, after all these years . . ."

She bowed her head, more tears lining her eyes and her hands folded in her lap. "I was a child, too," she whispered. "A selfish one. And I am sorry."

He leaned back, watching her. Looked as if he might speak again, but instead clapped his hands to break the dark spell his memories had woven around them.

"But we are children no longer," he said with another breathy laugh. "Either of us. Look what you've become." He gestured expansively. "The fucking Sun Priest of Tova!"

Not anymore, she thought. She said, "And you, the most notorious crime boss in the Maw."

"You flatter me," he said, a smile as cold and insincere as any the Sky Made matrons had mastered twisting his mouth.

And suddenly Naranpa realized she had made a mistake seeking out her brother, as if after all this time they would know each other at all, and that he would have any sympathy for her. It was folly of the highest order. Arrogance on her part, even.

But you are here for a reason, Nara, she reminded herself. *A reason bigger than your shame and discomfort with your past.* She had shrunk down in her seat as if his words had been physical blows for her to dodge, but now she straightened. She took a deep breath before she spoke.

"I've come because I need your help."

Denaochi steepled his fists under his chin and leaned forward. "I'm listening."

She could feel sweat on the back of her neck, and her heart raced under his gaze, but she forced herself to keep going. "Tova is in danger. And it needs your help."

"The *city* needs my help?" His voice was flat with disbelief. "I thought you said that *you* needed my help."

"Yes, *I* need your help," she admitted. "In order to help the city," she added hastily. "I need you to help me help the city."

A lopsided smile curved his lips. "What could I possibly offer the Sun Priest? You have assassins at your call, healers to do your bidding. The Sky Made matrons don't take a shit without consulting your star charts. What help could I give you? I'm sorry, the *city*. Unless . . . it's these very people who are the problem."

She swallowed.

"That's what it is, isn't it?" he said, voice soft with surprise. "You've been betrayed."

She thought he would laugh, mock her for her humiliation, but he only stared.

She smoothed her hands across her lap. "I seem to have acquired quite a few enemies, it's true."

"Anyone who rises as you have will collect them like flies." He leaned back, fingers tapping against his chin. "They hate you, don't they? Because you're not Sky Made, no matter how hard you try. You can't quite wash that Dry Earth stink off your skin, can you, Sister?"

She did not enjoy his all-too-prescient insight, but she knew he was not wrong. "I have had my challenges in the tower, I admit, but I want to be clear, Ochi. I am not here for me. I came to you because the city—"

He waved a hand, rolling his eyes toward the ceiling. "Oh, this talk of the city. I know you mean it, Nara. I see your sincerity. But they're trying to kill you, aren't they? Your precious priesthood wants you dead."

She shook her head. "Not the priesthood. The Crow cultists. An assassination attempt was made on my life. Two attempts. We caught the last man. He was killed before he could be questioned properly, but he bore the haahan."

"Carrion Crow does hate you," he acknowledged with a little more speed than she liked. "They would not hesitate to murder the Sun Priest, slaughter the whole tower if they thought they could get away with it. But they are much too smart to attempt an outright assassination. They know the other clans would turn against them. Plus, they bide their time for spiritual reasons."

"Waiting for the return of their god," she said, waving the nonsense away like the delusion it was.

"Be glad they've put their vengeance in the hands of an angry god and not taken up knives against you."

"You just said they weren't fools. Taking up weapons against the tower would be foolish, indeed."

"Exactly. I would suggest that if someone is trying to kill you, then you look a little closer to home."

She knew what he was implying, but it sounded preposterous, particularly in light of her recent dethroning. "If the priesthood wanted me dead, they have a hundred times a day to kill me in a myriad of ways."

"Ah, would any of them put the blame on Carrion Crow? But with the murder of their matron, perhaps they have decided they can no longer wait."

Had she heard him right? A chill slid down her back. "Yatliza died in her bed."

He *tsk*ed, waving a finger at her. "They pulled her body from the river. I have people close to every matron who report to me. It is the truth, although Carrion Crow is trying their best to keep it secret. The new matron and her Shield are no friends to the cultists, and my guess is if the cultists knew their matron had been murdered, Tova would run with blood. Their own blood, perhaps, but the damage would be done either way."

"But . . ." She shook her head. Murdered? "That can't be right." Skies, did Iktan know? She flushed, feeling like a fool. Of course Iktan knew. The question was why xe hadn't told her.

Denaochi narrowed his eyes, at first in confusion and then in mirth. "You really didn't know? How interesting. I assumed the priesthood were the ones responsible for her death." He smiled, darkly amused. "I think you've been trusting the wrong people, Sister. But, you see, you're not entirely wrong about Tova being in danger. There's a storm coming, true enough, but not from where you think."

CHAPTER 28

CITY OF TOVA (COYOTE'S MAW)
YEAR 325 OF THE SUN
(8 DAYS BEFORE CONVERGENCE)

> It is imperative that the dedicant forsake the kinship and du-
> ties that bound them before they joined the priesthood. Their
> only loyalty must be to their fellows within the celestial tower,
> else they risk crossed purposes and their true path becomes
> occluded by sentiment.
>
> —*The Manual of the Sun Priest*

Naranpa sat back, her mind racing. She had thought her situation complicated before, but she had only glimpsed the surface. Denaochi could see the entire cliffside.

He was up, pacing the room. She noticed he had a slight
limp, a drag to his left leg, and she pressed her lips together
to keep from asking. Another memento of his life, along with
the scar on his face and the missing fingers and burned hands,
no doubt. And all at once, again, her heart ached for the boy
he had been.

She knew she couldn't trust him. His indictment of her

was too fresh, his disdain for the priesthood too bitter. But she had come this far, and despite it all, he was helping her. And he knew things, had a grasp of the city that she from her tower did not. So she made a decision.

"There's something else you should know. The real reason I had to come to you, which now seems all too obvious."

He turned to her, his face a mask of suspicion.

"There are those in the tower who are advocating for the Knives to retaliate against Carrion Crow with the aid of Golden Eagle. Perhaps other clans, too, I don't know. Although I don't think Water Strider is part of their plans."

Denaochi nodded, as if her news didn't surprise him. "How long do we have before they act?"

"Surely until the solstice. They only decided yesterday after the riots. Right before they stripped me of my title and locked me in my room."

Her brother laughed, a low dry chuckle. "Well, well."

She swallowed back her embarrassment and focused on what was important. "We can't let another Night of Knives happen. It will rip the city apart."

"You may not believe it, but the bosses of the Maw care about this city, too. I know I disparaged your concerns earlier, but civil unrest does none of us any good. It hurts business, scares away pilgrims and tourists with cacao, particularly before the solstice. Whether the violence starts with the Odohaa or the priests, another Night of Knives would be the end of us all. Tova would not recover. The Crescent cities already regard us like a ripe fruit, waiting to pick us apart. Cuecola chafes at our yoke, and Hokaia would follow if they broke from the treaty. The Sky Made need only to make one foolish move to put us all at risk, and this infighting would do it."

Naranpa hadn't even thought about Cuecola and Hokaia. "Skies, Ochi. Have the Sky Made and the Watchers become so insular? So ignorant of what truly threatens us?"

His eyes bored into her, evaluating. The same look she had given him moments ago, before she decided to confess the entirety of her situation. She braced herself.

"You mentioned Golden Eagle before," he said, "that they have involved themselves. Perhaps the Sky Made know something of what's at stake and have plans of their own."

A wave of insight hit her. She felt like a fool. She accused the priesthood of being too focused inward, content to uphold the status quo, but she had been guilty of the same thing. Unable to look past Tova's nose and see the continent gathering at their doorstep.

"So what do you suggest we do?" she asked.

He snapped his fingers, the ones on his good hand, and called a name.

A sound from the shadowy corner where she had marked a presence and then forgotten it in the heat of their confrontation. A figure unwound itself from the darkness, pulling itself forward inch by inch until it resolved into a human shape, and then a woman.

She was neither plain nor beautiful, a bit like Naranpa herself, but where Naranpa was short, this woman was tall, and where she was rounded, this woman possessed a long, lean hunger much like Denaochi's own. Her hair was cut to the skin, and she wore a dress that covered her from neck to feet in a dark brown the color of river silt. She smiled, show-ing teeth.

"Tell her what you have seen in your castings, Zataya."

Naranpa's jaw dropped. "A witch?"

"She is my counselor," he said. "I trust her."

"Ochi . . ." Naranpa said, shaking her head. For a mo-ment there she had admired her brother, been impressed with his knowledge and savvy. But this? "Magic is a foolish man's crutch. It's nothing but sleight of hand and superstition."

The witch straightened, a flash of annoyance rippling across her shoulders. "You are not the only one who has learned to read the future," she said. "You may look to the stars, but we of the Dry Earth look to other signs. Fire and stone speak, too."

"Witchcraft," Naranpa accused. "It's not the science of the priesthood."

"Nara, please," her brother said, clearly exasperated. "You came to me for help. Keep an open mind."

"An open mind is one thing. But you are asking me to believe in folly." She started to stand. "I can no more bel—"

"You can!" he shouted, and she froze, startled to silence. "You can," he said, quieter, calmer. "If you want to save your-self and this city, you will listen, Sister. And you will remem-ber that while you have convinced yourself that you are Sky Made, you were born Dry Earth. This"—he gestured to the witch—"is who you are, not that tower. Now . . ." He ges-tured to her seat.

Stunned, Naranpa dropped back onto the bench.

Her brother ran a hand over his necklaces, as if the stones soothed him. He nodded. "Continue, Zataya."

"I have read the fire," she said, "and looked into the shadow." She pulled a palm-sized mirror pendant from her clothes and grasped it in her left hand. Naranpa shifted uneasily. She recognized the mirror as a scrying mirror, something used by the southern sorcerers.

"That's not Dry Earth magic," she murmured.

"Wait," Denaochi said.

Zataya closed her eyes and whispered an incantation. Naranpa strained to hear the words, but the witch's voice was too low for Naranpa to decipher.

Again, she repeated the chant, a soft buzzing hiss that filled the room.

They waited.

Again, the incantation. And again. Sweat touched the witch's hairline, her neck. She swayed on her feet.

Naranpa looked to her brother again, but he motioned her to patience.

Finally, Zataya spoke, her voice dark and sepulchrous. "A storm is coming across the water, and it does not rest!" she cried. "Dark forces from the south are gathering. As the sun grows weaker, he grows stronger."

Naranpa frowned. It sounded like theatrical nonsense. "I don't understand." She looked to Denaochi. "Who is he? And where in the south? Are we still talking about Cuecola? Can she see anything about Carrion Crow? What about Golden Eagle?"

"One question at a time," Denaochi murmured.

"All right. Who is he?"

Denaochi nodded. "Zataya?" her brother asked.

The witch seemed to focus harder, and now the tremors that rolled through her body were clearly visible. Naranpa's eyes widened as blood dripped from Zataya's hand. She must have cut herself on the mirror glass.

She opened her mouth to say something, but Denaochi shook his head. The lights above them wavered, sending shadows cavorting across the room. Naranpa rubbed her hands against her suddenly cold arms.

"What is happening?" she asked, her voice a whisper.

Zataya moaned, a low painful sound. Blood continued to leak from the hand that gripped the mirror. Her moan turned into a wail. The cords in her neck stretched.

"Stop her, Ochi," Naranpa said, nervous.

"She must finish."

"Finish what? She's hurting herself!"

"Leave it, Nara."

"No! This is reckless." She stood, ready to go to the woman and shake her free of whatever trance had possessed her. But before Naranpa could reach her, Zataya collapsed, falling to the floor in a heap. Naranpa reached to help her up, but the witch held out a bloody hand to stop her.

"Skies, Ochi! At least get her a bandage," she said.

"She's fine," he growled.

Another shudder rocked Zataya's shoulders. This was madness. They were both mad. Finally, Zataya opened her eyes. All Naranpa saw there was frustration.

"Well?" Denaochi asked, leaning forward.

The witch shook her head. "I cannot see the tool, only the result," she said, panting. "He's coming, and he brings the storm, but he travels in shadow. I can't see through the shadow." She looked at Naranpa. "But I did see something else."

Naranpa shifted uneasily. She didn't believe, but she didn't quite disbelieve, either.

"What?" Denaochi asked, eager.

"I have foreseen the death of the Sun Priest."

Brother and sister exchanged a look.

"And a way to stop it?" Denaochi asked.

The witch pressed herself to standing. She wobbled, unsteady, and Naranpa thought to help her, but again, she was rebuffed. Zataya made her way to the desk, where she pulled a handful of objects from a bag at her waist and dumped them on the desk. She rummaged through them with bloody fingers until she found what she wanted. First was a string necklace with a small figurine hanging on a pendant. Naranpa recognized it as her game piece from the patol table, the small obsidian bison.

"How did you get that?" Naranpa asked.

Zataya ignored her. Next, she held up a thorn. No, it was a stingray spine, twice as long as her hand and bone-white. A tool of the southern sorcerers and their bloodletting rituals.

"I'm not giving you my blood," she said flatly.

"You will if you want to live," Zataya shot back, her voice returned to normal and her strength apparently restored as well.

Naranpa glared at her brother. He spread his hands, blameless.

"No," she said.

"Nara, it's not so hard. Zataya knows what's she's doing, and right now she's trying to save your life."

"Your tongue, Priest."

Naranpa felt nauseated. At the prospect of sticking that spine through her tongue, yes, but also at the very idea of witchcraft. She had been taught it was not only false but anathema to the priesthood and their way of life. But then again, she had come this far, what was a little further?

She stuck her tongue out. The witch ran the spine through, quick and practiced. Naranpa's eyes watered, but the pain was brief and not as terrible as she had expected. Zataya caught Naranpa's blood in a small clay bowl and took it back to the desk. She placed the small bison figurine in the bowl, letting the carving soak in her blood. Once it was coated, she removed it and strung it onto the necklace. She held the necklace out to Naranpa, who slid it over her neck.

"What does it do?" she asked.

"As long as you wear it, I will hear you say my name and be able to find you no matter where you are."

"I thought you said this would keep me alive."

"This is all I can offer."

"But it's nothing!" she protested.

"Death comes for you, Priest, and soon. When it is inescapable, call for me, and I will find you."

Naranpa cupped the bison in her palm, doubtful.

"You can stay here, Nara," Denaochi said. "You can be done with that tower and those people. There is a place for you at my side, if you wish it. We can weather the coming storm together."

She looked up. He was watching her, face a mask. Part of her ached to stay, to run from the tower and never look back. But wasn't that what she had done as a child? She would not do it again. "I have to go back. But can you do one thing for me?"

His mask did not shift, but she could see she had disappointed him. Nevertheless, he said, "Name it."

"You mentioned you had someone close to Carrion Crow. Can you deliver a message for me? Written," she added. "You have that, do you not?"

Denaochi gave her a small mocking bow. He produced paper, ink, and a writing instrument from his desk. She thought he might be the kind of man who did not trust others to keep his records.

She sat, thinking of what she wanted to say.

She was taking a chance, assuming he could read. But he had been at the war college, so perhaps it was not such a risk to think he could understand written language. She wrote her message out in simple glyphs, folded the paper, and sealed it. She handed it to her brother.

"As soon as possible," she said. "To the son."

"I'll see it in his hands today," he agreed. "What will you do in the meantime?"

"I'll do what I've always done." She glanced briefly at Zataya. "Survive."

CHAPTER 29

THE TOVASHEH RIVER

YEAR 325 OF THE SUN

(4 DAYS BEFORE CONVERGENCE)

> Tovasheh is a terrible place. The rain is unceasing, and the food consists of things one draws up from its swampy environs. I do not recommend it.
>
> —*A Commissioned Report of My Travels*
> *to the Seven Merchant Lords of Cuecola,*
> by Jutik, a Traveler from Barach

The port city of Tovasheh stretched before them, a series of low wood and stone buildings in a sparsely populated mile of marshy delta. Winter had settled in along the more northern coast of the Crescent Sea, and the tropical climes of Cuecola had been replaced with reed-heavy wetlands that gave way to rocky yellow hills in the fog-shrouded distance. Ubiquitous clouds delivered a light but steady misting of chilling rain that didn't so much soak the landscape as continuously moisten it.

Xiala pulled a makeshift blanket around her, wet and miserable. She had salvaged it from the tarp that covered what was left of their cargo. It was stiff and none too warm, but it kept the rain out, and it was safer than using any clothing the crew had left behind. So far it seemed that her and Serapio's imprisonment had saved them from exposure to whatever illness had taken Patu, but she didn't want to take chances. Still, the blanket smelled musty and too well used for her liking. She still wore Serapio's extra clothes, but they were dirty, bloodstained, and getting musty, too.

"This town better have baths," she muttered to herself as she guided them in.

Annoyingly, the weather seemed to have put Serapio in a good mood. He stood at the bow of the ship with his cowl down, facing into the rain. The rain dewed his face and clung to his curling black hair in droplets. Some of his crows had returned, and they circled around him, taking turns landing on his outstretched hand to be petted. He stroked their long smooth feathers and murmured happy sweet nothings to them. They cawed back their pleasure loudly.

The docks resolved out of the mist, long log platforms stretching out from sediment mounds. Most were empty, and at first Xiala worried that some ill had befallen the city, but then she remembered that it was winter, and no ships were fool enough to travel the Crescent Sea this time of year. In fact, most were in dry dock somewhere, busied with repairs and waiting for spring.

"Like sane people," she commented, again, to herself.

She brought the canoe parallel to a platform, and Serapio jumped lightly from the deck, rope in hand, to secure the ship. He had assured her he could do the work, particularly with his crows helping him see, and she had taken his word for it.

She did the same, tying off the stern at the back thwart.

"I'll have to find the harbormaster," she said as she approached Serapio. "Maybe hire a few dockers to unload the cargo we have left. And a place to sell it, of course." She glanced at the sky. They had arrived late in the day. It would be dark in a few hours. Whatever she was going to do would take time, and she was running out of it. They could always sleep on the canoe again, but she was determined to find a bath and a bed.

"Do not forget we must be in Tova in four days." Serapio finished tying off the center thwart. She watched his hands work the rope, long fingers deft and competent. "That must be our priority."

"I thought Obregi didn't have ships," she said, surprised at his efficiency. "That's a solid knot." She reached out and tested it.

"We don't," he said, stepping back, "but I worked wood for a long time. Rope is not so difficult."

She grunted, impressed. "Secret talents."

He paused, face turning toward hers. "Yes," he said, in that way he had, as if she had accidentally stumbled upon a profound truth, but he didn't elaborate.

"And no, I've not forgotten. No haggling, just . . . sell." She winced when she said it.

He made a dry sound that could have passed for a laugh.

She straightened and looked around. Nothing but fog. "Where is that harbormaster?"

"I'm going to find us transportation upriver while you find the harbormaster."

She tilted her head, squinting. She had become accustomed to him in their days together, but he was still a sight. Black robe, red teeth, the cloth around his eyes. Even with all his haahan mostly covered, he was very, very strange. But then again, perhaps they were close enough to Tova that he'd blend in better than she did. Who knew? Maybe everyone in the Holy City looked like Serapio.

Mother waters, she hoped not. Not because he was strange, but because she was having enough trouble not wanting to constantly touch him, feel his smooth skin again, the rough scarring of his haahan, the salt in his lips, the feel of his hands.

"All right," she said briskly, already regretting letting her mind wander, "you go. I'll do the rest. Where should we meet?"

"I'll send a crow to find you." He shouldered an oversized travel bag and picked up a bone staff. She'd noticed the staff in his room on the ship, but she had never seen him use it. Perhaps the ship was small enough that he didn't need it. It looked part walking stick and part weapon, and he handled it well.

"Crows can do that?"

"Of course." And then he was walking away, staff in hand, travel pack on his back, his crows following.

• • • • •

She didn't find the harbormaster, but she did find a fisherman, a short boxy fellow morosely casting a net off one of the outlying piers. She traded a barrel of salted fish they no longer needed for directions to the harbormaster's home. It wasn't far, and she trudged through the empty fog-filled streets, wondering why she bothered. Did she think she would be able to return to Balam after this? Sell the cargo and stay in Tova or in this apparent craphole until spring and then return with a fresh crew and full purses? And what of Serapio? She hadn't let herself think past the Convergence, but now that it was imminent, she realized she didn't want to leave him. Not that she was attached, because she wasn't. Or at least, not that way. She didn't get attached. But he did intrigue her with his secrets, and they had an undeniable kinship, a shared connection. She didn't know what she wanted exactly, but she knew she wanted . . . more.

She found the house the fisherman had described and knocked on the door. After a moment, a woman answered. She was dark-skinned, darker than Xiala, and she wore her orange-colored hair in an elaborate bun atop her head. Xiala couldn't place her origin immediately. Somewhere on the continent, but that was about it.

She looked Xiala up and down, clearly judging her shoddy clothing and generally bedraggled looks.

"I'm looking for the harbormaster," Xiala said. "I was told he lived here."

"She lives here," the woman corrected her. "I'm the harbormaster."

Xiala managed a genuine grin. She had gotten used to Cuecola, where men seemed to hold most of the power. It was nice to be back on this side of the Crescent Sea, where women were often in charge.

"My apologies," she said. "I've just come into port. I'm docked out at the far pier. I've got some cargo to offload and . . ."

The woman had raised a skeptical eyebrow, hands on her hips. "You came in from sea? Just now? All by yourself?"

Xiala had known this question would come and had an answer with enough truth to it to feel authentic. "I had a crew. We set out from Cuecola, but most were lost at sea during a shipkiller. I and another survived, but the rest . . ." She lowered her head, and the sadness she felt for Loob and for others, even Callo, was real. Baat and Patu could rot in hell. "We were lucky to find shore."

"What fool lord sent you out in winter on the Crescent Sea?" the harbormaster asked, sounding outraged. "He must have been desperate."

"I just want to sell what's left of the cargo," Xiala explained. "Find a steam bath and a soft bed." She let some of her real desperation show through.

The woman's eyes narrowed. Xiala caught a glint of greed there. Ah, yes. That should help push things along.

"Come back tomorrow, then," the woman said. "I'll have dockhands to unload your cargo and find you a buyer. It's hard this time of year, but there'll be a few who want a jump on the season. Especially with what's happened in Tova."

Xiala frowned. "What's happened in Tova?"

"Tomorrow," the woman said, and made to shut the door.

"Wait!" She stopped the door with an outstretched hand. "Tomorrow's too late. I need to make a deal tonight."

"There's no one—"

"Please! I'll take . . ." She took a deep breath and steeled herself. "I'll take half of what you would normally offer. If we can strike the deal tonight."

The harbormaster paused.

"I'll throw in the ship," she added.

"Your ship that's been through a storm big enough to kill your crew?" The woman crossed her arms and glared down her nose. "The one that's likely ravaged and haunted?"

"For free." And stars and skies, that hurt. She tried not to wince. Serapio owed her on principle alone.

The harbormaster hesitated a moment before letting out an unimpressed snort. She disappeared inside while Xiala waited at the door, coming back a few minutes later in a wool cloak that kept out the drizzle and cold.

Xiala eyed her enviously. "Don't suppose you have one of those you want to sell?" she asked.

"Let me see your ship and cargo," the woman said. "If I like them enough to pay, I'll throw in the cloak for free."

It was as good an offer as she was going to get under the circumstances, so Xiala led the harbormaster back through the soggy evening to the pier where she'd left her hopes and dreams.

• • • • •

An hour later, Xiala was following a crow along the banks of one of the many inlet streams that ran through Tovasheh. The weather had settled in, finally turning to a steady rain, and she pulled up the hood of her new wool cloak and hugged it tight around her shivering body. In her hand she carried a bottle of xtabentún. The xtabentún was all she'd kept of the cargo she'd sold to the harbormaster. No personal belongings, no clothes. Nothing to her name, quite literally.

What's wrong with you, Xiala, she told herself as she drank from the bottle, *is that you can't keep a handful of cacao in your purse for more than a day, or a place to rest your head for a week*. And whose fault was that but her own? She wanted to blame it on her poor luck, on a faithless crew or a cursed deal. But this wasn't the first time she'd found herself reduced to a bottle of liquor and the clothes on her back. There was something else deeply wrong with her, something she had no desire to examine with any rigor. *At least this time*, she thought brightly, *you're not in jail and you're not alone*. It wasn't much, but it was something.

A barge came into view, a low flat-bottomed vessel anchored against the natural riverbank. Resin lanterns hung from poles at its fore and aft, and a rung ladder offered entrance down the embankment to the deck. It loosely resembled the fine canoe she'd just sold for nothing, but it was only half the length, and the majority of the black-washed deck was enclosed, leaving only a narrow expanse exposed on either side and a larger area at the stern that was wide enough for a gathering. The barge was attached to a harness, now empty, that faced upriver. Xiala squinted at the contraption but couldn't quite make out what was supposed to go there. A dozen men or a massive beast of some kind, or something completely different. Pole stations stood at each corner of the rectangular ship, no doubt used to keep the vessel from colliding with the shore while in motion and moving along in shallow water when whatever it was that pulled the barge wasn't employed.

Her guide landed on the thatched roof of the barge and gave a definitive squawk. She offered the creature a salute of thanks before taking the ladder down. Serapio appeared from the shadows as her feet hit the deck.

She startled, letting out a small scream. Her night vision was good, and she should have seen him, but he blended into the darkness here even better than he had at sea.

"I didn't mean to startle you," he apologized. "I heard the crow return."

"It's fine," she said, shaking off the spike of adrenaline. She looked around at their new transportation, but most of it was shrouded in the growing twilight. "Looks like you found us passage."

"A bunk in a room shared with three other travelers, but the captain assures me he can have us in Tova before the Convergence."

She grunted. Three others? Well, it was no worse than bunking with the crew. "That the room?" she asked, peering around Serapio's shoulder to the chamber behind him.

"Behind me? Yes."

She stepped around him and paused. He smelled clean. Like water and soap.

"Did you bathe?"

"In the river."

Her whole body drooped in disappointment. "Not a steam bath?"

"The river. It's very refreshing."

Which probably meant it was like sitting naked in a frozen pond. She wanted heat, not ice. But maybe it was better than nothing.

She peered inside through the reed walls. It was a tight fit, and sure enough three men were already crowded in, hunched over a dice game of some kind on the floor.

"Those our cabinmates inside?"

"Pilgrims," he confirmed. "Traveling for the solstice."

"Gambling pilgrims?" She laughed, skeptical.

He shrugged, unconcerned. "Did you find the harbormaster?"

"All sorted," she said. "And I got a new cloak." She held it out for his inspection, and then remembered he couldn't see it. "It's wool," she explained. "Water-resistant."

"Which reminds me." He picked up something from the ground beside his feet and handed it to her. It looked to be a bundle of cotton. She unwrapped it, and it came apart into two pieces. Clothing. She held it up.

"Is it pants?" he asked.

"And a shirt."

The clothes were simple but well made. The shirt was square, and the long sleeves were stitched at the shoulders. It looked a size too small, but it wasn't unusable. The pants were long and loose, but when she held them up, they came only to her calves. With sandals she would be cold, but if she could find boots somewhere, they would suffice. Both items were the same dull white as the clothes she wore now, but the pants had a colorful embroidery at the hem and waist, and the shirt was cropped. "Are these children's clothes?"

"I bought them from one of the pilgrims. They were to be a gift for a nephew. Will they fit?"

"I'm going to look like an adolescent boy with breasts and hips," she protested, "but . . ." She sighed. "At least they're clean."

They turned as a roar of victory emanated from the room where the pilgrims were. Good-natured shouting and benches being moved, and then the men were pouring out the door, loud and boisterous. The one in the lead almost ran into Xiala, the captain catching him at the last minute before they collided.

The man's eyes met hers, and Xiala saw that he wasn't a man at all, but a very attractive woman, hair cut short on the sides and pulled back tightly in a knot in a decidedly masculine style.

"My apologies," the woman murmured, and Xiala caught a hint of liquor on her breath as she smiled. The harbormaster had been the first woman Xiala had seen in weeks, and now this one, and she felt some tension she was carrying drain from her shoulders. She loved the sea, loved Cuecola with its majestic architecture and sophistication, but mother waters, it was good to be on this side of the Meridian.

"No apology needed," she answered, returning the smile.

The woman sized her up, a drunken flirty look. "Would you and your friend like to join us?" she asked. "My brothers and I are going in search of dinner and more drink. Maybe a gambling table if there's one to be found."

Her brothers were already pounding up the ladder.

"Go on, Xiala," Serapio said at her side. "Go enjoy your evening."

"What about you?" she asked, turning to study his face, but it was hard to catch his expression in the dark folds of his cowl.

"I can't give you what you want," he said quietly, just for her ears and with too much insight for her liking.

"So . . . ?" the woman asked, dragging a finger down Xiala's arm. Longing hit her all at once. Not for the stranger, who was attractive enough to make her evening exciting, but for the man beside her. The unavailable one. She cursed under her breath.

"No," Xiala said, resolute, "but thanks for the offer."

"Another time, then," the woman said lightly, and then she was clambering up the ladder, shouting for her brothers to wait up. Xiala listened to their laughter trailing away into the night, and exhaled heavily.

"Why didn't you go?" Serapio asked. "She seemed very interested in you."

"Shut up," she muttered, pushing him forward into the now-empty room. "Apparently, I don't want to have a good time with fun attractive people. I want to sit morosely in an empty room and drink alone with you instead."

She looked around at their temporary housing. It was luxurious compared to the canoe. A double bunk bed on either side of a room that was almost as long as the ship was wide, and two raised reed mats that ran along the far wall to make a total of six beds. A table in the middle of the room that the previous occupants had shoved aside to throw dice on the wood floor, and two long benches beside it. There were blankets that looked fairly fresh piled on each bed and a small window directly across from the door that opened to the outside. For two people it would have been perfect, but for six it was going to be tight.

"It's nice," she admitted, as Serapio felt his way forward with his staff. "It looks like they've claimed one of the bunks and the beds along the wall. That leaves us the other bunk."

"This one?" He dumped his travel bag on the correct mat.

"I guess I'm sleeping above," she said, eyeing the top bunk. Now that she was close, it didn't look all that steady.

"You can sleep with me," Serapio offered.

"Watch it, crow man," she said, laughing. "I've been on a ship for the past two weeks with a celibate. Offer now, and who knows what happens? I've only got so much self-control." But she was teasing, and he knew her well enough by now to know it. He gave her one of his half-smiles.

"What if I tell you a story?"

She paused in the act of draping her new cloak over the ladder to her bunk. "What?"

"We'll be in Tova soon, so it's time I told you what to expect when we arrive."

It was the same thought she'd had earlier. She felt their time together shrinking at an alarming rate. A few days in this room, on this barge, and then they would go their separate ways. And she would have to face her mess of a life and figure out what to do next. But mostly, she would miss him.

A chill rolled over her, not from the wet weather outside, but from a panic that made her stomach hurt. She pasted on a smile, which she realized was wasted on him, and said, "Sure! But first a bath!"

She bit her lip. She sounded like a fool. But he didn't say anything, didn't call her on her falsity.

He stretched out on the bed and tucked his hands behind his head. Pulled his cowl down so it covered everything but his mouth. "I'll be here when you're ready."

She grabbed her clean clothes, the soap that sat on the table, and the bottle of alcohol she had brought from the ship and hurried out the door.

CHAPTER 30

The Tovasheh River

Year 325 of the Sun

(4 Days before Convergence)

> I saw a terrible thing today. A dozen crows, small but fierce,
> attacked a much larger owl that had entered their territory.
> It was raiding their nests and had eaten a nestling. The crows
> attacked it with their beaks and claws, but the owl seemed
> to only see them as an annoyance. It even plucked one from
> the sky, breaking its neck before hurling it to the canyon
> floor below.
>
> —From *Observations on Crows*, by Saaya, age thirteen

Serapio was dozing lightly when Xiala returned. He had let the
lamp burn down to almost nothing, too comfortable to get up
and relight it. At night everything became shadows upon shadows anyway, and he saw just as well in full darkness as with
lamplight, which was not at all. But as the solstice drew nearer,
he had sensed the shadow within him growing, too, and with
it his perception had sharpened. He was still as blind as he
had been since he was twelve, but Xiala in particular seemed

to register more brightly, more intensely, in his awareness. He didn't know if it was because the god was growing within him, or if it was her Teek magic, but he sensed everything about her more acutely and missed her when she was gone.

He listened to her move about the room, trying to be quiet so as not to wake him. He wanted to ask her to join him again, to share the narrow bed, but was afraid she would say no. Fear. It was an emotion he had not felt in a while. Want was not something he had felt recently, either, but he experienced it now, a sharp pain in his chest. He wanted her close, wanted her scent of sun and salt and ocean magic in his nose.

He supposed it made sense. With Tova so near and his time coming to an end, of course he would have fears, have wants. But he had not expected them to center around this woman. He tried to remember some of the exercises his first tutor had taught him, the ones that helped him discipline his mind, but his concentration fell away as Xiala crawled into the bed beside him, warm and clean and soft.

"Move over," she grumbled, pushing gently at his shoulder. He slid over obligingly.

"This bed is only meant for one person," she muttered as she settled in. "And certainly not an Obregi giant."

"We could lie on the floor if you prefer," he offered.

"Seven hells, Serapio," she said. "I've been sleeping on floors for weeks now. A bed is what I want, even one too small for two." As if to make a point of just how cramped it was, she hoisted her leg over his and rested her head against his chest.

His heart rate soared, and heat gathered where her skin

touched his. For a moment he wished he didn't have to tell her what came next, that perhaps they could stay like this and pretend that Tova was very far away indeed.

"You know," she said, sounding sleepy, "maybe it's best you don't fuck."

He almost swallowed his tongue.

"I mean," she continued, "I fuck. A lot. The Teek aren't uptight about such things, and it's something I enjoy. But it's been kind of nice having a friend, too."

"I wouldn't say that I don't—"

"But don't you ever want to turn it off?" she continued as if he hadn't spoken.

He frowned. "Turn what off?"

"The old brain. I mean, if you don't fuck—"

"Please stop saying that."

"—and you don't drink, and I've never seen you relax. And that noise you make barely counts as a laugh. You're so serious. Doesn't it get old? How old are you, anyway?"

"Twenty-two."

"Hells," she muttered. "I'm five years older than you?" She sighed gustily and snuggled in closer.

They were silent for a while, and he thought about not telling her his story at all, but this might be their last opportunity to be alone. Once they were moving upriver and their cabinmates had returned, he would not have the chance. And he was unsure what awaited him in Tova the day before the Convergence. It had to be now.

"I am a vessel," he said.

"Hmm . . . ?"

"I am . . ." He wanted her to understand, but he wasn't sure how to explain it. He decided to start again. "I wasn't always blind."

"An accident?"

"No. It was purposeful. My mother did it."

He felt her shift under his arm, knew she had propped herself up on one elbow to stare at him. "How? Why?"

"She had her reasons. It made me a proper vessel. My eyes served as an entry point for the power of a god."

He felt her flop back down. Her arm draped across his chest. "I'm not sure I believe in gods," she admitted. "I mean, you've definitely got something happening, don't get me wrong. And your birds are undeniable. And the sun . . ." She trailed off.

"What is your magic if not the power of a god?" he asked, curious. "Is not your sea a goddess?"

He felt her shrug. "That's not Teek thinking."

"It is Tovan thinking." He thought of the Watchers and the Sun Priest and corrected himself. "Carrion Crow thinking. The old ways."

"Well, Teek is about as old as it gets."

"What happened to you there in your homeland that you can't return?"

It was only a moment, but he felt her stiffen, felt anxiety rise from her like a dark wave.

"My mother was an abusive monster, too," she whispered against his chest.

He did not think of his mother as a monster any more than he did himself, but he understood what she meant and that this was a confession, so he did not counter her.

"She and my aunt drove me out. Told me that if I ever came back, my life would be forfeit. Banishment is usually a death sentence for a Teek. We don't do well out in the mainlander world. We tend to meet poor ends at the hands of unscrupulous men or drink ourselves into an early grave."

"Is that what you're doing?" He had smelled the liquor on her breath when she arrived, remembered the balché from the sea crossing.

"I was giving it a shot," she admitted. She pressed a hip against him as she rolled onto her back, and he moved closer to the wall to give her space, but there was precious little to concede. They lay skin to skin, the long slide of their bodies touching.

"How does it feel to be going home?" she asked. "You're returning to your family, aren't you? Once we get to Tova, you'll go to Crow Clan. What did Loob call it? Odo? And then you'll be like a long-lost son. Will they all have red teeth and haahan like you, I wonder?"

"I am not returning to be reunited with my family," he said, his voice soft with surprise. Is that what she thought? "I told you I am going to see the Sun Priest, the Watcher in the celestial tower."

"Sure," she said, "but then what? What happens after that? I mean, once you've had your meeting with this priest, then you'll go back to your clan. Or will you go all the way back to Obregi? It seems a long journey for one day."

"Xiala . . ." He didn't know what to say. She made it sound so normal.

She waved a hand. "Never mind. It was only a thought.

I'm sure you'll be busy doing whatever the vessels of gods do. I'll just . . ." She sighed, long and heavy. "I'll find something. A job. But what kind of work do you think there is in a place like that for a Teek? The sea is distant, even now. I was in the river, and it didn't know me, Serapio. It didn't recognize me as its child."

He pressed a soothing hand to her head, ran a palm down the long plane of her hair. He could hear her soft sobs.

"Ah, shit," she said, her breath a soft hiccup. "Maybe I am drunk. And I think I left that bottle of xtabentún down by the river."

"Leave it," he told her. "Stay with me instead."

And she did, her breath steadying in slumber and her body limp against him. Only when he was sure she was dreaming did he begin to drift off, destiny untold, deciding that tomorrow was soon enough.

CHAPTER 31

THE OBREGI MOUNTAINS

YEAR 325 OF THE SUN

(5 MONTHS BEFORE CONVERGENCE)

And one day Crow came upon Eagle, who said, "Lo, Lord Crow. What fine feathers you have. I would like to admire them up close. Will you let me?" But Crow knew that she and Eagle were natural enemies and said, "You may admire me from where you stand, but come no closer. I do not trust you. It is in your nature to eat my kind." And Eagle, who had indeed intended to eat Crow, was chastened.

—From the Crow Cycle, an oral history of the Crow clan

"Did you kill the other tutors?" Powageh asked.

They were sitting under the giant pine outside Serapio's old rooms. He had been practicing calling the shadow. Shortly after they had met four years ago, Serapio had told his tutor about the trick with the mirror he had used to defeat Eedi. Powageh had listened and then scoffed.

"Only priests and magic users need objects to channel the god's powers, Serapio. You are something else."

"Explain."

"You are an avatar of the crow god. Your power does not come from somewhere other. You do not need to draw it from the sky or the fireplace or even your blood, although I imagine your blood would be quite potent." Xir mind seemed to drift off for a moment, lost in the possibility of Serapio's blood sacrifice. It should have been unsettling, but he was used to it.

"Anyway," xe said, concentration coming back, "Saaya already did that for you. It is inside you, now, all that power. Can't you feel it?"

He could. The shadow seemed closer to the surface of his skin every day, a living, rippling presence. When he let it come, he could draw it to his fingertips, feel its icy fingers dance around his own, hear the muffled roar of its arrival like the rush of beating wings.

"Is that what I will do when I confront the Sun Priest?" he asked. "Bring forth the crow's shadow to smother his light?"

"Her light. The new Sun Priest is a woman. But the body doesn't matter. It's the institution we're after."

Serapio said nothing. He was used to Powageh's rants against the celestial tower, the evils of the Watchers, the wrongs they had done to xir and countless others. He also remembered Paadeh's grievances of abuse as a child in a district of Tova called the Maw and how the woodworker had blamed his impoverished beginnings on the tower and the Sky Made clans. Serapio often wondered if his condemnation of the clans included Carrion Crow, but since he had already marked Paadeh for death after their first meeting, he did not bother to inquire. Eedi's complaint had been a strategic one. She wanted a weakened Tova so that her own people, a people who seemed to have soundly rejected her for a transgression she never made clear, could sweep in and conquer the Holy City. Serapio was happy to learn all he could from her, but he was not keen on her plan of conquest. When the crows forced her to fly, he did not mourn her.

"I said, did you kill them?" Powageh said, xir question cutting into Serapio's reverie and bringing him back to the present.

He thought carefully on how to answer. He decided that Powageh must already realize that he did if he was asking.

"How did you know?"

"That staff, for one. That was Eedi's. She would have to be dead for it to be in your hands. I knew it from the first time I met you under the tree, when you took me down with it."

Serapio ran a hand over his staff. "I made it my own." And he had, adapting the skills he had learned to carve wood to the more challenging bone. He had marked hand placements at both center and top with elegant and detailed designs that resembled the interlocking wings of crows.

"It is a spearmaiden's armament," Powageh said. "No one else carries a bone staff, and they are almost no more. It is the weapon of a different era, before the Hokaia Treaty."

"And now I carry one and have no interest in their Treaty."

Powageh sighed, and Serapio was not sure what xe was thinking.

"They were not good people, Powageh."

His only remaining tutor chuckled. "No, they were not. Are any of us? Am I? Are you?"

Serapio mulled the question over. It was a strange thing to ask. He had spent the better part of his adolescence being molded into what he was by these people: his mother and her co-conspirators. His father had all but abdicated responsibility for him from the day of his transformation, but in earnest after his seventeenth birthday, when Serapio had moved to a caretaker's cottage far from the main house. He did not know what Powageh had told Marcal to convince him to let Serapio go so easily. Perhaps not much at all except "burden" and "free of," but he had not seen his father since.

"Can a bad person become a good person by performing a good deed?" he asked.

"How do you mean, crow son?"

"If we agree that Paadeh and Eedi, and perhaps yourself, Powageh, are not good people, but you have trained me to a higher cause, the cause of justice, then perhaps you are a good person after all."

"The crow god a god of justice?" The old priest scoffed. "I've not heard that before."

"Vengeance, then. But what is vengeance if not justice?"

"Vengeance can be for spite. It can eat you up inside, take from you everything that makes you happy, makes you human. Look at what it did to your mother. Would justice do that?"

Serapio considered. He did not much feel like a human most days, although he was not sure what it felt like to be a god, either, despite Powageh's insistence that he was an avatar. And he thought that the thing that made him happy was vengeance, or at least the idea that he would travel to Tova and exact it for his ancestors since they could not do so for themselves.

"You did not train me for four and a half years to fulfill a promise of spite," he said confidently.

"Why did you kill them, then?" his tutor asked.

Serapio answered honestly. "Paadeh whipped me repeatedly. Often. He wanted me to make physical pain my friend and labored hard at it. But I forgave him that."

Powageh grunted noncommittally.

"But he also threatened my crows. Said if I didn't do as he told me, he would whip them, too. It would have killed them."

"He always was a petty tyrant of a man," Powageh muttered. Serapio could feel the weight of xir scrutiny. "So you killed him because he threatened your friends."

Serapio nodded.

"And the spearmaiden? Eedi? What did she threaten?"

"My clan."

After a while Powageh let out a heavy exhale. "She always did talk too much for her own good. Figured it would get her killed one day." Another sigh. "And how do you plan to kill me, crow son?"

Serapio had been thinking about this, too. "You saved my mother's life. Gave her shelter, loved her."

"I did."

"I do not think she would want you to die."

A startled laugh from the priest. "But my transgressions are many, Serapio. I have killed people in the name of the priesthood, many from your clan alone. You, the Crow God Reborn, the harbinger of vengeance incarnate, would let me live?"

Xir tone was jesting, but Serapio knew xe was serious. He had long ago realized Powageh carried a great burden, something dark that drove xir.

"Sometimes it is better to let one live with their misdeeds than to free them through death. A dead priest cannot atone. A live one . . . well, there is always the choice."

"Well, crow son," xe said, voice weary with the weight of age and choices, "perhaps my life has not been a mistake after all. But do not be so quick to grant me your mercy. There is one last lesson I must impart to you: your task on the Day of Convergence.

"The Sun Priest and the Sky Made matrons will arrive at Sun Rock before sundown. The Convergence should occur while the sun is just above the horizon line. The Convergence will last only minutes, twelve at the most, and those minutes you must use to your advantage."

"But there will be Knives," Serapio said.

"Yes, the Society of Knives will no doubt be there, along with the Sky Made matrons and their Shields. You will have to find a way through them all."

"You mean kill them."

"Yes, but once you have had your fill of blood, shadow will be your knife."

"What does that mean?"

"Saaya had a theory. It was only a theory, mind you, but she was right about so much. Right about shaping you, after all. She believed the Watchers had once been instruments of gods."

"Vessels?" Serapio asked, surprised.

"No. Or perhaps once, but no longer. The priesthood believes their powers are simply a product of natural talent honed through study, and there is merit in that opinion. For those of us who rose no further than dedicant, perhaps that's all there is. But Saaya believed there was a deeper essence in those that wore the masks, something that came in the moment of investiture as head of one's society that imbued them with a god's essence."

"What do you mean by investiture?"

"An ascension to rank."

"A ceremony, then. Sorcery," he said confidently.

Powageh's laugh was short and sharp. "Ritual magic? Perhaps, but the priesthood would kill anyone where they stand for heresy if they suggested such a thing."

"That doesn't make it any less true."

"Of course not. The crow and the sun are long enemies," xe continued, "some say from before the God War. Saaya believed that if the crow god at the height of his influence were to devour the essence of the sun invested in the Sun Priest at the nadir of hers, then the power in our world could be flipped to favor the crow."

"So it's not only the institution you and my mother are after, it is the god itself. The very ordering of the world."

Powageh said nothing, but Serapio could hear the breath rattling through xir faulty lungs and knew he had guessed right.

"You must think us arrogant fools," xe finally said.

"How will I kill her?" Serapio asked. "The Sun Priest. I would not ask such a thing of my crows."

"No, I do not believe your crows are meant for that."

Another heavy sigh, and Serapio could hear Powageh's reluctance to continue in xir belabored breath, the nervous shifting of xir feet.

"What do you fear, Powageh? Do not be afraid for me. I am not."

"And here I am sweating," the old priest said with a self-deprecating laugh. "Because in the end, I do not wish you to judge me harshly, but it is selfish of me to want your love."

Serapio's breath caught. No one had loved him since his mother, and he was unsure how he felt about the priest's declaration.

"Eedi said you are not my friends, that I must not get attached because I will be leaving."

"Ah, well, perhaps I should have had Eedi here to counsel me," xe said, xir voice a thin wavering laugh that dissolved into a quaking exhale.

"Are you . . . do you weep, Powageh?"

"Have I not earned a few tears?"

And suddenly he understood. "I am going to die, aren't I?" He had suspected it for a while, understood intuitively that the power he had inside him would consume him. He was a vessel. Powageh had said it from the beginning. He was the kind of vessel one must break to release what was held inside if one hoped to devour another god.

"I . . . skies and stars, boy. I *am* sorry."

"No," he said shortly. "My destiny has been inevitable since the day my mother closed my eyes, perhaps since she gave me birth. I am a vessel, am I not? The avatar of a god."

He cleared his throat. "Tell me what I must do." He only hoped that the pain would not be too great. He had made friends with it, yes, but it was a wary friendship.

"You must do nothing but exist," the priest said. "And when the time comes, you will speak your true name, your eyes will open . . . and you will exist no more."

He had hoped to witness the end of the Sun Priest and the aftermath of the crow god's justice, but he understood that it could not be. The Convergence would be his end, too, a final sacrifice to his god on behalf of a people he would never know, and who would never know him.

CHAPTER 32

The Tovasheh River

Year 325 of the Sun

(3 Days before Convergence)

They say to us,
Eat ash and drink bile
And be glad that you are spared.
Better we were dead and food for crows.

—From *Collected Lamentations from the Night of Knives*

Xiala woke up alone. For a moment, she panicked, trying to place the low ceiling of the bed above her, the slow motion of water below her, and the strong smell of an unfamiliar soap in her hair. And then she remembered the barge and the bath in the freezing river and the dent she had put in the bottle of xtabentún before coming back to climb into bed with Serapio.

She laughed, pressing a hand to her head. The look on his face when she had joined him had almost been enough for her to try to kiss him again. She had seen raw need there, and it had sent a satisfying thrill through her body. She was sure that if she had asked him for more last night, he would not have refused. But he had wanted to tell her something, something important, so she had not. Only now she couldn't remember what exactly he had said. Damn the xtabentún.

She sat up and swung her feet off the side of the bed. The pilgrims had returned at some point last night. She vaguely remembered voices and laughter. But they were all gone now, as was Serapio. She looked out the small window, trying to gauge the time of day, and guessed it to still be morning, but she had clearly slept in.

She slipped on her shoes, wrapped her cloak around her shoulders, and ventured out.

It was still raining, a steady drizzle that was like the sky continuously spitting on her face. The barge had moved up the Tovasheh far beyond the eponymous town. Stretched out along the riverbank were low grasslands browned by the winter and rocky yellow hills. It was a completely unfamiliar landscape, and she already missed the heat of the jungle and the salty sea air that permeated the southern side of the Crescent Sea.

She watched the world pass for a while, her mind on nothing more than the changing scenery. But then she realized that they were moving at a swifter pace than polers could account for and remembered that harness she had spotted the night before. Curious, she made her way to the front of the ship.

The harness was no longer empty.

She tried to process what she was seeing, but her brain was already having trouble focusing, the aftereffects of the drink from the night before. There was a creature. It had limbs, six of them, as big as logs, protruding from its body and then tapering to thinner but still tree-sized after the knee joint. The front limbs guided it forward, and the back limbs steadied the movement of its long body. A body half as wide as the barge itself. The middle limbs acted as paddles, moving them gently and efficiently upriver.

"Mother waters," she whispered. "What the hell is that?"

"Water strider," came a voice from behind her.

She turned to find the young woman from last night, the one who had invited her to join her, approaching her.

"Big suckers, aren't they?" she said, giving Xiala an easy smile. She wore a long shirt that hit below her narrow hips and tied at the neck. It was white and woven from a fiber Xiala didn't recognize. Black lacing edged the sleeves that came down to cover the woman's elbows. Fitted leggings and calf-length suede boots covered her legs and feet; turquoise pierced her ears and nose.

"I remember the first time I saw one," the woman continued. "It was just a baby, but I about shit my pants. Big as my whole body right out of the egg. My name is Aishe."

"Xiala."

"You're not from here."

"Cuecola," she lied. She didn't know this Aishe well enough to share her heritage, and if Aishe didn't recognize her telltale eyes as a giveaway, then she would just be the stuff of fairy tales, and it didn't matter.

"I'm Tovan born and bred," Aishe explained, coming forward to lean her back against the railing, still facing Xiala. "Clan Water Strider, in fact."

Xiala blanched. "Those insects are your namesake?"

"This one's named Paipai."

"It has a name?"

"They're actually pretty friendly. You can pet it later if you want."

"No. I'm fine." Xiala wasn't squeamish, but getting any closer to the beast seemed unnecessary. "Is it your pet?"

"My mother's husband's brother runs this barge. That makes him Water Strider, too, and my mother lends Paipai out for special occasions. He's very tame."

"What is the special occasion?"

"Solstice. Lots of people coming up for solstice." Her gaze roamed over the barge. "Well, normally there would be, but with the death of the Carrion Crow matron and the Sun Rock riots, it's put a damper on the festivities."

"The matron?"

"Matrons are the leaders of the clans. The Carrion Crow one died in her bed last week, week before? Anyway, there's rumors that it was no accident. And there was a riot at her funeral. A dozen people hurt and two Crows dead. Whole city on curfew for days. Anyway, it's enough to be a discouragement to tourists, to be sure. Plus, this weather?" She held out a hand to catch the rain. "Not surprising that so many country folk decided to stay home."

Did Serapio know the head of his clan had died? That he was walking into a city on the edge already? This had to be the news the harbormaster had alluded to yesterday. She'd forgotten to mention it, but in all fairness Serapio had admitted he didn't know anyone in Carrion Crow and wasn't there to reunite with his extended family, anyway. Maybe her death didn't matter, but a dangerous city certainly did.

"I thought you and your brothers were pilgrims."

"That was Tyode. He was joking." She rolled her eyes. "He's an idiot but mostly harmless. He sold your friend those clothes." She gestured toward Xiala with her lips. "You can borrow some of mine if you prefer. They'd fit at least."

Xiala frowned. "So, you're not pilgrims?"

"No, my brothers are security, and I take care of Paipai." Aishe looked her up and down, a long, evaluating look. "So, you're with the cultist. What did you call him, Serapio?"

"What? Oh, yes. Serapio."

"I wouldn't have asked you to join us last night if I'd known you were spoken for."

Xiala didn't know the phrase *spoken for*. It sounded like a Tovan phrase translated into Trade. But she got the gist.

"We are only friends."

Aishe smirked, face skeptical.

"Why do you call him a cultist?" It was another word she didn't recognize.

"He's not one? He sure looks like one."

"I guess I don't understand."

"The cultists call themselves Odohaa. They are followers of the old ways who hate the Watchers. You can ask my uncle about them. He knows more. Anyway, I came to get you to bring you back so you could see the fights."

Xiala was still trying to process everything Aishe had told her, but the last comment made her jaw drop. "Fights?"

"Sparring. Your *friend*"—she emphasized *friend* with a

knowing wink—"is incredible. He already beat Zash once, but he was going to take on Tyode and Zash at the same time. And blind!" She shook her head, amazed.

"Serapio can fight? We are talking about fighting?"

Aishe's eyes twinkled. "Oh, yes. You're in for a treat."

Aishe led her down the narrow side deck to the back of the barge. Here was a large open landing, enough for a dozen people to gather comfortably . . . or for three men to fight. A fourth man stood to the side, leaning on a barge pole, likely the uncle Aishe had referred to, but Xiala's eyes were on the center of the makeshift ring.

The two men she knew now to be Zash and Tyode stood stripped to the waist, soaked by the steady rain. One held a wicked-looking knife, half as long as Xiala's arm and tipped with obsidian. But Xiala saw the obsidian edge had been covered with cloth. Still, the side edge would cut flesh if not puncture. The other brother brandished a spear made of wood that he thrust forward. And dancing lightly around them both, avoiding knife and spear alike, was Serapio. He was also bare to the waist, and he had tied his hair back off his face with the strip of cloth that usually went around his eyes. He moved like liquid, swinging his bone staff in a wide, devastating arc.

"Touch!" the uncle yelled, and Tyode bowed his head.

Zash laughed. "You are too slow, Brother. That's three to one. One more and we lose."

Serapio must have struck Tyode, but it had happened so fast she had missed it. She looked over at Aishe, who raised her eyebrows in appreciation.

"It's not my fault," Tyode growled. "He doesn't follow my feints."

"You can't feint a blind man," Zash said, laughing.

"He's lucky is all," Tyode grumbled, and he straightened, shifting his knife from one hand to the other. "It won't happen again."

But it did, twice while Xiala watched, until their uncle cried, "Touch! That's five."

Tyode slumped to the ground, exhausted, but Zash stepped to Serapio, laughing.

"Stars and skies, Crow, where did you learn to fight?" he asked brightly, slapping Serapio on the shoulder. Serapio tensed. Xiala knew him well enough now to know he was unsure how to respond, so she hurried to his side. Grasped his hand to let him know she was there. It was warm from exertion. So often his skin was cool to the touch.

"My tutors," he said plainly.

"Well, your tutors must have been truly elite," Zash went on. "I've never seen anything like it."

"And blind at that," Tyode said, finally joining him. He was still winded, fighting to catch his breath, but appreciation lit his face.

"Blindness is only an adjustment," Serapio said. He appeared to have relaxed some, no longer looking like he wanted to flee the boisterous men.

"Well, it's an honor to have seen you fight," the uncle said, joining them. "I've only seen the like at the war college in Hokaia."

"Spearmaidens!" Zash said, snapping his fingers. "Remember Etze, Brother? The time he got thoroughly spanked by that spearmaiden?"

"And not in the good way," Tyode said, laughing.

"Spearmaiden?" Xiala asked. This was a side she had not seen of Serapio, another secret revealed. "Are you saying he fights like a girl?"

The brothers roared, her joke landing, and the uncle smiled. "Only the best girls in the Meridian. They won't train just anyone. Even those at the war college aren't always fortunate enough to train with the maidens."

"Is that what it is, Serapio?" Aishe asked. She had joined the group, and she looked at him slyly, evaluating. "You trained with a spearmaiden?"

"And a tsiyo, a Knife of the celestial tower."

Xiala could feel the small shock wave of awe ripple around them. Tyode rocked back on his heels. "Well, shit. No wonder I lost."

"No shame in that," Zash agreed.

"Who trains with such people?" the uncle murmured, looking at Serapio differently from how he had moments ago. It was a look Xiala recognized, one she had been on the receiving end of before. Part respect, part envy, and all wondering if she was a nut that could be cracked open to reveal treasures.

She said, "This is all very interesting, the fighting. But did I miss breakfast? I'm starving."

The uncle shifted his gaze to her, like he'd forgotten she was there. "Oh, of course. Where are my manners? You did pay for meals." He nudged his niece. "Get our guests some food. You." He flung a hand out at Zash. "Set a table up. We'll eat inside, out of this rain. And you." He moved to slide an arm around Serapio's shoulder, but Serapio deftly avoided his touch, and the man's arm slid to his side. "Ah, well, we'll talk. We've two more days to Tova and plenty to share, no? Plenty to share."

· · · · ·

They sat at a table in a room adjacent and identical to the one they had slept in, and the uncle, who insisted Xiala and Serapio call him Uncle, too, peppered Serapio with questions over a modest breakfast of corn cakes and river eel. She'd had better fare at sea, but she was hungry enough to clean her plate.

"The solstice, you say?" the uncle was asking. "Going back for the solstice?"

"That's right," Serapio answered.

"Looks to be a quiet one this year," Zash said.

"Usually Tovasheh is run full of tourists," Tyode added. "Gotta fight for room on the barge. We can charge premium rates to go upriver. This year, it's only you two."

Xiala said, "Aishe told me the matron of Carrion Crow died, and there've been riots, enough to shut down the city."

Serapio tilted his head. "What's this?"

"Harbormaster said the same thing," she admitted. "I meant to tell you."

"Will there be a problem getting into the city?"

The uncle shrugged. "Won't know until we get there but should be no problem for us. We're Sky Made enough to open a few doors if need be." He winked at Xiala, who gave him a weak smile. She still didn't trust the man.

"Aishe mentioned something about cultists, too," she said pointedly. "Said you could tell us more."

The man's eyes flashed to Serapio. "Aye, I think Serapio knows all about them." And there it was again. That hungry look.

She was sitting next to Serapio, and she leaned back so she could see him while also keeping her eyes on the uncle. "He won't elaborate," she said. "Perhaps you could tell me more."

Serapio stood, the bench scraping across the floor as he pushed it back, and they all startled.

"If you don't mind, I will rest now," he said.

The uncle stood, too. "Of course. If there's anything we can do to make your journey more pleasant . . ."

"That's not necessary. As long as we're in Tova before the solstice."

Aishe tapped Xiala on the arm. "There's not much to do on the barge but talk to each other and drink, but we do have some games. Do you gamble?"

"There's fishing," Zash added. "And there's nothing so calming as sitting and watching the world go by."

"In the rain?" Tyode complained.

"Sit under the eaves, you dolt."

"I wouldn't mind a game or two," Xiala said. "Win back our travel costs."

"Ho!" Zash said, laughing. "You think you're good?"

"At dice?"

"Game's patol," he said. "We invented it, you know. The official game of Tova."

"Well, allow me to beat you at your official game," she said with a smile.

That made them all laugh. Tyode rushed off to get the board and dice.

Serapio made to leave, and Xiala rested a hand on his arm. "You all right?" she asked. "It's okay if I stay and play?"

"Of course. I'm only going to rest. I'll be next door."

She pressed her lips together, wanting to say more but not in front of strangers. She settled on "I'll be over later."

And then Tyode was back with the game, and they were setting the board and shouting about rules and antes, and Xiala was swept up in the laughter and joy. By the time she had chosen her game piece, the uncle and Serapio were gone.

• • • • •

Xiala stumbled into their shared room near sunset to find Serapio sitting on the bed they had slept in the night before, a knife in his hand. She dumped a handful of cacao on the table in the middle of the room and dropped down on the nearby bench, smiling triumphantly.

Serapio raised his head.

"You won?"

"My share and then some," she declared. "Also got some clothes that weren't made for an adolescent boy." She thumbed the crimson fringe that edged her new white shirt. "Never play a sailor in a game of luck. We're favored by the odds."

"Callo wouldn't think so," he said.

She deflated, her good mood marred at the thought. An hour into their play, Zash had opened a barrel of balché, and she'd drunk with them. It had been the best time she'd had in months, and for a while she'd forgotten about their trials on the Crescent Sea.

She sighed, tugging a hand through her long hair. She leaned back against the table. "What have you got there?"

Serapio held up his hands to show her. "A carving."

She raised skeptical eyebrows. "You carve wood?"

He nodded.

"Another talent. First fighting, now woodcarving. Who are you?" She meant it lightly, as a tease, but it came out darker than that.

"It's a skill I learned as a teenager," he said. "I was a difficult child. Lost in my own world and admittedly unfocused. I had a tutor who taught me discipline through woodcarving." He pressed his lips together, as if momentarily lost in thought. "He was not a kind man. He beat me to teach me a tolerance for pain. But he also taught me to make beautiful things, to work with my hands." He held out his right hand to show her the piece he had been working on.

She took it. It was her. Well, not exactly her, but a creature of the sea with the upper body of a woman and the curving tail of a fish. He had rendered the individual scales in detail and was using his chisel now to draw long waves of hair so fine that they seemed to move.

"It's beautiful," she whispered, meaning it.

"It's for you," he said. "Once I'm done."

"Why didn't you carve on the ship?" she asked, curious. "All those days at sea and nothing."

"No wood," he said simply. An easy enough answer. "And what do you think of our hosts?"

She held the piece out, tapping it against his knee, and he took it back to finish. "Good people," she said. "Likable. Familial. Not so great at their treasured game." She laughed and ran a hand through her winnings.

"Do you trust them?"

"Enough," she said. "The uncle less. He looks at you strangely, Serapio. He wants something from you."

"I know."

She glanced over, surprised. "Do you know what it is?"

"He's Water Strider on his mother's side, which determines his clan, but he told me his paternal grandfather was killed in the Night of Knives. He's Carrion Crow."

"So he's family?"

"After a fashion."

"What does he want?"

He took up the chisel again, his hands turning and carving as they spoke. The soft scrape of the wood being formed whispered through the room.

"Aishe told you of the cultists, as she called them. The Odohaa."

"She didn't tell me much. Just that they're some kind of religious group that hates the Watchers. That's the priests, right? The same ones you're going there to meet."

He nodded, hands still moving as he formed the wooden figurine.

"She said she thought you were one of them."

"A priest?"

"A cultist."

"The uncle told me of the Odohaa," Serapio said, voice

thoughtful. "He said they pray for the return of the crow god. That there is a prophecy they follow that says their god will return and free them from the rule of the Watchers and restore Carrion Crow to glory."

She snorted. "I never much cared for prophecies and destinies myself. I prefer a clean slate in life, a woman's fate up to herself, not the sayings of old men and dusty scrolls. Besides, prophecies always have a way of going wrong, don't they? They promise you a savior, but that savior ends up eating babies or kicking puppies or something, and the poor gull who's the prophesied one always ends up dead. Besides . . ." She thought of her old crew and the dozens of crews she'd had through the years. "Prophecies are a breeding ground for opportunists. An excuse for bad behavior. Can't trust them." She rubbed her pinkie joint against the finger next to it. "They'll steal your very bones for a chance at destiny."

He had been working steadily as she spoke, but now he paused. "I don't think you understand, Xiala."

"Understand what?"

He was quiet for a while, but then he resumed working, deft hands on the wood, creating form from nothing. "I am the fulfillment of their prophecy."

Her first reaction was to laugh. Prophecies didn't like bedtime stories or let you borrow their extra undergarments. Prophecies didn't speak terrible Cuecolan and not know how to eat a damn fish. And they certainly didn't cuddle with you when you'd had too much to drink and were feeling sorry for yourself. But they did talk to birds and reek of magic and, stars and sky, make the sun fear them.

"Mother waters," she murmured. "You're serious."

He nodded.

"But . . . how? Are you . . . you're just a man! I thought prophecies required children of gods born to mortal women or something."

"Gods can be made in other ways," he said quietly. He worked the wood, hands never stopping. "Raw materials can be found and shaped, molded into a form that can contain a god."

"What does it mean, Serapio? That you're a god? What *is* a god? I don't understand."

"It is said that thousands of years ago our world was once populated with gods. They are our ancestors. But there was a great war, the God War, and many were killed. Those who were not killed in the war began to die anyway. Some say they were overcome with regret and withered, others say they lived, but they grew lonely and went into the far north, never to be seen again. And still others say they returned to the sky, which was their home before they came to earth. Wherever their blood was spilled or their bodies lay, great wonders happened. Mountain ranges burst from flat lands, rivers gushed water like divine blood, stars were born in cataclysm. And in everything, they left bits of their power—the sun and stars, the creatures of earth and air, the very rocks and rivers and seas. Once humans discovered that the objects, places, and creatures around them held power, they began to manipulate them for their own desires. Many societies call that witchcraft, pulling power from one source and putting it into another, usually an object for your own use like an amulet or a potion. The sorcery of the

Cuecolans and the southern coasts is similar, only they also complement the power transfer through blood and sacrifice to achieve ends that witchcraft could not fathom. The priests reject it all, saying that their study of the sun and stars is reason and not magic, but my old tutor believed it was not always so for them and the priests have only forgotten their magic."

It was all over Xiala's head, unfamiliar and, frankly, unwanted knowledge. But there was one thing she had to know. "And which are you?" she asked, voice a soft whisper.

"I am something else, although sorcery was used in my making. I am an avatar of a god. I am the object, the vessel, that contains the power, but unlike the sun or a stone or the sea, I am, as you say, a man. But not just a man, Xiala. Don't make that mistake." His head came up, his shuttered eyes meeting hers with unnerving accuracy. "I am also a god."

She shivered. Heard the beating of wings in his voice, remembered the feel of his magic, his power.

"I believe you," she said simply.

"Then you know why this bargeman and the Odohaa are interested in me. And why I must go to Tova and confront the Sun Priest."

Confront the Sun Priest. But that's not what he had said earlier, what the Odohaa wanted. "You mean kill the Sun Priest," she ventured. "You said you had a meeting with the Watchers, but what you meant was you are going there to kill them."

He nodded.

"Mother waters, Serapio, the whole priesthood?"

"They are a blight upon this world. They would destroy all the gods if they could."

"But there must be a hundred, maybe more. You can't kill a hundred people!"

"You have not seen my power manifest," he said. "Not truly. What I did to save you on the ship was but the smallest glimpse of what I contain. I am not afraid."

She had meant that it would be wrong to slaughter a hundred people, not that it was beyond his ability. She had wondered if he was hero or villain on the ship after the crows had come, and she wondered it again, now. And then something else occurred to her.

"So you're the one prophesied?"

He held out the figurine. It was a mermaid, beautiful and detailed, as fine as the best art by the best artisans in Cuecola. "A gift. So that you remember me fondly."

"No . . ." She heaved, the balché she'd consumed over the gaming table churning in her stomach. She pressed a hand to her mouth and kept it down, but her whole body had begun to shake. Because if Serapio was the one prophesied, then that could only mean one thing.

"Are you okay?" he asked, concerned.

She shook her head, but he couldn't see it. "No!"

"Do you need a healer?"

"Tell me I'm wrong," she whispered, horror shivering across her skin. "Tell me it's not true." She was crying, tears running down her cheeks as she tried to catch her breath. But it was no good. She was drowning.

"Tell you what is not true?" he asked.

"That you're going to Tova to die."

CHAPTER 33

CITY OF TOVA
YEAR 325 OF THE SUN
(1 DAY BEFORE CONVERGENCE)

> The Four Societies of the Watchers must always work together for the benefit of the people of the Meridian. If there is a disagreement before them, it shall be settled in Conclave before the full delegation of Priests and Dedicants. No subterfuge shall be tolerated, for the Watchers are a body of Reason and Science and beyond the petty squabbles of humankind.
>
> —*The Manual of the Sun Priest*

Naranpa had been locked in her room for a week after her visit to the Maw before Iktan came to visit her.

She had not been idle. She had convinced the servants, the girl Deeya and the boy Leaya, to aid her. Deeya had agreed to discreetly look for a possible message from Carrion Crow meant for her, and Leaya had agreed to carry a note to Ieyoue Water Strider letting her know of Naranpa's fate. And Naranpa had listened, just as she had when she herself was a servant, and tried to learn what she could. But being confined left her with scant opportunity to discover what the priesthood was planning.

Zataya's pronouncement of her impending murder had initially unnerved her, but the immediacy of the threat faded with the passing days. And seeing Denaochi again was an unexpected comfort in and of itself. But as the solstice approached, she knew her time to act was running out.

She had thought to tell the priesthood what she had learned from Denaochi, warn them of the storm coming from the south or the Odohaa's restlessness. But she suspected they already knew and did not believe or believed and did not care. And if she spoke now, she would have to explain Denaochi and her visit to the Maw, and perhaps reveal her outreach to Okoa and Ieyoue. No, best to keep silent and let them discover it on their own.

The Priest of Knives slid into the room on a whisper. Xe was dressed informally in soft gray, a long skirt and mantle, hair freshly shorn to xir skull. She was loath to admit it, but she still found xir physically attractive, beautiful even. Damn her traitorous heart. But at least she had the sense now to know she could not trust xir anymore.

"What do you want?" She tried to keep her voice calm and flat and hoped her roil of emotions didn't show on her face.

Xe leaned against the wall by the door and crossed xir arms. "The solstice is tomorrow."

"I'm well aware." She arched an eyebrow. "Have you decided to have me resume my duties after all?"

Xe almost smiled. "No."

"How's Eche?" She managed to keep the bitterness from her voice.

"He's competent. Not particularly creative, or smart, for that matter. But he knows how to play the political game. He'll do well."

"And me?" she blurted. She hadn't meant to ask, but she wanted to know.

Iktan sighed. "This confinement is only temporary, Nara, until after Carrion Crow has been dealt with. We're gathering support from the clans, and Eche is very good at that."

"You mean he's an ass-kisser," she shot back.

"Brown to his ears."

She smiled, despite herself, but her amusement quickly faded. Her hands were shaking again, but her voice was steady, almost light. "You know the rules as well as I do, Iktan. The Sun Priest serves unto death, so don't lie to me."

"An exception will be made for you. I would not have agreed to this without it."

She scoffed.

Iktan shifted, looking suddenly uncomfortable. She knew that look. Xe was going to ask her for something she didn't want to give.

"I need the mask, Nara."

Her breath caught. She looked involuntarily over to the narrow dressing table where the burnished mask of the Sun Priest was displayed. She had cleaned it after the riots, wiping Okoa's blood from the gold mosaic.

"Skies," she whispered, clasping her hands together in her lap. "Even now, I guess part of me didn't think this was real, that you would truly go through with it."

"It's real." Xir voice was not unkind.

Naranpa forced herself to stand. The walk to the dressing table felt like a march of miles. She lifted the mask and ran a hand over the broad cheek, admiring the craftsmanship. Wearing it had been the culmination of a lifetime of dreaming, twenty-three years dedicated to the priesthood. But all that looked foolish now, a child's dreams dashed to nothing.

She walked back and placed it in Iktan's hands.

"When is Eche's investiture?"

"After the solstice. We'll have to fabricate a reason why you have abdicated."

"Of course you will."

"Nara . . ."

"They were never going to accept me, were they?" she asked quietly.

"No," xe said. "The gap between Sky Made and Dry Earth is too vast."

She remembered Iktan had been born Winged Serpent. "And you? Was the gap too vast for you, too?"

"You know that I have never cared much for this institution, and certainly not to the extent that you have. I find it full of falseness and flattery, but I do like certain aspects of my work."

"The violence, you mean." She shook her head, rueful. "You always were a blasphemer."

"But I do very much care about you, Nara."

Her smile was soft and sad. "I wish I could believe you. So what happens to me now? Retirement? Perhaps I can join the river monks or grow a nice garden in the Eastern districts?"

"Would that be so terrible? It is better than death, is it not?"

Her whole body shuddered. She turned to face the window, her back to Iktan.

"Kiutue did you a disservice when he named you Sun Priest. It was an impossible thing he asked of you. It did not have to come to this."

She sighed. "Go, Iktan. You got what you came for. Just . . . go."

Seconds passed in silence. She turned to find herself alone. Only then did she allow herself to cry.

• • • • •

It hadn't been more than fifteen minutes when her door opened again. She was washing her face in the basin when she heard someone enter and turned, annoyed.

"Why are you back when I told you . . ."

But it wasn't Iktan in her doorway.

"What do you want, Abah?" she said, voice coated with distaste. "Have you come to gloat?"

The younger woman smiled, self-satisfied and indulgent. "Why would I gloat, Nara? I feel terrible about what's happened. But I think we can all agree Eche should have been Sun Priest from the beginning and now things are in their rightful order."

"I said what do you want?"

Abah sighed. "I do apologize ahead of time, but some of us talked, and we think it's best if you don't stay in the tower."

"I know. Iktan mentioned the Eastern districts after solst—"

"You misunderstand." Abah snapped her fingers, and four servants entered through the open door. They were big for servants, their brown robes stretching too tight across wide shoulders. And they looked too old. In fact, none of their faces was familiar.

"Who is this?" Nara asked, dread rising in her belly.

"Take her," Abah commanded. "But make it quiet. No one can know."

"No one can . . . ? Wait!" But the four men had seized her roughly by the arms and were dragging her toward the door.

"Stop!" she cried. "You can't—"

One of the men struck her across the temple. She swayed, catching herself against the man on her other side. He grunted and shoved her away. Her feet caught on the hem of her robe, and she went down hard on her knees. Her teeth rattled in her head, and she grunted as she bit her tongue.

"Get her up," Abah hissed.

Her arm was wrenched as they hauled her to her feet. Another man came into her room and dumped something on her bed. It took her a moment to register that it was a body. At first, she thought it was Iktan, and she almost screamed. But the body was the young woman who had been guarding her door since the last attempt on her life. It had required five men, but they had taken her down.

"Oh, skies . . ." She shuddered, nausea rolling over her in a heavy wave.

"Shut up!" Abah hissed. "There was no other way."

"Iktan will kill you." She said it with total conviction. Not only for her abduction but for killing one of xir dedicants.

"Not if xe's dead first."

Naranpa's laughter was high and hysterical. "You can bring

all the Golden Eagle guards you want into the tower. You'll never be able to kill xir."

Abah's face soured. "You overestimate that tsiyo."

"You have no idea what you've done."

"Enough." She motioned to the guard. He stuffed a rag in Naranpa's mouth, and two guards wrestled a brown servant's robe over her head, pulling the cowl up to hide her face, and then they were dragging her through the halls of the tower, off to somewhere else.

CHAPTER 34

CITY OF TOVA

YEAR 325 OF THE SUN

(1 DAY BEFORE CONVERGENCE)

> May you drown in shallow water
> May your song be never heard
> May you fall in love with a man
> May your mouth ever fill with salt

> —Teek curse

They arrived in Tova on a cold afternoon the day before the solstice. The barge had taken them through winding canyons of basalt cliffs that ceded to red rock and heavy currents. Without the power of the water strider to pull them through, Xiala imagined that the river route was impassable. In confirmation of her assumptions, more and more foot traffic appeared on the side of the river, and the barge made stops along the way to pick up travelers for the final miles upriver. By the time they had anchored at a pier that Aishe told her was the riverfront of the Titidi district, the barge was crowded with eager tourists and solstice pilgrims.

She and Serapio had spoken little since she had come to

understand that he was on a suicide mission. Oh, she'd yelled at him when she thought the others on the barge couldn't hear. Hissed words of frustration in his sensitive ears. Glared murderous looks in his direction. Even cried and begged until she was wrung out of emotion and words to convey it. He had seemed shocked that she even cared and then sat stalwartly through her ranting and raving.

At one point she had considered using her Song to change his will, but he'd given her a look, blind or not, that made her quake. She was sure he knew her plans and would never let it happen. She didn't think he'd hurt her, but on this one thing, she did not want to risk his goodwill.

"Are you still not speaking?" Aishe asked as Xiala helped her tie off the barge. Xiala had confessed she was a sailor herself the second day on their voyage, and since then she had helped Aishe and her family with the management of the boat, if only out of boredom and a way to avoid Serapio.

"No," she answered.

"What will you do now that you're in Tova?"

Xiala shrugged. She had no idea. She wasn't even sure Serapio still wanted her company, or if she wanted his. A day. He had only a day to live. It was frustrating and awful and absurd, and it made her swell with fury to think of it.

"My uncle wants to take Serapio to the Odohaa."

"Perhaps he should."

Aishe tied off the post and moved to the next one. "What will you do?"

Xiala's stomach sank. "I thought we would be exploring the city together, but now . . ."

"You can come with me."

She glanced over at her new friend.

"I mean, if you and he are done, I wouldn't mind your company." She grinned, the implied invitation obvious enough. "And if you're not done, my door is open in friendship, too." Her eyes took Xiala in, lingering and suggestive. "But that would be a pity."

Xiala laughed. Aishe was fun and easy, and despite her forwardness, Xiala felt no discomfort. In fact, her open manner reminded her of Teek customs. But Aishe still didn't even know she *was* Teek, and certainly didn't know what that meant. Xiala was sure that if she went with the girl, she would enjoy it. Days and nights of drinking and fucking and a clean farewell when they were ready to part ways.

But Aishe wasn't who she wanted.

"Are you ready?"

She turned to find Serapio at her back.

"What?"

"We are docked, and I promised to spend this day with you in Tova. Are you ready to see the city?"

"Don't do it out of obligation," she shot back, angry.

He frowned. "I don't. I . . ." He paused, his expression troubled.

"Let me leave you to talk," Aishe said, tying off her knot. As she passed Xiala, she touched her arm. "My invitation stands. Go to the Standard Dog near the Titidi Great House, someone will know it, and ask for me. They'll tell you how to find me." She squeezed gently, and then she was gone, leaving Xiala alone with Serapio.

Xiala crossed her arms and waited for him to speak.

His voice was hesitant, unsure. "I don't ask you out of obligation, Xiala. I ask because I want to spend my last day with you."

Every excuse vanished from her mind as her heart cracked. "Mother waters, Serapio," she whispered softly. "Why do this? Why? Aishe's uncle doesn't care about you. These Odohaa sound like opportunists who would only use you. You're so young. You've barely lived. You don't have to do this!"

"This is all I can do. I thought you understood that."

"I do, but . . ." She bit her lip, holding back the words she had said a dozen times before in the past two days. "Oh, hells," she muttered. "Who am I to convince you that life is worth living? I'm a mess. I've got nothing to offer you, nothing to show for my years. I can't even go home."

And it made sense to her all at once. Serapio, for the first time, was coming home. To a people who didn't know him, to a house he could never truly live in, even if all he could do was die for them. He would suffer what he must suffer because for one brief moment he would be more than himself. He would be all of Carrion Crow, the fist of his people, the sharp beak and talon of his god, and he would not be alone. And, Xiala knew well, being alone was no life at all.

"Will you spend the day with me or not?" he asked.

"Of course," she said. "I will not leave you until you ask me to."

He smiled, truly smiled. And her heart cracked a little more.

· · · · ·

They left behind their travel companions and headed up the steep steps to the Holy City. Xiala had heard Tova floated in the clouds, but she had not quite understood what that meant until now.

"Mother waters," she murmured. "Look at this place."

Titidi had begun its solstice celebration in earnest, despite Aishe's claim that the holiday crowds were thin this year, and the district's streets were lined with people. Many were dressed in skirts dyed the bright blue of a summer sky. Others wore furs and cowled robes to keep out the cold. Musicians played on the street, and the sounds of flutes and drums filled the evening air.

"Describe it to me," Serapio asked. "I want to know."

She smiled. He sounded like he had the first night he had asked her to explain Teek sailing to him, as curious as a child.

She told him of the people and the musicians and the beauty of the district itself. The gardens, frosted white with snow. The channels of running water that bordered the road, the great waterfall that ran through the district and that she could spot just to her left farther up. "There are trees here. Some kind of fruit tree, although now they are barren. And they've hung paper lanterns from them. All colors. Red, blue, green, yellow, and orange. Purple. More. They glow, Serapio, like stars against the night sky."

"And that scent. What is that?"

She breathed deeply. "Bonfires everywhere. The scent you smell is the wood they burn."

"It's almost sweet."

She inhaled again. "Spice and nuts?"

"No. Those I've smelled before. Something else."

She looked around and finally spotted what he must be smelling. She laughed. "Chocolate. Is that it?"

"Is that the same as kakau? I'd like to have some."

She led him over to a man selling the drink and bought two small cylindrical cups, one filled with the thick foamy drink.

"What do you want in it?"

"Chile."

"The hottest one," Serapio added.

She smiled at the vendor. "The hottest, then."

He added chile to the empty cup in her hand, and then she poured the drink back and forth between the cups in a long trail to let the ingredients mix. Once she was satisfied, she divided the rich liquid in each cup equally. She took a sip, and it burned her tongue.

"It's hot," she warned, but Serapio had already drained half his cup.

"What do you think?"

"Oh," he said, sounding happy. "It's very good. I had something like it once before, but this is even better."

"They call it the food of the gods."

He smiled. "I know. What else?"

She led him through the district, past children holding foot races and people dancing in the streets. She described it all to him—the ridiculous and the sublime, and he soaked it all in. As the sun began to set, they stopped at a stand where a woman was giving out candied figurines of the sun. Xiala took a figurine and gave Serapio half.

He bit into it enthusiastically, and dark honey dripped down his chin.

"Careful," she warned him, reaching out to catch the slow trickle before it could dirty his clothes. He grasped her hand before she could pull away. She froze, her breath catching in her throat.

He raised her hand to his mouth and began to lick the honey from her sticky fingers. Her whole body trembled. He paused with her thumb above his bottom lip.

"I never enjoyed food before I met you, Xiala," he said softly.

"Serapio . . ."

"Shhh," he said.

She held her breath as he continued to clean the sweet substance from her fingers one by one. And when he was done, he pressed his lips to her palm once before he let it go.

She exhaled loudly. "Seven hells," she murmured.

"There's something I want to give you."

"All right," she said, her voice shaking.

"The bargeman told me of a travelers' inn somewhere near. I'd like to take you there." He told her the name of the house. "I need you to lead us."

"What are you doing, Serapio?" she asked, voice unsteady. Her whole body felt weak, and all she could think about was the feel of his mouth against her skin.

"I'm giving you a gift. Let me do that."

He held out his hand, and she took it, and they found their way to the inn.

· · · · ·

Xiala had not known what to expect, but she had not expected this in all her years. The travelers' inn was built over a natural hot spring, and Serapio had secured a private room where the water gathered in a deep pool and steam came up through wooden slats in the floor.

Once the innkeeper had led them to the room and Serapio had locked the door, he took her to the wooden bench in the center of the room and sat her down. Carefully, slowly, he undressed her. Once she was nude, he led her to the bath, and she climbed in. She sank into the warm water with a sensuous sigh, closing her eyes and letting the tension and ache and sorrow of months fall away.

He washed her hair first, using the fragrant soap from a nearby bench to lather her head, his long fingers caressing her scalp. Once her hair was clean, he wet a cloth, added more soap, and washed her body. He started at her feet and worked his way up, slowly and attentively, taking his time.

The sleeves of his robe soaked through, so he pulled it over his head, discarding it in a corner. Through heavily lidded eyes she admired him. He was lean, perhaps a little too lean, but the haahan that covered his arms, chest, and back were softened in the low light of the bathing room. They told a story, she realized, of loss and sorrow and remembrance. *He wears his people's pain*, she thought, *and it is strangely beautiful.*

But that only made her think of tomorrow, which made

her brokenhearted all over again, so she closed her eyes and concentrated on his touch.

His hands followed the line of her body upward, massaging her calves and thighs, and when the cloth grazed the place between her legs, he paused. She opened her legs wider, an encouragement.

The first touch of his fingers shivered through her lower body like the kiss of lightning, hot with shock. She reached down to guide his hand, showing him what she liked. He followed her lead, and their hands moved as one. Slowly, the sensation became a warm hum that built until it crested. A wave of pleasure broke over her, and she moaned.

"Serapio . . ."

She clutched at his arm and tried to pull him closer, but he stopped her with a gentle kiss against her knuckles. He took her trembling hand, laid it across her belly, and continued to wash her. Each arm, fingers to elbow to shoulder, and across her breasts and finally the back of her neck.

When he was finished, he wrung the water out of the cloth and hung it across the bathing bench. She watched as he replenished the coals that warmed the room and set out a cup of cool water for her.

He gathered his wet clothes, took up his staff, and kissed the top of her head.

"I lied, Xiala," he whispered. "You were the one who gave me a gift."

And then he was gone, the door falling closed behind him.

Xiala sank into the bath and wept, her tears mingling with the bathwater and turning it to salt.

CHAPTER 35

CITY OF TOVA
YEAR 325 OF THE SUN
(1 DAY BEFORE CONVERGENCE)

> Even when armed with blade and bow, even with an army of
> a thousand at her command, a spearmaiden's greatest weapon
> is her tongue.
>
> —*On the Philosophy of War,* taught at the Hokaia War College

"There's a man here to see you."

Okoa looked up from the book he was reading. He sat in the library in the Great House, surrounded by ancient books made of bark paper and stones inscribed with words he could not read. Most of it was in Cuecolan, a language he was only passingly fluent in. And the celestial tower housed the books he really wanted to read, but it was surely closed to him now.

Although perhaps not. The message he had received from someone claiming to be the Sun Priest still sat in a drawer in his desk. He had read it a dozen times and still not been sure what it meant. It contained only three glyphs: Storm, Betrayal, Friendship. He had sent a message back asking for a chance to meet but had heard nothing, and then he had been distracted by the work before him and his promise to the Odohaa and a hundred other duties as the new Shield in a city on the brink pulling at him.

"Who is it?" he asked, rubbing his tired eyes. He half expected it to be Maaka asking why he had not returned. Okoa thought it better to cultivate a relationship with the Odohaa, at the very least so he could keep a watchful eye on them. He didn't want to be surprised by some midnight raid against the celestial tower that ended in horror. Another reason he was here in this library digging through these texts, looking for . . . he wasn't sure what. Something to convince Maaka that the Odohaa should bide their time? Or at least not take up weapons? He felt like a hypocrite. He was the one who had dismissed their belief in a resurrected god as folly, but now that they seemed to be shifting their sights to a more pragmatic solution to their vengeance, he found himself desperately wishing for some kind of sign the Crow God Reborn might be more than a madman's prayer.

"He says he's a bargeman from Water Strider but his grandfather was Carrion Crow from one of the lesser families. He says he has news you will want." The servant paused, hesitating.

"Go on."

"That the Odohaa would want."

That got his attention. He stood, pushing away from the desk. "Bring him to my private office. I'll receive him there."

The servant hurried off, and Okoa made his own way back to his rooms. He didn't want to discuss Odohaa business in a place where eyes and ears could be watching. It was bad enough Maaka had dragged him away and he had not returned to the Great House until the next day. Esa had been mad with worry, and Chaiya, his eyes blackened and his arm bandaged from wrist to elbow, had hugged him as if he had expected to never see him again. He had explained what happened and discovered two Shields had died before the fighting had been broken up by Golden Eagle's guard.

"They owe us for our dead," Chaiya had said. "And the injury to you."

"And they will pay," Esa had assured them both. "The Sky Made Council will see to it. The proper way." Which meant payment in cacao, not blood.

After the riots, it seemed more and more citizens were sympathetic to the Odohaa, if Okoa believed the snatches of conversation he heard in the hallways. It worried him, which pushed him all the harder toward finding a solution. He just wasn't convinced he would find it in books.

The man was there waiting when he arrived.

"I was told you have news for the Odohaa?"

The man blinked. "Yes, Lord."

"Go on, then. I haven't much time, and you'd best not waste it."

The man looked taken aback at his blunt manner, but he visibly rallied. "I have seen him."

Okoa frowned. "Seen who?"

"The Odo Sedoh."

Okoa's shoulders slumped. As much as he wanted to believe at this point, he found it impossible to think the Crow

God Reborn was traveling down a barge on the Tovasheh. He rubbed at his neck, lips tight with disappointment. "Listen, I am sure you think—"

"No!"

He looked up, alert, hand going to the knife he kept at his side.

"Please," the man said, raising his hands in innocence. "I-I know how I must sound, my lord. That you must get people like me coming to you all the time. But there was a man on my barge who . . ." His voice drifted off, and his eyes took on a sheen that Okoa recognized from the gathering at Maaka's home.

"You should have seen him fight. He said he had been trained by a spearmaiden of Hokaia."

Okoa snorted. "Impossible. They rarely train men at all, and they would never train someone not at the college. I was just there. I can count the men trained by spearmaidens on the fingers of one hand."

"Not just a spearmaiden but a Knife of the tower."

"A tsiyo?" That was even more outrageous, insulting even. He leaned forward, rubbing at the place on his jaw that was still healing. "He lied to you. No one but a tsiyo trains a tsiyo. It is a sacred order. It is not done." *And they are our enemies,* he thought. But he dared not say it to a stranger.

"I saw him fight!"

Okoa exhaled, frustrated. It was plausible this bargeman had met a man who was a good fighter, great even, but his claims were clearly a fraud.

"And he said he was the Odo Sedoh?"

"No." He shook his head. "*I* said he was. He said he came from Obregi, had the Obregi look about him, too, but he bore the haahan, and the blood teeth, and crows dogged his steps."

"Crows?"

The man nodded. "They came at his call. He talked to them, and . . ." His voice faltered as if he doubted his own words. "I think he used them to see. He did not catch me spying on him, but I watched him sit in his room alone lost in a trance, and I believe he flew with the crows."

"Farseeing." It was a magic he had heard of practiced by the sorcerers of the south, usually with the aid of a stimulant called star pollen.

"He was blind, my lord."

Okoa sat back, thinking. He was intrigued. The prophecies he had been combing through for the past week were vague and mostly useless. Religious rantings about old gods and blood magic. But they had all mentioned being able to commune with crows.

"And where is this man now?"

"Here, my lord. In the city. He told me he plans to confront the Sun Priest and her Watchers tomorrow at the solstice."

Okoa almost fell from his seat.

"Seven hells, man. Lead with that! Guard!"

The sentinel at his door stepped forward. "Call the Shield to me. I have a task for them. Go!"

The guard ran, and the old bargeman smiled. "So you believe me?"

"I believe this man, whoever he may be, is dangerous. He sounds mad, but a false god is just as deadly as a true one.

This city is on knife edge after Sun Rock. If he confronts the Sun Priest and can fight half as well as you seem to think, it will point right back to us, and we'll pay for his folly."

"He won't fail!"

"So you say. But I'll find your Odo Sedoh and decide for myself."

"You will see," the man said, nodding.

"I will." *And if I have to kill him to keep us all safe*, Okoa thought, *so be it.*

CHAPTER 36

Today I name Naranpa as my inheritor. Many of you, including my own Knife, object to this appointment, but you must trust that in my old age, perhaps I read a future in the heavens that you cannot. You may think her a puzzling choice, and you would be right. But often greatness comes from unexpected places.

—From the *Oration of the Sun Priest Kiutue on the Investiture of Naranpa in Year 325 of the Sun*

Naranpa was on a bridge. That much she knew.

She had slept on a dank stone floor. Her captors had dragged her down into the deepest reaches of the tower to levels she didn't know existed, remnants of the old city Tova was built upon. She kept foolishly hoping Iktan would show up, xir smooth emotionless voice calling out these brutal men and serving them back their own brutality in blood. She had always chided Iktan for xir murderous ways, but oh, what she wouldn't give for a little of xir violence now.

They'd come to a halt finally, and she'd been commanded to wait. Fervid conversation around her she couldn't follow, and then her hands were tied, eyes blindfolded, and gag tightened before she was unceremoniously tossed into the cell and left alone. She'd lain there for what must have been hours in the silence, nothing for company but the sound of water somewhere far off and her own breathing.

Finally, she slept.

She was awoken by the sound of the gate opening and rough hands dragging her to her feet. They marched her up the same steps she'd come down previously until they came to a door. The door opened, and a blast of freezing wind hit her full force. She shuddered and hunched over, trying to keep in some of her heat, but it was useless. They hauled her out into the cold.

Fresh snow frozen to a thin layer of ice crunched under her bare feet and glazed the hem of her robe. Her breath clogged her nose with ice, and her whole body shivered violently.

It was dark even through her blindfold. She was sure it was night or early morning, that last gasp of darkness before dawn. Dawn on the solstice. She wondered what Iktan was doing, if xe was preparing for the ceremony, or still in bed, or, as she feared despite what she had said to Abah, dead. She shook her head. Even now, she worried about xir fate.

Her feet hit the thick heavy fiber of one of the sky bridges that ran between Otsa and the other districts. Rough filament cut her feet, but they were so numb with cold the pain only dully registered. The bridge swayed beneath them as they crossed, and she imagined the great Tovasheh river below them.

"Stop!"

They stopped, and the hands that held her gripped her hard enough to make her cry out around her gag.

"What is it?"

The second voice was Abah's, and she was irrationally grateful to hear a familiar voice, even if it was her enemy's.

"We have to go back. There's someone at the Odo landing."

Odo. They were taking her to Carrion Crow. She had assumed Golden Eagle. She forced herself to concentrate and listen.

"We can't go back. We barely got her out undetected as it is. That damn tsiyo has razed the tower."

She smiled through shivering teeth. Iktan wasn't dead. But if xe was causing chaos in the tower, then xe wasn't the one waiting for her on the Odo landing, either.

"There's at least a dozen people, maybe more," the first voice said, obviously one of Abah's men.

Abah cursed, something Naranpa had never heard her do. "What are they doing there?" she whined. "It's not even dawn. We need to dump her body in Odo, or this won't work."

Ah, so that was her plan. Frame Carrion Crow for her murder to justify crushing them. Not because of the cultists; Abah never cared about that. They were only a means to an end. An end that involved Golden Eagle, no doubt, and resembled Denaochi's suspicions about influences outside Tova more and more.

"They're just standing there, but they're blocking the way. We've got to go back."

"What do you mean, go back? I just said we can't."

"It's dark now, but they'll see us when the sun rises if we stay here."

Nara laughed behind her gag. They were caught in the middle of the bridge.

Someone ripped the cloth from her face. "Why are you laughing?" Abah asked, some of her customary sweetness leached away by stress and the morning cold. "You'll be dead either way, Nara."

"Oh, Abah," she said, still laughing. "You always were too clever for your own good. Whose scheme was this? Eche's? No, he's too simple. I smell Golden Eagle's hand in this. What did they promise you? What did they promise him?"

Abah had narrowed her eyes and looked like she might answer when a shout rose from the Odo side.

"They've seen us!" a guard said.

Abah looked around wildly. "Cut her throat and throw her into the river," she finally said. "I'll find a way to salvage this."

The guards grabbed her, and she struggled, screaming.

"Wait! Take off the robe." Nara was still wearing the brown servant's robe they had disguised her in to move her out of her rooms. "If her body washes up in that, someone will suspect the tower."

Hands seized the neck of her robe and tore it from her body. The blindfold and gag came off, and her hands were untied. She stood naked in the middle of the bridge, Odo distant in the icy winter morning before her and Otsa behind her, no longer in her vision.

"The necklace?" someone asked.

"Leave it. It doesn't matter."

Naranpa blinked. Zataya's necklace, the small bison anointed in her blood. How had she forgotten?

"Zataya," she whispered. And then louder, "Zataya, help me."

"Nara, please," Abah chided. "Begging won't save you."

Nara smiled. Abah had not understood that she was calling for help. Now she only needed to give Zataya time to find her. And she saw only one option.

She used all her weight to throw herself against the guard on her left. He fell against the fiber railing, causing the bridge to tilt. Abah cried out, and the guards grasped for whatever they could reach, momentarily worried more about their own lives than Naranpa's.

She took the moment to launch herself at the railing, grasp the top, and haul herself over into nothing.

It was the fall she had always dreaded when she was a child in the Maw, her body plummeting to the rushing river below, the descent she was sure ended in death.

But to Nara, it felt like flying.

CHAPTER 37

And Grandfather Crow said to First Woman, tell me your stories so that I might know who you are and what you value. If your stories are of the glory of war, I will know you value power. If your stories are of kinship, I know you value relationship. If your stories are of many children, I know you value legacy. But if your stories are of adaptation and survival, of long memory and revenge, then I will know you are a Crow like me.

—From the Crow Cycle, an oral history of the Crow clan

When he left Xiala, he had planned to make his way to Sun Rock. The solstice festivities still filled the streets, and he passed through the people no more than a shadow. The world had been a wonder with her by his side, guiding him through the celebration. The sights and sounds and colors had come alive, superior in her telling to how they could have ever been through his own eyes. Those few hours had been the best he could remember, and for a moment, when she had shivered beneath his fingers in the bath, back arching and breath soft with pleasure, he had wondered what it would be like to be only a man.

Another life had flashed before him. One with clan and family around him, one where he called the beauty and spectacle of Tova his home, one where the Teek captain woke in his bed every morning, and they would drink chocolate on feast days and balché on a sandy beach and play games and laugh together. He would have friends like the brothers on the barge, and he and Xiala would grow old together surrounded by children, and he would care for his crows by carving them houses from wood, and the only revenge he would take would be in the pleasure of a long and well-lived existence.

His tutor Paadeh had once told him pain was his only friend, that he should welcome it as a lover. He had thought the man meant physical pain, the sting of his palm against Serapio's cheek. But he understood now that Paadeh had meant something greater. He did not know how to make the pain of leaving Xiala into his friend, and it sat heavy and foreign in his chest.

He stopped to take the pouch of star pollen from around his neck. He welcomed the shot of adrenaline that spiked through his body as he touched the powder to his tongue. He called for a crow to help him see through the city . . . and screamed.

Black wings filled his head. A great mind, keen and curious, reached out and touched his. He fell to the ground, heedless of the people who stepped around him, muttering about the Crow who had likely had too much to drink.

His heart pounded in his chest, threatening to burst, and one word came to his mind: *Benundah.*

Who are you?

He grasped for an answer, but he could not remember his name. And his name was inadequate anyway.

He thought of his life instead. The day on the balcony when he watched the crow devour the sun. The happy brush of feathers against his hands as crows fed from his open palm. Shadow at his fingertips as he called the crows down on the crew of Xiala's ship.

Grandfather. We were told you were coming.

Who told you? he thought.

The small ones. They speak of a mighty crow disguised as a man traveling toward the City. They call you Nightbringer and Suneater. Is it true? Do you come to eat the sun?

It is true.

Then how may we serve?

I need to see. Will you help me?

The distant cry of a great crow echoed across the canyon, loud enough to be heard over the revelry. People paused, listening, but when another did not follow, went back to their entertainments.

And Serapio saw everything.

He was inside the aviary where the massive corvids lived atop the black rock house. There was warmth and bedding, food and companionship. Rug saddles and bridles hung along a wall. A dozen other crows turned their attention to Benundah, as if they, too, sensed his presence.

How many are you? he asked.

The ones you see here, and many more in our rookery to the west. It is where we lay our eggs, far in the mountains away from humans, even the Crow clan.

I need only you, Benundah, he thought.

Then you shall have me.

She took to the sky, her wings wide enough to cover the risen moon. She soared across the city, lending Serapio her eyes, and he saw the Sky Made districts. Below them in the deep canyon, the river glinted silver in the moonlight. The woven bridges gathered frost that made them glow pale as spidersilk under the stars. And there in the distance stood the celestial tower.

It did not seem so big in Benundah's vision. A stone roundhouse, six stories high, set alone atop a mesa. Even now behind its walls were his enemies. Part of him itched to go now, to strike down those who had dealt the Crow clan such evil, who had tried to kill the Odo Sedoh's own voice.

Wait, he told himself. *You are meant to wait until the moment when darkness is at its fullest to strike. Do not become impatient now.*

He turned Benundah away from Otsa.

Show me Sun Rock, he asked.

She rode the drifting winds of the canyon east toward where he was in Titidi and showed him the freestanding mesa with its four connecting bridges and amphitheater. He saw himself in her vision, a still figure in black surrounded by a sea of color and revelry. He smiled as he saw the path Benundah showed him to the bridge and on to the Rock. It was empty now, dark and deserted under the thickening moon. Tomorrow it would be filled to overflowing with the matrons and their clans and the Watchers and, above all, the Sun Priest.

Snow had begun to fall, only a dusting. But the wind was starting to gust icy against his skin as flakes swirled around him.

A storm approaches, Suneater. It will bring the deep cold, the kind that may kill an unsuspecting crow. It is best you take shelter tonight and tomorrow go to the Rock.

I will sleep on the Rock tonight, Benundah. I am the only storm that matters now, and there is no shelter from what I bring.

CHAPTER 38

CITY OF TOVA
YEAR 325 OF THE SUN
(THE DAY OF CONVERGENCE)

> And brother shall not know brother
> And take him as his enemy, saying
> Your eyes are my eyes
> And your skin my skin
> And your mouth my mouth
> But we have been so long separated
> That you do not know me even when I stand before you.
>
> —From *Collected Lamentations from the Night of Knives*

Okoa stood in the aviary looking out at the three suns. Dawn had come late on the shortest and last day of the year, but when it did come, it was spectacular. The sun, heavy and low in the eastern sky, had split into three, each one a bright flare that burned low against the earth like a bonfire, its flames arcing upward to light the winter sky.

It had snowed the night before, but the snow had turned to rain and then ice, and now the world below him glittered frozen and iridescent in the morning light. He huddled in his crow-feather cloak and wondered what the three suns meant. Surely it was a sign, but was it one that favored the Sun Priest, or did it predict their shattering? The only ones who knew were the Watchers themselves, and he did not trust them to not bend the truth in their favor.

Okoa rubbed at his neck, trying to ease the tension in his body. He had not slept well. The crows in the aviary had been restless all night. He thought perhaps the weather had made them uneasy, and when he came up at first light, Benundah was gone. That wasn't unusual; she was allowed to come and go as she pleased. Nevertheless, something about it made him anxious.

He decided to wait for her, knowing she would never miss her morning feeding, but when she still hadn't returned by midday, he began to worry. He thought to take Kutssah or another one of the mounts out to look for her but decided he was being overly protective. She was a giant crow and a predator. There were very few things that could harm her.

Footsteps behind him, and Okoa turned to find one of the Shield approaching. He had sent them out across the city yesterday to look for the stranger the bargeman had named as the Odo Sedoh. They had reported throughout the day with no luck, and then one woman thought she had spotted a man matching his appearance in Titidi. He had sent someone to look further, but they had not been able to find him.

Another worry, he thought. The Odohaa, this self-proclaimed god, and now even Benundah was missing.

"Any news?" he asked the man.

"News, my lord," he said, "but it's strange news." He swallowed, looking uncomfortable.

Okoa grimaced. "Spit it out, man."

"We believe we found the man you were looking for."

"Where?"

"Someone saw him in Titidi last night and followed him. He crossed the bridge to Sun Rock."

Of course. He should have thought to look there first. If this Odo Sedoh was going to confront the Sun Priest today, it would be when she and the other Watchers were on the Rock.

"Go to Chaiya. Tell him to gather the Shield," he commanded. "We need to get to that man before the Sky Made clans and the celestial tower do." He could only imagine the havoc that would cause, the backlash that would rain down on Carrion Crow. "And send someone to my sister. Tell her no Carrion Crows go to Sun Rock for the solstice." He would tell Chaiya to put the great crows in the sky, too, out of Odo. Or they could go to the rookery, where they would be safe.

He glanced at the sky. It had darkened markedly, and bands of shadow painted the ground at his feet. The sun and moon were moving into alignment as they neared sunset, and Okoa knew without a doubt that when the sun was at its weakest and Tova was under the sway of the eclipse, the Odo Sedoh would strike.

Which meant he had precious little time to get there. Where was Benundah? If his mount was here, he could be on Sun Rock in a matter of minutes.

"There's one other thing, Lord Okoa."

He had almost forgotten the man was there. Hadn't he told him to call the Shield? "What is it?" he asked, irritated.

"We found your crow."

He frowned. "Benundah?" His chest tightened. "Is she all right?"

"She appears to be fine, Lord, but she's on Sun Rock with the Odo Sedoh. It appears she sheltered him there all night."

CHAPTER 39

Сıтʏ оf Tova
Yeаr 325 оf тне Sun
(Тне Dаʏ оf Convergence)

And knives shall break against him
And wise men lose their rhetoric
No succor to be found
The sun, diminished
Unto death

—Prayer to Odo Sedoh, recorded at a meeting of the Odohaa

"They do not look so terrible," Serapio observed. He was sitting under the wing of the great crow and ran a hand through her black feathers as he watched the priesthood come. He had taken another dose of the star pollen so he could observe their arrival, and Benundah had allowed him to share her vision.

Looks are deceiving, Benundah warned him. *They have killed many Crows.*

"My tutor described them as monsters. I expected them to be something from a nightmare. But they are only humans in bright clothing."

He watched the four priests who led the procession. They wore long robes with matching masks—red, white, black, and yellow. He decided those must be the leaders of the societies. He marked the one in red first. His tutor had told him the Priest of Knives wore red. That was the one who would be hardest to kill.

Serapio let his gaze drift to the priest in the yellow mask. He leaned forward, eager. His tutor had told him the Sun Priest was a woman, but this looked like a man. No matter. The individual behind the mask meant nothing to him. He was here to put an end to the priesthood and, if Powageh was right, change the very balance of the world.

More priests filed in after the masked ones. Dedicants, he remembered his tutor calling them. Priests in training whom he would destroy before they could grow and infest.

"And who are the others? In gold and green and blue?" Blue he recognized from Xiala's description yesterday. "They are the Sky Made clans, aren't they?"

They are.

"And where is Carrion Crow?" he wondered.

Your own clan was smart enough to stay away today, Odo Sedoh.

My own clan, he thought to himself. *I have a clan, a family.* His gaze turned toward the black cliffs of Odo just visible to the southeast. *I do this for you. Please forgive me.*

He waited, Benundah silent with him. He relaxed against her strong chest, under the shelter of her wing. He only regretted they had not been able to fly together at least once.

They were singing now, the priest and clans, words about

banishing the darkness and welcoming back the sun. But it was too late for all of that.

The shadow grew as the daylight dimmed, just like it had when he was a child. The singing grew louder below him, more desperate to his ears, as the crow god swallowed the sun.

"It is time for me to go, Benundah," he said.

I know. Travel well, crow son. And I will see you when this is over.

"Benundah . . ."

I understand. And with a great flapping, she launched herself into the sky. Serapio broke his connection with her, his last vision of himself looking up, his face infused with joy.

He was alone. His mother's last words to him rang through his head.

You must go home to Tova . . . there you will open your eyes again and become a god.

He had two obsidian knives in his belt, and he took one now. He used his free hand to spread the skin of his eyelid tight and, one eye at a time, sliced along the narrow line of scar tissue that held his eye shut. His teeth cut through his lip as he struggled to hold in a scream, and blood filled his mouth. More blood poured from the wounds, and the pain doubled him over, but he didn't stop until both his eyes were open.

He was still blind. The damage had been done to his sight long ago. But he did not need human vision to see by the light of the black sun.

He cupped steady hands and caught the blood, using his

palms to wipe the sticky substance through his hair, slicking it back from his face. He hauled himself to his feet and stripped off his shirt, exposing his haahan. He took his staff in hand like a weapon and called shadow to his fingertips. It oozed from his skin and grew to encircle him lovingly, a cloak of darkness to ease his way.

There was only one thing left to do. To say.

For a moment, fear gripped him. He didn't want to die. He had accepted his fate so easily before when Powageh had told him what must be. Even when Xiala had berated him aboard the barge, he had not wavered. But now, with the moment at hand, he wanted . . . different. He wanted to be Serapio. But he had not been Serapio since he was twelve. "A vessel," he reminded himself. Not a person, not a man. A weapon. He forced himself to breath, letting the scent of his own blood fill his nose, his mouth. And the doubt passed through him, leaving him only resolve and purpose.

"I am the Odo Sedoh," he whispered.

He felt himself fracture into a million pieces, felt the darkness suffuse him and break him apart and put him back together in his true form. He screamed, euphoric, and the world trembled at his coming.

The crowd below him had stopped singing, and he sensed more than saw their confusion. Confusion turned to terror as the Odo Sedoh moved among them and began his slaughter.

He swung his staff, and bone shattered bone. Movement to his right, and he ducked and turned, shifting the staff to one hand and sweeping it wide, taking men off their feet. He brought the staff up, and it connected with soft tissue. He pulled back, then jabbed forward, and the softness collapsed into a slick wetness. A woman screamed as she fell.

More came, and he took them down. The shadow around him expanded, and where it touched the dead, it fed, leaving only ash and bone in its wake.

He could smell their fear now, hear their too-quick panicked breaths and the quiver of terrified hands that held weapons that would not save them. He grinned, drinking in their terror, and a dark satisfaction filled his heart.

The clans scattered. He let them go, his focus only on the priesthood.

The Knives came for him. Once they were close enough, he dropped his staff and drew his own knives.

They fought, the tsiyo striking like a pack of wild dogs, trying to bring him down in pieces. But he knew their methods and their poison blades and anticipated each attack. He was too fast, too unpredictable. He became a whirlwind. Untouchable. Unknowable. Inevitable in his destruction.

He slew them all.

He slit the throat of the priest in white, and she collapsed, striking her head against the rocks.

He sliced the black-masked priest across the back of his knees when he tried to run, and then climbed his back to punch his blade into his skull in quick succession until he stopped moving.

The Priest of Knives fought the hardest, and for a moment, he was pushed back, but then he called the shadow to his hand as he had once long ago and threw it. The Knife stumbled, blinded. He kicked the priest in the chest, sending them tumbling. He ran, sliding on his knees to come in low enough that the Knife had barely recovered when he tore his blades through the priest's belly, opening it hip to hip.

At last there was only the Sun Priest.

He imagined what the priest must see before him. The crow god come to avenge his children, his teeth red and cheeks and hair stained with blood. His body carved with remembrance and his eyes endless pools of shadow.

The priest ripped the mask from his face, his brown eyes wide with terror. He said words, but they were unimportant. He cried out, but there was no one alive on the Rock to hear.

"My old enemy," the Odo Sedoh whispered in his voice of a thousand wings. "I have waited a long time for my revenge. Forgive me if I savor it." He breathed deep, the pleasing smell of death filling his nose. The dark satisfaction that had bloomed before, now flowered in its fullness. He could not keep the wide smile from his face.

He reached out with shadow, a tendril of power that penetrated the priest's chest like the sharpest blade and sought the essence of the sun god within. But he found nothing.

His nostrils flared. The black veins in his neck strained, and darkness leaked from his eyes like pitch.

"You are not the Sun Priest." His voice was thunder, dark with rage. It was the cry of a murder, thwarted. "You are a lie."

"Please!"

He cocked his head, seeking. She was here, somewhere. Not too far for a crow to fly, not so hidden he could not find her. But his time was short and this body he rode was failing. He must reconsider.

Something pricked his side. He turned his attention back to the false priest. He had broken a metal piece off his golden mask and used it to stab him in the stomach. He pulled the projectile out, examined it, tossed it to the side.

The false priest fell to his knees, and for the insult and the lie the Odo Sedoh used his obsidian knives to take his head.

CHAPTER 40

City of Tova
Year 325 of the Sun
(The Day of Convergence)

> A smart Teek survives the storm, but a wise Teek avoids
> storms altogether.
>
> —Teek saying

Xiala stood on the balcony of the Standard Dog with the other patrons and watched the eclipse obfuscate the setting sun. The servants moved through the room, extinguishing all the lights, torch and resin alike. And she saw the same happening on the streets and, from her vantage point on the balcony, the next street and the next, until the whole district was dark. And then the districts around it, the one barely visible across the canyon and even Sun Rock itself.

She shivered in the darkness. It was like being at sea under a black cloud at midnight, save for the thinnest crescents of red that glowed on either side of the black hole that had once been the sun. People began shouting around her, yelling for the sun to come back.

She tapped the nearest woman on the shoulder.

"What's happening?" she asked. "Why did they smother all the lights?"

"It's part of the ceremony," the woman explained. "All light must be put out with the end of the year. But don't worry. Even now the Sun Priest is lighting a new fire on Sun Rock. Runners will take the fire to all four districts of the city, and all new fires will be set by her fire. A new year!"

Xiala nodded her thanks and moved away. Her hands trembled as she took a drink from the bottle she clutched by her side. She had been drinking since she woke up and came here, determined to find Aishe and forget last night. But she hadn't worked up the nerve to ask about her friend, and the only thing in her head was the memory of Serapio's hands on her body, his mouth as he sucked the honey from her fingers, the touch of his lips against her head.

She tried to remember why she had let him go. Why she hadn't fought harder. She was Teek, and Teek were stubborn. Teek didn't give up. And she had her Song, a power that could change a man's will. Why hadn't she ignored his protests and just forced him to stay?

The crowd was singing another song, and someone had begun stamping their feet impatiently, calling for the return of the sun. She looked around at all these strangers. She used to like a crowd, love a cantina, but all of it seemed sour now. Empty.

"Fuck this," she said. She grabbed the nearest patron, a man in a flowered cape, and shoved the bottle at him.

"Here," she said. "My treat."

The man looked confused at first, but when Xiala smiled and insisted, he took it and thanked her.

Xiala wound through the balcony crowd and down the steps until she was back on the street. Crowds of people milled about in the darkness or gathered by bonfires that were waiting to be lit with the new year's fire. She could feel her Teek eyes widening, shifting to take in what light they could, but it was so dark she had difficulty seeing her feet before her. She muttered apologies as she bumped shoulders and avoided obstacles, moving through the crowd. She didn't realize where she was going until she was at the landing of the bridge to Sun Rock.

She hesitated, looking out at the expanse. She could see something was happening on the Rock. Darkness, darker even than the false night around her, roiled over the mesa, churning like a living thing. She thought she heard screams, faint and distant. She couldn't be sure over the singing and shouting. The woman on the balcony had said that a runner with a torch would come over the bridge, so she squinted into the blackness, looking for any sign of an approaching light.

Something was coming. Something big and churning that set the bridge swaying. The thick braided cables rocked and strained against their stone bases. Screams—she was sure there was screaming now—grew louder.

The churning mass revealed itself all at once. Dozens, no, a hundred or more people were running toward her, shoving and pushing to get across the bridge. She watched in horror as the great span tilted, and a woman dressed in a bright blue dress toppled over the edge. Another followed her, a body too dark to identify.

Xiala blinked. It had happened so fast she couldn't be sure she had actually seen it. The shadows were thick, even with her improved eyesight, and no one had stopped or cried out. The mob was still coming, and she ducked to the side just as bodies streamed across the bridge. Their solstice finery was torn and bloodstained, eyes wide in shock or broken by fear.

Her mind tried to take it in, tried to process it all.

"Serapio," she whispered. She knew without a doubt they were running from him.

She shoved her way into the crowd, fighting against the flow as best she could. But there were too many people. She didn't make it far before she was pushed back, farther away from the Rock and back to Titidi.

No! She would fight. She reached for her Song, and it came, wild and fierce, to her lips. She lashed out, a sharp weapon to drive her way through the crowd.

The people around her halted as if suddenly frozen in place, but her Song didn't reach far enough through the stampeding throng, and those who couldn't hear her trampled the others. They went down without complaint, crushed underfoot.

She choked, horrified, and modulated her Song, softening the command, lowering the pitch to soothe, not wound. She thought of gentle waters and star-filled nights. She thought of laughter and good food on a sandy cay. She thought of childhood stories shared with a captive audience of one. And it worked. People slowed, calmed. She raised her voice loud as she could, and everywhere she reached, people quieted.

She pushed through pliant bodies, still Singing. Made it back to the bridge and well onto the bridge itself. She smiled around buoyant notes. It was going to work.

Suddenly, the air shifted. A dark gale, shards of ice like glass, hammered down across the bridge. It whipped her hair, stinging, across her face. Sliced her skin open, sharp as obsidian. Froze her from the inside like ice crystals on a lake, deadening nerves and thought.

Her Song faltered and died.

Everywhere around her, people were falling, stumbling, wracked by the same unnatural wind. She was on her knees, clutching the thick rope of the bridge, sure the gale would throw her off into the canyon below.

And then it stopped, but it was all she could do to hunch down against the railing, gasping, reeling from the pain, and trying to breathe. Panic rolled through the crowd like a rogue wave, and what calm she had been able to Sing drowned on a fresh wave of terror. The crowd surged around her, dragging her to her feet and back toward the landing. Someone kicked her, an accident, and then an elbow struck her cheek. Another blow, this time to her back, and she stumbled. A man hauled her up, and it was all she could do not to go down underneath indifferent feet.

Ground beneath her again, slippery and churned by a hundred boots and shoes. Hands pushed her, tore at her sleeves, shoved her directionless through the streets of Titidi. People shouted and pointed. She couldn't understand their words, but she lifted her head enough to follow where they were looking.

In the sky above Sun Rock, the sun hung suspended. It was an enormous disc on the horizon, neither rising nor setting. The moon had stopped, too. It cast its shadow across the sun, eclipsing it entirely. A black sphere now rested where the sun had once been, only the barest slivers of light showing along its edges.

Everything else was darkness.

CHAPTER 41

City of Tova (Coyote's Maw)
Year 325 of the Sun
(The Day of Convergence)

Today Saaya discovered a *working* in one of the forbidden volumes that is meant to bring back the dead. She brought it to me as eager as a child who had found a stray puppy and hoped to keep it. I read the text and was not persuaded. I encouraged her to focus on the more promising theory of divine transference and leave these ideas of resurrection behind. To harness the latent powers of a god into a single human vessel. Surely this was the highest of magics that would make even the Sun Priest in his high tower break with envy.

—From the Notebook of Lord Balam of the House of
Seven, Merchant Lord of Cuecola, Patron of the
Crescent Sea, White Jaguar by Birthright

Zataya used a long pole, the same kind the river monks used, to fish the body from the Tovasheh.

"Foolish woman," she muttered as she waded out into the slow-moving tributary to haul Naranpa from the water. "What did you do to end up in the river?"

The witch motioned the two teenaged girls with her to grab the once–Sun Priest by the armpits and drag her the rest of the way to shore. They dumped the naked and water-logged body on the barren muddy riverbank. They were tucked well under a heavy rock overhang away from the eyes of anyone who might be traveling the river. Not that anyone was. Solstice celebrations raged on as they neared the hour of the eclipse; all eyes were focused upward, not down into this fissure in the earth.

Naranpa looked surprisingly fresh. Her face was slack, but her skin had not taken on the waxy coating or gaseous bloat of bodies that lingered in the water. Zataya guessed by her appearance that she had not been in the river more than a few hours, and perhaps had not even been dead when she entered the water. She ran rough hands over Naranpa's body, inspecting her chest and back and probing her head under her hair, looking for wounds. But there was none. The woman had not been dumped in the river but had gone in alive and intact.

"A small blessing," the witch muttered, lowering Naranpa's head gently to the rocky ground.

Zataya's two apprentices had kindled a small dugout fire. They huddled around it, trying to warm themselves after their wade into the river, but Zataya grunted and pushed them out of her way. Down here in the deep canyons, they were well away from the winds and frosted air at the top of the cliffs; Zataya thought it almost warm.

She retrieved a bag of herbs from a string around her neck. She reached in, scooping out a handful, and dumped them into the fire. They crackled and hissed, sending up a fragrant white smoke. She fanned the smoke toward Naranpa and then motioned the girls over to take up her task.

Satisfied, she turned back to the body. She drew an obsidian blade from her belt and, with a well-practiced cut, opened a long gash in her arm. Blood welled bright and red. She held the wound over Naranpa and let the blood drip down on her chest and belly, even across her face. She signaled to the girls, and they knelt by the body, using their hands to spread the blood evenly across Naranpa's cold skin while Zataya bandaged her wound. Zataya watched until she was satisfied that the priest was thoroughly coated. Only then did she shrug the mantle from her own shoulders to cover the body.

She paused with the blanket poised over Naranpa's face.

"Open her mouth," the witch said, and one of the girls complied. Zataya tucked a smooth white lump of salt beneath Naranpa's tongue before dropping the blanket over her head. Then she made her way around the body, making sure the edges were tucked in tight and no air could get in or out. Done, she dropped to her haunches to admire her work.

"What happens now?" one of the girls asked.

In truth, Zataya wasn't sure. She worked usually in earth magic—charms of finding, small fortunes told, potions and cures for ailments and colicky babies. But her mother's mother had traveled widely and had learned some of the blood magic of the southern sorcerers. She had taught her daughter, who had taught Zataya. But for a Dry Earth witch who had never actually performed such sorcery and in truth had only learned about it at third hand, it was very possible that nothing would happen. But she had promised Denaochi that she would try everything possible to save his sister, so that was what she intended to do.

Down here in the depths of the Maw, it was much too dark to have any use for the sun. Its light never reached this deep in the canyon. But Zataya shivered all the same as shadows spread across the city and the meager daylight disappeared altogether. She heard faint cries far above them, echoing down through the walls of the canyon. The eclipse must have begun.

"What happens now," the witch told the girl, "is we wait."

CHAPTER 42

THE CITY OF TOVA
YEAR 1 OF THE CROW

Today I observed a crow funeral. One fledgling had fallen
from the nest and brained itself against the ground. Throughout the day all the crows of Odo came to visit the corpse,
talking loudly among themselves and bearing witness to their
fallen companion. I asked my uncle about it, and he said that
the crows are only warning the others about a fatal danger
so that they do not repeat and perish as well. But he did not
hear the crows weep, as I did. He did not behold their terrible
sorrow.

—From *Observations on Crows*, by Saaya, age thirteen

Okoa flew over Sun Rock on Benundah's back and despaired.
The ceremonial grounds had become a wasteland. Bodies
were strewn across the amphitheater, or what was left of bodies. Many had been reduced to nothing, only dark smudges
against the red rock earth. The rest fanned out from the center in a disquieting symmetry, as if their arrangement had a
hidden deeper meaning.

He had studied war, but he had never seen anything like this. It turned his stomach, made him nauseated at the level of destructive power the Odo Sedoh had wielded. And he was convinced this man was indeed the Odo Sedoh. When Benundah had come to him in the aviary and urged him onto her back and brought him here, there was no longer room for doubt.

Although Okoa had no idea what being the Odo Sedoh truly meant. In all the Odohaa's talk of a god reborn and vengeance, he had never imagined the reality of it. It had always seemed something far off, a noble battle between the dogged and underpowered cultists and the cruel Knives and their Sun Priest. But below him were people—just people—and he had no idea how to process it all.

Benundah cried out and made for the middle of the circle. He tugged at her reins, forcing her to bank and soar clear of Sun Rock. He wasn't sure it was safe to land, even for her. But she shook her head, fighting his control, and turned back to the amphitheater, again. This time he let her lead, and she circled twice over the center, crying out in a voice he had not heard from her before. It was raw, primal, and it shivered down his spine, reminding him Benundah herself was a creature of magics.

Directly below him in the center of the circle of the dead he saw a figure. Small from this height and lying on his back. Benundah screamed again, and he knew it was him.

"All right," he said to his mount, resting a reassuring hand against her shoulder. "I'll go look."

She immediately descended, swooping low to land at the

lip of the amphitheater. Okoa slid from his saddle and took in the scene before him. The first thing to hit him was the stench. It smelled of death, of emptied bowels and viscera, and over the offal stench was the sweet and coppery scent of blood and the familiar must of crows.

He did not want to go down into the pit, but he had no choice. He breathed deeply through his mouth, squared his shoulders, and drew his knife before descending the stairs. He had been here only two weeks ago for his mother's funeral, and countless times before that for celebrations and ceremonies, but now it seemed an entirely different place, unfamiliar and haunted.

He picked his way across the killing grounds. He recognized the bodies here. There were a handful of people arrayed in Sky Made clan colors, likely household guards, but mostly he saw the corpses of priests. A cluster of red-robed dedicants he knew to be tsiyos in training splayed out like the plucked petals of a ruined flower, a spiral of twisted limbs and torn bodies. He shuddered. If he had not seen it with his own eyes, he would not have thought such domination possible. All his life, the Knives of the Watchers were untouchables, demons from every Crow child's nightmares. Even recently, they had bested him and his Shield. But here they were, mowed down like so much grass in the field.

As he moved closer to the center, he found the bodies of the masked priests. They were arrayed in a line of four, as if stacked side by side in sacrifice. The first was a young woman, her long burnished hair clotted with blood from a blow to her scalp that had shattered her mask of white dawn in two and likely killed her instantly. He reached down and delicately pulled the bottom half of her mask away, revealing a young face, soft and pretty even now with a red gash opening her throat. He amended his cause of death.

He had never seen any of the priests unmasked, but it gave him pause to see a young woman so . . . normal . . . revealed as a priest.

Beside her was an older man, his head crowned with wisps of white. His face was collapsed entirely as if half of it had melted, skin, bone, and flesh fusing into something grotesque. His black mask had been carefully set atop the broad expanse of his stomach, empty eyes staring upward at nothing.

Next was the headless body of a man. Cupped in his hands was what must have been his missing head, still wearing the radiant mask of the Sun Priest. Okoa bent to remove the mask, accidentally sending the severed head tumbling to the earth. He fought the urge to vomit.

He stared at the man's face, thinking. Did that mean that the woman Sun Priest he had met at his mother's funeral was not here this day? That eased something in his chest. He was not sure he wished her dead. And suddenly the message made more sense, and so did why he had not received a reply to his inquiries. Betrayal . . . he wondered what had happened within the walls of the tower. Wondered if he could have made a difference. Wondered if the woman was, in fact, dead after all.

There was movement to his left, and Okoa startled so badly he almost fell, a shout of alarm on his lips. He raised his blade, ready to defend himself. It was the red-masked priest. Okoa approached warily, but it was clear the priest was in distress, a deep fatal gash ripping low horizontally across her stomach, blood leaking from the wound to soak her red robe, turning it black. She had her hand pressed to the wound, fighting to keep her innards intact. She might be alive now, but she would not be for long.

Okoa gingerly lifted the mask away.

The woman was unfamiliar. She didn't seem the same priest who had sliced his jaw open at the funeral. Her breath came in syncopated pants, tight and short, as she struggled to hold on to what little life was left her. Her long hair had come loose and stuck to her wide forehead in wet ribbons. Her gray eyes searched Okoa's, pleading.

Okoa stared at the woman, his emotions a tempest of confusion. Here was a fearsome Knife before him. Not just a Knife but the Priest of Knives. And just as he had been strangely moved to see the red-robed dedicants, he was similarly moved to see their leader.

"All human after all," he said quietly, and Okoa did the only thing he could do; he gave the Knife his mercy.

He found the Odo Sedoh surrounded by crows. They must have come while Okoa was crossing the Rock and tending to what was left of the Watchers. The birds circled the figure, calling to one another in distinctive bursts and clicks. Okoa recognized some of the smaller residents that shared the aviary and the surrounding nests of the Great House, but others seemed different in size and build—smaller beaks, feathers more blue than black, chests a different circumference. Voices echoed from above, and he looked up to see the great crows from the aviary circling overhead, adding their strident cries to the chorus.

Crow ceremony, he thought, and let them say their farewells.

After a moment, he stepped gingerly through the circle of crows and stopped, eyes wide. He had only noticed the crows on the outer circle and those in the sky. But there was an inner ring of corvids nestled against the man's body. At first, he thought they were sleeping, they looked so peaceful, but the truth dawned slowly, and to Okoa's horror, he realized they were freshly dead. Each bird had settled against the bare blood-painted skin of the man's chest, wings spread like a blanket. His breath caught as he realized the crows must have sacrificed themselves for the man, but to what end? Had they joined him in battle, or only come to him after his collapse?

Okoa had never been a particularly religious man, but he prayed now, simple words of thanks to the dead crows for the lives they had given, before he reached down to push their black-winged corpses away.

The Odo Sedoh was not a large man. He was tall for a Tovan, stretched leaner and thinner than most of his kin, and certainly not as broad or muscled as Okoa was, but his wide cheeks and mouth resembled Okoa's own. His face ran with rivulets of dried blood below eyes closed as if in sleep, and his hair was matted with it. The bargeman had said he had been blind, but Okoa could not tell either way. His upper body was carved well if not skillfully, showing a hand with more enthusiasm than practice. All told, the man could have easily been one of his cousins.

Okoa had decided he would not leave the Odo Sedoh here among his enemies, so he bent and lifted him in his arms. He was light, as if made from bird bones. Okoa pressed an ear to his chest. He thought for a moment he heard a heartbeat, fast and stuttering, but he couldn't be sure. He did see that despite the blood matting his hair and coating his bare skin, the wounds on his body seemed superficial; there was a gash on his stomach but it was far from a fatal blow. It seemed hard to believe this man could have caused so much bloodshed, created so much carnage, and escaped death himself. But as Okoa looked again at the dozens of crows at his feet and circling above, he found himself reordering what he believed and what he did not.

Okoa stepped around the crows, who took to the wing as he passed, loud cries reverberating across the canyon. He made his way back to where he had left Benundah. She fussed and squawked when she saw him, or was it that she saw the Odo Sedoh? He remembered that she had sheltered him the previous night, and a tight spike of jealousy pricked his heart. But that was foolish. Benundah and he had a bond forged over years, and besides, this man was surely dead, or at the least at death's front door.

Benundah bumped her head against Okoa's shoulder so forcefully he had to catch himself.

"What are you doing?" he asked her, and she bumped him again, as if chastising him.

"Do you want to see him for yourself?" he asked. She ruffled her feathers, a kind of affirmative, so he held the man out and let his crow inspect the body. She prodded at the man with her beak, blowing puffs of air over his blood-caked form, until she finally seemed satisfied. She spread her wings, a sign for Okoa to mount.

He draped the man over her broad back before climbing on behind him. Once in his seat, he pulled the man upright until his body rested in the cradle of his own and his legs straddled Benundah's wide neck. He wrapped an arm tight around his chest and grasped the reins with his other hand. The balance would be tricky, but he knew Benundah would be careful.

The great corvid took to the air, breaking through the circle of crows above them. Okoa had been so preoccupied with the battlefield below him that he had failed to notice the sky. Time appeared suspended, the world in deep blue twilight between day and night, and the eclipsed sun quivered in bands of barely seen red behind the swollen moon.

He shivered, unsettled. First the triple sun at dawn, now the halted eclipse. What did it mean?

Benundah wheeled west, away from the aviary, and he pulled her steady. But she fought him, forcing them west. West to the rookery, the safest place for a crow. A thrill shivered down his spine. He had never seen the rookery, no human had. But he trusted her to know best.

He hugged the Odo Sedoh tightly to his chest to keep him from slipping. The man's head lolled back to rest on Okoa's shoulder. At first Okoa thought it only the wind, but then he realized the man had purposefully tucked his head in the crook of Okoa's neck. Okoa inhaled sharply as the man's eyelids fluttered open.

"Hold on!" Okoa shouted over the wind. "If you can hear me, hold on. We're going home."

ACKNOWLEDGMENTS AND CREDITS

I've always wanted to write an epic fantasy with the scope, scale, magic, and intrigue I found in my favorites of the genre and set it in a fictional secondary world inspired by the pre-Columbian cultures of the Americas. So much of epic fantasy is set in analogs of western Europe that I think most readers believe that all fantasy must be set in a fake England in order to even be considered epic. Happily there seem to be more and more epics set in secondary worlds influenced by various cultures in eastern Europe, the Middle East, and Asia, but it still seems incredibly rare to find a fantasy inspired by the Americas. I think part of the reason is the persistent myth that the indigenous cultures pre-conquest were primitive and had little to offer, when the opposite is true. Here were master architects who built massive pyramids that rivaled anything in Egypt and created citywide sewer systems when London was still tossing its waste in the streets. Here they built high-rises that housed thousands. Here they tracked the equinox, the solstice, and the movement of the heavens with stunning accuracy. They wove cotton and traded turquoise and shell and feathers and cacao along trade routes that stretched across continents. They lived and laughed and loved. They were, in a word, epic.

That's not to say this book is a history book. This is pure fantasy, where I liberally mixed cultures and made a lot of stuff up (giant insects and talking crows among them, although the crows are closer to the real thing than you might think). Nevertheless, there are some aspects peeking through that I wanted to mention. The navigational skills of the Teek were inspired by traditional Polynesian sailing methods. The languages in the story were drawn from Yucatec Maya for the Crescent Sea cities and from Tewa for the Tovans but, again, with exceptions made for the fantastical.

A lot of generous people helped make this book better:

A huge thanks to my disability consultants. In many indigenous cultures, physical disability does not hold the social stigma it does in mainstream Western culture and in fact can be a sign that the individual is "god-touched." Serapio is certainly god-touched, but I wanted to make sure he was genuinely human, too. Thanks to the book *The 33 Worst Mistakes Writers Make about Blind Characters* by Stephanie Green, which got me started. Thanks to Rose Johnson Tsosie for sharing her experiences, particularly in "blind school," which inspired Serapio's tutors and his woodworking. Thanks to Elsa Sjunneson for reading the manuscript and helping me avoid bad tropes, understand adaptive technologies, and tease out the difference between learning a skill and getting a superpower. Any mistakes or offenses in the depiction of Serapio's blindness are entirely mine.

Thanks to Kate Elliot, who helped me with the early research on the maritime Maya and pointed me to the scholarship in the field. Thanks also for the talk at WorldCon. Miles, it is!

While a lot of Cahokia did not make it into this book, I very much enjoyed learning about the great city and hope it comes around in the next one. Thanks to Annalee Newitz for her insight into Cahokia, including her excellent article you can google and read.

Thanks to Critical Mass, especially those folks who read my 100,000-word manuscript in five days. Heroes without capes, every one. Thanks to Emily Mah, SM Stirling, Lauren Teffeau, and Sara Nichols. Thanks also to J. Barton Mitchell, Sarena Ulibarri, and Matt Reiten.

Thanks as always to my husband, Michael Roanhorse, for getting me through the writing process with coffee and infinite patience. Thanks to my daughter, Maya, who drew the initial maps of the Meridian and Tova and who is #TeamBroCrow.

Thanks to my agent, Sara Megibow, for making sure I got the chance to write this book.

Thanks to my editor, Joe Monti, who read the first draft of this book when it was entirely different and said, "It's okay, but it's not great." That annoyed me so much I completely rewrote the book, and now I hope it's a little closer to great. Thanks for shielding me from the BS and taking the heat so I wouldn't have to. You, sir, are definitely great.

ACKNOWLEDGMENTS AND CREDITS

Thanks to the folks at Gallery/Saga Press for believing in this book and working to get it out in the world, including Lauren Jackson (LJ) and Madison Penico.

Thanks to Robert Lazzaretti for taking the imaginings in my head and turning them into amazing maps. It is a fantasy writer's dream to get one map, never mind two!

Thanks to the brilliant Hugo Award–winning artist John Picacio for the stunning cover artwork. I am infinitely grateful you agreed to join the team. You are making your ancestors proud.

I read a lot of books. Here are a few that may interest you: *Gift of the Crow*, by John Marzluff and Tony Angell; *A Scattering of Jades: Stories, Poems, and Prayers of the Aztecs*, translated by Thelma Sullivan, edited by Timothy Knab; *The Chaco Meridian: One Thousand Years of Political and Religious Power in the Ancient Southwest*, by Stephen Lekson; *The Maya*, by Michael Coe and Stephen Houston; *Envisioning Cahokia: A Landscape Perspective*, by Rinita Dalan, George Holley, William Woods, Harold Waters, and John Koepke; *Cahokia: Mirror of the Cosmos*, by Sally A. Kitt Chappell.

1/22-∅
6/24-∅

City of Tova

Otsa

Tsay :
Golden Eagle Clan

Tovasheh River

Sun
Rock

Odo : Carrion Crow Clan